REVELATION

Book 1 of The Ancient Hopes Broken Trilogy

R.P. Miller

Published by Dragon Scribe LLC
www.dragonscribellc.com
dragonscribe@dragonscribellc.com

Cover art by Morano

Revelation

First Edition
ISBN-13: 978-0-9969902-7-1

To those who always believed.

THE KNOWN WORLD

KEY:
- DWARVEN STRONGHOLDS
- CITY-STATES
- CAPE TOWN
- CITY OF SAND
- HANNES
- CRESCENT CITY
- KAMPAIA
- MECCA

BARREN OCEAN

SEA OF HEADS

SAUROMATIAN JUNGLE

AFRIKAAR

SOUTHERN OCEAN

ORC BOGS

THE GOLD DESERT

MOUNTAINS OF HOPE

EAST AGER

KINGDOM OF FEATHER COAST

COLD SEA

CLIFFSIDE GULF

GOBLIN ISLES

KINGDOM OF EAST AGER

POINT PROVINCE

2 — FORDELL AND THE COLD SEA CATHEDRAL

3

1

TRUPPOR

NORTHERN HOLY RIVER

FEATHER COAST

6 GARETH

4 TRIKKLE

ERIC'S RIVER

5 — MECCA AND THE CATHEDRAL OF POWER

MOUNTAIN PROVINCE

SACRED ISLE

7

SOUTHERN HOLY RIVER

10 — ELINCIA AND THE CATHEDRAL OF THE WHITE FEATHER

MOUNTAINS OF HOPE

8

FIRE PASS PROVINCE

KOBOLD WOOD

FIRE PASS CATHEDRAL

11 — ZEPHYR HILLS

9

13

12 — FARROW AND THE SOUTH SEA CATHEDRAL

14

PEARL

CLIFFSIDE GULF

PENINSULA PROVINCE

16

CATHEDRAL OF NEW BEGINNINGS

GOBLIN ISLES

15

TLES: 1 OLAVINLINNA   2 EILEAN DONAN   3 PORTCHESTER   4 PREDJAMA   5 THE CITADEL
ED CASTLE   7 ALBRECHTSBURG   8 CONWY   9 ALMOUROL   10 ALCAZAR   11 MANZANARES
EAUMARIS   13 HARLECH CASTLE   14 CAERNARFON   15 HIMEJI   16 MATSUYAMA

Prologue
(Tarik)

The great wall of Fire Pass was smooth and unscathed, an indomitable barrier that shone darkness and absorbed all light. The single tunnel that ran through its center could not be lit by a torch. Even the west side of the wall radiated black despite two pools of flames that left a natural bridge leading up to the gate. These pools were the origins of two twin rivers of lava that hugged the black wall and snaked their way north and south, slowly getting cooler and hardening into rock as the leagues continued deep within the impassable Mountains of Hope. Fire and molten lava erupted like great fountains from the pools, often splashing the bridge with droplets of flame.

"Shiva must be angry this day..." muttered Tarik Ziyad. He looked down over the wall and watched the Northern River of Flame bubble with its intense heat. He stood looking out of a small stone window in one of the two lush rooms inside the barracks reserved in case of the presence of a Constable, the military leader of a province.

"Ancient Shiva will stay angry as long as she is trapped, and trapped she will stay," remarked Nolasco, the high priest of Fire Pass Cathedral, as he quietly slipped inside Tarik's room. *Had he chosen a soldier's path instead of the path of a priest, he would be a physically imposing man,* Tarik thought. Most men who claimed heritage to the old empire in the north were bigger than those with native ancestors. The high priest wore a tunic made of white feathers and matching silk pants. A large pearl ring decorated his left hand, just as a silver circlet with a black chip embedded in the front adorned his forehead.

"Long has the time been since the curators, our gods, have banished her," Nolasco began, his gray eyes solemn. "We thank them for her imprisonment; else we would live in quite a different world."

Tarik knew the legend of the dragon Shiva. It was said the curators, the gods of Reproba Caelum, had banished the fiery dragon to her prison beneath the very place he stood.

Nolasco continued to preach. "We owe much to the curators. Our kingdom prospers in a land bathed in security rather than flames."

Tarik smiled. The Kingdom of East Ager was anything but secure. He had just ended the War of Fire in his own province, the Peninsula Province. Goblin armies had traveled from their isles for unknown reasons to unleash war. Giants raided from the north, barbarians to the west still dreamed of reclaiming their lost land, and the provinces acted more like separate entities without a king to unite them. Only Reproba Caelum held the four provinces united as a kingdom, and it was the six high priests who enforced its control from their cathedral fortresses.

"News of your victory in the War of Fire has spread. The vile goblins have abandoned the Peninsula Province and returned to their islands. It's the mark of a true leader when he can summon so many to fight for him. The Army of Truth is a powerful force when the levy is added to your standing army."

"When a man fights to protect his home, others in the same peril will join him," Tarik responded. "If I had not been commanded here with all haste, the levy would be home tending their fields and enjoying the company of their families. I doubt anything short of another war on our soil would bring so many willing conscripts."

"And we all pray to the curators that there won't be another war in the Peninsula Province," the high priest said. Tarik studied Nolasco with crystal-clear blue eyes, hoping there was no hidden meaning behind Nolasco's words. "But you must come; Anuke wishes to speak with you."

A summons from the goddess, Tarik thought. Anuke was the goddess of Fire Pass Cathedral. She was often depicted with a bow, and according to Reproba Caelum, she was tasked with leading the dead to the Sacred Isle. It wasn't uncommon for a priest or Constable to be summoned by the one of the gods, but it was considered a great honor.

Tarik was hesitant to go after the few words he shared with Nolasco, but he knew he couldn't turn down the summons. He had thought his order to bring the Army of Truth was due to another attack on the pass by the barbarians in the desert, but everything seemed quiet beyond the wall. There was something else.

They can't afford to make me a martyr. There's too much unrest as is. Adding my corpse to the pile... no. I'll be safe.

He followed the high priest into the hall, his enchanted armor making no noise. The armor was a deep blue with silver veins running from the bottom of his steel leggings up his cuirass and down his pauldrons to the edges of his half-gauntlets. The veins even snaked up the shaft of the spear that was strapped to his back.

They walked down six flights of stairs to the ground floor without a word. Waiting patiently at the bottom of the stairs stood a soldier in a breastplate formed of metal strips that wove in and out of each other in an intricate knot pattern. It was the armor commonly worn by the cavalry in the Army of Truth – and those who could afford the armor and the horse were mostly those of noble birth. In a province so far to the south, the light armor served well in the heat, whereas the heavy cavalry of the other provinces would likely roast in their full shells of steel. The soldier was Varro, one of Tarik's two Lieutenant commanders in the Army of Truth. "Sir, the infantry has arrived."

"Set camp. You and Paulus are to meet me in my tent when the moon is visible. Alert the sentries that none other than the soldiers of the Army of Truth are allowed inside the camp, and that none in the Army of Truth are allowed out unless under orders from myself." This brought a raised eyebrow from Nolasco. "We wouldn't want to cause any trouble with the soldiers garrisoned at the Pass," Tarik explained with a casual glance.

Varro brought his leather covered fist to his chest in the form of a salute and turned away to fulfill his Constable's orders. The slender Lieutenant commander strode away easily despite the falchion, a single-edged one-handed sword, that hung at his side. Tarik had always valued Varro as a loyal soldier. *Not long now until your loyalty is truly tested.*

Tarik and Nolasco continued through the barracks. One was protected by his enchanted steel armor and fighting prowess, the other by a feathered tunic and the faith he held in his gods. The soldiers garrisoned in Fire Pass watched them walk by in silence, looking up from their rest to regard the unlikely pair.

Once outside, the last rays of the sun fell upon Tarik's short cropped hair, highlighting the specks of brown that still shone amongst the gray. That same sun shed its fading light on the second largest cathedral in East Ager. Marble statues of past high priests decorated the exterior, perfectly etched replicas of the once living. The cathedral itself was a dull yellow, built from stone that could only be found on an uncharted island far to the west of Mundus no living captain could navigate to. The stone was made even more beautiful by the white veins that wound up its sides like cobwebs that stretched out in no particular pattern. Reproba Caelum, the only religion tolerated in the Kingdom of East Ager, made a huge show of power at the holy ground known as Fire Pass.

Five smaller towers with their own white runes surrounded the central domed chapel and made up the cathedral. Each was connected to the chapel with an arched bridge, their runes merging with those on the central chapel. Where they met high on the wall, near to where the actual dome of the roof began, the white veins shifted to a swirl of green and blue. They formed breathtakingly beautiful supports for the largest stained-glass window in Mundus. The Cathedral of Fire Pass was a perfect imitation of a five-pointed star, the symbol of Reproba Caelum.

The bleak landscape upon which the cathedral sat only accentuated its beauty. Black volcanic rock made up the surface – a sharp contrast to the colored structure. It was magic and magic only that held the cathedral, the barracks, and the wall secure over the unstable ground.

Tarik and Nolasco walked up to the two wooden doors leading into the chapel. A pair of soldiers nodded to their high priest as they opened wide the massive doors. Tarik felt their gazes, thick with distrust, wash over him, but when he returned their looks, their eyes fell to the ground. Tarik was a man of great renown and strength, and few could lock eyes with him.

The chapel resembled a field. Thousands of paper flowers were carefully placed to maximize their beauty throughout. Hundreds of small white crepes lined the cobblestone walkways and small clearings, with many more yellow, green, and blue behind them. Large red, black, and purple roses lined the walls.

Small sets of stairs led to the balcony that hugged the wall. Tarik knew it granted a wondrous view of the cathedral. It was in the balcony that people sat to listen to the words of the priests, though few were able to travel all the way to this cathedral to hear the words of Reproba Caelum.

No priests were present in the chapel, only the hard working acolytes and the few pilgrims who dared venture so far from home for a view of the cathedral. The acolytes moved with the pilgrims, blessing them. Their robes were all white as snow, unmarred by dust or grime.

Tarik continued to follow Nolasco along one of the paths, but he couldn't keep his eyes from wandering up to the image that loomed over his head imbued in the stained glass window. It was an image of the seven curators banishing Shiva. Two great spiraling horns were on her head, and spikes ran down her back all the way to the great tail that was wrapped around her body. Flames shot out of her open mouth, leaving rows of razor sharp teeth behind. It was taught that the curators banished her right under Fire Pass Cathedral, and it was she who made the Rivers of Flame sprout from the beneath the earth.

The seven curators in the image surrounded the demonic beast. They resembled men and women with large, white wings, except for one with black wings. Behind the feathered gods was the bright sky, a sky that stood for hope despite the enemy they faced.

Once in a large clearing situated in the back of the chapel, the pair came to stone steps that led up to the altar. Nolasco called a nearby acolyte to his side. Tarik watched as unknown instructions were given, and the acolyte immediately called to his brothers and sisters. In each cathedral there was a high priest, five priests, and any number of acolytes.

The acolytes came to the clearing and formed the sacred symbol, the five-pointed star. Together as one they began a slow quiet chant that built up in its intensity. From each of their hands came a swirl of color. From one acolyte came a stem of blue representing water, from another came green representing air, then yellow to represent earth, and a brilliant white branched forth from a fourth acolyte to meet inside the star. Together they twisted into a rope of magical colors and rose straight up into the air.

The fifth acolyte spoke, but his words weren't loud enough to be heard. From his angle Tarik could see one of the other acolytes snicker at him. He blushed, spoke a word Tarik didn't understand, and tried again.

"The cathedral is closed for all pilgrims," boomed the enchanted voice of the acolyte, sending his words echoing off the stone of the cathedral. A dim green sparkle seemed to come out of the speaking acolyte's mouth, resembling dust particles caught in a ray of sunlight. "We hope that the glory and the might of the curators have touched the heart of all: the heart of the most powerful lord, the heart of the richest merchant, and the heart of the most humble farmer."

Those inside the chapel began to filter out the doors. They had a long walk to get to the small town that stood just over a league to the east on stable ground. Tarik noticed the flowing silk garments of merchants mixed with the coarse wool of hard working folk. Though their clothes might have been different, all of their eyes were open wide. "They're in awe," muttered Tarik under his breath. A few moments passed until the doors were drawn shut by the exiting acolytes. Tarik was alone in the huge chamber with Nolasco – or so he thought.

Nolasco began to mutter words under his breath that Tarik didn't recognize. He took a step back to watch the next spell, but his sixth sense, the keen sense of a warrior, told him to be wary. Though he didn't know the words, he knew they meant magic.

From the other side of the paper meadow came a blue-streaking arrow, whizzing over the flowers toward Tarik. "*Alveus Silicus*" he cried as he dove, feeling his armor become lighter. He felt an impact on his right shoulder, but the enchanted armor stopped the arrow from completely piercing. The sheer force of the attack left a numb feeling tingling beneath his pauldron. Tarik jumped back to his feet and pulled out his spear, the same spear he had used in so many engagements fighting with his army.

Tarik was hit again by another arrow on his breastplate. The magical arrow sank in only enough to stick into the enchanted armor, but the impact knocked him back a step. Tarik gave a grunt and whispered, "*Cruor Peto.*" He turned and made a mighty sweep with his spear that aimed to take out Nolasco's legs. Just before the spear made contact, Nolasco faded away into an ethereal form, a blue mist in the shape of a human. He appeared ten steps further back among the flowers, and the spear passed through the mist. Green and yellow energy surged forth from Nolasco's hands and met a purple force that erupted from his circlet. The colors bonded together and bathed Tarik in their light. He immediately felt the weight of his armor return as Nolasco dispelled its magical qualities. Another arrow flew in; this one burying itself deep in Tarik's left shoulder, blasting through the now cumbersome armor as though it was paper. Tarik stumbled back under the blast, but managed to keep his feet.

Tarik felt a cold sensation snake its way through his body from the arrow. His muscles began to spasm as he fought for control of his limbs against a chill that threatened to paralyze him. Gritting his teeth and pushing through the magical sensation, Tarik threw his spear straight at Nolasco.

Nolasco saw the spear coming and raised his right hand. A gust of wind streaked across him. The missile was too close and too massive to be pushed completely aside, and it struck him hard in the hip. The heavy blow caused Nolasco to do a half spin before falling among blue pansies, bathing them in a color more fitting for the roses that lined the paper garden.

All control of his body lost, Tarik fell to his knees. His body was stiff. He had no power over his muscles. He could hear the sound of beating wings. Dust flew up from the stone finding its way in his teeth, leaving a dirty taste in his mouth. Tarik heard feet come to rest on top of the altar behind him.

"Tarik Ziyad, the famous commander of the Army of Truth. I think you have something that I need. *Brevis. Levo.*" Tarik felt his hair dance as a strong wind turned him around and lifted him off the ground. He now faced his captor hanging in mid air.

It was Anuke, the female curator of Fire Pass Cathedral. Her beautiful white wings were neatly folded behind a golden breastplate that was fashioned to fit her womanly curves. A short, studded leather skirt hung down over her strong thighs, and the straps of her leather sandals wove up her shapely feminine legs.

Anuke's blonde hair poured forth from underneath an open-faced bascinet that circled an unblemished face. Her full lips were taught with rage and pulled tight just below angry eyes filled with demand. She, like the other curators, would have been an image of pure beauty were it not for the anger that distorted her face.

Another curator stood behind her in the shadows. His white wings were folded protectively around his body, hiding everything but his gaunt, pallid face. His sharp features were similar to Ares, the god of war and the curator of the Cathedral of New Beginnings.

Tarik recognized the figures in front of him, but he made no move to speak. He knew what they wanted, but instead he held his tongue.

"How many have you shown? How many know the truth?" Anuke demanded from beneath her helmet. Tarik said not a word. "Answer me!"

"How is it that I, a mere *mortal*, could have something that the *goddess* Anuke desires?" Tarik responded.

Anuke's right and left hands shot out. She whispered more words of power. A fiery red light streamed out along with a bright blue. Yellow, green, white, and black poured out as well, twisting and turning together like writhing, hungry snakes.

From a necklace with a black chip that hung around her neck came a shining purple light that made each of the colors glow brighter than they already were, causing them to surge with power. As one, they struck Tarik's chest.

Tarik felt his insides burn as though a wild fire was eating away at his intestines. His skin turned to ice, concealing the fire within. He screamed in agony, but when the pain subsided, he said nothing. Tarik's body then seemed to want to explode from the inside out, causing intense pain in his gut and the feeling that he was going to rip apart. In an instant the air around him closed in like a wall, crushing his body against the outward push from inside. He screamed in agony, but when it came to an end, he said nothing. Tarik then became weak, his body rotting. He could smell his own decaying flesh, even managed a glance at a withering hand. He could hear his dying lungs wheeze for breath, and he could feel dead skin fall from his face only to have it replaced so that it could crumble away again and again. The seconds stretched on until they felt like an eternity for Tarik, until at last Anuke pulled her hands away.

"Are you ready to share?" she asked in a sweet voice. She walked toward the Constable, her lips turning to a wicked grin. "You need only whisper it in my ear," she said, her face coming close to his. Tarik said nothing.

"You appear to be having troubles," the other curator said in a bored, mocking tone. "Perhaps you should allow me a try. You elders lack the imagination of my generation."

Anuke turned from Tarik relieving him of her hard gaze. "Do not dare presume equality with me! You will witness their stubborness firsthand soon enough. And you will do as you're told from those of us who know better." She looked back at Tarik and slapped him across the face, a treasure compared to his earlier pains.

"Have it your way," she spat. "And know that everyone you know must die for your blasphemy. Good-bye Tarik Ziyad, enjoy your afterlife."

Anuke took a hop back that was enhanced by a single beat of her wings and landed beside the other curator. Her left arm came up, bow in hand, as her right pulled an arrow from the quiver on her hip. The arrow pounded Tarik in the chest, ending the numb feeling in his body. Just as his eyes were closing, he saw Anuke take wing toward the fallen Nolasco.

Chapter 1
(Anne, Galavon)

A warm, humid breeze spiraled over the Goblin Isles, passing over the broken tribes of small green-skinned creatures. Far above, it could make out a tattooed shaman performing rituals with flames, calling to their god. A sudden shift in its course brought the gust down low enough to blow out one of the sacred fires. It then continued its journey across the scattered islands, leaving the goblin rites behind.

The zephyr eventually found its way to the beaches off the eastern coast of the Peninsula Province where it gently played with the long hair of three young girls gathering shells. A stream of giggles accompanied the gentle breeze through tall southern trees and over lush green grass, but they were soon left far behind. A city, Pearl, crossed under the path of the spiraling air, and the late warm season draft came down to swoop through an open gate with strong iron bars. Down the streets it went, at one point catching the aroma of a warm apple pie and carrying it to a nearby thatched rooftop.

"Mmmm," let out Anne. "That one's apple." She poked her crystal, light blue eyes over the edge just in time to see hands set the simmering treat on the windowsill next to four other pies. "I bet that one is for the Fall Festival too. She won't even let us have a bite!"

Anne watched her brother Cecil take a look over the edge with similar crystal blue eyes inherited from their father, Tarik Ziyad. Both had slim bodies and small noses with skin goldened by days spent in the sun, though Cecil's shoulders were broad from working with a sword. Anne's heart shaped face resembled their father's, while Cecil had inherited their mother's long face.

A door opened somewhere down the street, and Anne quickly grasped a handful of Cecil's brown, straight hair. With a tug, she pulled him back out of view.

"I heard a merchant came in today from the Mountain Province just in time for the celebration tonight," Cecil whispered. "He'll probably be the last merchant from that far north until after the cold season." Anne could tell where her brother was going with this. "Forget the pie. It'll only get us in trouble. We should go see what he brought. Besides, I'm supposed to meet my tactician tutor at midday in the library, and you're supposed to help mother prepare for tonight." Anne hated to disappoint her brother, but she had a different idea of how to spend their time.

She squeezed her lips together and slowly shook her head back and forth in refusal. Even her curly brown hair swayed from one side to the other in another breeze as if saying no. She knew how to convince her brother. "Do you remember the time we slipped away from Caernarfon Castle to explore the bank of the Sparkle without a whole mess of soldiers following us around?"

"Yes, I remember. This is different. We're older now."

"And how father himself actually followed us?"

Cecil sighed. "Yes, I remember." Anne already knew she won.

"We didn't follow the rules then, and we found the bones of a dead wyvern with father in the shallows. Look, I still have the pearl we found in the clam there. See?" Anne pulled up her necklace to show her brother the pearl that decorated her neck. It was bigger and brighter than an average pearl, just like the rest of the pearls that came out of the lake situated beside the city. Ever since Anne had been given it, she had never let it out of her possession, though she kept it hidden and out of sight by her father's orders. "Sometimes when you don't follow the rules, good things happen. You discover things."

Cecil slumped his shoulders and motioned for Anne to continue.

With her brother convinced, Anne told Cecil to create a diversion while she snagged the pie. Her brother normally didn't take orders well, but Anne knew that she could convince him of just about anything. It had always been like that. Together they climbed down from the rooftop with Cecil helping Anne down the last jump. They shuffled around the other side of the building, garnering a confused look from the home's owner. Soon they were in the narrow alley between houses looking across the street at the windows to the bakery.

Anne noticed a group of kids who had seen maybe ten Twil, Twil being the shooting star that marked the end of the cold season, pretending to be fighting off a goblin invasion right next to the window. One was even pretending to be her father, Constable Tarik Ziyad, barking orders to his friends against the make-believe enemy. The plump woman who had baked the pies crouched outside under the window tending her herbs now that her cooking was complete. She was a widow, her husband tried and found guilty of heresy only two Twil ago. Now she ran the bakery by herself and like many struggled under the heavy taxes imposed by Reproba Caelum.

Anne shoved her brother out from the protection of the alley. He had seen seventeen Twil, one away from becoming an officer in his father's army. The thought of his role in this childish attempt to steal a pie was embarrassing him immensely, Anne knew. She watched as Cecil walked out to the middle of the street and brought his hand over his mouth in mock surprise. He yelled loud enough for everyone on the street to hear. "Look, a dove with a hurt wing!"

The children playing turned their heads, the fight apparently coming to a standstill. The battle commander, the boy pretending to be Constable Ziyad, waved his wooden waster high into the air and shouted, "To the bird!"

The army ran down the street yelling, all thoughts of formation gone. The baker's widow, Mrs. Brown, watched the group depart. Her pudgy face soon focused once again on her herb garden. Then came the cry, "Hoist me up, I'll find him!"

That cry brought Mrs. Brown up to her feet and into the fray. She took off her gardening gloves swatted the would-be rescuers as though they were cudgels. "Aye, ye just try and get up on that roof! I 'ave two hands here that be saying otherwise! Ye the new thatcher in town? Ye just leave the poor birdie alone!" Mrs. Brown yelled in her thick southern accent.

The distraction created the break Anne needed. She ran across Muffin Street, replaced the latest pie with a silver penny, and ran back into the alley. The hems of her light green skirt were stained with dirt from the garden. The pie was warm in her hands as she began to pick her way to a small door on the side of the city wall, avoiding any who might reveal her latest ploy.

Her slippers made little noise on the cobblestone alleys, and the only major street she had to pass was East Peri Street. It ran alongside the eastern portion of the wall. Pearl, the name of the city, was circular with four gates. The gates faced northeast, northwest, southeast and southwest. For one who had lived around the city as long as Anne though, it was no surprise that she knew of the small sally door facing directly east.

As she made her way across the street, her final barrier, she looked at who was positioned for guard duty at the door that day.

"Porter Mann..." Anne whispered, immediately recognizing the young soldier leaning on his spear in the heat and humidity. He was fifteen Twil, slightly overweight, and outfitted in a leather brigandine. A leather brigandine was a vest with small plates of metal riveted between two pieces of leather. A deep blue patch that reminded Anne of the ocean with a white pearl was sewn on the breast of the brigandine to show he was a soldier of the Peninsula Province. Decorating his neck was a white seashell necklace. After the battles, the officers of the Army of Truth could count their losses by the number of corpses found with the shell necklaces.

Porter used to be a friend of Anne and Cecil before he joined the Army of Truth like so many other young boys during the War of Fire. The goblin raids were so numerous at this time that Tarik had accepted boys as young as twelve Twil to begin training. He would use them to cook, fletch arrows, deliver messages – anything to free up his real soldiers. Keeping Pearl and the larger towns free of crime fell under the duty of the Army of Truth as well, and it was another way Tarik kept the young soldiers out of harm's way. Now that the war had ended, Anne expected most of the young soldiers to return home, especially those like Porter who weren't exactly natural born warriors.

Most of Anne and Cecil's male friends were either in training like Porter or were spread across the Sparkle, the salt water lake beside Pearl, diving deep into its depths in search of clams that might yield one of the valuable pearls the city was named after. The young women were married by now, also in training, or too involved in helping out with their father's household to play games with the two.

"Looks like a fun job, Porter," Anne said as soon as she was near enough for him to hear. She noticed sweat beads on his forehead, so she added, "A little hot outside for brigandine armor, isn't it?"

"We 'ave to wear 'em on guard duty," he replied in his southern drawl, standing up straight as soon as he realized it was Anne. He wiped off his brow. "But it be the beginning of the cold season tomorrow." Anne noticed the slight tremor in his voice as though he was nervous, and his eyes kept glancing away from her to the ground. Many of their old friends had become this way as they got older. They no longer saw Anne as a friend, but instead as the daughter of the Constable.

"Porter, I need to get through this door. Could you open it for me?" Anne looked around behind her to be sure there was no pursuit. There wasn't.

"Why don't ye use the main gate?" Porter asked. He rubbed his hands and tried to look her in the eye. He only managed it for a moment before looking away again. "I can't let ye out this one. It be against orders."

Anne didn't think he would take guard duty so seriously. Every possibility came to mind in seconds, along with their downfalls. Her thoughts found their way to the stiletto dagger strapped to her calf underneath her skirt. Her father had given it to her for protection. While the straight, slim blade was as common as the boy soldier in front of her, the hilt had a beautiful twisted handle. Her father told her it came from the Sauromatian Jungle, where its past female owner used its magical properties to hunt men. Whether the stiletto held magical properties or not, Anne wasn't sure, but it was a beautiful weapon she could use to convince her old friend to open the gate.

She thought this method a little much for an apple pie. Besides, she wasn't even being pursued. She could have made it out of one of the main gates without any questions asked. But then again, that wouldn't have been any fun.

"You think you might let me out for a piece of this?" she offered, pulling the pie out from its meager hiding spot behind her back.

He leaned in. "Is that apple?" Despite his few seasons of training, without a battle beneath his studded leather belt, Porter was still only a boy.

"It is," Anne assured him. "First one in Pearl since, well, probably the War of Fire! I'll give you a piece if you let me pass." She watched him with her crystalline blue eyes. Anne could tell he was still unsure, but she couldn't allow him to say no.

Without waiting for an answer from her hesitant friend, Anne withdrew her stiletto and cut out a slice of the pie and placed it in his gloved hands. "Don't eat the bottom, there's still polish on your gauntlets. You may open the door now."

Porter fumbled with the keys before finally opening the gate. It led out to the green fields east of Pearl. Anne ran down a slight slope as the ground leveled out and crossed a pasture where one of the stables let their horses nibble on the grass. Once through the small pasture she came to a farm filled with women collecting the harvest and preparing to plant the cold season crop.

With most of the men gone, the women of the Peninsula Province were forced to take up such duties. They were a strong people though, and despite the heat and hard work, Anne knew the women would finish the harvest. They may not be able to tend as many fields as they would have had their husbands and sons been home, but there would be no food shortage, only tighter belts.

Anne then started uphill. The land around Pearl was mostly flat besides the hill the city rested on and the small bump where Anne traversed. At the top, she sat down underneath the huge leaves of a maltree and recovered from her run. She gazed out at the land her father had fought to keep safe from the goblin invasion.

To the east and south, forests and farms stretched as far as Anne could see. The farms grew bananas and kerplums in the warm season and vegetables in the cold. Further south there would be more stables she knew. Pearl lay to her west, with the Sparkle stretched out behind it hiding its elusive pearls. It was the only saltwater lake Anne had ever heard of. Two highways branched out of the two northern gates, both leading to the Fire Pass Province. The northwestern highway went to Zephyr Hills and the famed Fire Pass Cathedral, the other to Port Farrow: a major city situated on the Southern Holy River.

She wondered why none of the other Constables had come down those highways to help her father against the goblins. It was as though each of the provinces were on their own, like there was no Kingdom of East Ager.

The southeastern road led to the Cathedral of New Beginnings and the town Asaph that had grown around it. Anne had traveled there with her father a few times during the horse fair in the early warm season. Her father had managed to keep the goblins from raiding that far inland, keeping them contained on the east coast. The southwestern road hugged the coast of the Sparkle and led to Caernarfon Castle along the Cliffside Gulf.

Anne closed her youthful eyes to bask in the shade of the maltree, shade that would have been considered hot by any not used to the southern heat. She put her arms behind her head and waited for her brother to join her.

She finally saw him strolling through the fields. She could tell it was Cecil by the clean, sleeveless blue tunic he wore. She was jealous of that, it looked much cooler than her long dress. As he made his way to the bottom of the low hill, Anne could see the unhappy look on his face. She laid back again and closed her eyes to wait for his tirade.

"Anne, I know it's only for fun, but we must start acting our age. And our rank." he said. "After this next Twil I'll be an officer, and how will men look up to me if all they can remember is me stealing pies? And you, you're nearly old enough to be married! You should be making your own pies! And you gave Mrs. Brown a silver penny for that pie! A silver penny! You can buy at least ten pies with a silver penny!"

Probably closer to fifteen, Anne thought, but she didn't say it out loud.

"You know word will get back to mother."

Anne ignored his last comment. "Took you long enough to get here. Let's eat!"

Anne explained why a piece was missing, talking continuously while she downed the greater portion of the pie. She knew her brother wasn't listening as he lounged against the trunk of one of the maltrees and nibbled on his piece, but she continued on anyway. Her brother was like that - constantly focusing on doing his duty and letting the simple pleasures like a hot apple pie escape him.

"You know, we should check out what the merchant brought," Anne suggested, stealing her brother's earlier idea while licking her fingers clean. "There's bound to be something interesting. I heard from one of the monks that Constable Eudes from the Point Province was able to reopen trade with the Free Cities. In fact, he told me that the people who live in the free cities are either really tall or really short. Naturally they're tall since they come from the old Empire, but some are short because they have dwarf blood in them.

"But the orcs are right there too, along with the elves. Does that mean the people are green and brown, light skinned, or both? It just doesn't make any sense to me." Anne paused to think. What was the point of her story?

"So are you all right with checking what the merchant brought?" she finally finished, turning her thoughtful blue eyed gaze to her brother.

Brother and sister headed back toward the city after filling up on the pie. They were headed to the Green, the open square in the northern part of the city to look at the goods brought by the merchant.

"Galavon! Help me with this barrel," demanded Torvil in a deep, gruff voice. He was the head of the caravan guard.

Galavon helped the huge man lift the heavy barrel from off the wagon bed and carefully set it down beside a table littered with an assortment of items ranging from pots and cups to various weapons. The latter were supposedly from the Free Cities, but the trade routes to those far northern cities were among the most dangerous due to brigands. It wasn't even odd to be attacked by raiding giants from the Giant Islet in the Cold Sea. Those brave enough to attempt the journey and lucky enough to survive it usually brought back one or two exotic weapons said to be enchanted.

Inside the barrel were shiny red apples that came from the Mountain Province. They had been carefully stored in the wagon to prevent them from bruising during the long trip from Mecca. It was the third of three barrels, the first two having already been sold to various shop owners so they could prepare for the city's annual feast.

After setting the barrel down Torvil stood up straight, revealing his great height. With broad shoulders, a jovial but scarred face behind a fluffy red beard, Torvil and his enormous great sword stood as the barrier between bandits and Galavon's father's cargo. It usually only took one look at the big man and his rough lackeys in their assorted steel and leather armor to dissuade any sort of ambush.

Galavon looked the opposite of the huge guard. His brown hair was short and neatly trimmed. There were no calluses on the palms of his hands, nor was he decorated in scars. He was an average height, but lanky rather than broad. He stood just under eight span. High cheekbones defined Galavon's hairless face, and his innocent green eyes showed that he had lived an easy life.

Galavon traveled with his father, Patrick Hostleton. Born in the bustling capital city of Mecca situated between the Point and Mountain Provinces, Patrick devoted his entire life to trade, especially after the death of his wife, Galavon's mother. His family had always been merchants who traveled the Great Trade Circle. The route went from Mecca down the Southern Holy River to Farrow, from there by ship to Elincia, then up the highway to Gareth before embarking on a barge back to Mecca through Eric's River and the Sacred Lake. Each of the cities stopped in were the centers of trade in that region, bringing goods ranging from produce and iron to silk clothing and delicacies. The trade route had made his family wealthy and established connections in every province but the Peninsula Province.

Galavon's mother, Tara, originated from the Mountain province. Her green eyes and light skin were traits common to the people who lived alongside the mountains in the forest. Those forests were dominated by giant oaks that left little sunlight for vegetation to grow below. It was from Tara that Galavon got his green eyes.

"I'm off to find an inn, maybe a lass to add some entertainment to the evening," Torvil said with a gruff chuckle. "Here's some advice: go and find yourself a lil' entertainment too!" After a hearty laugh, Torvil set off down the road to find some 'entertainment.'

"I also have certain dealings I must procure," said a voice from the other side of the wagon. Galavon turned to see his father, Patrick, walk out from behind a wagon filled with iron bars they bought in Mecca. They were mined in the Mountains of

Hope. "You're in charge of the wares set out for the public," he said. Patrick's right hand fiddled with a round iron pendant that hung from his neck on a plain chain. The pendant had a crude carving of half a sun and a crescent moon pressed together. "Give good prices," he continued. "I don't want my name spoiled here." His gray hair and thin face made him look stern.

Patrick turned and walked away before Galavon could respond. He looked like a noble walking these streets in fine silk that had been tailored by one of the guilds in Farrow – the best you could find in Mundus. The exquisite clothing reminded Galavon just how strange it was for them to leave the normal trade route for a destination that failed to offer more than a few coins.

"Yes, father." Galavon said to the empty space where his father had stood. He turned to the stall and saw three of his father's guards standing watch near the tables to prevent theft, but his eyes were drawn to the crowd that had gathered. Because they usually sold items in bulk to agents who would in turn sell them to lesser merchants, the items at the stall were various trinkets they picked up at different towns. Galavon smoothed out his dark green tunic and straightened his brown leather belt. He often did a better job of scaring away customers rather than selling things to them.

Hopefully I won't mess anything up today.

"Hello," he said kindly to an older woman looking at a shiny pot. "That pot comes straight from Trikkle, a mining city in the Mountain province that gathers ore and crafts things such as this. They've begun to put copper on the bottom to speed up the heating. It's as fine a pot as you'll ever find."

"Ohhh," squawked the woman, turning the pot in her dirty hands before putting it into Galavon's. "It be far too fine fer me, seems more fit fer a castle."

"Oh, no ma'am, it's reasonably..." Galavon started, but the woman disappeared leaving the pot in his hands. Looking down the table he noticed some young boys with wooden swords staring at an axe. It had a half moon blade on one side with a spike on the other. Galavon dropped the pot and hastened to them.

"This is meant for a warrior. See, it has the mark of Barbuta on the blade, from up north outside of the kingdom. Barbuta is the city-state by the Cold Sea that battles raiding giants."

An "ooh" emerged from the boys as Galavon straightened the axe for emphasis. He beamed in their admiration. It wasn't often anyone was impressed with him. "Ave ye ever been to Barbuta?" asked one boy in that strange southern accent.

"I can't say that I have, but I have seen a giant."

Their mouths hung agape.

"I hope I get to travel like ye one day," another boy squeaked.

"Maybe if you can find me at the Harvest Festival I'll tell you about it. I'm busy now, but if you find me I'll tell you the whole story." They scurried away through the growing crowd, and Galavon let out a chuckle. He had never actually seen a giant, but while in Gareth with his father he had seen a slain giant's harpoon; a huge javelin with a barbed end that the gigantic creatures used to catch whale. Galavon searched the tables for someone who looked as though they meant to purchase something.

He looked to the barrel of apples and found a true crowd of people who intended to buy some of the red fruit that was so rare this far south.

Father's agent must not sell them outside of Farrow, these people are acting like the apples are gems!

He walked toward the barrel and explained where they came from. For two copper pennies an apple, Galavon began to hand them out and collect the small amount of money.

In the larger cities where the trades were made in bulk with huge amounts of coin passing between hands, Galavon had learned the worth of a coin. Ten copper pennies were equal to a copper lot, ten copper lots were equal to a copper mark, and ten copper marks to a silver penny. Ten silver pennies equaled a silver lot, and ten silver lots a silver mark. Ten silver marks made a gold mark. Galavon simply remembered copper to silver to gold, penny to lot to mark – except there was no gold penny or gold lot. One gold mark was the equivalent to one million copper pennies. Most people in East Ager would spend their entire lives without seeing a gold mark.

As the crowd around the apples dispersed, Galavon noticed a girl looking among the items. She looked to have seen maybe fifteen or sixteen Twil, just a few Twil younger than himself. She was looking down and had curly brown hair on a bright, heart shaped face. She was dressed in a nice, if somewhat dirty, light green cotton skirt. Usually shy of pretty girls, Galavon couldn't help but walk toward her with Torvil's advice still ringing in his ears.

"Hi, are you looking for anything in particular?" he asked with kindness in his voice. She kept her head down looking at the items.

"No, just looking. Thanks."

"Are you sure? I have…" Galavon stopped. The girl raised her enchanting, crystal blue eyes that were so common in this province and met his gaze. Galavon lost all concentration and felt his stomach turn into a knot.

The girl stared back, neither blinking. They simply looked into each other's eyes, the light blue into the soft green; the soft green into the light blue.

"I was wondering how much this pot would cost me," asked a young man at her side, holding up the copper pot the old woman had put down earlier. Handsomely dressed in cotton so light it could have passed for coarse silk, the newcomer held his chin high and looked down upon Galavon. His long, narrow face made him look arrogant. "Oh, I seem to have left my coins at home," he finished as soon as the girl's eyes darted to the ground. He put the pot back on the table, and Galavon noticed he looked as strong as one of his father's guards in his sleeveless tunic. "Come on, Anne." The young man grabbed her arm and began to walk away through the crowd.

Coming to his senses, Galavon yelled, "Wait!" The pair stopped and turned, the young man's eyes filled with suspicion and the girl's with anticipation. "Will you be at the feast tonight?" Galavon dared to ask.

The girl's mouth partly opened in a silent response. Before she could speak, the young man she was with interrupted and said in a dry tone, "Probably." They disappeared around the corner.

"Excuse me sir, could ye tell me the price of…" began a portly man with a goblet in his hand.

"Who was she? And who was that man with her?" Galavon interrupted, still staring at the corner where the two had disappeared.

"The two you were just talking with? Those were the Constable's children, Lord Cecil and Lady Anne. You won't find a more dutiful son or a more beautiful maiden in all of East Ager." The man studied Galavon's face. "She's the pearl of the province and destined for a great man."

"I wouldn't doubt your words..." Galavon mumbled, his vision still on the corner.

"Now about these goblets, sir, what sort of glass are they made from, because my wife would love to have a new set."

"Oh, oh yes. The glass is from the Feather Coast, we picked them up in Elincia..."

With the crowd dissipated and the sun hanging low in the sky, Galavon began to put the items that were not sold back into the wagons. It had been a fairly successful day, but because they were probably the last merchant to come this far south with the intent of selling goods rather than buying them, it was to be expected that things would sell. Selling odd trinkets, however, didn't even come close to the usual profit along the Great Trade Circle, and once again Galavon began to wonder why his father had decided to leave the normal trade route this year.

Once he finished loading the items, Galavon hoisted himself onto the back of a wagon and watched the folk of the city set up for their celebration. Having seen most of the cities in the kingdom, Galavon wasn't sure that Pearl should even be considered a city.

His thoughts mostly lingered on the girl he saw while selling his father's wares. "Anne," he whispered to himself, remembering the name the man had given to her. He had never seen anyone like her. Galavon had seen beautiful women before, women men would consider far more beautiful than this girl, but there was something about her that had ensnared him. It didn't help that she was the daughter of a Constable. Even though he came from a wealthy merchant family, Galavon knew there were lines that were not crossed in the Kingdom of East Ager. Powerful nobles were beyond even the richest merchants, though this Anne didn't dress or act like any noble woman he had even seen.

"You're still out here?" asked Darak, one of the guards under Torvil's command. He was alone in the dim light. "You should be getting ready for the festival. I'll watch these scraps. Your father got rooms at The Angry Maiden on East Peri Street."

"All right. Thanks." Darak was different than the rest of the guardsmen. He kept himself clean and didn't smell like a pigsty. He didn't use foul language or avoid speaking with Galavon. He kept to himself mostly, and kept his face hidden beneath a hood no matter the heat. Galavon jumped down off the wagon and waved back at Darak, just catching sight of his indigo eyes from beneath the hood.

Galavon followed the path the wagons laden with goods took earlier that day back along East Peri Street. The cobblestone streets seemed out of place in such a small city, but unlike a large city, they were kept clean. The houses were fairly small, but even the ones with single floors stretched high into the air so that in the summer the heat would rise to the ceiling, and the cooler air would sink to the floor. Galavon only knew that because the houses built in Farrow were similar.

Finally, he came to a large building with an open door streaming light onto the darkening street. "The Angry Maiden" was painted in red letters over the door, and the sounds of chatter echoed from inside. Galavon could hear Torvil's deep laugh among the voices. A narrow alley ran alongside the inn with small clumps of hay littering the ground. Galavon passed the entrance of the inn and followed the alley to the stable.

In the first stalls were his father's horses. They were mostly work horses to pull the carts, but there were also Plainstriders. He bought them once they got off their ship at Marcil, a bustling town built around Conwy Castle along the Southern Holy River. Tall, lean, and good for long journeys, Plainstriders were the most common breed in the Kingdom of East Ager.

The other stalls were filled with Southern Jigglers. They were smaller, surer on their feet, and arguably the most intelligent of the different breeds. They were common this far south because they dealt with the heat and humidity better than the big horses. When a skilled rider rode them, it seemed as though they were dancing, legs coming up to their chest and heads held high. Their "dancing" was made even more beautiful by the long white hair that grew just above their hooves called feathers.

The only horse breed not in a stall was a Charger. They were huge horses that carried fully armored men further north. In the southern heat Chargers didn't fare as well as in the cold.

Galavon saw a pitch fork rise and fall at the far end. He took a hesitant step inside. "Hello?" Galavon asked. One of his father's horses neighed. The pitchfork stopped, and the head of a young man popped out. This was the second boy his age that Galavon had seen around town not dressed as a recruit.

"Did you come with the merchant? Hostleton?" The stable boy had a lot of the visual southern traits – they all seemed to have the same curly brown hair and were shorter than the men further north. He did lack the light blue eyes though. His were a walnut brown. His nose was spotted with freckles which gave him a friendly look.

"Yes. I'm Galavon Hostleton. I'm looking for my bags."

"I took them in for you. Second floor, third room on the right." He stepped into the hallway. "The name is Saoirse, Saoirse Ire. My friends call me Sao." He nodded as a greeting. "Either my mother or father should be at the desk; they'll point you to your room. If you're lucky it's my father, the inn's named after my mother."

"Thanks," Galavon responded, awkwardly smiling at the joke. He was always shy around new people. He wasn't sure what to say back. He went to turn but noticed a bizarre weapon at Sao's side. It was a claw with three blades made of a fiery red metal. The exotic weapon looked strange on the stable boy.

"That's an interesting weapon," Galavon said. He tilted his head toward the weapon at Sao's side.

"This?" Sao pulled the claw from its sheath. He twisted it in the air between them, the light from the low sun reflecting off the red blades. "Since the war, everyone with business outside the walls started keeping some sort of weapon on them. Lieutenant Commander Varro himself gave me this.

"During the War of Fire, he killed one of the goblin shamans. This one was fighting with fire all over his skin. As soon as the weapon was knocked away though, the flames went out. Varro killed him and picked up the weapon."

"Is it magic?" Galavon asked.

"I don't know. It's blasphemy to use it if it is. Not long ago Mrs. Garun, the cobbler's wife, came across an old weapon when she was cleaning out her attic. She asked one of the monks about it, and before the season ended she was taken away as a heretic. All she did was ask about it!"

Similar stories were told all across the Kingdom of East Ager. The only legal way to use magic was to become a monk or a priest and dedicate your life to Reproba Caelum, even if it was through an old weapon or trinket. Otherwise, you were hunted down. Galavon was surprised Sao could even keep the weapon.

"Anyways, someone will point you to rooms," Sao said. "I have to get back to work if I want to make it to the festival smelling like something other than horse manure."

Chapter 2
(Anne, Galavon)

"If ye ever to become a good wife, ye must be here to help. Ye need to learn how to..." Anne stood in front of Margaery, the older woman who helped her mother run the household. It seemed to Anne that Margaery actually did everything, so she never understood why she was to learn the art of needlework or food preparation. She would rather be learning to wield a sword or go horseback riding. The things a lady were supposed to do were boring.

Extremely boring.

"Your father should have allowed me to send you and your brother to another estate," Lady Ignava commented. She sat with a straight back in her husband's carved chair sipping from a delicate cup. "That's how the nobles in the other provinces raise their children. Constable Eudes of the Point Province sent his only son Guy to another family. Even after losing his eldest."

Lady Ignava looked like the very essence of the northern nobility with ties to the old empire. She was tall, had a sturdy build, dark straight hair and of course, the long face. She was proper and predictable. Everything Anne was not.

"Are you listening to me? A pie, Anne? A pie?" The last sentence sounded like a snarl. "We could have baked you a dozen pies here!"

"Yes, mother," Anne said back in a monotone voice. Baking pies was no fun. Stealing them was. "May I go now?"

"Go wash," she said with a wave of dismissal. "I'll send a clean dress for tonight, you've absolutely ruined that one. We must look our part in the festival, especially with your father's absence."

Without waiting for another comment that might mean she'd have to stay longer, Anne darted toward the exit of the Great Hall. Tapestries decorated the wall, and a thick, intricate carpet ran down the center. Anne's father had planned the resistance from the goblins with his commanders in that room. Lady Ignava decided the punishment for her daughter.

Hanging a left out of the hall, Anne went up the curving stone steps that led to the right wing of the second floor. The third floor was for the less important servants due to the rising heat, but the second was for the Ziyad family, guests, and revered servants. This wing was a neat but sparsely decorated hall with four doors. Her room was at the end of the hall on the right, and Cecil's was directly across from it. Margaery also had a room in this hall, along with a spare room that was kept clean for guests.

Anne stepped onto the cool stone floor of her room and turned to shut the door. Once it was shut, she walked to her feather bed and fell back onto it, arms outstretched, and eyes looking up at the stone ceiling.

All she could see was the smiling face with green eyes.

She had been paralyzed! She had never been at a loss for words before; she even prided herself with her quick thinking. It was as though his face had knocked the breath out of her, and now she couldn't stop thinking about him.

If only Cecil hadn't pulled her away. She knew he was just being her big brother, but she wasn't even able to learn his name. "Sometimes he just cares too much," she whispered. Anne sucked in a deep breath and slowly let it out.

A knock at the door tore her thoughts away from the young merchant. "My lady? I ave' brought a dress fer ye to wear tonight."

"Come in!" Anne sat up on her bed as a maid walked in with a dark blue cote-hardie adorned with gold fringes. "Ahh, thank you Isabella."

Isabella, like Anne, had all of the qualities of a native from the Peninsula Province. She had curly brown hair, a heart-shaped face, crystal blue eyes and skin golden from the bright sun. Though she was not as slim, if she hadn't been Anne's father's age they could have passed as sisters.

"Yer welcome my lady," the maid said as she came in the room and carefully laid down the dress. "Lady Ignava wishes fer ye to be the symbol of the province, so she sent this dress fer ye to wear. It be quite beautiful. I 'ave also set up a bath in yer washroom fer ye."

Isabella was the kindest of the maids and always sent to help Anne. Anne fumbled with the buttons on the back of her skirt in an attempt to get it off. There was always that one button in the middle of her back that she couldn't reach, no matter how she twisted her arms. "Isabella, do you think you could…"

"Yes, ma'am, of course."

"Isabella, you don't have to call me ma'am. I've known you since I was born." She slid the garment off her body and stepped out of the pile of dirty cloth that had been her skirt. She turned to face the maid clad only in her chemise.

"I'm yer maid, my lady, no matter how many Twil I've known ye."

Moments later, Anne was sitting in the tub in her washroom, getting her back scrubbed as her hair absorbed the nutrients of the shampoo Isabella had lathered on top of it. The water was cold, but it was a nice reprieve from the heat outside.

"Isabella… have you ever met someone… a boy… that you couldn't seem to get out of your head?" Anne asked staring straight ahead into the soapy water of the bath.

"Yes my lady, he be with the Army of Truth right now, wherever it may take him." The scrubbing slowed for a moment. "I'm waiting fer the day that will bring him to me, or the night that will take me to him."

The scrubbing renewed to its original pace. "Ave' ye met a boy? I'd 'ave thought ye knew all the boys around here."

"Well, sort of. I never got to actually meet him or even learn his name. Cecil pulled me away before I could say anything."

Isabella laughed at that. "Before *ye* could say anything? Must 'ave been an interesting meeting." Isabella grabbed a pitcher of water from off a nearby table and poured the water over Anne's head without warning, washing the coat of shampoo off. Her curls fought against the water immediately, some already beginning to coil despite being drenched.

"I suppose I'll see him tonight. Maybe then I can learn his name." Anne rose up from the water and stepped out of the tub. Isabella dried her with a thick towel before giving her a robe to put on.

"If my lady be still thinking about him, I hope ye can learn it tonight as well." Once Anne was dry, Isabella held her shoulders and gave her a tight hug. Looking into her eyes, Anne thought she saw a tear. "Let's get to yer room so we can get ye in that dress."

It wasn't long until Anne sat in a bumpy carriage with the Lady Ignava sitting across from her. Anne's arms were folded tight against her chest. She stared out the window of the carriage, and her chin jutted out in a scowl to let her unhappiness be known. The mood was palpable.

I don't understand why I have to ride in this bouncing box! she thought. She could see her brother riding beside them on his warhorse Babieca. Babieca was so large for a Southern Jiggler he could have been mistaken for a Plainstrider were it not for the feathers around his hooves. He joked with one of the guards before letting Babieca loose and running ahead.

Laughter and music greeted her as the carriage passed under the gate and they entered Pearl. They rode all the way to the Green where hundreds of people were seated at long tables drinking their fill in the last bit of sunlight as torches were being lit. Many seemed to have already consumed a healthy portion of ale judging by the noise, but Anne couldn't blame them. The feast itself couldn't start until they arrived, and Lady Ignava never made it to any occasion on time. She would find some excuse to force tardiness, whether her hair had to be perfect, or her dress was too wrinkled. She claimed it reminded the people of who they were.

Still, Lady Ignava did look like a noble. She was always well dressed, and her long face made her a handsome woman. Her gray eyes and pale skin made her stand out in the city.

The carriage came to a stop and Anne stormed out of the carriage first. She stomped her way to Cecil's side, Babieca now being led off to a stable by Cecil's friend, Sao. Sao's parents owned one of the inns in town, The Angry Maiden.

"Don't forget to smile, this is a feast after all," Cecil whispered to her. "I just hope there's more pie."

Anne couldn't stop her lips from curling up in a half smile as she watched Lady Ignava emerge from the carriage and gracefully walk to Cecil's other side. She gave Anne an angry look when she noticed the smile, already suspecting foul play. Anne let the smile take up her whole face.

The three of them climbed the steps of a raised dais situated in front of the other tables. Cecil stopped behind their father's chair. The crowd that had gathered below stopped their talking and looked up to the platform. Anne waited patiently behind her own chair. With their father's absence, it was up to Cecil to begin the feast.

Cecil stood in front of the entire city in a dark blue doublet with brass studs. Under the doublet was a shirt the same blue color with gold along the tip of the collar and the edges of the sleeves. He perfectly matched Anne's dress. Looking at the two of them, there could be no doubt they were related to the province's hero, Tarik Ziyad, and the silence given to them by the people below showed their respect for the family that had rid them of the goblins.

"In my father's absence, I take his chair." Anne scraped her heavy chair back and sat as her mother and brother did the same. Then Cecil continued."We all thank curator Ares for this feast and for our victories. May he forever watch over his own land!" Light clapping came from all seated below, followed by the holy sign from the more devout: thumbs to shoulders, chest, then right thumb to forehead. Ares was the curator of the Cathedral of New Beginnings, the god that warriors and farmers were supposed to pray to. "And now, let the feast begin!" That was when the real applause erupted.

Immediately food was brought out to the tables. First it came to Cecil, where her brother would sample a bite before passing it on. There was rainbow trout from nearby springs, octopus from the Sparkle, freshly picked green beans, pig complete with one of the apples brought by the merchant in his mouth, roasted kerplums grown just outside the city walls, and many more dishes. If something appealed to his taste buds, like the seasoned, stuffed duck, he would cut off a piece for himself before passing a portion to Anne or Lady Ignava. Their plates were full before half of the dishes had been brought, so he waved the rest on so everyone could enjoy the bounty of the feast. The ability to hold a celebration such as this so soon after the war showed the strength and resolve of the people that lived in the province.

"Anne! Small bites!" Lady Ignava snapped. Anne looked up innocently with three slices of an apple fried in cinnamon and honey stuffed in her mouth. Anne ignored her though. The feast was on in full, and what good was a feast if you couldn't eat as much of your favorite food as possible?

Anne grabbed for the goblet of wine that sat in front of her to wash down the apple. She had never had ale before, Lady Ignava would never allow it, but Anne wouldn't mind trying it. The way the townspeople drank it down below, she felt it was more her style than the tart, watered down wine in front of her. *Well, maybe it's not tart, but I'd still like to try ale.* She took a giant gulp before looking at Cecil.

He sat calmly looking out at the common folk below. His plate was empty, and his wine glass was full as he swirled it around in front of him. Anne thought it strange how easy it was for Cecil to sit in front of so many people and lead the feast – he had taken on duties such as this for the past Twil while Tarik won the War of Fire. It seemed natural for him.

"You know, the wine is meant for drinking," Anne said. She took a gulp of her own to show him. "Like you told me, this is a feast! Loosen up! I'm sure yours isn't mostly water."

Cecil laughed at her and took a small sip. "I'm loose! But you be careful! It can't take much more than half a glass of wine to make you too festive."

Anne let her earlier scowl creep back to her face after she gulped down the rest of her wine and stared at her brother. Cecil laughed in return before taking another small sip of his own.

Sitting above everyone, Anne could see everything. She saw mothers feeding their young children, old men telling stories, and many young women talking with each other. Boys her brother's age were few and far between, although she recognized some who had left the city earlier in the season to gather pearls out of the Sparkle. It didn't surprise her they took a short break from their perilous dives to the bottom of the lake in order to enjoy the celebration.

Her eyes came to rest on one young man. It was the merchant from earlier. He was dressed in a doeskin doublet the color of grass with tan, silk pants to match. The outfit made his green eyes darker, and the jumping light of the torches on his soft face with the high cheekbones made him more captivating than he had been earlier.

He looked out of place seated at the table. Anne assumed the men around him were his guards meant to protect the goods. He seemed nervous in their company and focused on eating.

"Very nice entrance, my boy!" said the fat man sitting on the other side of Lady Ignava at the high table. The sudden statement tore Anne's focus from the merchant. It was Fragtos, the Baron of Pearl, the man in charge of the city. Though only priests were allowed to buy the large pearls, the taxes from these sales made Baron Fragtos wealthy. The Harvest Festival was the only time the Baron gave back to the city. The thin quiet woman who sat beside him was his wife Mara, the Baroness. Anne couldn't recall ever seeing her eat, even at the feasts.

"Your mother must have taught you to be fashionably late; I know your father was never one to show his position, or to be late for that matter." This comment came from further down the table from a man dressed in monk's robes. He was the nuncio of Pearl. The nuncio coordinated the movements of monks throughout the Kingdom of East Ager to help mend wounds and cure the sick. Anne always enjoyed the monks' stories of travel. The nuncio were only boring old men with an air of self importance. They didn't help to rule like the priests or high priests, but they did enjoy the easy life of a heightened position that didn't require them to travel. The positions were often given to nobility who were unable to perform magic, though some nuncio's did have the ability.

"I do try to teach them how to be civil," Lady Ignava commented as she nibbled on a blackberry muffin slathered with thick honey. Honey that thick could only have come from the Point Province, probably costing a fortune. "But try as I might, it was I who forced our fashionable tardiness, or else my darling son would have been here earlier." She brought her lace napkin to her chin to dab away at nothing.

"Earlier? The guest of honor? That would have been disastrous!" Grease ran down the Baron's chin from the giant chicken leg he was devouring. Anne couldn't help but laugh when she watched the Baron say "disastrous." The word sent his second and third chins into jiggling spasms and turned his face red. The grease dripped down onto his red silk tunic to join the splashes of wine that had ruined it earlier in the evening. Other members of the high table agreed with the baron – these included Cecil's tutor and a few Viscounts from the surrounding area.

Anne turned her focus back to the merchant. He was blushing at some joke made by the huge man who sat beside him. He was handsome even while blushing. She wondered what the man could have said to make the merchant boy so embarrassed.

"At least be discreet about it." Anne felt her cheeks turning red at Cecil's comment. She was sure she matched the merchant below.

"Anne, you're a noble. He's a merchant. I'm putting an end to this once the dancing begins."

"You won't say a word to him!" Anne said. " I will not…"

"I'm not sure you'll be able to." Anne turned and found Cecil's friend Sao with a grim look on his face behind the platform. Most of the girls around Pearl knew of Saoirse Ire, as he was infamous for his freckles and kisses. "There's a soldier, Captain Gherro. He has news."

Cecil excused himself from the table while the seated nobility murmured among each other, curious as to what could call away Cecil's attention in the middle of the feast. Lady Ignava silenced the gossip with some line or another about military matters. Sao led Cecil out of the Green.

What could have happened? Goblins?

Anne felt abandoned on the dais without her brother. Lady Ignava and the other nobles were not very good company. She gazed out at the crowd and tried to be discreet as she studied the merchant.

"When I said you should find yourself a lil' entertainment, I didn't mean the Constable's daughter!" Torvil whispered into Galavon's ear with a gruff chuckle coming soon after. He leaned back and made a crude joke to the woman sitting in his lap.

It was true though. During most of the feast Galavon and Anne had been sneaking looks at one another in-between bites. Anne didn't seem to mind being noticed, but Galavon tried to sink deep in his wooden chair due to the unwanted attention.

A loud knocking came from the table on the raised dais. The fat man Galavon's father had been doing dealings with earlier in the day stood, and the entire Green fell silent.

"Unfortunately, it would seem our young Lord had to be excused, so I take it upon myself as Baron of Pearl to move on to the dancing!" Immediately the food was removed from the tables before they were lifted up and carried out of the center of the Green. Two old men, a monk, and a few younger women took up instruments and started to play.

As soon as the music began, the people of Pearl got to their feet. While the first song played, Galavon searched the crowds of women for Anne. With so few men, most of the women were sitting in the seats along the sides glaring at the lucky ones who were able to procure a partner. A number of them danced with children or each other and laughed all the while. Many left for the inns and taverns where they hoped to find a different sort of celebration.

Torvil had already left with the crowd, and Galavon's father hadn't come to the feast. The other members of the guard weren't around either, probably helping Patrick with his business. Or else they were taking care of their own business, as Torvil was doing.

Galavon couldn't find Anne within the throng of women, and as soon as the second song began to play, a girl his age came and asked him for a dance. She had the customary blue eyes from the region, darker blue than Anne's, and frizzy straight brown hair. Her smile was inviting though, and with Anne nowhere to be found along the sides, he agreed and took the girl's hand.

Galavon was no novice dancer. He loved music, and even learned the basics of the harp in Mecca during their short stays between the trading seasons. He knew all the essentials for dancing, whether at fine balls thrown by the nobility in Mecca when on a rare occasion merchants were invited to attend, or in town and city celebrations encountered during travels with his father. He was swift but smooth, calculated and gentle, knowing just when to turn and how quickly to do it. Often music and dancing were the only remedies to his shyness.

Galavon took the girl's hand gently and raised it above her head. She walked around him as the dance was supposed to be performed. The song was "The Shadow Sonata," a favorite throughout the Kingdom of East Ager in most wealthy houses. Galavon was surprised they were playing it at the Harvest Festival.

As she came around, he placed his hand carefully around her waist before setting her off into a slow spin. There were no words to the song, only a slow, dark tune meant for dancing.

"Ye are quite the dancer," the girl giggled as they continued to dance. "I'm glad I got to ye before the other girls had a chance."

Galavon let go of the girl and did his own slow spin before coming to grasp her right hand with his own. Though his dance movements flowed together like a finely woven tapestry, Galavon wasn't sure what to say. "Thank you. You, uh, are a good dan..." Galavon stumbled on a side step. Anne was dancing in front of him with the Baron, looking disgusted with the overweight man and scanning the crowd. The Baron talked to another couple beside them and did more rocking than dancing.

"Sorry about that," Galavon said. "I suppose I'm not quite as good you thought."

"It's all right, I would 'ave been completely lost halfway through this song without ye leading," she responded. "It's the Baron's favorite." An older soldier of some rank slid past the two dancers and moved to the Baron. The officer whispered something in his ear that caused the Baron's eyes to go wide. The song came to an end and the fat Baron excused himself and followed the soldier out of the Green.

"I would love to 'ave another dance with ye," the girl said a sweet voice. He heard her words, but his eyes were fixed on Anne where she stood in the middle of the dancers.

"It was nice dancing with you, but I think there's another I should dance with." Galavon replied distantly.

"Perhaps a little later then?" the girl asked.

"Perhaps." The clapping that was coming from the onlookers came to an end as the next song began. Anne started to walk out of the crowd, but before Galavon could even consider being shy, he clasped Anne's shoulders.

"Do you, do you suppose I could have this dance?" he asked with uncustomary courage. Anne turned and gave Galavon a smile while he looked down into her eyes.

"Certainly," she said. Galavon took her by the hand and led her back among the dancers. He hoped his hands wouldn't get cold and damp. The music started, more lively this time and accompanied by a woman's voice. They brought the palms of their left hands together and began to dance.

This song had no set dance attached to it – it was the sort of music Galavon expected to hear at a Harvest Festival. It was upbeat and energetic, bringing clapping and laughter from the onlookers.

Once they began, Galavon didn't say a thing. At first his nervousness set in, so he looked into the crowd. However, the knot in his stomach faded with each note, and he found he couldn't keep his eyes off of Anne. He felt content sneaking looks at her as they danced. They continued in silence beneath the noises of the rowdy crowd.

I'm such a fool. No one else my age has problems talking to girls.

Then the song reached its end. In the clapping that followed Galavon stood looking at his feet. Without the music, he was only the shy merchant with no words.

Another tune began. It was another lively song. Galavon looked up from the ground as Anne flashed a smile and her face beamed.

"'A Harpist's Broken String!' I love this song!" Without giving him a chance to speak, Anne moved Galavon back a few steps so that he was across from her in a line of three. All of the dancers made these lines standing across from their partner with their backs against another line of three creating a column of dancers that spread down the Green. Galavon could see Anne's excitement as she waited for the appropriate part to start dancing. It made him smile. She returned his smile with one of her own as soon as it came time to dance.

At least this broke the awkward moment.

All the couples walked toward each, then back. Toward each other again, and spun around switching positions. This was repeated, putting them back into their original spots as the singer began.

> *"In the city not far from here,*
> *Gathered a crowd,*
> *A harpist to hear!*
> *It was said he could win a tear,*
> *From all the beautiful maidens dear!"*

The couples then moved close again, grasping hands above their heads to form a tunnel.

> *"He played one note,*
> *and then two,*
> *But just as the maidens began to woo…"*

"This is my favorite part!" Anne said, her hands firmly grasped in Galavon's. Then all together, singer, dancers and those watching burst out with the chorus as the couples on the right side of the tunnels danced through to the other side.

> *"It went pop! Pop! Pop!*
> *A maiden's broken dream!"*

Galavon and Anne danced through the tunnel.

"Pop! Pop! Pop!
Fate can be so mean!"

The last couple moved through.

"Pop! Pop! Pop!
A Harpist's broken string!"

The singing ceased as the couples moved close together again. One arm around the other's waists and their free hands clutched together, the dancers moved to the right in beat with the fast pace of the music. Once all the way to the other side, they clasped left hands together and moved all the way to the left.

"You're a good dancer! Do they play this in the other provinces?" Anne asked. They skipped back to the right.

"I only heard it once in Farrow during the Spice Derby, but it wasn't nearly this much fun!" They made their way back to the center and stepped apart from each other.

"See you at the last verse!" Anne yelled over the music. Everyone clapped hands before turning around to face their new partner as the next verse rolled out.

Galavon was now face-to-face with another girl. She was short with curly brown hair and a huge lump of a nose. He smiled politely to her and went through the motions of the dance for the second verse.

"The harpist was like snow in the Spring,
Or even a bird,
Without a wing!
He was a crown without a king,
So he put down his harp and started to sing!

He sang one note,
and then two,
But just as the maidens began to woo…

It went crack! Crack! Crack!
A maiden's broken dream!
Crack! Crack! Crack!
Fate can be so mean!
Crack! Crack! Crack!
A Harpist's broken string!"

Everyone clapped their hands together and turned back to their original partner.

"This is the last verse!" Anne told Galavon as they made their first approach. "It's the same as the first verse but faster – be ready!"

It took no time for the players, dancers and singer to race through the song. When it came to the part of the dance where the lines moved left and right, everyone broke apart and danced the best they could to the fast music. The dancers whirled to the left and spun to the right trying to keep pace.

"A harpist's broken string!"

"I need a break from dancing," Anne said amongst the roar of clapping and laughing from the bystanders. She was breathing hard, and Galavon thought a break would be nice as well. "Would you come with me to get something to drink?"

"Sure," he said. The nervousness was coming back.

Side by side they walked out of the dancers to the table where drinks were still being poured. Galavon poured Anne a cup of water. She broke the silence when they sat down in some of the chairs on the outside of the dancing area.

"So I've danced with you, but I still haven't learned your name," Anne said. She took a drink of water and waited for his answer.

"Galavon Hostleton. It, uh, is a pleasure."

Come on Galavon! You can at least talk to her!

Anne rolled her eyes. "Well, Galavon, if anything is a pleasure, it's dancing with you! Even when there are more men around it's hard to find a good dance partner. You said you heard that song once?" she asked.

Galavon nodded. He couldn't help but look away when he muttered, "Two Twil ago while I was in Farrow." *Come on, she is going to think I'm an idiot if I can't even look at her!*

Anne took another drink of her water. "I'm impressed you can remember it. My brother still hasn't learned it, and he's been to a ton of these."

Galavon chuckled. Her easy tone made him feel more relaxed. "It's not too hard when Anne Ziyad is leading you through it."

Galavon dared to look back at Anne then. She was looking down into her cup. "I suppose it isn't too difficult to discover my name around here. Pearl may be a city, but everyone knows most everyone." She turned her blue gaze to Galavon. He managed not to look away. "Everyone except new merchants, that is. Why is it that you and your father came at such an odd time? If you're from almost anywhere north, your travels back through the cold won't be much fun."

Galavon could tell Anne felt comfortable around him already although he was almost a complete stranger. It amazed him, and it made it that much easier for him to continue talking to her. "I'm not sure. My father seems to have business with the Baron."

"With the Baron? That dullard?" Anne laughed. "Your father must be serious about his business if he's working with him."

She doesn't know Patrick. "I believe he wants to travel to Farrow once he's done here so we can finish the Great Trade Circle before it does get too cold." *I wish I could stay here and get to know you better,* he thought.

"Don't you miss home? I mean, I've been away from Pearl before, but never for more than a season. You're from Mecca aren't you? I heard someone mention it at your booth earlier today."

Galavon didn't respond immediately. He took a few seconds to think, and when he spoke, he spoke slowly. "Mecca is no more of a home to me than Farrow or Elincia. It's just another place on the map to do the books and wait out the weather."

A young recruit walked up to Anne. He looked nervous. "Jorno? What's wrong?"

"It's not my place to tell ye my lady, but ye are to head home immediately. Yer horse is waiting by your table. I'll be escorting ye."

Galavon watched as Anne's eyebrows crinkle together in thought. "I think I'll walk home, it's not too terribly far," she said.

"I don't mean to argue with ye my lady, but I was told to escort you," Jorno said.

He looks sad and confused.

Anne turned her head toward Galavon, making her curls bounce on her head. "Galavon, would you mind being a gentleman and escorting me home?" She smiled at him, her lips curving up at the sides because she already knew what the answer would be.

Jorno looked wide eyed at Galavon. Galavon stared at Anne with the same unbelieving eyes. The words "It would be my pleasure," stumbled out of his mouth, and Anne roll her eyes with feigned exasperation.

Taking advantage of the dumbfounded recruit, Anne said, "See there, it's settled. Thank you, Jorno, for delivering the message. I hope whatever is troubling you works out for the best. Come along Galavon, we wouldn't want to leave Lady Ignava waiting for too long." Anne got up and strode off toward the Southwest Gate. Galavon looked helplessly at the recruit before following behind.

"I can't believe she's making me leave," Anne said. She led Galavon to the gate. "Oh, wait, I bet it is fashionable to be late *and* to leave parties early. How silly of me." An exaggerated sigh escaped her lips once she finished.

One of the sentries posted at the Southwest Gate approached Anne as the pair walked underneath. "Anne, ye must be getting home faster…"

She used the same tactic with the sentry as she did with the recruit. She answered swiftly and gave him no time to respond. "I'll be all right, Galavon is going to walk me home. Thank you for your concern." Her brisk dismissal stunned the sentry. Together they walked through the gate at a quick pace out into the warm southern night where the stars and the moon lit their path.

Once through, the sounds of horses galloping in the distance could be heard coming closer. Anne turned them off the road. "There seems to be a lot of traffic. I know another route across the fields. Maybe then we won't see anyone else to pester us."

The cosmos offered just enough light for the two to avoid any loose stones lying in the grass. Clouds were coming in quickly from the west over the Cliffside Gulf, covering up some of the glow. Step after step they walked without a word passing between them, until Galavon made the first comment. He again felt confident in her presence.

"I was a little shocked when you asked me to accompany you."

Anne turned her face toward him, her features highlighted by the dim light of the stars. "Why is that? Who else would I ask to walk me home?"

"A soldier? Your brother? Someone you met sooner than a dance or two ago." Galavon said. She laughed out loud, a sweet sound to Galavon's ears.

Yes, finally you can talk!

Her quiet laughter faded and her face became serious. "I'm not really sure why, to be honest." Within the next step, Anne managed to find his hand with her own.

The nervousness came back. Galavon looked straight down at the ground in an effort to avoid looking at her face.

"Will you and your father be making this a permanent stop?"

Galavon nodded before mustering the courage to look at her. He noticed how her hair bounced on her shoulders, and her eyes danced with excitement. "He really needs a new agent to bring his goods here from Farrow. The side trip is too dangerous for him. Maybe I can talk him into letting me do it until he finds someone else."

"That would be nice," she said. She squeezed his hand. "I wouldn't mind getting to know you better." It was then that the clouds caught up with the couple, and a light shower began to fall on them. This was unusual – most of the rain in the south was closer to torrential downpours.

"Mmmm, I love the rain!" Anne broke apart from Galavon to run ahead and twirl in the falling droplets of water. Her dress spun around, and her curly hair began to stick to her face.

Galavon smiled at her enthusiasm. All the noble girls and women he had ever met would be upset with being rained on if they were wearing such a beautiful dress. Well, upset if they were just getting rained on, no matter what they wore. "Come dance with me!" she begged. He couldn't resist.

They locked both hands together and danced beneath what stars were left shining through the clouds. They didn't follow a dance pattern like they had during "A Shadow's Sonata," or even "A Harpist's Broken String." The soft patter of the rain was their music, and they danced however they felt. At least one hand was clasped in the other's hand at all times.

They danced the rest of the way as the rain passed by, moving slowly and not worrying about how long it took them to get there. Both were out of breath and grinning at each other when they arrived at the Ziyad Manor. The manor was like a small castle, with a courtyard and a low wall as tall as a man that wrapped all the way around for minimal defense. The bottom windows had thick wooden shutters and iron bars, but the second floor's rooms had giant arched windows that led to porches and allowed maximum circulation. There was one entrance with an iron gate from the front that faced the road.

When Anne tried to open the gate that led into the courtyard, she found it locked. "I wonder where all the guards are. I was going to ride back with my mother."

Galavon shook his head back and forth like a dog, sending the droplets in his hair scattering. "Should we call for someone?"

"If I wasn't in this dumb dress I would just climb the gate and unlatch it. It wouldn't be the first time. Do you think you can manage it?"

Not wanting to disappoint or look like a coward, he nodded. He walked up to the gate and using the bars like a ladder, climbed up. He hoped he didn't look too ridiculous climbing – the gate was wet and he slipped more than once. He could hear Anne giggle below. Once at the lip he pulled himself over the edge. One foot at a time he began his descent down. On the ground, he unlatched one side of the gate and pushed it open.

"Thank you, Galavon."

The courtyard sparkled in the moonlight due to the fresh rain. Walking up the steps that led to the huge wooden doors that barred the way inside, they kept their hands clasped together. Galavon stopped before the last step, and Anne turned around when she made it to the top. With Galavon a step below her, they were face to face.

"Thanks for walking me back." She said. Anne first looked down at her feet before looking back to Galavon. "Will I be able to see you again?" she asked hesitantly. The clouds in the sky opened up completely, allowing the full light from the heavens to fall upon her face. Galavon smiled at the hair sticking to her face. Without thinking, he brushed one of the strands away.

"I have a room in the city, so I should at least be here for another day. If you want to meet me sometime tomorrow…"

"Why don't you come here around midday?" After Galavon nodded in agreement, Anne's voice became softer. "I had a good time tonight." She blushed. "Good night."

Instead of turning to walk inside, Anne slowly leaned forward. Their lips brushed in the slightest form of a kiss.

"I'll see you tomorrow," she whispered as she pulled her face away from his. She turned and disappeared inside.

In his bliss, Galavon blindly walked back to Pearl along the same path they took across the fields. Due to the travels he made with his father and his shyness, Galavon had never had time for a girl, and that light kiss from Anne was his first. He felt weightless, and the return journey seemed to take no time at all.

When Galavon made it back to Pearl, the tables and benches had been moved. He smiled when he walked through the Green where he had danced with Anne, and he made his way to The Angry Maiden.

Upon entering the common room, he found the festival was still going on for some. A few old men gambled in the corner as a young boy attempted to play the flute. The female servers were harassed as they passed, and some of them even ended up in a patron's lap.

"Galavon!" Torvil's voice boomed, his words almost slurring. "Your father is looking for you!" The girl in his lap gave him a playful look, and Galavon noticed it wasn't the same red-haired woman that Torvil had been with at the feast.

His father was staying in the suite on the first floor. He walked down the long, dark hallway that separated the room from the rest of the inn. He knocked before entering.

"There you are. Sit." Patrick Hostleton sat at a desk in the back of the room and motioned for Galavon to have a seat on the chair in front of the desk. "Our plans have changed."

Galavon sat in the chair. His father was a hard man in a way that was different than the guards he hired. Despite traveling with him for a number of Twil, Patrick treated Galavon as one of his men, not as a son or a friend.

Patrick shuffled through some papers on his desk. He didn't bother to look at Galavon. "I find that I like the weather in this area, and I grow too old to continue traveling. I have decided to stay here for the time being."

Galavon just managed to keep his mouth closed. His father owned a mansion in the Silver Square in Mecca and a house in Farrow, Elincia, and Gareth. Why would he stay here? "You aren't going to travel the Great Trade Circle anymore?"

Patrick looked up for a second. "Are you deaf or just stupid, boy? No. I will make no more travels. As I said, I am growing too old. I've seen over fifty Twil in my lifetime. Your mother was much younger than me."

Galavon's mother had died in childbirth. Everyone who knew her told him he looked just like her, as if he had walked out of one of the small mountain towns himself instead of being born in Mecca. Light skin, lithe form, high cheek bones and green eyes.

"You shall continue our family's trade in my absence."

I will continue it!?

"You know the Great Trade Circle, you know my contacts, you know what goods to buy at what cost, you know where to take them." He then slid a letter across the desk toward Galavon along with his plain iron pendant of the sun and moon. "And now you have my word that you have taken over the travels for the time being if any should doubt you." Patrick looked him over.

Galavon's eyes grew big looking at the parchment and pendant in front of him. His father had worked hard to become a member of the Trade Guild, a powerful organization in Mecca. Galavon couldn't believe he would throw that away. He picked up the simple token on its plain chain, the pendant slowly twirling. "And everything you've worked for? You're going to give it all up?"

"I don't intend to give anything up. Where's the profit in that?" Patrick's voice grew louder. It wasn't often that Galavon questioned him. "But you will do as I tell you without questioning my decisions," Patrick said in a stern voice. Galavon averted his eyes but still felt his father's hard stare.

"Now take the letter. Wear the pendant. The iron bars go to Farrow where you pick up the normal order of silk. You will then take it up the Feather coast and back to Mecca."

Galavon nodded. It wasn't as though he could refuse. It was an important job, finally! He would have to tell Anne of his new plans when they met tomorrow.

Patrick looked down to a stack of papers on the desk and began to write on them. "You will depart as the sun rises. I suggest getting as much sleep as you can."

But Anne... "Tomorrow? Father, do you think we could wait until..."

"No!" Patrick snapped. "Our agent in Farrow has already been informed of our irregular timing and has gotten an order together. It would be suspicious if you stayed here longer. You have all the information you need. Torvil and his men will be waiting for you outside of the Northeastern Gate as the sun rises."

He tossed a large pouch of coins at Galavon's feet. "It's filled with copper and silver. There is one gold mark in case of emergency. I expect no emergencies and the gold mark back. Torvil will receive his pay when he gets you to Mecca, no sooner." Patrick's head bent back over the papers.

It was the closest to a good-bye Galavon knew he would receive. Patrick was not a successful merchant by being nice. Galavon slid the chain with the pendant over his head and scooped up the bag of coins and letter. He stood out of his chair and turned for the door. "Good luck, Father," he said over his shoulder.

"I'll need more than luck," Patrick mumbled just as the door closed behind Galavon.

Chapter 3
(Galavon, Anne)

*A*nne,

I've been sent away on urgent business to complete the Great Trade Circle for my father. I will return as soon as I can. Please forgive my sudden departure.

> *Don't forget about me,*
> *Galavon Hostleton*

Galavon looked over the note with weary eyes. He wasn't sure what to write, other than the fact that he was leaving and sorry for the sudden trip. This was the fourth draft, and every time the letter sounded too formal.

It's just my luck father would begin to trust me as soon as I get the courage to meet a girl. I'll finish this trip and be back for you Anne. No matter what happens, I'll be back. He felt silly for such a romantic thought, but it was how he felt. He yawned and folded the parchment in half.

He was already packed, having put his travel clothes in one bag and the finer clothes he would wear in the cities in another. Another two bags were filled with books he read to pass the time riding in the wagon, and yet another was filled with other odd items such as blank parchment, quills, a brush, and other miscellaneous items he may need on his journey. Galavon could barely manage to carry all of them.

He was dressed in a simple, dark green cotton tunic and brown leggings with a leather belt strapped around his waist. Hanging on the belt was the pouch his father had given him, pulled tight and filled with copper and silver. The silver marks were hidden amongst his travel sacks, and the gold penny was in one of his boots for extra protection. It amounted to a small fortune, and Galavon was surprised his father had given him so much. He also had a small one-sided knife that he used for small tasks and to eat with while on the road, as well as the odd pendant with the moon and sun around his neck.

Coming down the stairs into the darkened common room, Galavon found that the festival had finally come to an end. The innkeeper was nowhere in sight, but Galavon saw some maids cleaning the floor and benches.

"Excuse me," Galavon said to one mopping a puddle of spilled ale underneath a table in the dark room. He dropped a bag to free one of his hands. "If I left you with a note, could you get it to Anne Ziyad? I have coin." Galavon produced a copper lot from the pouch at his side.

The barmaid gave him a weary look, but her eyes jumped at the sight of the copper. "Suppose I could do that for ye and the extra coin." She took the coin then the letter. "Good as delivered."

"Thanks."

She stuffed the coin and note in an apron pocket before turning her back on Galavon to continue cleaning. He stepped out of the inn on to the cobblestone street unsure if the note would ever make it to Anne.

The city was empty this early in the morning. Galavon saw no one as he made his way to the Northeast Gate, and with only a line across the horizon that was the rising sun, his shadow wasn't even there to follow. Another yawn escaped his lips, and he struggled to keep his bags from falling over.

He found Torvil and the other guards waiting for him. Galavon was familiar with only a few of them. Like most guards, they came and went with almost every stop. Torvil handed the reins of his horse to Kavar, a small dirty man who covered himself in knives and a single short sword. He seemed to be asleep on the second cart bench, but he took the reins.

"I heard your father put you in charge. If I hadn't drunk enough ale to drown a fish last night, maybe we'd celebrate."

Galavon smiled at Torvil's uncanny humor. Torvil had been traveling with Galavon's father for many Twil, and Galavon knew him the best out of all the guards. Still, Galavon wasn't completely comfortable around the aggressive, loud man. "That's all right. Where can I put my bags?"

"Your father is keeping two of the carts here."

Of course Galavon thought. His father usually used two wagons to carry his own personal supplies, Galavon's bags, and the odd trinkets he had Galavon sell to the public. Without Patrick making the trip, he kept the wagons.

Torvil grabbed the bags with one hand, easily lifting the load Galavon had been struggling under. "You pack like your father," Torvil mumbled. "I'm sure there's room somewhere." He tossed Galavon's bags on top of the iron ore in the first cart without regard for their contents.

"But before you climb in the wagon," Darak said behind Galavon from the top of his horse, "there is something else." Darak was the guardsmen who had relieved Galavon from watching the goods the night before. The cowl of his cloak still hung low over his face, as was usual for Darak. His gray Plain Strider had a quiver on the saddle along with his bow and two small saddle bags. Hanging on his left side was a long curved dagger that looked exotic with runes on the blade that ended at a handle covered in bronze wire. Galavon had never seen him draw it, but then again they were rarely in danger as long as they stayed along the Great Trade Circle.

Darak was leading another horse behind him. "With limited space in the carts, your father sent an extra horse. His name is Kid." He passed the reigns to Galavon.

Galavon's eyes grew wide in panic. *I don't know how to ride a horse!*

Galavon had always read a book from one of the benches of the carts. He had ridden a horse before, of course, but never for any real distance. Or recently for that matter.

"It isn't often your father gives anyone a gift." Torvil grumbled while retrieving his own horse. "I'd take it and not say another word."

Galavon fumbled his way up the back of the brown horse, not sure what to think about Torvil's attitude. He never spoke to Patrick in this manner.

It wouldn't surprise me if father told Torvil he was really in charge.

"Not quite the expert rider, are you?" Darak said once Galavon was situated on top of the horse. Kid shook his black mane. Darak watched from his own mount. His face was completely hidden beneath the shadow of his cowl. "You got up on the wrong side. I'd say after one completion of the Great Trade Circle, you'll be far beyond a novice. Well, at least you won't get sore anymore." Galavon caught the flash of a smile appearing in the shadow of Darak's face – a rare sight. Galavon lightly squeezed with his legs like he remembered to induce Kid into a walk.

The sun peaked over the horizon, lighting the dirt road ahead as they started the most dangerous portion of their trip at a slow pace. Galavon had no trouble controlling his horse at a walk. He rode to the right of the wagons beside Darak, who stayed quiet and stared straight ahead. He wore a simple leather breastplate and pauldrons over a padded shirt. His hair was dark and shoulder length, and not even a shadow of a beard appeared on his face beneath the cowl of his hood. His unique indigo eyes were alert, but his body seemed relaxed.

Torvil rode at the front of the column, fast asleep on the back of his horse. He was dressed in the same clothes he had worn the night before, except now he had on a black leather belt with iron studs that matched the strap that ran at an angle up his back. That strap held his flamberge, a true two-handed sword with a wave in the blade favored by the barbarians who lived in the Gold Desert.

Just behind Torvil steering the first cart laden with iron ore was Angar. Resting beside Angar on the cart bench was a mace, a mace that Galavon couldn't see anyone else being able to wield. Angar had to be well over nine span when he stood up straight, even taller than Torvil, so it was no wonder to Galavon that he was in the cart instead of on horseback. Always quiet and not exactly a scholar, the other guards claimed Angar's grandfather had been a giant. He wore a leather vest that matched his stringy brown hair that hung over a simple face with an over-sized forehead.

Kavar, the dirty man with all the knives who had held Torvil's reigns, steered the second cart. He too drifted off into sleep, but luckily the horses didn't need much direction and simply followed the cart in front of them. Occasionally the early morning sunlight would reflect off one of his blades and temporarily blind Galavon. Kavar was crude and usually gambled away his wages as soon as he earned them. Galavon thought he talked too much and didn't trust him.

Galavon wasn't overly familiar with the rest of the guards, but they were equally as intimidating as the others in their own unique way. In total there were six of them, and none usually said two words to Galavon besides Torvil and Darak.

Galavon was slowly being rocked to sleep by the lulling steps of Kid. He hadn't exactly gone to bed early that night, not with the walk back and his head filled with thoughts of Anne. He struggled to stay awake, too afraid that he might fall off. The sun continued to rise, as did the heat, and Torvil finally called a stop.

"This heat could fry a dragon egg." Torvil proclaimed. "Take the horses to the shade until this heat eases up a bit."

As soon as all the horses were tethered, the group of guards took their own seats in the shade offered by trees along the side of road. Judging from the position of the sun, Galavon figured it to be just before noon. Galavon sat apart from the guards and thumbed idly through one of his books.

Dust from the road had already begun to cake itself on his clothes, and the smell of body odor shifted through the air. The dust and sour stench were familiar to Galavon and didn't bother him in the least. Who was he trying to impress out here, the Mother curator Neith?

"I'm telling ya, I got them both in one night!" Torvil exclaimed, becoming himself again after the nap on the back of his horse. Despite the shade offered by the tree they were seated at, Galavon could feel himself sweating. The moisture in the air made him feel as though he was swimming.

"Bah, you haven't the energy for two dances in one night!" said one of the other guards. "Now as for me..."

"She isn't for counting!" Another said cutting him off. This guard was rubbing the sides of his head as though trying to get rid of a headache. "You know as well as I she is the cheapest..."

"And you be one for the talking?" the first guard shot back, spittle flying out of a mouth that boasted less than half of its teeth. "How about that 'Margaret' you danced the night away with? We all be knowing you weren't the first she danced with!"

Normally they kept this sort of conversation quiet around Patrick, but Galavon found himself entertained as he listened to their claimed exploits of the previous night.

"All of ya shut it! No matter who we were lucky enough to dance with using whatever amount of coins we managed to dig out of our pockets, it was Galavon who got to spin with the Constable's daughter!" Kavar said leaning in with a grin on his dirty face. "That is a story I want to hear!"

"Constable Tarik's daughter?!" Angar exclaimed, looking away from the group to where Galavon sat. Surprisingly his voice was not as deep as one would expect from the giant man.

"No wonder we left so early!" Torvil boomed. All the men had a laugh at this, and Galavon couldn't help but smile awkwardly. He kept his mouth closed and continued to feign reading. To say anything would only lead to more, much cruder jokes. Galavon always found it easier to stay quiet. Only Darak refrained from making comments. He sat alone as well, as was his custom, with his back against a tree and the cowl of his forest green cloak pulled down over his eyes.

"All right, that's enough boys. While the sun is beating down we should catch up on some of the sleep we missed." Torvil gave a pause and then looked at Galavon. "Whether we missed it because of a simple tavern wench or the Constable's daughter!" More laughter followed, but the guards spread out in the shade to find some rest. Galavon put away his book, used his saddle as a pillow, and closed his eyes.

Though he was tired, sleep eluded him, so Galavon watched the others around him. One of the guards poured water over his bald head, Angar snored like a rutting pig, Torvil kept watch on the road, and the others were resting.

"Not able to sleep?" Darak asked from beneath the shade of his hood. Galavon couldn't believe he kept that hood on, it felt like Shiva's own breath outside!

"No, not really. I'm not used to sleeping in the middle of the day." Galavon sat up and ran his fingers through his hair and wiped some of the sweat from off his face.

"Sometimes it's better not to ignore a joke like that," Darak said.

"If I would have said anything they only would have continued," Galavon responded. "I noticed plenty of trades that went sour because my father couldn't ignore a joke like that."

Darak considered the notion. "There's nothing wrong with learning from another's mistakes. It saves you the trouble of having to deal with the consequences. The only thing you must be careful with is making sure that it is a mistake."

"What do you mean?"

"People have a great deal of respect for your father, because he doesn't let other people make him their fool. In fact, I'm guessing you only observed that happening to him once or twice."

"I can only remember once."

Darak chuckled from under his cowl. "If you go about it the right way, jokes like that can end."

"They don't bother me. I'm fine." Galavon put his head back down, quickly tiring of the conversation. Darak usually spoke little during the trips unless it was with Patrick or Torvil, and Galavon wished that trend would return.

"They may not bother you, but if Anne Ziyad heard them making that sort of joke, would it bother her?"

Galavon brought his hands back behind his head in an effort to get comfortable on the saddle in the ensuing silence. He tried to change the subject. "We're heading to your home now, aren't we?"

"My home..." Darak said. "My home is not in East Ager. My home is over the Mountains of Hope. Your father only found me in Farrow." Darak said. The guard was lean and of average height. Despite the low cowl of his hood, Galavon could feel Darak's purple-eyed stare. "Better get some rest. And think about what I said."

Once the heat became bearable, Torvil announced they were going to continue. Their pace was the same, and eventually they came upon a group of riders who identified themselves as Outriders from Pearl.

"We ride up and down this road twice every seven moons all the way to Lonely Hill, the last town in the Peninsula Province. The road is safe up to there, but no one watches past it.

Not even the Knights of the White Wing ride that bit of the highway. The furthest south they go is Farrow."

"What dangers are there past Lonely Hill?" Torvil asked in a gruff tone. Galavon moved up to listen better, but he felt certain that the soldiers' information would be more useful to the guards rather than the merchant.

"Just the usual. There are always reports of bandits from the Albus Veneficus. The manticores that roam the hills have moved north out of the heat, although there still may be a few of the young males hanging behind. The weather should begin changing soon, so it won't be long before they come south again."

"Bah! Manticores are just lil' kitties with wings and long stingers. We'll be fine," Torvil replied with a chuckle.

"If manticores and bandits don't bother you, then maybe a sighting of the Crows will," the captain said. "It's rumored twenty or more of them are to land in Farrow by ship, and we heard that in Lonely Hill. No telling when they'll reach the port."

"The Crows, eh? That is trouble. I wonder what sort of 'blasphemy' is bringing so many this far south from the Cathedral of Power." Torvil cracked his knuckles nervously.

There were two orders of knights within Reproba Caelum. There were the Knights of the White Wing whose goal was to protect the followers of Reproba Caelum. The base of their operations was the Cathedral of the White Feather. The other group was the Holy Order of the Black Wing, but they were more commonly known as the Crows. They tracked down any who disagreed with the teachings of Reproba Caelum and dealt out the punishment. They were widely feared across the Kingdom of East Ager, and usually they traveled in groups of two or three, not twenty.

After trading information the two groups continued on their way. Other than that brief encounter, the ride that day was uneventful.

The party kept moving even as night descended. The maltrees along the road were beginning to thin and give way to open land. "This is your last night in the deep south, my boys," Torvil yelled from the front of the column. "Tomorrow we're sleeping in beds at a Lonely Hill inn. The Fire Pass Province, infested with manticores, hiding bandits, and bellied with troll hovels along nearly every stream! Our kind of place, eh?"

Galavon wasn't sure he'd be able to stay awake. He knew the plan was to ride through the night and sleep while the sun was at its brightest, but during their usual travels it was the basics: sleep at night, travel during the day. It didn't help that he was sore from a full day of riding. Galavon was positive he had never ridden on a horse so long in his entire life.

The night continued on, and Galavon was sure he dozed off a couple times before being woken by a misstep from Kid. A welcoming vision came at last to Galavon though. It was the sight of the first rays of sunlight stretching across the sky. *Only a little longer, then we'll break. Torvil only wanted to get a good start.* The early rays turned into a morning full of sunshine. He looked around with sleepy eyes and noticed that most of the other men seemed drowsy as well.

Galavon squeezed Kid with his legs, once, twice, until finally Kid moved into a lazy trot. His legs ached with the extra effort and bouncing. He hoped he got used to riding sooner than Darak supposed. He moved up to the front beside Torvil. "Let's make camp here and start up again once the sun eases up this afternoon."

Torvil's bearded face turned toward Galavon. "And lose the good riding weather? Did you see how much of the day we lose to the heat boy?"

Galavon didn't expect Torvil to combat his order. Galavon opened his mouth but nothing else came out.

Torvil gave a deep "hmmph" in response to the silence. "You're the one in charge. You want to stop, we stop."

I don't want to stop, I have to stop. If I had it my way I'd have stopped before we left.

"Stop playing with your food," Lady Ignava snapped. Anne and Lady Ignava were sitting together for the morning meal alone in the Great Hall. Anne was poking at the food on her plate with her fork. She hadn't had much of an appetite since she heard the news of her father late last night when they found her in her bedroom. The guards who usually manned the gate of the manse had been sent out into the night to find her.

The two were coping with Tarik's death in different ways. Anne wore a plain, wrinkled black dress, and her hair was disheveled. She knew she slumped in her seat, and her eyes felt heavy.

Lady Ignava looked her best and displayed no outward signs of emotion. Her nose was pointed high in the air as usual, making the trip for her food twice as long as it could have been. Her hair was done up into a bun on her head, decorated with a net of silver. Her crisp black gown matched with its silver trimmings and her pale skin. She looked neat and orderly in her mourning.

"I'm not hungry," Anne responded to Lady Ignava's command. She continued to stare down at her food and slide it around on the plate.

"I'm sick of your attitude!" Lady Ignava exploded, standing up out of her chair. "Do you think you're the only one who is upset about your father's death?" Lady Ignava forcefully calmed herself and sat again. She smoothed out the wrinkles from her dress and pointedly stuck her nose back into the air. "In times such as these, we the nobility must set a good example. If we fall apart, then those who look up to us will fall apart as well."

Anne looked up from her plate. The two had never gotten along, but for the first time Anne believed her mother offered good advice. Anne straightened her posture in an effort to give an outward sign of stability. Lady Ignava looked pleased, if not a little surprised.

"Good. See, we are better than the common people, aren't we?" Anne's respect went diving yet again.

"I've had Margaery read through some documents your father had written in case this very thing happened," Lady Ignava commented between bites. Her face remained disturbingly calm. "He seems to have known Cecil would be forced to leave and has left me with a note that we are to go to Caernarfon Castle immediately. However, I have too many things to do here, so Margaery has gathered an escort for you, and a messenger has been sent. I can only imagine we are to retrieve some blessing or another from Duke Briel. The customs and logic of this province continue to elude me."

Anne always enjoyed visiting Duke Briel in his castle on the strip of land between the Cliffside Gulf and the Sparkle.

Constables were the most powerful and influential of the nobility because they commanded the army, but those who controlled the largest and wealthiest tracts of land were Dukes and Duchesses. Counts and Countesses were also powerful Lords and Ladies, though their estates were not as large. Viscounts managed smaller tracts of land beneath the Dukes and Counts. In the Peninsula Province there were three Dukes, each of which controlled a different castle and the surrounding land.

"As soon as you return, we'll have a funeral service for your father, and I will have completed arrangements for you to travel to Mecca. You're to live there with my sister and learn how to be a lady so you can be wed. I can't think of any decent noble who would marry you in your current state. At sixteen Twil I was already pregnant with your brother and running your father's household. Now go change, you are to leave soon."

Anne got up from her chair and slammed it back under the table before turning to leave. Shouts of protest sounded behind her, but Anne stormed out of the Great Hall. Her father had died. Her brother was gone. She was to be married. *I hate being a noble,* she thought bitterly. *I hate it, I hate it!* The steps up to her room disappeared quickly beneath her.

Once in her room, Anne slammed the door. She then whirled toward her bed where the floor length mirror revealed her reflection. Her bottom lip stuck out, and her eyebrows crinkled up close together in an expression that spoke of anger. *Maybe Cecil has been right the whole time, maybe we do need to grow up.* Anne tried to mask her anger by putting on a face that lacked emotion. Though she had none of Lady Ignava's features, looking back from the mirror was a face Anne believed would better fit the older woman.

A small smile crept to her lips looking at the odd image of herself with a cold, separated look in her eye. The smile quickly faded though, and tears began to roll down her cheeks. She couldn't believe her father was dead.

She left the mirror behind and walked to her dresser where she pulled out some of her riding clothes – a comfortable billowy shirt, a thin brown belt with brass studs the same color as her tight cotton riding pants, and leather riding boots. Anne sniffed and tried to wipe away her falling tears, but one after another they continued to fall. She finished her outfit with a black ribbon in her hair. Turning back to the mirror, she now looked more like herself. Well, despite the trails left on her cheeks from her tears. She thought she had used them all when she first heard the news late last night.

"My lady," a quivering voice called from the doorway. Anne turned to see the door open. It was her maid, Isabella. "I 'ave packed yer bags for the stay and yer escort be waiting in the courtyard for ye. It seems the captain wants to leave a little earlier than planned," she said softly. Her cheeks were tear-stained as well, and her voice was queasy. Anne suspected many of the servants were sad. Her father was kind and well liked. "Be there anything else ye need?"

Anne knew she was forgetting something. "Actually, yes." She walked to the small desk in her room and pulled out parchment, quill, and ink. She hated that she only just remembered the merchant boy Galavon, but with the news of her father her fairy-tale dreams had come to an abrupt end. The least she could do was leave a note and hope that the future might lead them to one another again.

Galavon,

    Sorry for canceling our plans, but I must leave. If you're not here when I return, be sure to find me the next time you make your way to Pearl.

                      - Anne

"Could you give this to one of the guards to give Galavon? He's supposed to be meeting me outside the gate today." Isabella smiled at the name and nodded. Anne knew in that smile that Isabella knew Galavon must be the merchant boy. "Will you be traveling with us to Caernarfon Castle?" she asked her maid.

"I will," Isabella responded. Her curly hair stirred in the breeze from the open balcony doors. *She really is pretty for a maid,* Anne thought. The maid's eyes shined like Tarik's. Most people's eyes did if they were truly descended from the oldest inhabitants of the Peninsula Province. For a second, Anne thought she was looking in the mirror again, except for the wrinkles around Isabella's eyes.

"I'll be waiting with the escort." The maid then turned and walked out of the room into the stone hallway. Stunned for only a second by their similarities, Anne continued packing.

Instinctively she reached for the pearl that hung around her neck. She felt the familiar bump underneath her shirt and realized she was missing the other item she always kept on her - the stiletto. Anne walked back around her bed to the nightstand, though only yesterday she would have done a belly flop, twirled around, and bounced to her feet once she was on the other side. She grabbed her dagger from the dresser top and slid it in the belt that hung around her delicate waist. While she was by the open arched doors that led to the balcony of her room, she stepped out to see her escort.

"A monk and three soldiers... is that Porter Mann?" Anne couldn't help but giggle despite her sadness. *This trip might not be so bad after all.* With the thought of making Porter's first real mission the most difficult he would ever encounter, Anne rushed out of the room and ran down the curving stone steps, her usual smile creeping back to her face. She leapt over the last three steps and hit the stone floor running in an attempt to leave her woes behind. Just before she opened the big doors that led outside, she realized how childish she would look running out of the manor. She remembered Cecil's words about her acting her age and rank. She willed herself to a calm walk as she opened the oak doors.

In the courtyard were, as she saw from her balcony, three soldiers and a monk. Two of the soldiers, Porter included, were on foot in leather brigandine armor carrying the Army of Truth's main infantry weapon – a heavy spear that rose eleven span into the air. Strapped on their backs were round shields painted dark blue with a white dot in the middle. Cecil had explained to Anne that they only put the shields to use when they were in battle formations, that the heavy spears were more effective with two hands unless supported on either side and behind.

Now closer, she recognized the man leading her escort. It was Captain Philial Marlow, armed and armored like the cavalry in the Army of Truth. He had a breastplate formed of silver interlacing metal strips sitting on his broad shoulders, a bow on his back and a falchion at his side. Sitting tall atop his Southern Jiggler, he looked every inch a noble. He had a strong jaw, short cropped hair, and the blue eyes of a native, but even more than that, he had an air of surety about him that was common in those born into leadership.

He was the fourth son of Duke Esmund Marlow, the second most powerful man in the Peninsula Province, falling only below the Constable. Duke Marlow controlled Castle Matsuyama to the east and a large amount of land that nearly stretched from the coast of the Goblin Sea to the Cathedral of New Beginnings. Anne knew the Duke as an old, stubborn man who was a devout follower of Reproba Caelum. His lands were hit hardest by the goblins in the war, and he openly blamed the Ziyad family for it.

As the fourth son, Philial Marlow wasn't to inherit any holdings or land. He had joined the Army of Truth as soon as he saw his eighteenth Twil, just before the War of Fire. Because he could afford his own horse, he was assigned to the outriders in Pearl. While patroling, his troop was ambushed by the Albus Veneficus, and as the sole survivor he was able to bring back two of the rogue magic wielders as prisoners. He was promoted to captain, a great honor for a soldier so young.

The Albus Veneficus fought against the enforcement of Reproba Caelum as the only religion. Some of their small bands included men and women who wielded magic, a thing forbidden by the curators unless you were a monk or a priest. They were seen as blasphemous bandits, but it was nearly impossible to eradicate them as they hid amongst the masses of loyal followers. They struck against Reproba Caelum like a mosquito – annoying, but hardly a threat.

The monk traveling with the escort was dressed like all the monks who were sent out from the cathedrals. He wore a rough cotton robe dyed white and a five-pointed star that hung from wooden beads around his neck. In the middle of the star glittered a pearl from the Sparkle. He was the oldest in the escort, and looked to have seen fifty Twil.

He kept his gray hair so short it might as well have been shaved off. A straggly beard the same color clung to his chin. Leather sandals protected the soles of his feet and allowed him to stay as cool as possible in the heat. The monks of Reproba Caelum traveled all over the land. Every tenth day they gathered all the Followers, those who practiced Reproba Caelum, which was supposed to be everyone, and gave praise to the curators wherever they could find room. The nobles who lived close to the cathedrals would attend a gathering in the chapel with a priest or even the high priest.

"My lady," the young captain said in a deep voice devoid of emotion. He bowed from his horse. "I'm terribly sorry for the loss of your father; the whole province mourns."

"Thank you, Captain Marlow, for your kind words," Anne replied quietly, playing the lady as best she could. The words still stung, and she wished he wouldn't have said anything.

He nodded. "Philial. Captain Philial."

Anne winked at Porter, but the recruit only paled and looked away. *Oh Porter, I'm still the same girl you used to play with when we were younger.*

Isabella walked up with one of the stable boys leading two horses. One of the horses was a work horse laden with heavy saddle bags stuffed with the things Isabella packed for Anne. The other horse was a Southern Jiggler, and it pranced beside the stable boy to Anne's side, sending the feathers around its hooves dancing.

The ride to Caernarfon Castle would be a short one. The journey took most travelers two days moving at an easy pace, traveling only in the early morning and late afternoon. With the cold season approaching, the trip might even take less time if they were able to continue through the hottest part of the day. Anne mounted, and they walked out the gates. Anne wasn't surprised Lady Ignava didn't come outside to see her off, nor did she particularly care.

All were quiet in the beginning of the trip. Anne suspected that Captain Philial and his soldiers would stay that way. Captain Philial was solemn and stony-faced, and Anne imagined not the most companionable officer. He led the way on horseback, and the two young soldiers walked at the rear. The monk walked along Anne's left, and Isabella led the work horse to her right. Though she tried, there was no way for Anne to maneuver her horse out of the circle so she could ride ahead on her own. It was pleasing in an odd way that they expected nothing less than a mad dash from her.

The day was hot, sticky, and boring. They started in the worst of the heat, though it wasn't as bad as it would have been in the middle of the hot season. The recruits behind her were trying to be perfect soldiers by keeping a quiet vigil. Isabella never muttered a word, and Captain Philial seemed only interested in the road ahead. The heat was scarcely bearable, and more than once Anne had to wipe sweat off her face and hold her hand to her nose in a poor attempt to block the body odor coming from the lightly armored recruits behind her.

She mostly thought of Galavon, the merchant boy she had the met the night before. It was better than thinking of her father. She imagined that Galavon wasn't really a merchant, but a hero in disguise traveling the land. She could picture it despite his outward awkwardness. If he treated everything like a dance, he could do anything.

I only spent one evening with you, she thought, *and already I can't shake you from my thoughts.*

The group took their first break under the shade of some maltrees by a freshwater spring along the road. It was a common breaking point for travelers. When they resaddled, Anne finally found someone to talk to.

The monk, Jericho, was Anne's source of entertainment. His short gray beard moved with his lips when he smiled, and his bright eyes were always looking to Anne as though he had found salvation there. He told her stories about his travels as a monk and the great cathedrals of Reproba Caelum.

"Our province be blessed," he said, pulling up on the wooden beads that held his star. He pointed out the pearl. "Monks be all given a pearl from our own Sparkle when they join Reproba Caelum. They be bigger and brighter than the average pearl, and the curators make 'em a gift to those who spread Reproba Caelum's teachings. Only we may be in possession of one." His accent marked him as being born in the south.

Anne had to fight to keep from touching the pearl that hung beneath her shirt. For a brief moment it reminded her of that perfect day she found it with her brother and father. The three of them had laughed together during their exploration of the shores. It was one of the few times they had been alone together. She shut her eyes for a brief second and willed away thoughts of her father, refusing to show sadness in front of the others.

She changed the subject. "Do you mostly stay in this province? I've only been to the Cathedral of New Beginnings, and I hear it's small compared to the other cathedrals."

"The Cathedral of New Beginnings may not be the biggest, but parts of it be the oldest," Jericho said in defense of his home cathedral. "Unless assigned to a province's army, we be sent to travel between the different villages and towns to pray and to help the sick, as Mother Neith would 'ave us do." Neith was the curator of the Cathedral of Power, known as the Mother. When people were sick or injured, it was to Neith that they prayed. Although Neith was never pictured with a weapon, only the healing touch of her hands, it was she who was in charge of the Crows, the order of Reproba Caelum that dealt out punishments for blasphemy.

"Some of us be lucky enough to be assigned to castles or cities," he continued after a brief prayer to Mother Neith, "under the care of the local nuncio. They be usually old and quite knowledgeable about Reproba Caelum. There be only three true castles in this province, but farther North they be more common. I was assigned to serve under a nuncio many Twil ago at Almourol Castle. Countess Gillian controlled the castle there. She sent out patrols along the river to keep the trolls from raiding the flat boats that travel downstream to Farrow. I often traveled with the patrols in order to mend the wounds of the soldiers."

"Larith is the nuncio assigned to Caernarfon Castle, so he's in charge of all the monks there," Anne said in response. "Duke Briel protects the shore and the Sparkle from pirates, so I've seen Larith work with magic. He says the magic monks use is called White Magic." She looked to her right over the head of Isabella at the Sparkle glittering in the sunlight. She could see small boats out in the distance and imagined the sailors diving far into the depths in search of the pearls. If a crew managed to find a single pearl, they could live happily off of their earnings for the rest of the season. "Do you know any magic other than white? The goblin shamans use Fire."

"Fire be forbidden to all but a special few. Perun decides who can learn magic, and I was not deemed worthy fer more than white." Perun was the chief curator. He ruled from the Sacred Isle, the place where the dead were escorted by another goddess, Anuke.

"What's it like casting spells?" she asked the monk eagerly.

Jericho looked up at her smiling. Anne figured he was asked that question often. She regularly asked monks about it, and she delighted to hear it described each and every time.

"It be much like running a race, or sword-fighting, my lady," he said quickly, as if he had answered the same many times before. "Ye draw energy from deep inside yer gut to your fingertips. It's almost as though ye are filling up with water and ye let it squirt out through yer fingers. Of course, fer more powerful spells it's more like a gush, but if ye let out too much energy ye can kill yourself. Ye must know your own strength. The other magics be different from what I understand, though I've never experienced 'em."

"Why don't you teach me some? I bet I could learn." Her horse stumbled over a stone in the road. Anne reached out to gently pat its neck.

"My lady, Perun grants the power to wield magic, not I!" Jericho said with a chuckle, and he returned his gaze to the road ahead.

Anne turned and looked between her horse's ears with a sigh of disappointment. She didn't like to accept no as an answer. She snapped her head back to Jericho in an instant, her right eyebrow raised in question. "If that's true, how do the Albus Veneficus use magic? Or the goblin shamans?"

At the mention of the Albus Veneficus, Captain Philial looked back. Jericho shut his eyes and made the five-pointed star of Reproba Caelum with his thumbs; he touched them to his shoulders,then his chest, and ended by resting the thumb of his right hand on his forehead as the pinnacle of the star.

"Forgive her, Mother Neith, she is but an ignorant child to question her faith with such ideas." Anne looked back at Porter for support, but his eyes were wide, and his mouth still hung agape at her question. No one dared question the teachings of Reproba Caelum.

It was just a question.

"My lady, ye must watch what ye say, else ye will offend the curators." His smile was gone. "Those ye speak of get magic from the fallen beasts that thought themselves greater. They trade their souls fer it. The goblins ask fer it from Shiva, and the Albus Veneficus from another great beast banished some time before."

"Then let's see if Perun will grant me the power!" Anne exclaimed. "I know it's illegal to use magic if you're not part of Reproba Caelum, but if I'm not part of it, why would Perun grant it to me? I'm not asking Shiva for it." Anne could hear Isabella chuckle at the logic. It was a solid argument, and Isabella knew as well as Porter that the priest had dug this hole himself – Anne wasn't going to stop unless she was completely defeated, and she had a different notion than most about what 'defeated' actually meant. "If it's impossible then you have nothing to fear!"

Jericho sighed in exasperation before agreeing to try and teach her at their next break. They continued onward until the sun began to set in the west and cast brilliant colors of orange, red and pink across the Sparkle. Like the fingers of the divers, the colors reached across the salt water lake searching for pearls. Nearly all the pearls found in the lake were found while the sun was either setting or rising. If they caught the sunlight right, they reflected back a brilliant rainbow.

"We'll stop here." Captain Philial motioned to a clearing. Anne saw a small deer scurry off in the fading light. "Eat a snack, dinner will be late. I plan to travel a good distance while the sun isn't out." He wiped sweat from his brow, dismounted, and tethered his horse to a nearby tree.

Porter took the reins from Anne and took care of her horse while she grabbed some food. Heath, the other recruit, scanned the roads. Anne thought this was kind of silly – she couldn't imagine a safer road between the capital of the province and Caernarfon Castle. Captain Philial pulled out his flint and lit a torch from his pack.

Anne watched Jericho pointedly avoid eye contact with her and eat a piece of bread with a thin slice of yellow cheese. *You're not getting out of it,* she thought. Once she had eaten, she strode up to the monk, her plans evident on her face.

"All right," he said. He motioned for Anne to squat down beside him. "With the fading light, I'll show ye the easiest White Magic spell." Jericho held out his hands as though cradling an egg and muttered "*Subluceo.*" A small white ball of light came to rest in the air above his right palm.

"The key be to clear yer mind and create an image in yer head before ye command it with the Holy Tongue. Energy will surge through yer body, and ye allow just enough to seep through yer palms to form yer image. Don't allow too much through or ye could pass out. Or worse." Suddenly Jericho began to laugh at himself. "I don't know why I even told ye that, ye won't be able to conjure the light. Even during the training for monks that be chosen by Perun, most don't get it the first few tries. It be difficult to block everything from yer mind and then create so vivid an image in yer head.

"Once ye 'ave the ball of light, ye control it with your mind. It becomes second nature, until ye are able to control two." He separated his left hand. *"Subluceo."* Another brilliant ball of light appeared. One hovered while the other rose into the air before coming back down. "Controlling more than one be a toll on the mind." The second ball of light folded in on itself in an instant and disappeared. "It be like growing another arm and trying to use all three. It be awkward and requires practice."

Anne had seen the simple conjuring of light before, but her eyes were wide at the show. "How do you make them disappear?" she whispered to the monk.

"Two ways. The first be if the energy runs out. It be like a candle. If all the wax melts, there be nothing left. The second be to command it to disappear with yer mind." The last globe disappeared then, leaving Anne in darkness.

As her eyes adjusted, she began to envision her own ball of light floating easily above her open palms. It was a simple thing for Anne to do: she often pictured things in her head while she was daydreaming. *"Subluceo,"* she said

She felt something deep in her gut come aglow. Energy she had never felt lit up inside of her. The warmth filled her chest before gently traveling down her arms. She could feel it stream from her hands like water from a watering can. She immediately cut off the strange feeling.

A tiny globe of light appeared above her palm.

In its dim glow, Anne could just make out the shock on Jericho's face. His eyes were as wide as a silver mark.

The glowing light disappeared. Silence followed.

"Let's get moving," Captain Philial called, walking to his horse. He motioned for the two recruits to light their torches.

"But you're not a monk! You've said no vows!" The anxious monks looked at the others.

Captain Philial was adjusting the straps to his saddle bags on his horse. The two recruits, Porter and Heath, we re trying to light their torches with little luck. Isabella was packing the left over cheese and bread. No one had noticed.

"Ye must not tell them what happened! Tell no one! If the high priests hear of this they'll send the Crows… they'll send the Crows after me!" He immediately outlined the five-pointed star on his upper torso again and prayed for forgiveness.

Anne was shocked. She had tried to cast that simple spell a million times. It had never worked before. Anne walked to her horse and mounted, trying to disguise the excitement that welled within her like the new energy she had discovered.

As the journey continued and the darkness of the night got deeper, Anne's excitement was not enough to keep her weariness at bay. A full day's journey just after a late breakfast usually wouldn't tire her much, but she had gotten little sleep the night before after hearing the news of her father. She looked behind to see how Porter and Heath were holding up.

Both of their eyes hung at the corners with weariness, and the spears they had held high at the beginning of the day were used more like walking sticks. Sweat stains were visible through the leather brigandines by the light of their torches. *I hope the real soldiers don't get tired so quickly!* Anne thought. She stifled a yawn with the back of her hand.

Isabella seemed all right, except that she kept readjusting the sack of provisions she carried. Anne reached down to grab it and placed it behind her on the saddle. Isabella gave her a nod in thanks and continued to walk.

Jericho seemed too worried to be tired. He whispered prayers of forgiveness in the dark and slid his shaking hands over his shaved head. In his nervousness, he fiddled with his star necklace imbedded with the lustrous pearl.

Captain Philial sat unwavering on his mount as he had been the entire trip. He showed no signs of fatigue that Anne could discern.

The ride was silent before they came to a halt after a few extra hours of travel. They stopped in another clearing along the bank of the Sparkle, the stars shining on its surface. Wispy clouds drifted overhead, every now and then blocking even the starlight. Isabella lit a fire and prepared the provisions she had brought for dinner while Captain Philial explained to his soldiers how they were supposed to set camp.

Anne took care of her horse and brushed him down. He was grateful for the care and the oats she gave him. Anne snuck away for a few minutes to try and cast the spell again, but her attempts went without success. Tired and frustrated, it wasn't long before she wandered into the light of the fire to eat.

"My lady, this be no delicacy, but it be all I 'ave for ye," Isabella apologized as she handed Anne a bowl of stew with chopped carrots and salted venison.

"That's all right, Isabella, I wasn't expecting anything fancy. We're on the road after all." She took a bite of the food and thought she could have been happy with anything.

Captain Philial, Porter, and Heath came to the fire after a while and began to eat as well. Jericho was the last to grab a meal, but he was startled to find to that no one had prayed. "You must thank the curators for what they have provided. Make the sign and bow your heads." The others did as they were instructed.

"Ares, we thank your glorious wings for these soldiers to keep us safe, and for the food you have blessed us with from your earth. May your sword never dull, and may you keep us safe from the fire." Anne always thought it was funny that the god warriors prayed to was the same god farmers did. Soldiers and farmers didn't want the same thing, even when the farmers were forced to arm themselves and act like soldiers.

Porter and Heath talked among themselves afterwards, avoiding eye contact with Anne. *Do they really think I've changed since they became soldiers? I'm still the same girl, even if my fath-, I mean brother, is the Constable.* Thinking of her father again, Anne choked back a tear. She had wept constantly the night before until her chest hurt from sobbing. She didn't think she had any more tears to give.

Isabella laid Anne's cot out for her, and Captain Philial took the first watch that night. Lady Ignava refused to travel without a large tent and a real bed, but Anne didn't care so much for those comforts. She curled into a ball on her pallet, placed a bit apart from the others. She was grateful for the small amount of privacy. With her father still fresh on her mind, she sobbed herself into a dreamless sleep with Isabella beside her attempting to comfort, but Anne felt the wetness of the maid's silent tears behind her. The Sparkle stretched out behind them, silently still in the dead of the night.

"Porter," she absently heard her voice say, stirring her from sleep. *Did I just say that?* She opened her eyes and propped herself up on her elbows before wiping the sleep from her eyes.

"Porter, I think Heath found something in the water. Come check this out." A small thud sounded as though someone stepped on something."Shhh! Don't wake the others!" her voice whispered sharply. She could see the dark form of Porter grab his spear and begin following a shadow to the edge of the water.

Anne squinted her eyes together and peered into the darkness beside her. *Am I dreaming?* Beside her Isabella continued to sleep despite the noise. Anne got up and followed Porter to the water's edge.

"I don't see Heath anywhere," Porter said with a yawn. "I thought you said he found something."

The figure he followed was cloaked in darkness. From the dark form, Anne heard her voice again. "It's in the water. Come deeper. It may be a pearl." The figure walked through the shallows with the obedient Porter Mann behind. The water rose to their ankles, shins, and then to their knees.

"Porter, don't go!" she heard from behind her. It was Captain Philial, running to the bank with bow in hand. "It's a water djinn!"

Porter brought his spear into both hands, ready to strike. He wavered for an instant. "Anne?" he asked, confusion evident in his voice.

"It's not me, Po   rter!" Anne yelled out. She thrust out her hands, pictured a perfect round sphere of light, and yelled, *"Subluceo!"*

The energy she felt earlier came to her call, filling up her insides with a pure glow that shined down her arms and out of her hands to form a ball of light. The sphere she formed was huge, as big as Anne herself. The light it emitted was bright enough to light all of the surrounding area and force d Anne to shield her eyes. Becoming dizzy, Anne wavered where she stood and could barely force her mind to keep the massive glowing globe intact. Its light reached over the bank and into the water, lighting the dark form.

Bathed in the bright light of the spell, the figure was no longer shrouded by darkness or its illusion. It hunched over with scaly skin and bulging muscles. Nearly as tall as a troll, the beast had small fins on its shoulders. Its head was wide like a frog's, and it had a blue fin that stretched from its forehead down its back. Small, black beady eyes squeezed shut in the sudden light, and the creature flinched back a step with its short, powerful arms covering its eyes.

Porter, fear evident on his face, drove his spear forward. The point pierced the creature through its stomach. The glint of steel shined a dull red when it emerged from the creature's back. Its webbed hand grasped the shaft of the spear. The water djinn's muscles tightened as it pulled its body along the smooth wood in an effort to reach the recruit. The djinn slid down the pole with an evil hiss, leaving a slick trail of red.

His courage gone, Porter let go of the spear and fell backwards into the water. Captain Philial sent a barrage of arrows toward the creature. Arrow after arrow thudded into the creature's scaly skin. Porter scrambled back while the creature shrieked and gurgled in pain. Unable to walk any further, the creature grasped Porter's spear both webbed hands and fell to its knees. The water djinn let out one last hiss and fell over into the shallows. A splash erupted, and ripples from the creature's fall started off on a journey in all directions, with a slight tint of crimson mixed in with the salt water.

Still light-headed from her spell, Anne stumbled past the light, bringing her feet into the water. She closed her eyes and leaned forward, her hands on her knees.

"Anne!" It was Captain Philial's voice. She opened her eyes.

She saw two bodies floating in the lake. They had bruises around their necks. One of them had a robe bobbing in the water around him, the other wore brigandine armor.

Unable to continue standing, Anne fell forward as the light from her globe blinked away.

Chapter 4
(Anne, Galavon)

"I've never seen her like this," the muffled voice of Duchess Dara said from the other side of the door. "From the minute she rode through the gate she's been sad, sick, and exhausted. She needs to talk to someone, and I demand to be let in to see her."

"I be sorry my lady, but orders from yer own husband won't permit me to allow it."

"To Shiva's own prison with your orders! I'm the lady of this keep, and I order you to move!" Silence. "I will send my Duke of a husband to Shiva's prison with your orders!" After a primal grunt, Anne heard the echoes of angry footfalls striding farther and farther away.

Anne sat at a wood desk in the antechamber to her own lush suite, listening to the activity outside. The tower she rested in was the Eagle Tower, a tower saved for the Constable and his family. They had stayed at Caernarfon Castle often during the seasons before the goblins attacked the province. Being one of the three true castles on the peninsula, Caernarfon Castle was handsomely outfitted, and the rooms Anne sat in now were no exception. She didn't share them with her family on this trip, though, and it made the rooms seem empty.

The antechamber had a thick carpet that led to a desk situated at the end. While it was not an enormous desk, the crafted wood came from a rare snow oak, a huge tree with white wood that grew in the forests of the Mountain Province. The four legs were carved into white wyverns, and their heads met the desktop with pearls in their mouths. The sides were carved with interlacing stars. They were seven pointed instead of the Reproba Caelum five. Each intricate star had tiny symbols carved inside that went in a pattern: a flame, a wave, curves for wind, a mountain, a skull, and a round symbol Anne believed was a Pearl. The most beautiful of the tiny symbols was the only one not to follow the pattern. Instead it showed up sporadically between the others as if it held them all together. It was a dragon, and it graced only seven of the stars with its presence. The desk was the oldest piece of furniture in the keep.

On both sides of the desk was a banner of the province: a simple stitched pearl on a dark blue background. The two sidewalls each held a tapestry depicting different battle scenes between the white wyverns over the Sparkle beside the keep. The battles took place once every hundred Twil, and the amazing view offered by Caernarfon Castle could be matched by nowhere else. No one knew why the great beasts fought to the death in pairs over the salt water lake, but as sure as the heat in the warm season, they came.

Sconces fashioned to hold scented candles were strategically placed in various parts of the room, as well as a hanging chandelier, but instead of their flickering gold light the soft white glow of an orb lit the antechamber. Anne sat behind the snow oak desk, moving the light around the room with a blank expression on her face.

She had woken that morning in the bed she normally occupied when visiting with her family. Isabella had been in one of the elegant chairs that decorated the room, anxiously waiting for Anne to awaken. She told Anne what had happened.

The beast had been a water djinn, a creature that tempted people into the depths of an ocean, lake, river, or stream and drowned them unmercifully. They would watch travelers and use mimicry and a sort of illusion to induce them into the water. After drowning them, they would take the corpses of their victims deep into the depths and eat them. Earth djinn were common in the ruins of the empire far to the north, and tree djinn lived around Kobold Wood in the fig trees that grew on the edges. All were equally dangerous and cunning.

Captain Philial hadn't hesitated once Anne fell on the bank. He had commanded Porter to pack up the camp and start immediately for Caernarfon Castle. He then threw Anne over his saddle and made it to the keep late the following morning.

Captain Philial, Isabella said, pieced together the events of the night for his report once the others arrived. The water djinn began with Heath before killing the monk. The djinn's next target was Porter, but because Porter was so loud in following the beast, he had woken not only Anne but the captain as well.

Anne could tell that her maid hadn't slept since being woken up last night. Dismissing Isabella to get some rest, she now waited. What she waited for, she wasn't sure.

She watched her small globe race around the room. Despite having summoned such a large globe that night with the water djinn, this was all she could manage. She assumed it was because she didn't cut off her energy when creating the light by the lake.

"Ah, Yulin!" said a slow, winded voice of an old man. "A finer lad to guard our province's pearl couldn't be found in all of

Mundus. Ares would be proud to have you under his wing in any task."

The voice came from the other side of the door, but Anne knew it was Larith. He was the nuncio assigned to Caernarfon Castle by the high priest of the Peninsula Province. A nuncio acted as an ambassador of Reproba Caelum to prominent nobles in a province, offering advice and the word of the curators as well as taking charge of the monks in the area.

"Thank ye Larith, but I just be doing a soldier's job." Anne could hear pride in the soldier's voice. "I assume ye 'ave written orders that allow ye in her quarters? The Duke be worried fer the girl."

"Of course." He sounded ancient. There was a slight rustle of paper.

"Everything be in order," she heard before the faint sound of footsteps faded away. She assumed he was dismissed.

The carved door that led into the antechamber opened to reveal Larith in all his glory. The skinny old man had age marks on his face and on his bald head. His ears were pointy, but not as long as an elf's – at least, Anne didn't think they were from the pictures she had seen. The star with the pearl that hung around his neck seemed to weigh him down, hunching his back. His white robe hung loosely on his skinny frame, and instead of sandals he went barefoot. His lips were thin, but they were set on a smiling face. Anne saw his eyes go to her hovering white globe, but his face never lost the smile. He calmly ignored the light and shut the door behind him.

"Anne Ziyad, pearl of the province," the old nuncio said in his slow voice that made him sound wise. "It has been far too long since you have graced us here with your beauty! It's a poor day the day you come bearing ill news, along with being ill yourself."

She brought her globe to the desk in front of her and stared at it. "I'm not ill."

Her globe of light disappeared. Confusion splayed itself across her face. *I hadn't dismissed it! It should have lasted longer!*

Another appeared above Larith's right shoulder, once again bathing the room in a white glow. "Unfortunate, I must say." Larith shuffled his way in front of the desk and leaned heavily on one of the chairs. "It seems you've mastered that trick easily enough. Quickly too, I might add, even for one with pure southern blood." He tried to study her face, but Anne stared down at the desk. She wasn't sure what he was talking about. *Pure southern blood? Lady Ignava isn't from the Jebel-A-Tarik Province.* "It was foolish of you to cast a White Magic spell when you're not sanctioned to do so. You have set a dangerous path for yourself."

Anne looked up immediately, ready to defend her actions. She had *literally* shed light on the beast. If it hadn't been for her Porter would have died. If Perun had deemed her worthy of White Magic, why not use it?

But before she could fully open her mouth to combat his words, Larith added something. "Foolish, but brave." He motioned toward the door. "Shall we continue this conversation on top of the Chamberlain Tower? We can catch the last of the sunlight. A bit of sunlight is good for my tired bones. Besides, I enjoy having a pretty girl help me up the steps."

Larith allowed his globe of light to dissipate as soon as they entered the stairwell. It had large windows to let in a cool breeze from the Cliffside Gulf, and sunlight poured in to light the stone passage. The last of the warm season flowers decorated the windowsills.

"Larith," Anne began as she helped the old nuncio down the stairs, "why would Perun…"

"Quiet, my dear! One should be wary when stumbling down a dangerous road. You wouldn't want the wrong ears to hear your words. I shall explain everything as soon as we reach the top of the Chamberlain Tower. A visual aid always helps in teaching the young."

Anne bit her lip to stop her questions from escaping. With her free hand she drew back some of her curly locks from her face.

The pair drew no attention from passing servants, only smiles at the kind remarks they received from Larith. They passed through a set of doors and came to a portion of the wall where they passed soldiers on guard duty looking out over the gulf. They passed through the Queen's tower, where the Duke's quarters were, and continued on to the Chamberlain Tower. The Chamberlain Tower was filled with nothing but books, making it the largest library in the Peninsula Province. They entered from the wall into the third floor of the tower.

Each level of the tower was a single room. This room, as most were in the Chamberlain Tower, was round with circular bookcases covering the walls. They were only missing at the door and where the stairs protruded from the wall. These floating steps slowly spiraled around the inside of the tower. No windows decorated the walls so that the humid, salty air wouldn't hurt the books that filled every inch of space above and below the seemingly unsupported stairs. Somehow the tower room remained a pleasant, cool temperature no matter the season. A chandelier comprised of small glowing globes hung from the ceiling to give light to the room.

"You know, I designed this tower in my youth when the castle was being built by Duke Briel's grandfather," Larith said. They climbed the staircase to the fourth floor. "Well, forty Twil at least seems like youth when you become as old as I have. The high priests demanded this castle be built to help solidify Reproba Caelum here. That is why it looks so different from Castle Himeji and Castle Matsuyama – those two castles were built by the people who lived on the peninsula long before Reproba Caelum. This tower was built just before the last time the white wyverns fought their battles over the Sparkle. Quite a sight to see from the top, I assure you. But even with the roars of the victors and the screams of the dying, it feels right knowing that the natural traditions of Mundus continue. For with natural continuance, we shall continue."

The pair reached the fourth floor and Anne helped Larith up the first step to the fifth. The fourth floor perfectly resembled the third except that there was no door – just books and books, a chandelier with the glowing orbs, a simple wood table set in the center with chairs, and the spiraling staircase. Their progress was slow. "Larith, that was nearly a hundred Twil ago, and you said you had already seen forty?"

"Yes, child, I have been blessed with a long life it seems." Larith reached out to touch the wall of the tower as they climbed. "The stone for this tower in particular was especially expensive. It came from a goblin fortress built hundreds of Twil ago. As I am sure you've noticed, it has the power to expel heat and moisture, making it safe for my books."

The sudden change in subject from Larith's age made Anne wonder, but she didn't press it. "How did they make it?"

she asked. Despite their many visits to Caernarfon castle, she had never been told how the tower kept cool.

"The secret has been lost for many Twil, the books long destroyed. The goblins, however, hand their knowledge down by oral tradition. It is they who made these very stones. Somehow they have taken out the stone's ability to heat up. It must have something to do with their affinity to fire, as befits a race that worships ancient Shiva." They both fell silent. East Ager seemed to be in a constant struggle with the creatures and men who worshipped the ancient dragon. They reached the fifth floor. Again it was filled with books and a simple table with chairs. Their footsteps echoed in the circular space. They continued their ascent.

"What about the lights?" Anne asked. "The chandeliers that hang in each of the rooms? Where did they come from? How do the globes never fade?"

Larith smiled, spreading his thin lips to flash a full set of teeth. *No man his age should still have all of his teeth*, Anne thought. "I made them myself. The materials to craft them were also very expensive." The old nuncio looked proud of his work.

"You made them yourself?" Anne asked incredulously.

He chuckled at her disbelief. "Yes, yes, I crafted them myself. It's likely I'm the last in all of the Kingdom besides the curators who know the art of enchanting."

"How did you learn? Can I learn? I've never seen them anywhere in all of the province but here and in the Cathedral of New Beginnings. What sort of…"

"Do you ever give anyone the chance to answer your first question?" Larith asked her. With Anne duly silenced, he offered what little explanation he was willing to give. "When I had only seen a few Twil, I was fortunate enough to travel Mundus and leave the Kingdom of East Ager far behind. During these adventures, I made new friends of old ones and discovered myself besides."

His ending riddle made no sense to Anne, but she knew she would receive no more of an explanation. They entered the sixth floor.

"Perhaps one day you will be able to learn, but it is a very big perhaps. You must keep your control over White Magic a secret while the curators rule over the province. And not only this, but you must learn how to control other magics as well, again, all in secrecy. You are not part of Reproba Caelum, and many would see you killed for blasphemy despite your noble title. Or perhaps for your noble title." Anne felt like a fool for trying to learn White Magic. She didn't ask any false gods for the power, but how would she be able to convince anyone else of that fact? That must be why Duke Briel kept the guard at her door.

"Larith, where are all of your monks? Aren't you supposed to be in charge of them here?"

"I enjoy my privacy here in the tower. Besides, there is nothing in the castle that I can't take care of myself. No, they are in the town below the cliffs or sent off with patrols. Monks were made for the road, child." There was a longing in his voice. Anne tried not to laugh picturing the nuncio slowly wobble from one village to the next. They entered the seventh floor of the tower.

"If I knew I was going to have to climb these things at my age, I would have asked for the Great Hall, not a tower." Anne giggled despite herself and helped Larith up the last of the steps to the top of the Chamberlain's Tower. The afternoon's slanting sunlight hit their faces as they exited the seventh and last floor onto the roof.

From the height advantage, the lay of the land sprawled out in front of Anne's eyes. To the west was the Cliffside Gulf. Small islands dotted the blue expanse. To the north the Mountains of Hope rose into the sky, though from the distance they seemed to only be hills. Of course to the east lay the Sparkle, making it seem as though Pearl were surrounded by the lake. The coast snaked off to the south, and the late afternoon bustle in Caern, the port town carved into the cliffs beneath the shadow of Caernarfon Castle, looked like a flurry of ants with the sounds of seagulls cutting through the air.

"So tell me, Anne," Larith said between huge intakes of fresh air, "in the dying light what strikes you the most from this view?"

Anne looked toward the Cliffside Gulf. The water stretched so far her vision swam in its endlessness. But even while she looked at it, there was an urge to turn toward the Sparkle.

Sunlight glistened off the water of the lake, but unlike the gulf, it was still. There were no great waves crashing against its shore , no large ships built to withstand rough waters. It was serene, calm, and pacified.

"The Sparkle, with the city just visible behind it. " Anne fiddled with her pearl necklace. "It's my home. Always has been, always will be."

Larith nodded. "You know it, and you love it. I suspect you will give up much to do what is best for the people there. It's where your heart lies." Larith turned his gaze to the land that stretched out to the southeast, the heart of the province. The fading light of the day hit his eyes and for the first time Anne noticed their color. They were not the crystal clear blue of a native to the region. No, they were a bit darker, as though someone splashed a bit of purple in the blue to make the color deeper. "Your brother answered the land to the southeast. He'll be a good Constable after some time."

Anne flinched at the mention of Cecil. It reminded her of too much: his parting, her father's death, and the floating dead bodies of her escort.

"What about you, Larith? What direction are your eyes drawn to?"

Larith turned from the southeast and walked to the northwest. He looked across the gulf and beyond the mountains. "My journey for answers took me far beyond the Peninsula Province. Far from East Ager. The more answers I discovered, the more questions I needed answered. I fear the truths that I learned will soon become common knowledge, and with them will come a flood of violence and a torrent of tears." The old nuncio looked back to Anne. "I shall begin by saying that Mundus is a much harsher place than you know it to be, and the Kingdom of East Ager is no exception. The answers to your questions will come in time, and I suspect the number will grow as well."

"If I was stronger with white magic I might have been able to save them," Anne said distantly looking back to the Sparkle.

"Perhaps," Larith responded. "Perhaps not. It's difficult to assess the past with 'ifs.' I will teach you more, Anne. Soon enough the people of your home will need all the help you have to offer."

True to its name, Lonely Hill was quite possibly the loneliest place Galavon had ever stayed in all of his travels through the Kingdom of East Ager.

Maybe thirty people inhabited the village, perhaps sixty when the farmers who lived outside of the palisade walls came in for the meager protection they offered. Just outside the village, Galavon and his guards were greeted by true southern rain. Rather than the drizzle Galavon had experienced walking Anne home, the drops of water were the size of his fist and came down in a sheet. The group might as well have been under dozens of buckets filled with water.

The rain had turned the streets to mud. There had been no stable for the wagons, forcing the guards to watch them from under the miserable protection of an overhang. The five rooms in the Moon's Crest Inn had been filled with fleas, and the poor food might have turned away a scavenging manticore. The road was more welcoming.

Lonely Hill was two day's ride behind them now. The days had been uninteresting travel down an empty road through the endless plains of the Fire Pass Province.

Galavon pulled back on his reigns to bring Kid to a stop. It was dark, but the sun threatened to peak over the horizon at any minute. Curious as to why Torvil called for a stop while it was still dark and cool, Galavon walked his mount to the front where Torvil questioned Darak in hushed tones.

"You're sure?" Galavon heard Torvil whisper. Darak nodded and dismounted from his horse. He winked a indigo eye in Galavon's direction. Torvil turned and addressed the company.

"Half a league ahead there's an ambush laid out for us by the Albus Veneficus," Torvil announced loud enough for the band to hear.

The Albus Veneficus were renegades in East Ager who rebelled against Reproba Caelum and practiced magic in secret. They were more common in the Peninsula Province, but Galavon had heard talk of a another group hidden away in the Mountains of Hope who were said to be masters of Wind Magic.

"There are only ten of the Shiva-blasted bandits, but they have a shaman. They probably think they'll have this fight easy. There's no way to avoid it."

Questions ran through Galavon's head. *How did Torvil know their number? How did he know they had a shaman?* Half a league was too far away to know these things.

Torvil went about spreading the mercenaries around the wagon. He mostly split them in pairs, except for the huge man Angar. "Angar, you're up front. And by the fire of Shiva when they come out, keep your mouth closed! Galavon, you're with me on the right side. Tie the horses to the back wagon, we don't need them getting injured."

The company nodded and moved to obey. Galavon tied his horse and moved beside Torvil. He was nervous.

"Galavon," Darak said. Galavon turned. Darak pulled an ash staff from the back of one of the wagons. "I bought this in Lonely Hill. It's a good traveler's weapon. You should take it."

"I, I dont know how to use it," Galavon stuttered.

"You hit them with it," Torvil muttered.

Galavon's eyes grew wide. "Maybe I should wait here until after..."

"Stay between myself and the wagons, and you won't have to use your stick," Torvil boomed.

"You'll be fine, " Darak assured him. "It's just in case."

Galavon nodded. He tried to keep his fear under control as he walked behind Torvil beside the wagons. He didn't see where Darak went. He gripped the staff tight and looked for any sign of the bandits. Something like this would never happen on the Great Trade Circle. By Shiva's own prison, they were about to fight a shaman! A shaman! They'd be lucky if they weren't all burned alive!

Perhaps I'll never see Anne again after all.

She had been a regular visitor in his thoughts during the long days of travel. He wondered if she would forgive him for not being there the day after the feast. He wondered what she was doing. He wondered a lot of things about her really, but he knew now wasn't the time.

"Torvil, how did you know about the ambush?"

"Quiet! Stay between me and the wagons!"

Galavon kept his questions to himself after that. He felt more like the iron bars in the cart than a man.

Angar brought the first cart to a stop, bringing the entire group to a halt. It was mostly dark still, but the world seemed to glow in the early morning. The familiar line of pink and gold couldn't even be seen over the horizon, but the stars began to fade in the sky. Galavon chanced a glance at Torvil, and he seemed nervous as he looked around at the sky.

"Well, what do we 'ave here?" said a man ahead on the road. Galavon could barely make out his form. The lack of light made his short sword a shadow at his side. "Looks to be as though ye brought me an early gift for the passing of Twil!"

A tense feeling hung in the air. No one responded to the bandit.

The stars continued to fade in the sky, and the earliest rays of sunshine broke free from the darkness. With the growing light Galavon could just see the flash of a smug smile printed across the blurred face. "I be only asking once. I want…"

Torvil's booming voice broke off the man's speech. "Forget it, there's no time! Attack!"

A hundred things happened at once. First, a silver flash cut the air so quickly that Galavon wasn't even sure he saw it. Angar charged at the talking bandit brandishing his giant mace. Two men in rags jumped up from the tall grass beside the road and made their own charge at Galavon and Torvil. Torvil's flamberge made a mighty arc keeping the two attackers at bay. The sound of steel on steel could be heard on the other side of the cart.

Torvil made another swing at the two attackers. The quicker of the two darted inside of the swing, assuming that Torvil would be unable to bring the blade back in time to defend. His assumption was correct, but just as his blade neared its mark, an arrow from one of the guards on the wagon hit him in the shoulder. The steel point pierced easily through rags and flesh, coming out on the other side more red than gray. A look of pain crossed the man's face, and he brought his attack up short. Rather than bring his blade back around, Torvil smashed the man in the face with the pommel of his sword, making Galavon think the man didn't have chance even without the arrow.

The voice of the first bandit called out over the ring of steel. "Ceridwen! What are you waiting for? Burn them!" Galavon could see the man dancing around Angar's mace. The guard with the bow on the wagon turned to fire at another bandit who emerged from the woods in front of the wagons.

Torvil ducked as a crude arrow whizzed by his shoulder, imbedding itself in the wagon.

The amount of action stunned Galavon, making him immobile. Once he regained his senses, he took a step back toward the horses tied behind the wagons. He was useless and worried about the arrows. With daylight coming in, the darkness concealed nothing, including the strange scene behind the wagons.

A thin woman emerged from the tall grass. Her brown hair was streaked with grey and might have been curly was it not matted and dirty. She had light blue eyes and a nose that resembled the beak of a lark: long, thin, and pointy enough to spear a worm. Her movements were slow, like she was trudging through mud. She plodded toward the center of the road at a snail's pace. Galavon assumed she was steering clear of the brawl. Avoiding the end of one of Torvil's massive swings, Galavon backed further toward the end of the wagon train. He tripped backwards over a rock and hit the ground. The bandits were fighting desperately now to defend themselves, and they kept glancing at the sluggish woman.

Galavon watched as the wounded man attempted to block one of Torvil's heavy blows. The result was the blade being flung directly toward Galavon. He scrambled to his feet to avoid it. The horses tied to the back of the wagon reared, and Galavon backpedaled even further. He clutched his staff tight and never let his eyes leave the melee.

Within minutes it seemed the bandits were either too wounded to continue or dead. None retreated, as though they still believed hope remained. Galavon closed his eyes, took a deep breath, and let out a sigh of relief with his head pointed upwards. He watched the last star fade from the sky.

Then there was a silver flash, and he heard the sound of the woman behind him stumbling forward.

Galavon whipped around and saw confusion on her face, then anger. She raised her hands and closed her eyes. In his fright, just as she began to speak, Galavon slammed his staff against the side of her head and watched her fall unconscious to the ground.

At the sound of the crack, the guards looked over to see Galavon standing over the woman. The remaining bandits threw down their crude weapons.

"Tie them," Torvil bellowed. He then turned and made his way to Galavon.

"I, I didn't know if she was dangerous. She looked threatening all of a sudden, so I just..." Galavon wasn't sure how to finish.

Without a word, Torvil bent down and rolled her on her back. Fresh blood wet the side of her hair. He did a rough search over her body, making no effort to be gentle.

"Torvil, I know she was unarmed, and a woman, but I wasn't sure if..." Again, Galavon didn't know how to finish the sentence. He had just hit a woman on the side of the head with a staff. *Not only am I coward, but I hit a woman.*

Finally finding what he was looking for, Torvil ripped off an arm band hidden beneath the rags on her arm. Before Torvil hastily put it in his pocket, Galavon noticed a large uncut ruby in the middle of it.

"Stop quibbling," Torvil growled. "She was dangerous." As if she was no heavier than a bag of feathers, he threw the limp woman over his shoulder before turning back and walking to the wagons. The quick movement combined with the rough search over her body dislodged a hidden pouch that hit the earth. Still shaking from the fear of the fight, Galavon scooped up the pouch slowly. He looked at it for a moment before following after Torvil who was almost to the second wagon.

While the mercenaries tied up the surviving Albus Veneficus, Galavon walked to the side of the road and sat in the shade offered by the back wagon. There were no trees in the area, just tall grass dancing in the wind. Cupping his left hand, he emptied the contents of the pouch into it.

Galavon expected another raw ruby like the one he saw on the shaman's armband. Instead, in his hand was a large polished emerald. It was dark green, uncut, and the size of his fist. He marveled at how the early morning light made the dark green stone seem to glow in his hands.

Galavon placed it back in the pouch and hung it from his belt. He sat watching the yellow grass shift in the wind.

"Galavon."

Galavon tore his eyes away from the swaying grass. Behind him was Darak, looking even more haggard than the mercenaries who had fought. He had black rings under his eyes.

"Time to go?" Galavon asked.

"Yes. There's still time to travel before the worst of the heat. The weather is already beginning to feel cooler though, so the stop won't be long."

The bandits who could walk were kept between the two carts secured by a rope. Their more injured comrades were sprawled on top of the iron in the first wagon. The woman was tied in the last wagon with the chains that used to hold the iron bars in place with a dirty rag stuffed her mouth. The prisoners meant they would have to travel slower, but from what Galavon heard from the mercenaries, Albus Venificus brought in a good bounty if you could prove that's what they were.

Darak insisted on riding last in the column, and Galavon decided to join him. The mercenaries were busy boasting about their victory. The only injuries to the group had been shallow cuts and a huge bruise taken by a sling. Kavar, the dirty little man, walked with the prisoners and threatened them with his knives.

"Torvil told me you knocked out the shaman," Darak said. He kept his gaze on the woman as if he was waiting for her to try and escape.

Galavon turned red. "I suppose I did." He felt embarrassed. "She didn't do anything during the fight."

"I'm sure she would of done something if she could have. A shaman controls fire, Galavon, and yet she is more than a shaman. She has an understanding of White Magic as well as Fire Magic." Though his hood fell low, it didn't conceal his exhaustion. "The old tribes that lived here called those that could wield more than one of the elemental powers a mage. You knocked out a mage, Galavon."

The mercenaries ahead busted out into laughter. Kavar was still threatening the bandits, much to their amusement.

"Where were you during the fight?" Galavon asked.

"I used to hunt the Albus Veneficus when they were more numerous years ago. When they were much more dangerous." Darak said. "I played my part." Galavon thought he saw a smile underneath the cowl of his hood.

Soon the heat was too much to bear, and a lone, scraggly tree could be seen on the side of the road. Galavon's mind still raced from the ambush, and the heat only made it worse, making him dizzy. He felt as though he might topple off his horse. He had to call a stop.

Galavon was nervous about issuing a command, but he needed the stop, had to have it. He needed a break. He took a deep breath to steady himself and slow the spinning in his head. He stood in his saddle. "Angar!" Angar, who was driving the second wagon, turned around. "Tell Torvil we'll wait out the heat under this tree."

The big man looked surprised. "All right." Galavon heard the command get passed up, and he thought he heard Torvil say something about a worthless yelp.

The group settled under the little shade. The wagons themselves blocked more of the sun. Rather than fight for an area under the lone tree, Galavon crawled under the wagon furthest away and closed his eyes.

Sleep refused to come. The small skirmish replayed in his mind over and over again. The red point of the arrow coming through the bandit's shoulder, the sound of steel clashing on steel and, more importantly, his inability to help. He had frozen. Galavon fiddled with the pendant his father had given him.

Hushed tones came from the side of the cart.

"A pearl, you said? I should have kept searching after I found the ruby." The voice was deep. Galavon was sure it belonged to Torvil.

"I took the pearl, but it's drained of magic. It's a tradition of the Albus Venificus to separate themselves from their first stone so they're not bound to it. But she can't use Fire Magic without the ruby, and there are no White Magic spells she can cast to help herself escape." Smooth voice, even while whispering. That one had to be Darak. "Besides, Galavon needs rest. It was his first fight."

"Bah! He needs rest? He was more of a hindrance than…"

"Easy, my friend. The others are far enough away not to hear anything, but Galavon is sleeping under this wagon."

"He sleeps like a rock! A roaring dragon couldn't wake him! The boy doesn't have the heart to fight or the charisma for trade. He's too shy and too scared. He'd have no clue what to do with the iron in Farrow if not for his father's connections." Torvil let out a sigh.

"Experience will change him. He wasn't raised to be a fighter, and perhaps the stars don't have it in their pattern for him to be a merchant either."

A heavy chuckle came from the voices. "You mean the curators, not the stars, don't you? It seems the battle took a bit out of you as well."

"Yes, forgive me. The starlight faded quickly, and I had to focus the dimming power. If it weren't for Galavon hitting the shaman when he did, you might all be ashes."

"Hmmph."

Two pairs of footsteps padded away. One was light and barely audible while the other was heavy. Galavon rolled on his back. Was he a failure at everything? He knew he couldn't fight and hadn't thought of trying to trade without his father's contacts. He opened his eyes and stared up at the bottom of the cart.

Two light blue eyes bore down on him from between the boards.

"The one you know as Torvil doesn't seem to approve of your actions," said a voice from the direction of the eyes. It was a powerful, feminine voice.

Galavon looked around from under the cart. None of the mercenaries moved from beneath the tree.

"They can't hear us. You heard the secretive one. I can still use White Magic."

Galavon had heard Darak mention the pearl. That meant she had had a ruby, a pearl, and unbeknownst to Darak and Torvil, an emerald.

It was common knowledge that pearls from the Sparkle were outlawed by the high priests, but Galavon had heard of other stones being illegal to have in your possession as well . Although harder to find because they couldn't be found in the Kingdom of East Ager, certain stones from specific regions of Mundus were only sold to the priests of Reproba Caelum. To be in possession of one was considered a crime severe enough for death.

Galavon didn't know where the stones could be found, didn't even know the names of most. Galavon could only think of one other stone besides the pearls from the Sparkle.

His mother Tara had lived in a small town by the northern section of the Mountains of Hope. Only agents of Reproba Caelum were allowed to have emeralds from deep in those mountains. They could be recognized by their dark color and slight aura, or glow. The aura marked them as property of the curators, and the law was strictly enforced.

The voice came again. "My mind couldn't grasp the magic of the emerald, despite all the things my mother taught me," the mage said. Her eyes continued to bore into Galavon. "My mind is too distracted by the methods I must use to cast White Magic and Fire Magic."

Galavon looked back at the Albus Veneficus with a puzzled expression. He was taught the curators granted magical abilities. Those who used it without their blessing were granted the power from lesser, evil gods. But the mage just said her mother taught her? And what did she mean by the "magic of the emerald?"

Galavon caught a glimpse of white teeth between the boards as the mage grinned. His confusion must have been clearly etched across his face. "A child of Reproba Caelum, are you? The bit about Perun granting magic is a lie that took hundreds of years to become accepted, and there are still some of us who remember the truth. The only things that decide whether or not you can use magic are your own abilities and the possession of certain stones."

She lies, Galavon thought. *She must be.* He felt the pouch at his belt for the emerald.

"Judging from your green eyes, either your mother or your father lived in the Mountain Province. Your heritage makes you an ideal candidate for the emerald, for Wind Magic. Yes, the magic usually comes easier for those with links to the natives of the region the stone can be found."

Galavon finally found his voice. "You're lying. I'm not a priest, Perun wouldn't grant me the power," he whispered.

A sharp laugh erupted from above the boards in his mind. "So you don't believe me do you? The only reason the high priests claim that Perun grants them their power is because they control the trade of the stones. Everyone must be taught, but not by any god I assure you."

Only a member of the rebel groups would make that claim. Of course Perun granted the power! Everyone knew it.

"I don't believe you. No one has ever learned without Perun's blessing unless they worshipped an evil god."

The light blue eyes lit up with amusement. "The curators must alter the history books a bit as well to keep magic to themselves. Allow me to fill you in on a brief introduction to the Kingdom East Ager's true history.

"Years ago there was a great empire across the Barren Ocean. Mundus is a far larger place than what we know it to be. The empire stretched so far that they founded their farthest colonies in our lands, lands they called Ager. This I'm sure you know.

"For some reason the mainland of the empire was utterly destroyed, leaving the cities here vulnerable. Wars for dominance over the cities erupted and resulted in how we know them today – as independent city-states that are only remnants of what they used to be.

"During these wars food shortages were not uncommon. The cities are too far to the north to plant year round, and they didn't have supplies coming from the rest of the empire. Masses of people made their way further south.

"These lands were already inhabited. There were three human tribes, each of which specialized in a different branch of Elemental Magic. The settlers had never encountered Elemental Magic before coming to our land. They originally found difficulty because of your people who lived in the Mountain Province. They specialized in Wind Magic, producing seers with the emeralds that were in abundance in their area. They worshipped the green dragon that lived in their mountains.

"Without magic of their own the settlers were unable to move into your ancestor's territory. Instead they turned east and faced the other races. That is why the Point Province is the most heavily populated region in East Ager. This is where most of the settlers from the old empire found themselves, faring better against giants than Seers."

"That's common knowledge. The nobles in the Point Province almost all have gray eyes and bigger bodies. They say they are descended from the empire," Galavon said out loud.

"They also inherited stubbornness and no imagination," she retorted forcefully. "Which means their magical skills are weak. They settled all along the Feather Coast and established the Kingdom of East Ager. The first king, Louis I, was able to keep peace in the area until Shiva, the fire dragon worshipped by the tribe in the Fire Pass Province, let loose his chaos and ravaged the land."

"And then the curators ended the chaos by imprisoning Shiva. I know the history."

"Yes, they did," she snapped. "Now, are you going to let me continue before the rest of your group is ready to leave?"

Galavon nodded his head.

"Anyways," she continued, "without magic the young kingdom was being devastated by raids from the fire tribe, their goblin and troll allies, and occasionally even the dragon Shiva.

"At this point the curators came into the scene. They were few but powerful with magic. Louis I struck a deal with them, claiming they were gods and forced his men to worship them. The curators began to teach their followers how to wield magic, and with the addition of the curators' priests, Louis I was able to force the fire tribes away from the border and beat them back to Fire Pass. The tribes gathered here because it was where Shiva rested, and they hoped she would win the fight for them. Louis I and his army fought the tribes in a great battle. The battle on the ground was fierce, and overhead the five chief curators did battle with Shiva until they successfully sealed her beneath the ground at the pass.

"Louis I forced the fire tribe into the desert and the wall was built to keep them out of East Ager. The Fire Pass Province is now known as the holy land to those people, and they claim their god Shiva promised it to them. Since then they have dwelled in the desert and are known as barbarians. The twelve tribes still exist today.

"Another brief war was fought with the seers in the forests around the mountains, but they were less numerous than the fire tribes, and their green dragon remained hidden in his mountains. Louis I's son Charles II looked to the south to expand his growing kingdom.

"Giants from the north and goblins from the east divided his forces, so his battle with the clerics in the Peninsula Province was drawn out, lasting many years, finally ending with his son Louis II. The clerics were skilled at fending off magic, but they were eventually defeated by sheer force. Only the goblins and kobolds have held on to their land at the insistence of the high priests, though other beasts still live in the less populated corners of the Kingdom of East Ager.

"Due to the constant battles necessary to hold the Kingdom together, King Lothair established the Constables to govern the secular needs of the different provinces. That's why most of the nobility in East Ager claim origins from the Empire, at least everywhere but on the peninsula. The nobles of my people made a deal in order keep their places in society. The Ziyad family is no exception – they have the blood of the ancient rulers of the peninsula.

"The early kings had absolute power, claiming the curators chose them before they were born to rule, and that the throne was theirs by divine right. They chose the high priests. However, when the line ended with Louis V, the high priests seized control, also proclaiming that they had been chosen by the curators. They have been ruling ever since."

Galavon looked away from the mage's eyes. Staring at the dirt on the highway he was lying on, he considered the version he had been taught. It was basically the same, except there was no mention of the lack of curators when the settlers moved into East Ager. Louis I, or as the history of East Ager knew him, Louis the Pious, was always portrayed as a hero, only fighting for defense. To hear him described as a conqueror was odd.

I can't believe what she says. The stones are only stones. The curators are the true gods. Perun grants magic.

Galavon rolled out from under the wagon into the heat. He rubbed his eyes from the sun, but he hoped it looked like he had just woken. Darak walked toward him leading Kid.

"Rested? It's time we left."

Galavon grimaced before nodding and felt the insides of his thighs. They were already saddle sore, but he refused to continue looking weak in the mercenaries' eyes.

Chapter 5
(Sheik, Saoirse)

"Before the recollection of men, Mundus was dark. Chaos ruled all. Chaos did not believe in justice. Law did not exist – it was no place for mortals. In this time Chaos gave birth to the curators.

"Perun, the Father, was the first, though many followed after. He saw beyond the destruction and believed he could make a just world. Perun wrestled the world from Chaos, his father, so that he and the other curators could lead Mundus to peace and stability. To his servant, Lleu, he gave a spear to lead the poor and the gift of song to encourage them. To his youngest and most reckless son, Ares, he gave a short sword to battle the enemies of Reproba Caelum. Perun sent him to tame the wilds for the farmers. To Esus he gave an axe and great knowledge of water to help the merchants and sailors in their travels. Astarte, Perun's beautiful sister, received a sword and was charged with the protection of all who followed Reproba Caelum by creating the Holy Order of the White Wing. To his other sister, Anuke, he gave a bow so that she could escort the dead to the Sacred Isle in safety. To his wife the Mother, Neith, he gave no weapon, but charged her to raise the children of Reproba Caelum in the correct teachings, leading to the creation of the Holy Order of the Black Wing. For himself, Perun the Father kept the gift of magic. These seven curators, our seven gods, continue to lead East Ager, and even all of Mundus, to security."

The priest made the holy sign, touching his thumbs to his shoulders, his chest, and ending with his right thumb on his forehead.

With the recollection period finished, the first phase of worship in Reproba Calum, Sheik Nasseri left his place of honor beside the priests behind the altar. After making the five-pointed star himself, Sheik Nasseri's small frame made its way on similarly short legs to stand behind the altar crafted to depict Esus lifting a flat marble slab. He faced the priest at the altar, made the sign again, and watched him return to the others along the wall. He turned to face the Followers who attended. The altar sat on a stage, and he used his height advantage to look down upon those in attendance.

No hair grew on Sheik Nasseri's face, and he had a wide nose. Dark brown hair fell just above his gray eyes. The chainmail he wore was kept silenced by the black vest he wore over it, which also concealed a necklace with a large, uncut ruby. Gold buttons ran up the middle keeping it tight across his chest. A black coat that fell to his ankles hung open and also had the gold buttons. In his hand he held a black rod with gold butt caps on both sides. If there was murmuring during the recollection period presented by the priest, not even a fly dared to disrupt Sheik Nasseri, Lieutenant of the Holy Order of the Black Wing. Those present stared up at him from the places they stood in the cathedral – no seats to ensure a Follower's full attention.

"Before I give the Brahma, I have a message from The Mother." Sheik could sense the unease of the priests behind him. He hadn't warned them of this.

Sheik gazed out upon the crowd.

This is the filth that considers themselves Followers in Farrow?

"The Mother's teachings have failed to come this far south. Shiva's breath haunts it with its heat, leading me to believe Farrow is not only a city of trade, but also a city turning from Reproba Caelum. A city turning to chaos." Sheik's voice had a high pitch that rang through the South Sea Cathedral.

"And what of the Followers in Farrow? Less than half the nobility came today, the last day in eight. Is it new to celebrate Perun's victory on the eighth day? I think not. And of the peasants? The peasants are even fewer in attendance on the Day of Victory! Of merchants there are hardly any!" Sheik's face was red, and his gestures were sharp and quick. His look was hard, and few dared to meet and hold his eyes from the crowd. He continued.

"Fishermen set their wares across the street from the cathedral. His voice grew loud. "The black market flourishes. Heathens like the Albus Veneficus likely wander unknown through the crowds." Lieutenant Sheik Nasseri brought his rod up high and slammed it down on the marble altar. A sharp crack echoed throughout the cathedral. It was the only sound.

"And you! The few who attend, the few who believe themselves to be true Followers allow the South Sea Cathedral to look like this!" Sheik spread his arms wide, motioning to the cathedral.

Red brick made up the walls, with more brick pillars throughout for support. Smoke stains darkened the red above bare sconces, and statues of all sizes and shapes decorated the sides. The major source of light came from the high window above the altar, a large stained glass depicting Esus holding his axe in one hand and a bag of coppers in the other. The rooms beyond were for the priests and the acolytes.

"Spider webs hang in the dark corners, dirt lies between the aisles, moss grows low on the stone outside. This cathedral lacks the sheer size of the Cathedral of Power, the gold of the Cathedral of the White Feather, the bells of the Cold Sea Cathedral, the stained glass of the Fire Pass Cathedral, falling even behind the Cathedral of New Beginnings and its garden. This cathedral is known for the stink of fish outside its plain wooden doors, and the stench of horse manure in the streets from your wicked races!"

Sheik continued his hard stare and found many of the people sweating under his gaze. He was breathing hard now. He slowed down his pace.

"There are only two types of perfect men: the dead and the unborn. But if you are true Followers of Reproba Caelum, if you truly wish to reach the Sacred Isle and life everlasting, then surely you abhor the poor state of Farrow. This city must be cleansed by those who are still true to Reproba Caelum. If you believe in security rather than chaos, you will help to make Esus proud."

Sheik paused. There were murmurs among the Followers in the cathedral, many in agreement. Vows were made by the men and women to serve the curators true. Sheik raised his free hand to silence the talking.

Your vows should have been made sooner and all of this could have been avoided, filth.

"Due to these and troubles foreseen by the curators, I have been instructed to enact new laws in the city. It is not the cry of the bird that brings the flock to follow, but the act of flight itself. To begin, all raw iron coming in and out of the city shall be seized. Reparations for these seizures will come at a time seen fit by the high priests. We must keep such materials out of the hands of our enemies." The silence brought on by fear was cast aside by outrage, but the sounds of displeasure lowered enough for Sheik to continue once he rose his hand into the air for silence.

Traitors of the curators! All of them! If it were up to me, I'd burn them all.

"New taxes will be placed on the sales of spices and perfumes." The objections returned with more force. The taxes on these items were already high, as was the danger in getting them with the threat of pirates. The merchants had to make the trip far off shore around the Peninsula Province and the Tew islands. "The sale of weapons is forbidden without express permission from a priest. No ships are allowed to leave port without new documentation that must be signed by a priest."

Shouts filled the Cathedral. "Is this discontent?" he screamed back. "Is this refusal to accept the word of the curators as law?" The shouts died down, but a man stepped forward and climbed the first steps to the altar before turning to address his fellow worshippers.

Lieutenant Sheik could not tell how many Twil the man had seen, but he saw speckles of gray in his brown hair. The man's belly stuck out far beneath his silks, marking him as wealthy. A trimmed beard covered his face.

"I am a devoted Follower of Reproba Caelum, always have been! Why should I be subject to such laws? I trade silk for iron and ship out of Farrow on the Goblin Sea..." Shouts of approval echoed behind the man.

Perfect. One early example solves many problems later.

Sheik stepped out from behind the altar into the shadow of the large man bellowing his discontent. Sheik's hand shot up and grabbed the back of the large man's silk tunic, and with surprising force threw him to the side where he landed on the steps and rolled to the base. Four men from the Holy Order of the Black Wing rushed forward to keep the pair separated from the crowd.

"You dare disobey the word of the curators?" Sheik asked the man. He descended to the bottom of the steps and stood over him, the room now hushed. The crowd stared at his back while the fat man cowered against the steps. Sheik's black rod snapped down and cracked against the merchant's meaty thigh. The rod came back up and he swung it at the man's face. Sheik's victim managed to bring his fleshy arms up, but three of the stinging blows brought his arms low and the rod snapped in again on his nose. "The word is law from the curators, spoken to the high priests, and relayed to you by me. To disobey the curators is blasphemy." Blood sprayed on to the floor as Sheik delivered an additional blow for good measure. He then turned back to the people once he ascended two of the steps.

Yes. That has done the trick.

The four Black Wing soldiers threw the fat man off the steps. The crowd of Followers had moved back when the beatings began Sheik was glad to see, and the man crawled toward them leaving smeared blood on the stone floor. Pleased and covered in blood splatter, Sheik walked back to the altar.

They always cower before a showing of strength. It will also be true for the Peninsula Province, with the Ziyad family as my example.

"These laws will be posted for all to observe. Now, let us all close our eyes, and I will give the Brahma."

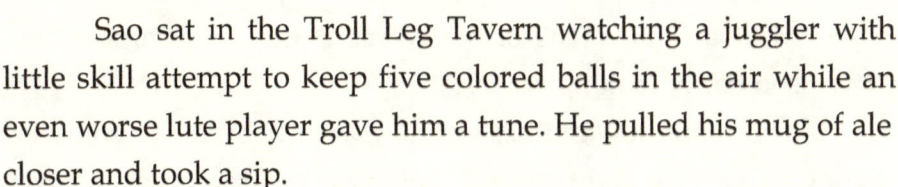

Sao sat in the Troll Leg Tavern watching a juggler with little skill attempt to keep five colored balls in the air while an even worse lute player gave him a tune. He pulled his mug of ale closer and took a sip.

Sao made a face in his mug and hoped no one saw it. *This stuff is rotten. I've always preferred ale over wine, but this stuff could choke a vulture.* He put the mug back on the splintery table and tried not to let his tongue touch the insides of his cheeks for fear of getting another taste of the sour ale.

He sat in the middle of the room surrounded by loud, boisterous men. The tavern was so crowded that Sao shared his round table with strangers squeezed in elbow to elbow. Ugly women with bent backs brought out more cracked mugs whenever a man yelled for it. The unsightly women received pinched bottoms and a copper penny for their efforts. This tavern catered to men who woke early in the morning and gathered in the Common Square where they hoped they would be chosen to do work most men refused for wages a man could scarcely live off of. Here they spent their meager coin on cheap ale.

"Ahh, get that beast off the stage!" yelled the man to his right. Another man yelled, "I've only six fingers, and I juggle better than that!" More unruly patrons joined in, and Sao cast his own voice to the lot, trying to sound gruff.

The juggler stooped down to pick up a dropped ball, but a thrown mug sent him scurrying off the stage.

So that's where the cracks come from.

"Bah, it's impossible to get a good show around here," the balding man to his right complained. He had hard features that were forever tanned by the sun. They marked him as a field worker. "The decent performers go to The Peak."

"I'd say that's true of the women, too," Sao said to him. "I've seen better looking horses."

The man took another swig. "I wish I could say you were wrong. That one right there," he said pointing to a younger, plump barmaid facing the other direction, "Sweets they call her." She turned around and gave Sao a clear view of her long face, tiny eyes, big nose and protruding teeth. "I say it's a face only a blind man could love."

"She looks like an overfed Charger with that long face," Sao said, cringing.

"Haha, aye, that she does! This one here is Marti." He motioned to a woman in her middle years walking by with more mugs in her hand. She smiled at the man as though he was a regular. He pointed to her calves, the only part of her legs not covered by her long skirt. With a quick glance before she disappeared among the patrons, Sao was able to see hair thicker than most men's.

"If we shaved everything but her ankles, she could pass for a Southern Jiggler," Sao said.

Laughter erupted from the man. The deep tone mixed in with the noise of the tavern, and splashes of ale spilled onto his lap and on the floor.

"All we need now is a Plainstrider." Sao stood and feigned searching the common room. He sat back down soon after with a shrug. "Nope, none of them are pretty enough!"

The rest of the man's ale spilled as he roared out in laughter.

Sao smiled at the laughing man. *It wasn't that funny.* He forgot how terrible the drink was and took a big swig. He managed to get it down but went into a coughing fit at the sour taste.

"The name is Winfrey," the man said between gulps of air. He shook his head and thrust his free hand forward, palm open.

Um, uh... "Babieca. It's a pleasure." *Cecil's horse's name?*

"Well, Babieca, it's nice to meet you. You from around here?"

"I work outside the city in a stable. How else could I know my horses so well?"

Winfrey shook his head. "I'm no brewer, but I know good ale when I taste it." He downed what was left in his mug, sending froth trickling down his chin.

"I disagree with you there, Winfrey, if you believe this to be good ale."

"Bah, all ale is good ale."

Sao slid his mug toward the man. "If all ale is good ale, then all horses are good horses."

"With enough good ale they are."

It was Sao's turn to laugh. "Winfrey, I'm glad I ran into you tonight. You're a man of wisdom."

"I've been called many things in my years, but never a man of wisdom." Winfrey grabbed Sao's mug and started to drink out of it.

"So what do you do in this city besides drink and make strangers laugh?"

"Same as most. I find work where I can. And before you ask, I don't know of any, and if I did I'd take it myself! But as far as things go, I'm one of the lucky ones. I have a daughter who takes care of me."

Sao put on a look of disbelief. "Winfrey! You have a daughter and didn't tell me? I thought we were friends!"

"You're a stable boy. I'm not feeding my sheep to the wolves. She has a future ahead of her. She is one of the pretty girls you were talking about being on The Peak. She is a servant in Castle Manzanares. Aye, one day she could be a chief maid if she works hard enough!"

"You're right then, Winfrey, she is without a doubt a breed I am not familiar with. I am, after all, only a stable boy." *Maybe not a servant to the Constable himself, but this is my way into some real information.* "But if you don't mind me asking, out of curiosity, how many Twil has she seen?"

"I'm telling you now, Babieca, she won't like your curly hair or your freckles. You're too short for her." He paused, smiled, and nodded his head. "But she has seen the star eighteen times."

Perfect. "Winfrey, what do you say we get some more of that sour ale you like so much? I'll pick up the next round." Sao raised an arm and motioned for two more mugs from the woman Winfrey named Marti.

Sao had traveled with Cecil all the way to Zephyr Hills, but his friend remained camped with a few loyal followers on the south side of the city with the Army of Truth on the north. Cecil was wary of reaching the army without gathering information from the city about what awaited him in camp. Sao had volunteered since he was the only one able to pass in the city as something other than a soldier or even a native to the Peninsula Province. Cecil himself couldn't go either. If Tarik had been assassinated as the soldiers claimed, Cecil could be a target as well.

Of course, that wasn't the story Sao heard in the city. To hear it told in the taverns, Tarik Ziyad had attempted to kill their High Priest Nolasco, making the constable a traitor to the

Kingdom of East Ager. It was a dangerous place in the city now for anyone from the Peninsula Province. The peasants took revenge wherever they could find it, and coins too for that matter.

It was a volatile situation in Zephyr Hills, and Cecil needed more than rumors. Sao could give more than rumors if he could get into Castle Manzanares. Or knew someone there. Constable Edward of the Fire Pass called the castle home, and this Winfrey had a daughter who could at least get him on the Peak. Zephyr Hills was made up of seven hills, the Peak being the largest of the seven. It housed the noble and the wealthy, and on its top sat Castle Manzanares.

Marti arrived with the ale and a smile on her face for Winfrey. "I think she likes you, Winfrey."

"Bah, she knows my pouch jingles. That's more than most around here can say." Winfrey immediately began to down his new mug of ale.

Sao stared into his own, regretting buying himself another round instead of just one for his new friend. "Let's get out of here, Winfrey. If you're daughter can get us on the Peak, I'll buy you something worthy of being called ale."

Chapter 6
(Galavon, Anne)

"**I** can teach you to use its power. I know you want to learn. You're hungry for the knowledge. You aren't a fighter, you aren't a merchant – are you a seer? Free me, and we'll find out together."

The woman's voice haunted Galavon's thoughts as they traveled along the road. She pelted him with argument after argument, tried time and time again to persuade him to help free her.

Just keep going. Farrow isn't far. Just keep going and you can make it back to Anne.

"Since you so avidly follow Reproba Caelum, Follower, mind if I shed a bit of truth on it?" the voice asked. Galavon knew she mocked him for opening a tome from the wagon and reciting the Brahma earlier that day since no monk was present. He couldn't respond to her questions, so he knew she was going to tell him her answer even if he didn't want to hear it. "Their five pointed star stands for five magics: white, fire, water, wind, and earth. This is common knowledge. What most don't know is that the old tribes used a seven pointed star, the true star, for magic: white, black, fire, water, wind, earth, and one other known as dragon. These are the true seven elements, not the lie the curators tell to control magic."

Galavon bounced up and down on Kid. It was midday, and that woman would not get out of his head. Farrow wasn't much further ahead, Galavon knew, and he couldn't wait to turn in the Albus Veneficus and rid himself of her.

"That's what they're doing, you know. Controlling magic. They buy all the stones and give them only to priests. Sure they give pearls away to monks, but pearls are the most available and are used for healing. Acolytes and priests get the others, and they only leave the cathedrals when the curators need them as fire power. The Kingdom of East Ager is forced to worship them because they control magic! Can't you see? What gives them the right? Security? They imprisoned Shiva, but what about the goblins, the trolls, the giants? What about bandits? They bring a false sense of security. They only bring control."

Only when they stopped to rest through the heat of mid-day did Galavon find any sort of reprieve, and he was only able to by wandering off into the tall grass. Luckily, the sun was shining now in full force, so a break from her relentless torrent was about to come to a halt.

"We stop here," Torvil commanded, bringing the group to a halt. "Second to last day on the road before Farrow. Pull the wagons off to the side so we can get some rest."

The carts were moved off the road, and Galavon made sure to stay clear of the mage. Farmhouses and ranches had begun to show up on the hills as they neared Farrow, but they were still spread out and far between. The endless plains of swaying grass still dominated the countryside. Galavon walked into the grass hidden from view while the mercenaries prepared a meal of scraps and hard bread - a meal he didn't mind missing. Alone and without distractions, Galavon pulled out the pouch he took from the woman and dropped its contents into his hand.

The emerald's shape and color could not have been more perfect. A breeze swooped in and made the grass rustle beside him. "You grant me magic then," Galavon said to the stone. "Not Perun."

Galavon closed his eyes and let the wind swirl around him as it did the tall grass. He imagined making it blow harder, so hard the longer stalks of grass would whip his face, so strong that he couldn't hear himself think.

The breeze died off and silence returned.

Galavon shook his head. "I can't believe I tried that."

"Looks like it didn't work," a voice said behind him. Galavon jumped to his feet and turned around. Darak stood behind him. "Did you get that stone off the mage?"

"Yes," Galavon said.

"And what makes you think Perun doesn't grant magic?"

"Nothing, now." Galavon rubbed the emerald with his thumb, feeling the bumps and imperfections of the uncut stone. He was nervous. Someone knew he had doubted Reproba Caelum. All it took was once to be branded a heretic.

"That's good. You're a Follower, Galavon, you don't need that stone. I'm not going to take it from you. In fact, here." Darak produced the armband with the ruby. He handed it over along with a large but smoky pearl. "Turn them in with the mage when we make it to Farrow. Promise me."

"I'll give them up when we turn her in." Galavon felt embarrassed. "Don't tell the others I tried to use it."

"I won't."

"Thanks, Darak." Galavon followed him back to the camp and ate a small meal. He found a quiet place and drifted off into sleep.

When he woke it was late afternoon, and he could hear voices coming from the road where the wagons were being readied by the guards. Travar was there harnessing the horses, and the dirty man gave an evil looking grin in Galavon's direction.

That man truly unnerves me.

" ...all of it. And no one gets paid."

"Bah! Shiva blasted Crows never did bring good news with them," Torvil said.

Galavon walked out from behind the last cart. Torvil and Darak stood with a middle-aged merchant talking in front of a single cart and two mercenaries.

"I'd be careful throwing that name around. The Holy Order of the Black Wing is headed down this road with a Lieutenant. I heard he beat a group of Followers in the South Sea Cathedral for not being devout enough."

"Thanks for the information," Darak said. "May Esus watch over your travels and trade."

"And you as well." The merchant snapped his reigns and continued down the road toward the few farmhouses they had passed on the highway.

"What was that about?" Galavon said walking up to Torvil and Darak.

"That man was a merchant who makes his living selling wares to the farmhouses around Farrow," Darak said. "He told us the Crows arrived in Farrow with a new law and are confiscating all iron ore."

"What?" Galavon responded. "We can't go to Farrow then! If we lost two cart loads of iron ore…"

"Merchant boy speaks the obvious," Torvil retorted. The big man was turning red and looked frustrated. "What then, since you pay me, should we do?"

Continuing forward was not an option. The loss of the iron ore would be a huge financial blow, one Patrick would undoubtedly blame on him. If the whole caravan went back, they would run out of supplies, especially with the prisoners. The group would have to split, some going back to Pearl with the iron and some continuing into Farrow. It was the only thing that made sense. They could all meet back up in Pearl and let Patrick decide what was best from there.

"We're going to have to split the group. Send a few ahead to turn in the Albus Veneficus and the rest can take the iron back to Pearl until this law is reversed."

Going back meant he would be able to see Anne sooner. He had thought a lot about her during the last few days of travel when he wasn't getting pestered by the mage. He could still remember her curly, dark hair and crystal blue eyes.

Strange, he thought, *how I only spent one night with her but can't seem to get her out of my mind.*

"You should send Torvil and the men back with the iron," Darak suggested.

That wasn't what Galavon wanted to hear. "Why?"

"You need to determine how long this ban on trading iron is going to last, so you can report to your father. I too have things I need to accomplish in Farrow, so I'll accompany you. We won't be far behind the others."

Galavon ran his hand through his straight hair, but a breeze flew through and messed it up again. "I suppose that makes sense."

"Dust on the road ahead!" The call came from Kavar. He stood on top of the cart he had been harnessing to the horses.

"Crows. Come on boys, we have to move these behind that rise." Torvil and the rest of the guards got the horses moving. Galavon and Darak stayed on the road.

The dust cloud soon became visible from the road. The heat had made fast work of the puddles brought in from the rain. The group came into sight soon after at a trot, working their Plain Striders hard in the heat.

The lead rider could not have stood as tall as Galavon's shoulders, though it was hard to tell while he was mounted. The rider slowed his horse, making the fifty men behind him slow as well. Black defined the man's clothes in every aspect other than a bit of gold here and there. When he stopped in front of Galavon and Darak, an expression of curiosity came to his long face, and his wide nostrils flared.

"Good morning. The Mother's blessings on you." The high-pitched voice had an air of superiority to it. Though the black rod with the gold caps hung on his other side, Galavon knew it was there. This had to be the Lieutenant of the Holy Order of the Black Wing.

"And on you and your men, sir," Darak said. He bowed his head and Galavon did the same. Galavon would have spoken, but he was too nervous to make his voice work.

"They tell me there is little traffic on this stretch of the highway. What are two travelers doing on the road by themselves?"

"We are..." Darak began before the man on horseback stopped him with a motion.

"I would like to hear it from the young man." Galavon felt the man stare at the top of his head. "That is a large coin purse at his side. He who holds the money holds the swords they say."

"We are, uh, traveling from... Pearl," he managed. The short man's stare froze his blood and made thought difficult.

"Pearl, eh? And what may I ask were you two doing in that cursed province?"

Galavon waited a second to get his thoughts in order, and he focused on not stuttering. "The Fall Festival, sir. We came to the Peninsula Province for the Festival."

"And your return journey? How is the road ahead?"

"Ares protected us from bandits. The Mother herself watched over us." Galavon looked up at the man and tried to smile, but he was sure it came out as a more of a grimace. He made the Reproba Caelum five pointed star with shaking hands: both thumbs to shoulders, chest, and one on the forehead.

The Crow let silence take over. The Lieutenant looked over at the grass. A clear trail of bent stalks marked the passage of their wagons and horses, but they could not be seen behind the small hill. Galavon rubbed the back of his neck nervously.

He felt the chain of the pendant his father had given him. He fiddled with the it, not knowing what else to do with his nervous fingers.

Beside him, Darak produced a similar amulet, though much finer, from beneath his tunic. Darak said in an even tone, "We had business in Pearl."

When did Darak get that?

The Crow looked askance at Darak's amulet. Galavon began to wish he had followed Torvil behind the hill.

up at the Crow's face. "Let's move!" And like that, the Holy Order of the Black Wing rode by, fifty men in black uniforms, chainmail, and blackened steel maces. They were not traveling at an easy pace.

Galavon produced his own pendant, the one his father had given him before he departed. "What are these?" he asked Darak who had already hidden his in his tunic.

"Badges. I'll explain once we're in Farrow."

"Could we use them to bypass the laws? Still sell the iron?"

"They have their uses, but they don't exempt us from taxes."

They walked along the trail left in the grass by the wagons and found them just behind the hill. Galavon suspected the Lieutenant wasn't fooled by their words. If they hadn't had the pendants...

"Made up your mind, boy?" Torvil walked around one of the wagons. He crossed his muscled arms.

"Uh," Galavon started nervously. "Darak and I will press on to Farrow with the prisoners and follow the rest of you back to Pearl. I have to discover how long this ban is going to last."

"We're taking Kavar, too," Darak said. "He knows the... narrow streets of Farrow."

Torvil nodded and got the rest of the men moving the carts. Galavon didn't feel as though he had made the decision, it was almost as if Torvil had to approve his orders. Even stranger, Galavon felt as though Darak was truly making the calls.

Within no time the wagons were moving southwest again, taking all the horses but Kid. Galavon managed to reduce his things down to one satchel. The bag hung over the back of his horse, and Galavon held his reigns in his right hand. He rested the butt of his staff in his left stirrup.

The bandits were tied in a line with the woman at the back under the eye of Kavar and his knives. The small man kept himself happy by sharpening them where the prisoners could hear the sound of whetstone on metal.

"You know," Kavar said once they started their trek toward the city. "I bet we could get more coins selling the stones on the black market instead of turning them in." Darak walked at the front of the procession, unable to hear the words.

"He's right," said the familiar voice in Galavon's head. "If they're taking iron they're preparing for war, and that means they won't be able to pay you. Set us free!"

"We could just kill them here and not even worry with them. That's what will happen to them anyways, " Kavar finished.

It's not about the coin, Galavon thought as he continued riding, acknowledging neither Kavar or the mage. *We're doing the Kingdom of East Ager a favor by turning them in. We're doing the curators a favor.*

"You will learn soon enough the mistake you're making," the mage said in his head.

The sounds of metal clanking together and wooden axles creaking echoed down the road from behind a turn in the grassy plain. Not long after a wagon appeared with a single driver.

The man could have been Darak's brother, judging from what Galavon could see. He wore a wide-brimmed straw hat that left his face in shadows and covered everything above the top half of his ears. Cheap cotton fabric covered the rest of his thin frame, and a simple wooden bow lay beside him on the driver's bench.

"Darak, it's good fortune that I've run into you," he said. He stopped his cart in front of the line and smiled, briefly flashing violet colored eyes from beneath his straw hat.

"It would seem the Peninsula Province is receiving a great deal more attention than it deserves."

Darak turned to his companions. "Galavon, Kavar, I need a moment."

Galavon nodded and climbed off Kid. He held the horses' reigns beside Kavar and the prisoners. "A chance meeting, huh?" Kavar said. "There's no such thing as chance when it comes to Darak."

Only a few seconds passed before Kavar said, "To Shiva's own prison with it! I deserve to know what they're talking about." Kavar walked to the back of the wagon, trying to look inconspicuous. Every now and then Galavon noticed him straining in their general direction.

Galavon sat on the edge of the road and didn't pay the discussion any attention.

"Ziyad.... body..."

Galavon's head shot up at the mention of the Ziyad family.

Kavar chuckled. "Worried about your toy?" he mouthed back.

Darak and the odd man became much quieter then, making it impossible for Galavon or Kavar to decipher anymore of their words.

"From what we can hear, it would seem the Ziyad family is in some trouble," said the voice in his head. The woman spit in the grass beside the road before continuing her one-way conversation with Galavon. "Family had it coming.

Tarik Ziyad never cared for Reproba Caelum, but he was too afraid to fight for what he believed in."

Galavon didn't care about Tarik. He didn't want anything to happen to Anne.

"That means that mercenary of yours is something more. Probably a spy." The woman spit again. She spit more than any man Galavon knew.

The secret conversation finally came to an end. Darak left his friend on the cart and strode toward Galavon and Kavar. "There's been another change in plans," he said. "You two take the brigands and turn them in. I'm ending my contract with your father, Galavon. I require no pay. Good luck with your trading."

With no other words exchanged, Darak left their group to join the mysterious man on the wagon.

"Wait, Darak!" Galavon said to his back as he jumped on to the cart. "You said you would explain..."

"Yes, just ask your father. Or Torvil." The man with the straw hat then urged his horses with a snap of his reins.

"Wow, that's it?" Kavar asked once the wagon disappeared down the road. He stood in the middle of the road watching the two disappear. "Looks like we can do what's best for us now." Kavar went to the lead Albus Veneficus, grabbed his hair, yanked his head back, and cut across his neck with one of his many knives.

Galavon watched crimson seep through the thin line. The small leak turned into a torrent, staining the front of the man's dirty tunic. Gurgling sounds accompanied bubbles around the slit in his throat. The man's eyes grew wide, and his hands searched for a way to stop the bleeding. With his life force leaving, the man crumbled to his knees, fell on his side in the dirt, and swam in a pool of himself. His wide eyes went blank.

"Kavar what are you doing!? We're turning them in!" The prisoners went into a frenzy, trying to run each way and getting nowhere. They screamed, lashed out, tried desperately to free themselves. Kid, usually a calm horse, neighed at the confusion and pulled free from Galavon's grasp, knocking his staff to the ground.

"I'm telling you, the officials will require the stones for proof. They'll take them, but they're worth so much more!" One of the prisoners tried to fight back, but Kavar grabbed him by the tunic and stabbed him in the stomach, sawing up so that his punctured organs fell to the ground.

"Kavar, this isn't about the money! This is about doing the right thing! I have plenty of coin, I'll give you extra!"

"Give me back my ruby and I'll take care of this lunatic," the woman said out loud.

"You do, that's right! You also have the stones. Perhaps I kill you as well, then I can make my way to Barbuta and live like a king." A prisoner took a swing at Kavar, but the weight of his dead fellows stopped his blow short. Kavar stabbed him in the side of the neck.

"Give me the ruby, and I'll stop this."

"Aye, I think being a king sounds like great fun. Hate to do this to your father, Galavon, but I'm sure you understand – a man has to do what a man has to do to survive. Well, survive in comfort at least." He dispatched a wounded prisoner and started toward Galavon.

Frightened, Galavon took one step back, then another. Kavar kept advancing. The dirty man had a twinkle in his eye.

Galavon sent his right hand up his left sleeve and stopped on the ruby's strap.

"Kavar, there's no need for this! Stop! We can turn them in, and I'll pay you more than what they're worth!"

A vicious smile crept up on Kavar's face. The facial expression spoke volumes, but nothing Galavon hoped for. "And let this opportunity pass? I think not."

Galavon undid the strap around his arm and tossed the ruby in the air toward the woman. He saw Kavar make a leap in his direction, so Galavon made a leap of his own further away.

"*Incendia Telum.*"

Galavon landed hard on his shoulder and turned on his back to defend against Kavar. Instead, he saw a thin beam of fire shoot from the mage's hands and catch Kavar in mid-air. Once the beam touched him, the dirty man erupted into flames. He hit the ground screaming and rolled around in the dirt to try and put an end to the hungry fire. The smell of burning flesh and hair made Galavon bury his face in his arms, but then the screams still found his ears. They lasted only a few moments.

Galavon mustered up the courage to turn around and found the woman bent over Kavar's still burning corpse. In her hand was the knife Kavar dropped when he started to burn, and it dripped fresh blood. The smell and sight of the gore on the road made Galavon turn back around and vomit in the grass.

A hand rested on his shoulder. "I'm not sure I've properly introduced myself. I am Ceridwen, a mage of the Albus Veneficus. It's a pleasure to make your acquaintance, Galavon."

Galavon heard the few prisoners who were left drag their tired feet to Ceridwen behind his back. When the sound stopped,

Galavon knew they were waiting for the same thing he was waiting for – waiting to figure out what would happen to him.

"What are you going to do to me?" he asked.

"I'll make a deal with you," Ceridwen responded.

Galavon raised his head and stared at the swaying grass. *Perhaps I will live.*

"You come with us. Let me see if I can teach you how to use Wind Magic, the magic of your ancestors. If you still believe Reproba Caelum is the right way after the cold season, then you're free to leave. Do we have a deal?"

Using the back of his hand, Galavon wiped the rest of the vomit off his mouth. He got to his feet, still keeping the rebels at his back.

"I know you're afraid to question what you've known your entire life, Galavon, but Reproba Caelum is now your enemy as much as it is ours if you wish to try and save that Ziyad girl. The Crows are after her now, and you know as well as I that does not bode well for her. Come with us, and let me give you the ability to save her."

"And if he says no, Ceridwen?" one of the men asked behind him. She didn't bother to respond. Galavon felt her stare on his back, unwavering.

To say no means I die. To say yes means I live, but will I truly ever see Anne again? But there's a chance with yes.

"I'm yours," he whispered.

"A good choice. I can't say that any other decision would have been a wise one."

"There are seven different types of Elemental Magic," Anne recited. "Following the seven-pointed star, and starting with the pentacle, they are dragon, black, wind, fire, water, earth, and white. Opposite elements are across from each other."

"Good. Now draw the Elemental Star and label it."

Anne sat in the seventh floor of the library. The stone walls hid the sun, and there were no voices other than hers and Larith's bouncing off the books. The lights she had admired so vehemently only days before now drove her crazy with their constant luminescence. She missed real light; she missed the sun.

Anne rolled her eyes and pulled a scrap of parchment close. Her quill tip found the ink jar. To begin, she drew a small circle, the beginning of the Elemental Star. With seven quick jabs she placed seven dots an equal distance from each other and the middle circle, with one directly above. Next, she drew a straight line from the top middle dot to the circle, connecting the two by barely brushing the outside left of the circle. She then drew another line from the same dot brushing against the right side of the circle. She did the same with the next dot.

"Larith, I've drawn the star a million times, can I learn a new spell?" Anne still only knew how to make the globe of light.

"No."

Anne sighed and continued drawing. She went around the circle connecting each dot to it with two lines.

"Why can't I just draw it in one motion? It's possible. I already figured out how to do it."

"Anything done in one motion is far from perfect. Perfection takes time and practice." Larith sat on the other side of the table staring at an old tome.

Anne connected the bottom left dot. "Larith, did you ever notice that if you left out the middle two dots you would get the Reproba Caelum five-pointed star?"

"And if you did that you would be omitting two important dots, similar to how Reproba Caelum omits two important elements." The old man brought his nose out of the book and smiled at Anne. "You're astute, did you know that?"

Anne returned the smile with a grin of triumph. She focused her attention back on the drawing. She connected the left middle dot, making sure her lines were straight. Two more lines finished her star from the last dot. Each point of the seven-pointed star was perfect.

Starting from the top and going to the right around the star at all the points she labeled D for dragon, F for fire, Wi for wind, B for black, Wa for water, E for earth, and Wh for white. The Elemental Star was complete.

"Done. Can we learn magic now?"

Larith chuckled. He stood from his chair and shuffled to her table. "Soon, soon! There are things you must learn before spells. Now what stone goes with what Elemental Magic?" he asked while making his way beside her.

"Ruby with fire, emerald with wind, onyx with black, sapphire with water, citrine with earth, and pearl with white," Anne said in a single breath as Larith made it to her chair.

"And dragon?"

"Dragon shell. I didn't say it because it's not a stone."

Larith smiled. "Soon you will learn the locations of these all these special gems," the old nuncio said in his slow voice.

"Larith, why is wind with a green gem? Wouldn't citrine make more sense for wind? And emerald with earth, since it's green?"

Who are we to question the Creator? He deemed it so, and so it is." He scrutinized her star. "Look at this, Anne."

Anne looked up at the old man's wrinkled face. She wondered how old the nuncio really was.

"You see what happens when the dots are evenly spaced? The lines never go through the center of the circle and they're all an equal size and distance."

"Yes," Anne wiggled in her seat and decided to sit on her hands to prevent any more movement. She didn't know how much longer she could stay in the tower drawing the star over and over again reciting what Larith told her.

"How are the elements divided on the star, Anne?"

"Wayward elements are separated from Tame elements, each directly across from its opposite. Dragon is on neither side because it is neither and has no opposite."

"And why are they divided?"

"Wayward elements are difficult to control. The elements sometimes do as they wish and ignore the caster's commands. Fire and black are hungry, wind unpredictable. Tame elements always do as you command, so long as you cast them right."

"And what happens if we mix Wayward and Tame elements with elements besides their opposite?"

"The spell is powerful and difficult to control. Larith, I do pay attention to you when you talk about these things."

"Yes, yes I know you do. Now tell me what happens if we mix opposites."

"You said opposites attract. They're put opposite each other to remind mages, those who wield more than one Elemental Magic, that they are the most easily combined into stronger spells. Mixing Wayward and Tame spells that are not opposite is dangerous and should be done with caution."

Anne felt Larith lean heavily on the back of her chair. She wished he would have let her come to him instead of the other way around. Whenever she tried though, he said never slowing down kept him young – but he looked pretty old to Anne.

"The last bit you recited is important, Anne, even if you never learn another magic. You can combine opposites, but only combine Wayward and Tame if you have extreme control over them."

One of his age-spotted hands stuck out a finger and touched the F. "What do we call a person who only casts fire?"

"Shaman," Anne dutifully responded.

Larith moved to the next letters, Wi. "And wind?"

"A seer. Necromancer for black, sahagin for water, druid for earth, and cleric for white. Like me. I'm a cleric."

The finger then traced her star, following each of the lines. Anne bounced in her seat. "From dragon to the center there are two lines. From fire to the center there are two lines. For each of the elements there are two lines. It doesn't matter whether they are Wayward or Tame elements." He continued connecting all the dots with his finger. Anne tried to keep still through the monotonous movements of the old man. "Do you have any idea why there might be two lines connecting to the center." He lifted his finger from the sketch.

"To make the star pretty?"

"Well, that it certainly does. It is in fact another reminder to the caster, whether they're a cleric, a shaman, a druid, or a mage. The lines tell us that there are two sides to each element's power. It can be used for good, or it can be used for evil."

"And in-between too. There's a space between."

Larith chuckled. "Yes, yes I suppose. That is an awfully large space compared to the lines."

"Larith," Anne asked. "Why doesn't Reproba Caelum include black or dragon in its star?"

"Reproba Caelum offers order, stability, and life. Black Magic takes these things away, no matter how strong the wielder, if they use too much of it. It's addictive and dangerous. Dragon amplifies spell power, giving a great deal of strength to those who are able to use it. It makes the use of even Tame Elements dangerous."

"Just because they take them out of the star doesn't mean they don't exist. They're still dangerous. Maybe more so, because not as many people know about them."

"A true statement, Anne." Larith straightened from the table. "Let's go outside, I believe you have a strong foundation."

Anne helped the old man to the stairs and to the lower level. Once they reached the bottom he patted the top of Anne's curly brown hair. "Now remember, to the others I'm healing you from your traumatic experience. Don't mention what you've learned to any but myself." Anne nodded. "Good girl. Let us go to the stables."

They exited the Chamberlain Tower from the door that led to the battlements. From there they walked to the Queen's Tower, down a stairwell, and then into the Great Hall.

The Great Hall of Caernarfon Castle could seat two hundred. Two rows of tables ran up its center from one end of the stone hallway to the other. Because it never got too cold on the peninsula, only two empty hearths on each wall welcomed Anne and Larith into the room. Seven tapestries filled the wall space in between, and they were known as the "Peace Tapestries." One was of a hunt, another of a woman baking bread – none of the scenes were violent. Several doors also decorated the walls.

A thin, dark blue carpet ran beneath the legs of the tables, and it stopped at the steps leading to the raised dais at the end. A carved table sat on top of it, with chairs enough for seven. A huge arched window loomed behind the table granting light and a view of the Cliffside Gulf. Chandeliers also hung from the ceiling.

They crossed through the empty room, their footsteps creating an echo. A sea breeze flew in through the big window and unsettled the Peace Tapestries, causing them flap back and forth. They exited through the main doors opposite of the dais into the lower ward. It was a plain double door of thick solid wood, reinforced with a band of iron running across its middle.

Larith lifted his nose once they got out of the shadow of the keep. "Smells like rain tonight. We should get done with this quickly."

"Rain?" Anne asked. She let go of his arm and twirled in the sunlight, nearly causing a maid to drop a bucket of water. She let her blue skirt swirl around her ankles and stretched her arms out to feel the warmth, though they too were covered up. "But it's beautiful outside! Not a cloud in the sky."

Larith didn't stop moving. He continued toward the stables. "Yes, yes, the sky is clear, the same color as your eyes. But there is a wind coming in from over the gulf, and it will bring clouds. Now come help this old man to the stables, he still prefers being helped by a pretty girl."

"And this pretty girl is going to be stolen for just a minute, you dirty old man," said another voice walking up from the small garden beside the Great Hall. It was the Duchess, Lady Dara Briel. She reminded Anne of her mother, Lady Ignava, by the way she held herself. Her chin found the air above her nose inviting, and her dress looked spectacular every day. Her gown stole the true color of the sun and made her smile vivid and inviting. A gold chain hung around her neck, but the bottom of it lay hidden in her bosom. Her long hair once shined like gold, but gray took over as the dominant color.

Duchess Dara's personality, however, strayed far from Lady Ignava's. Where Lady Ignava was cold, the Duchess was fiercely caring. She made everything around the castle her business, whether it was personal or not.

"Aye my beautiful Duchess, as you wish. I'' be in the stable visiting with an old friend."

The Duchess giggled like a girl and watched the old man hobble off. She turned, all smiles, to Anne. "It's been three days, and I rarely even see you at meals! Come, it's time for girl talk." Anne nodded and allowed her hand to be taken and led into the small garden to a bench. She tried not to be too stiff as they walked, but the smiling Duchess trying to act like a teenager made her tense.

The day felt warm rather than hot, the perfect weather that is only achieved during the change of the seasons. The pair came to a stone bench in the shade, and Anne did her best to keep her dignity about her. Her ankles were crossed, her back straight, and her hands rested in her lap.

"You know, Larith used to call me 'pretty girl' and beg me to help him hobble around." The Duchess smiled, and Anne thought it transformed her into a younger woman. She must have been beautiful when she had seen fewer Twil. Duchess Dara sighed and again faced Anne. "Anne, we both know how silly men can be, especially men who have any rank associated with their title. My husband and Captain Philial are no exception to this rule, I assure you."

Anne wasn't sure where this conversation was leading, but she knew there had to be a reason for having it alone. The Duchess became quiet again after studying Anne's face, and Anne cursed herself silently for letting her facial expression betray her confusion. She stroked her fingers through her hair.

"Captain Philial could seduce the curator Anuke with his muscles, don't you think, Anne? He's close to your age I believe."

"What?" Anne exclaimed. She had never thought about him that way. "Captain Philial is nice enough, I suppose. That is if you don't mind someone who takes things too seriously. Which I do."

I prefer merchant boys who know how to dance.

Duchess Dara let another girly giggle escape her lips. The sound was funny coming from someone with wrinkles.

I'm not dumb, Anne thought. *I'm not going to tell you anything just because you're trying to be my friend.*

"Then why don't you tell me what happened that night by the Sparkle? Girl to girl, no boys here to mask the truth."

The Duchess smiled, waiting for the story. Anne couldn't decide why no one had told her yet, but if no one had, there was sure to be a good reason.

Duchess Dara leaned in closer, her gray eyes big. "Come on, you can tell me everything." The chain around her neck came forward with her, and the awkward position brought the pendant hanging on it out of the top of her dress. The five-pointed Reproba Caelum star hung in the air between them, rocking back and forth.

"I'm sure whatever they told you is the truth. I was sick, I don't recall much of the night." She took her gaze away and watched a giant kerplum leaf sway in a breeze fresh off the gulf.

Silence took over the garden, though the everyday sounds of the keep could be heard in the little garden.

The Duchess sat back, trying to hide the frustration on her face. "I'm sorry to hear you were feeling so terrible. Well, you better hurry off to Larith."

Anne didn't waste a second. She got to her feet, curtsied, and scurried out of the garden, her curly hair bouncing along for the ride. She wasted no time sliding past workers on the way to the stables either, though a couple of times she bumped into them rather than sliding past. She found Larith in the last stall, alone. It was unlike the others, fully walled off and spacious. Larith sat inside stroking an old Southern Jiggler.

"This is Friedrich VIII. He used to be the Duke's horse, but he's gotten old like me. Not everyone has forgotten about the old fellow though." Larith patted the space between his eyes before stroking down his muzzle and rubbing his nose.

The feathers above his hoofs were tattered, but his brown fur remained intact and soft. His shabby mane shone at some point, Anne was sure, but the short stringy strands lacked any luster. His round eyes were gentle. "He's a sweet horse," Anne said. She stroked the side of his ample belly; Friedrich never moved.

"It's sad though, the stable boys won't take an old man's advice and cover his neck." Larith took one his wrinkled hands and brushed up the short shabby mane. There were two large black flies with bulbous eyes. "He can't quite move like he used to." Larith plucked the flies off one at a time and squished them between his thumb and pointy finger. The grotesque insects made a soft "pop" both times. Larith wiped his hands on some hay. Blood trickled down Friedrich's neck.

"Blood flies," Anne said. "Those sores must be painful."

Larith nodded. "He's the only one who gets them. That's why I visit him on occasion." The old nuncio hovered his hand over one of the fresh sores. "*Resarcio.*"

Larith flinched, but Anne saw the little bits of muscle beneath string together quickly and replace what the blood fly ripped away. The skin grew over too, sprouting fresh brown hair to match what was on his neck.

"Larith, let me try the other one!" Anne exclaimed. "What was the word again? Resacio? I just do the same thing, picture it healed, right?" Anne's words flew out of her mouth faster than was possible to understand. "I'll look at your spot. Then say the word. Not too much though! I learned my lesson."

Larith chuckled, but it brought him into a coughing fit. Anne stopped talking and waited until the old man could speak. "This sort of White Magic is different, and infinitely more dangerous."

Anne opened her mouth to question what he meant, but she thought better of it and let the old man continue.

"It's dangerous for the patient because the healer must know everything that is wrong. You're not just putting skin over the wound, you're mending tissue. To heal, you must picture everything being healed, not only the top of the wound."

Anne nodded enthusiastically. She understood. She could do that.

"It means if you wish to pursue the art of healing, we will have to spend a great amount of time pouring over books and studying anatomy, learning how and why the body functions as it does. Is this the direction you would like to go with White Magic?"

"What else could I learn?"

"Mostly mind tricks," Larith said slowly. "Speaking to someone's mind rather than their ears, muddling their thoughts."

Anne bit her bottom lip and thought about her course of study. "Can't I learn both?"

Larith smiled. "Of course you could, though both require a great amount of practice and study. It would be difficult to be proficient in both. I would suggest choosing one path for now."

I want to help people. I want to help everyone I care about. "I want to heal."

"Because White Magic comes from the user, everything you heal you will feel. Heal too much, and like creating too big a globe of light, you'll create enough pain to kill yourself."

"I still want to heal."

"Place your hand over the sore then." He grabbed her small hand with his own and placed it hovering over the bleeding hole. Friedrich slapped away at another fly with his tail. "Focus on picturing the tissue come together first. Here, it helps to clear away the blood." He dabbed at the spot with the sleeve of his robe. "The tissue is stringy, so imagine it stringing itself together. The word is *resarcio*. Say it to me without picturing anything."

"*Resarcio*."

"Good, now give it a try." Anne focused on the sore, now clear of blood. She could see the walls of the tissue, the pink standing out against the hide around it. A moving picture of Larith mending the other sore sat vivid in her mind's eye still, and she used it.

"*Resarcio*."

Anne felt a sharp sting on her neck. She flinched and slapped at the spot, losing her concentration. The bite was painful.

"Focus, Anne. I warned you that would happen."

Anne envisioned the process again.

"*Resarcio.*"

The sharp sting returned, and though Anne flinched she managed to concentrate. The sinewy tissue started to come together, much slower than Larith's had. The strings of muscle found their partner on the other side before coming together and filling the gap. Subconsciously, Anne pictured the skin coming together next. It grew instantly, covering up the tissue beneath still at work in repairing itself. The pain on her neck stopped.

"No, no! I wasn't done yet!"

Larith patted Friedrich. "It's all right. The wound was only a bug bite. It can heal properly on it's own, but that is the sort of the thing we must avoid. You must learn what the healing will look like without being shown, in case you see something new. You must know the shapes of the bones, the thickness of muscle, the location of organs, what disease certain symptoms mean. You must familiarize yourself with all of these or risk making things worse for your patients. If all of this were not enough, you must also learn to concentrate on healing while ignoring the pain you will feel."

Anne felt her shoulders droop. "Does this mean back to the library?"

"Anatomy, second floor."

Chapter 7
(Anne, Galavon)

Two knocks on her door from the antechamber woke Anne. She wiped tears from her eyes, a common occurrence when she woke now. Her dreams were always of her father.

Will I ever wake again without tears?

"Lady Anne, ye must wake up." The voice was Porter's, his southern accent thick. She rolled out of the blankets and let her feet hit the floor. No sunlight came through the window in her room, only bits of starlight that was able to sneak through the wisps of clouds that traveled through the night sky.

What is he doing here in the middle of the night?

She threw a cloak over her chemise and wrapped it around her body. Anne knew her curly hair stuck out in all directions, but she didn't bother with it – it was only Porter. She shuffled across the floor and swung the door open.

Porter stood in full battle array; he wore his brigandine armor and carried his spear. The recruit immediately turned his head away once he realized Anne was in her chemise. "Could... could..." he stammered. "Could my lady, um, dress to travel?"

Anne smiled and tried to wipe away the streaks from her tears that she knew were on her cheeks. "Of course. One second Porter." She giggled at his averted eyes. "And we're friends, you don't have to call me lady." She pulled the door shut and went to change.

For travel, huh? She lit a candle before putting on the now clean clothes she had worn to Caernarfon Castle: a comfortable billowy shirt, a thin brown belt with brass studs, tight cotton riding pants, and leather riding boots. Once again, she put the black ribbon in her hair to remember her father.

Anne tucked her pearl in her shirt. She never went without it, not even while she slept. Her stiletto rested on the night stand, and she reached for it as well. She thrust it in her belt and walked into the antechamber.

"Porter, what's going on?" she whispered. She wasn't sure why she whispered, just believed it to be appropriate. "Are the wyverns here? Have pirates been spotted? Is Larith all right?!" she asked, slowly getting louder with each question.

"Quiet, please my lady," another voice spoke in a whisper. This voice was mature and commanding, deep and sure. It came from outside the antechamber in the hall. Porter led her that direction. The voice belonged to Captain Philial.

"If my lady would follow, the circumstances will be explained." The tall captain walked ahead, assuming she would follow – which she did. Porter followed her from behind. The trio walked down the stairwell and across the lower ward into the Great Hall through its main doors.

The walk from one end of the Great Hall to the other seemed to take days. Only three torches were lit for the entire hall. One burned by the main doors, while two more crackled in the center of the hall. They created shadows that danced around the dais.

Duke Briel and Larith sat together on the raised platform. Anne had not seen Duke Briel much during her stay besides at meals. He was many years his wife's senior, and gray hair covered his head. He was kind, but firm, much like her father Tarik.

"Sorry to have you woken at such an awkward time," the Duke said. He wore a robe loose around his frame. "I too am unaccustomed to these night time forays."

The Duke shifted his gaze from Anne to Larith, who nodded. The two seemed like old friends. "The three of you have been full of questions since your arrival, and I believe it's time you received answers."

Philial didn't move, but Anne heard Porter shift his weight. Larith avoided eye contact with her.

"Anne Ziyad used White Magic though she is not part of Reproba Caelum. You all wonder why and have approached the question in different ways. Captain Philial brooded over the subject and kept his sword arm busy with my guards. Porter, you prayed in town with a traveling monk. Anne, you didn't question your ability. You have embraced it and grown in the art of White Magic."

Porter shuffled his feet again, and the shield on his back scraped against one of the studs on his brigandine armor. The resulting sound pierced the silence of the hall.

"Perun does not grant magic," Larith said, finally speaking. "Anne, show them your necklace." Anne pulled it free from her shirt. He nodded. "The stones and the user's own abilities grant magic. Reproba Caelum is a false religion, created to control Elemental Magic."

"B-b-but, I'm sure there be another reason!" Porter said. He did the holy sign of Reproba Caelum with his thumbs and edged away from Anne, all the way to the wall. He looked to Captain Philial for support.

"He speaks the truth, Porter," Duke Briel said. "I know it's hard because it's all you have ever known, but..."

"No! It's hard because Reproba Caelum be the truth!" He pointed a finger at Anne. "She must 'ave made a deal with Shiva, the Djinn, or some other beast! She must 'ave!"

"Quiet down, boy!" Duke Briel snapped. "Control yourself! We don't need the entire castle awake. That will happen soon enough I fear."

"Certainly you have evidence that what you say is true," Philial said in his deep voice. His father, Duke Edmund Marlow, was known to be a devout Follower. He would have been raised with a heavy Reproba Caelum influence.

"We do, captain," Duke Briel answered. "Constable Ziyad entrusted it to me before he marched to Fire Pass. He didn't know what they had planned for him there.

"You three were called here because of new events." Duke Briel pulled his hands off the arm rest of his chair and leaned forward. "They have charged your brother with treason against the curators, Anne. The Crows move to your manse outside of Pearl even as we speak, to search for evidence of heresy against your family, which I guarantee they will plant. It's a tough judicial system to beat when your accusers are your judges. There is no doubt your own story has spread despite our best efforts, and they will come here searching for you as well. You must leave."

"You want us to be traitors too? Is that it?" Porter asked, finding his voice again. Anne couldn't believe him. They used to be friends, and now he was willing to let her be taken by the Crows?

"I can see the recruit's concerns, my Lord," Philial said. "If you want us to escort Anne to safety, we'll be sacrificing our lives in East Ager. We'll be running from refuge to refuge, and if the Crows want her badly enough, they'll be at our heels the entire way."

"That would be true were it not for the circumstances," Larith responded. The old nuncio seemed more alive than ever. "The Duke and I, along with others, have been waiting years for an opportunity such as this."

"Larith, of course, has known the longest, but there was no evidence. All we had was his word until Constable Ziyad discovered Ares' corpse. The corpse of a god." He stopped there and looked the three of them over. Anne turned to look at Captain Philial, expressionless as ever. She looked at Porter, who shook his head in disbelief.

"This revelation changes everything. If the curators are mortal, why must we suffer under them? Why must we surrender our wealth, our friends, our family to Reproba Caelum? Why must we fear? Why must we submit? I will no longer surrender, fear, or submit anything! They don't know how many of us stand together. With your brother, Anne, comes the might of the Army of Truth. When the province learns they assassinated your father, we can rid ourselves of the lies. With the truth, we can rise and rule ourselves again in the Peninsula Province."

Anne blinked at the Duke. A civil war? Against all of the Kingdom of East Ager?

And I don't have a choice, Anne thought. *I'm a fugitive if they ever learn I used White Magic. And if anything happens to Cecil, I'm the last Ziyad.*

"We ask that you two, along with some of my household guards, travel south out of harm's reach with Anne. Take the long route down the coast to Castle Himeji. She'll be safe there. A messenger will be dispatched to Lady Ignava, and we will hopefully see her safe at Castle Himeji soon after your arrival."

"Castle Himeji? Duchess Hamilton, the Lady Ayn, knows your plans?" Captain Philial asked.

"Yes. Many of the nobility have joined our cause, and the Lady Ayn is one of them. With Tarik's evidence and the list of atrocities committed by Reproba Caelum growing every day, little persuasion is necessary. But now we need Cecil to convince the common folk and the army. Without those, we can't hope to achieve anything."

"I don't want to go south. I want to help!" Anne exclaimed. "A revelation like this... the people will need me! I can help convince them!"

"As your strength increases, Anne, you will be able to help. For now, though, you help the most by keeping out of harms way," Larith responded.

"And what of my father?" Captain Philial asked. "Duke Marlow? What does he say of this coalition?"

Duke Briel took a deep breath. "We have not approached him yet. We fear his response. He is a known devout Follower."

They have two out of three Dukes, the most powerful people besides the Constable himself. Soon they'll have the Army of Truth. Duke Marlow wouldn't stand a chance unless the other provinces marched south.

"Larith, its time. Show them," the Duke commanded. The old man nodded his head, muttered a few indistinguishable words, and the front doors of the chamber slammed open. Wind rushed inside, extinguishing one of the torches. The force sent Anne's curly locks to brush against her face and rub at her smooth cheeks.

The wind swirled down the hall. It swept beneath the long table and pushed out a large coffin. The force left it crooked, but it was close enough for Anne to reach out and touch.

"Their bodies are different than ours," Larith explained. "They live almost as long as elves, sometimes up to a thousand Twil. This attribute lengthens the decomposition of their bodies as well. That is why he looks as though he died yesterday. It will be a year or more before the body begins to smell and rot."

Anne took a step closer to the coffin and knelt down on her knees. She was the first. Porter stayed against the wall and stared off into darkness, refusing to look. Captain Philial stared from over her shoulder. She brought her small hands to the lid and threw it aside, causing it to bounce on the floor, the sound echoing through the mostly empty hall.

The figure inside looked like a sleeping man. The armor he wore shined bright, and Anne wouldn't have been surprised if it was crafted of pure silver. Yellow runes were etched on the rims of the breastplate, and a red tunic of fine material cascaded out from beneath it.

No, the material is white. The red is blood.

She noticed because the white wings behind his back and head were splotched with the same color.

"You're looking at Ares." Duke Briel said. "He's a young curator. When they die at their cathedrals, a new curator is sent from the Sacred Isle to replace them. It seems their young are similar to ours. He believed himself to be invincible. A stray arrow from a goblin raiding party proved otherwise." The Duke stood from his chair. "This is why the high priests targeted your father, Anne. They knew he had the corpse, and hence the ability to prove that Reproba Caelum is false to lords, ladies, everyone. They feared what a man with his power and influence might be able to accomplish with this sort of evidence. This is why the great lords of the Peninsula Province band together. We band to end the murders, like your father's, and to end the lies. We will drive out the false and support the truth to create a home where we do not live in fear of the atrocities of Reproba Caelum."

"Is that enough proof for you?" Larith asked the two soldiers in front of him. "Proof that they are not immortal, that they are not gods?"

Porter slumped against the wall as his legs gave out from underneath him. He still didn't look at the corpse. "It must be true," he whispered.

Philial nodded.

"Then gather your things and say your good-byes. The two of you are escorting the pearl of our province. Philial, you're in command. Porter, you're to accompany him. Meet your party at the gatehouse." Both were hesitant, but they finally did turn.

"And keep your lips sealed," Larith called after them, "until the appropriate time has come."

The Great Hall found silence with their departure, but only for a moment. "What about my brother? Will he be all right?"

"We know little about your brother." Larith said. "Sometimes the Duke receives word from Lieutenant Commander Varro, other times the wind will bless me with bits of information."

"He's trudging through the fire of Shiva," Duke Briel said, cutting in. "We have supporters watching over him, but there are many who would see him dead. Without him, we could lose the Army of Truth. We need him. We travel as soon as the sun rises to Pearl, where Larith and I hope to intercept him and invite him to our cause. Your father's cause."

Anne nodded. She worried for Cecil. He was strong and intelligent, but sometimes he needed her, and she wasn't there. But once Larith was with him, he would be fine.

"There are a few more things you should know about me, Anne." Larith said in his slow meticulous voice. "In all my travels, I have acquired a better understanding than most of the magic of Mundus. Because our lessons can't continue, I want you to take this." Larith pushed up from his chair and produced a leather-bound book from within the folds of his robes. The old mage wobbled on his legs. "This will help to teach more of the history and give you a better understanding of all magic." He stroked the worn leather book fondly as though he did not want to part with it. "Focus on White Magic, but do not forget there are other branches of elemental power. And as you read, you will discover there are older magics that few remember, and even fewer can practice."

There's more than Elemental Magic? Anne thought. She walked up the dais. With one last look at the book, Larith reluctantly handed it over to Anne. He eased back down into his chair.

"Let your power with White Magic grow, and soon you will be able to help your brother and all those you love."

"How long have you known? About the curators?" Anne asked.

"A long time. My path in life taught me a great deal. An odd path, I assure you. As you can see, I'm a nonbeliever, yet I serve as a nuncio. A very odd path."

Anne nodded. There was a lot to take in. More questions came to mind. "If Reproba Caelum is a false religion, what's the real one? Are the old religions right? Does God even exist?"

The old man leaned forward in his chair and stretched out a wrinkled hand to cup Anne's chin. They felt leathery, and in the torchlight Anne could see blue veins racing underneath the skin of his hands. "Perhaps the one true religion died out years ago, leaving none to know the true god or gods. What I do know is that we all share Mundus, and if a religion requires inequity, suffering, or murder, that is not a religion I wish to practice. We can only lead the best life we are able to and try to know our creator through their creations."

Duke Briel spoke next. "Your maid gathered all of your things. You should meet with everyone at the gatehouse."

Anne thanked the Duke and kissed Larith on the cheek. Though this night he didn't have his usual carefree attitude and funny jokes, she would miss that side of the old man as well as this more somber one who seemed to be the keeper of all knowledge. Knowledge she believed she now held in her hand.

The two lit torches flickered in the dark, and shadows danced at the edge of her vision as she walked down the Great Hall. Her steps were muffled by the carpet. She felt as though she was one of the shadows, silently slipping through the night leaving not a trace.

"And Anne," Larith called out from down the hall. His voice echoed. She turned. "The secret to your dagger lies in its name, *Alius*. Grip it, call its name, and let its power flow out. Its the way of all items forged with magical attributes. " Anne nodded, though she was sure they couldn't see it. The last bit seemed unimportant compared to all she had learned.

She stepped through the doors into the night. The clouds overhead drifted by on a journey of their own, causing portions of the courtyard to shift from glowing with starlight to fading into absolute darkness. Anne walked toward the gatehouse. The wind blew away the clouds and just for a moment the entire courtyard became bathed in the stars' silver glow. It reminded Anne of her last night in Pearl, though it didn't last, as new clouds moved in overhead.

Anne noticed two figures leaning against the stone wall. She couldn't see the face of the soldier, but she recognized the other as one of the girls who helped serve food during the meals. She had a thick body and a chubby face. She also had the most beautiful hair Anne had ever seen. It cascaded down her back to her waist like honey-colored silk. Individual hairs never strayed, and even with the lack of strong light, it shined.

The front figure bent its head over hers, and she disappeared for a moment under the kiss. A shadowed hand ran down her locks of hair. The two embraced in a hug, and the serving girl ran off along the wall and disappeared behind the stables.

Must be one of the guards saying good-bye.

Anne felt a smile creep to her face. Despite all that she had learned tonight, it was good to know that some things about the world would always be true. Love would always exist.

I suppose that's the last I'll see of Galavon. I hope he leaves in time to avoid being caught up in all of this.

So much was happening it was hard to even remember what the young merchant looked like. With effort, a great deal of effort, she pushed him out of her mind. There was too much else to worry about.

Anne continued to the gatehouse. Waiting there was a wagon loaded with food, five men she didn't recognize, and Isabella. The maid looked as though she had recovered from her long nights without sleep, but lines still showed around her eyes that must have been from worry.

Isabella came to Anne and wrapped her in a hug. "Larith told me," she said. "Cecil will be fine. Ye know how strong he is."

Anne nodded against Isabella's shoulder. She wondered if Larith had told her everything, including about the corpse of the curator.

They stopped hugging and Anne turned toward the main building of the castle. Isabella kept a hand on her shoulder. The touch felt comforting. Isabella had always been more motherly toward Anne than Lady Ignava.

Captain Philial came to the group leading his horse. Porter followed soon after, and the group was complete: five household guards, two soldiers, Anne, and her maid.

Anne rode in the cart beside Isabella. Captain Philial led the group from the front on top of his Southern Jiggler, while the rest of the men formed a circle around the cart. Anne noticed Porter take position as far from her as he could.

He must think I'm a monster.

Captain Philial turned and looked over the small group before they departed. Anne could see how women found Captain Philial attractive. He had an air of confidence, a hard but handsome face, and determination. He began to speak while Anne studied his features. "You all know why we are leaving. We must protect Anne and get her somewhere safe. Do you understand?"

The men did not speak, only nodded. *They all seem so serious.*

Captain Philial led them through the gatehouse and down the winding road. The clouds above kept them veiled from sight, but the captain chose to go around Caern rather than through it. The mood of the group was somber. No one uttered a word.

They're probably wishing they were asleep in their beds.

The roar of the ocean beating on the cliffs to their right accompanied them through the night once they passed the coastal town. The road they followed ran right along those steep cliffs. The weather felt fine for traveling. The cold season on the peninsula rarely reached severe temperatures even during the night.

The town sat not too far behind the traveling group when the sun peaked its head over the horizon. The morning was foggy, and the wispy clouds from the night turned into dark angry creatures of the sky. Rain would find them on the road.

Now that the sun granted them a little light to see by despite the dark clouds, Anne looked at the soldiers surrounding the wagon. They were mostly solid built men, older than Captain Philial. They didn't carry a spear like Porter or most of the infantry in the Army of Truth, but rather held on to axes and broadswords. They served Duke Briel and only Duke Briel, not the Army of Truth. It was common practice for the nobility to command a small household guard that followed their orders and not the orders of the province's army.

They took to following Captain Philial easily enough. He rode in front, his eyes searching for any signs of danger ahead like he did on their trip from Pearl to Caernarfon Castle. His silent vigil didn't surprise Anne.

The other guards began talking in hushed voices, as though they didn't want to disturb the tranquility of the morning. They spoke of trivial things - horses, weather, and ale. Anne wondered when and if they were told the truth about Reproba Caelum.

The only sound coming from Porter was the echo of his boots on the dirt road. Anne felt bad for her friend. She never realized that he was so devoted a Follower. Judging from his stooped shoulders, Anne assumed he still felt unsure about the situation.

Anne noticed something shine on his shoulder against the leather brigandine. A lock of blonde hair was clipped there, close to his heart. Anne could see him touch it for reassurance every once in a while.

Porter Mann? It couldn't have been!

Anne thought back. She remembered the girl's face and her hair, and the man had been cloaked in shadows. But the hair on his shoulder proved he was the soldier.

Thinking of Porter and his mysterious love made Anne think of Galavon yet again. She wondered what had happened to him. If she was moving all over the province from castle to castle, would she ever see him again? She hoped that she would. Memories of the merchant boy brought back the lyrics to the song they danced to together. She whispered them.

"In the city not far from here,
Gathered a crowd,
A harpist to hear!
It was said he could win a tear
From all the beautiful maidens dear."

Another voice joined hers from the wagon. Isabella joined her voice with Anne's. They sang a little louder.

> *"He played one note,*
> *And then two,*
> *But just as the maidens began to woo..."*

Porter added his voice to theirs. Though barely audible, the recruit added a little something to the song.

> *"It went pop! Pop! Pop!*
> *A maiden's broken dream!*
> *Pop! Pop! Pop!*
> *Fate can be so mean!*
> *Pop! Pop! Pop!*
> *A harpist's broken string!"*

"A harp?" Galavon asked. He sat with his back against a lone tree and his legs stretched out in front of him. His traveling clothes were smudged with dirt and streaked with sweat. He wouldn't have been surprised if he smelled worse than Kavar ever did.

"Yes, a harp," Ceridwen snapped. She wasn't the kindest of teachers. "To speak with the wind, you must befriend the wind. You don't get to choose to use Wind Magic, it chooses you. You're having problems with that, so play for the wind and let it choose you."

Galavon looked at the harp. The neck running along the top had a poorly mended crack in it, and the tuning pins were starting to rust. "Where did you get this from?"

"The same place we got the horses. We stole it! Now let me hear you play." Ceridwen stood over him with her arms crossed.

The past few days of trying to learn Wind Magic had been a waste. Galavon didn't understand how he was supposed to talk to the wind. He tried the words Ceridwen taught him, strange words like *brevis,* but they did nothing. Somehow he was supposed to hold a conversation with the wind, or hum to it. He thought Ceridwen might strangle him until she discovered he knew a little of playing the harp.

"I haven't played the harp in a long time," Galavon said testing the first string. "I won't do any spells just playing, will I?" He pulled out his knife and tried to adjust a tuning pin.

"No. You won't. You're building a relationship with the wind by playing. Now play!"

Galavon buried the blade of his knife in the dirt and started to play the instrument. He felt as rusty as the old harp. It was a miracle it still had all of its strings. He plucked one of them and allowed the wind to carry it off into the sea of grass.

"Good. Play the tune I taught you to hum. Play it for the wind. Let it hear you." Galavon felt uncomfortable beneath her scrutinizing stare, but he started to play. The strings rubbed against his smooth fingers. He knew he would get calluses on his finger tips from playing, making them match the hardened skin on every other part of his body.

Galavon began to hum and tried to match it with music from the harp. The tune was so simple, it didn't take him long at all to play a simplified version. As she often did when Galavon started to hum the tune, Ceridwen sang.

"Look to death's deep,
Where the dragon sleeps.
Look to the lake,
Where the dragon mates.
For the dragons are Mundus itself.

Look to the fire
At the dragon's pyre.
Look to the sea
Where the dragon will be.
For the dragons are Mundus itself.

Look to the mines
For the dragon shrines.
Look to the sky,
Where the dragon flies.
For the dragons are Mundus itself."

Her harsh voice sounded odd singing. Ceridwen took a breath before she fell back into her normal attitude. "Listen while you play," Ceridwen commanded. "Each element is cast differently. White by focus. Earth by runes. Fire by rage. Black by life. Water by trance. Wind is cast by asking."

"By asking?"

"No questions," Ceridwen snapped. She spit in the grass. Galavon thought she was nicer in chains. She had certainly spit less. "There are only a few who practice Wind Magic. The emeralds are found in the Mountains of Hope, sometimes in deep caves, sometimes high on a peak. The few that are discovered are hoarded by Reproba Caelum, and less than half of those emeralds even find a person to use their power. There are far fewer seers than clerics and shaman, or even druids and sahagin. Only necromancers are fewer in number."

"The Tame elements generally accept a user if they have the ability to use its power. Fire and Black Magic want nothing more than to be unleashed so they may spread their destruction. Wind chooses who can use it and if a spell will even be cast. The spells don't always work as the caster sees fit, which makes it a Wayward element rather than a Tame one."

Galavon grimaced. He hit a wrong note and destroyed the tune with an unsettling ring. If he wanted to befriend the wind by playing an instrument, he would have to get much better. "So what's the point of learning Wind Magic if it's unpredictable? Couldn't it fail me when I need it the most?"

Galavon expected the mage to yell at him for missing a note or asking a question, but he was surprised. "I'll be honest with you – wind is not considered the most important of the elements. Its inability to be dependable and precise makes it a poor choice for fighting."

Ceridwen was often harsh and angry, but every now and then Galavon could see her soft side. *Fire Magic and White Magic suit her well.*

"Wind Magic does, however, allow the caster to send messages over long distances. Many call it 'the whisper of the wind.' This one spell makes a seer invaluable. This is why we need to find someone wind will accept."

Galavon nodded in understanding. One spell is why they wanted a seer. The ability to send messages would make coordinating attacks easy and planned assaults go smoother. Galavon hoped he could become a seer and learn to use Wind Magic – he had never been a valuable part of anything.

"Good. Breaks over. Let's get moving!"

Though he wanted to be important, Galavon definitely felt out of place with the small band of Albus Veneficus. Every one of them looked like a brigand, talked tough, and gave Galavon looks that promised death. He was, after all, in the group that had killed many of them. They didn't know how to walk a horse – a canter was the slowest they traveled. Galavon had been sore from learning to ride with Darak, but the constant bouncing of their canter rubbed the insides of his legs raw. Bruises the size of his fist developed between his legs, and even the thought of walking hurt.

The group packed their meager items and traveled at their normal break neck pace. Galavon's horse, Kid, gave him trouble on more than one occasion, especially since he now had to try and to keep his satchel, staff, and harp from falling. It was all he could do as a novice rider to keep the Plainstrider under his control. The few breaks Ceridwen did allow weren't breaks for Galavon, either. They were breaks for the horses. He spent all of them trying to use Wind Magic to no avail.

Galavon didn't understand how he was supposed to talk with the wind. Even his teacher couldn't use Wind Magic, else she would have kept the stone for herself.

"All right, that's enough," Ceridwen called out after another long, hard ride. The brutes traveling on their stolen horses came to a halt. "There will be rain this afternoon, I can feel it under my skin. Mother always said she wished she had a sapphire to make me a sahagin."

Sapphire for Water Magic, huh? I wonder where they come from.

"You men find a troll hovel dug into the hills, or some other shelter." Ceridwen sighed and spoke much lighter. "We'll have to go all the way back to Marcil." Galavon was the only one close enough to hear her.

Marcil? By Castle Conwy? We still have a ways to go.
The men spread out to look for anything that could work as a shelter to pass through the rain. Most of their horses were work horses they had stolen from farms, not meant to ride with a passenger. They had left that region far behind now, and they rarely saw a farm.

"Is finding a seer so important?" Galavon asked. "If you let me go I can make my own way to a town or somewhere near. You could travel faster without me."

"Yes, actually it is. And if you knew what was best for you, you'd be trying to learn as hard as Shiva is trying to break out of her prison."

Galavon knew what she really meant. If he wasn't any use to them, they would kill him. He would never see Anne again. He had to learn Wind Magic.

These rebels aren't much better than Reproba Caelum if you ask me.

Galavon let Kid nibble on some grass and tried to rearrange his stuff. He could hardly hold the harp, reins, and staff. The satchel he tied to the saddle. While fiddling with his luggage he asked, "How do the seers communicate with each other?"

"Through the wind. *Veho Affatus.* The wind then carries the message to the other person's ears. I don't know the specifics, only the words. And very few words for Wind Magic, at that." Ceridwen scanned the men's progress and patted her horse's neck.

"The others couldn't learn it either?"

"Them?" Ceridwen asked. She motioned toward her fellow Albus Veneficus with her head, who were now fanning out. "They each had a few days to learn it, but I knew if I couldn't grasp it, they couldn't either. Now I'm giving you a few days. The difference between you and them is they are still useful without magic."

It was obvious she was in charge of the group. She made all the calls – when to stop, what to steal, where to steal from, when they ate, what they ate. Galavon found it a relief not to be struggling with leadership like he was earlier in his travels, but the mage was brutal. Her verbal assaults had the other men running.

Or maybe it was her command over Fire Magic and White Magic that gave her authority.

Would they listen to me if I learned Wind Magic?

Galavon wasn't fond of asking her questions due to her callous remarks, but he had no choice. She made it clear that he had no value to the group unless he could use the emerald. He obviously was not a warrior. It seemed his only skill lay in dancing, and that wouldn't help the Albus Veneficus unless they planned on stomping out the curators with a harvest festival. Under normal circumstances he wouldn't have even considered joining the group, but he had not really had a choice.

Galavon strapped on a leather frog to his belt while Kid was still. He was given the frog from the corpse of one of the dead rogues. Galavon untied the leather strings on the front, fit the neck of the harp inside the leather, and tied it back. It was made for an axe, but it fit the harp with perfection. Galavon was grateful something finally worked.

Finally something fits right.

The men came galloping back together, claiming to have found an old troll hovel in the side of a hill – exactly what Ceridwen expected. It was a blessing no troll was inside. More than once Galavon heard the men say it was odd not to have encountered any of the man-like beasts traveling through the plains.

Galavon felt as though he had better control on the horse now that one hand was free. He climbed on Kid's back and reached out to scoop up the reins, but Kid felt his neck free. The Plainstrider took off while Galavon fought to grab the reins. He could hear the men laughing while he struggled. Unable to grab them, he dropped the staff, swung his feet over the side, and bailed off the tall horse.

Kid gave a half-hearted buck before settling down to nibble on the grass again. Over the laughter he heard Ceridwen's powerful voice. "You break that harp and I'll break your fingers! Now get back up, the rain will be here soon!"

Galavon gathered his lost weapon. He walked toward the horse and threw the reins back over his neck. He jumped on Kid's back and slid his feet in the stirrups without thinking about the soreness in his legs. The horse could sense his irritation and allowed Galavon to lead him to the others. Again, the group took off in a canter, leaving Galavon struggling behind bouncing up and down.

Is it really necessary to race to a hole in the ground?

A cold wind blowing in from the southeast hit the group. It came ahead of a group of threatening dark clouds that quickly took over the sky. The wind blew in and flung bits of dirt strewn up from the horses in front in Galavon's face. He shut his eyes to try and keep it out, but then he couldn't see. It was apparent Kid didn't care for the dirt either, because he slowed down to a stop to avoid the dust cloud. The cold wind continued to blow.

"How am I supposed to keep up when I can't see?" Galavon exclaimed to no one, frustration beginning to boil over. "My horse won't listen. I'm a heretic. I have to learn Wind Magic, or I die. I find a girl, and I have to leave her." He squeezed lightly with his legs and urged Kid to a walk. He stayed a good distance behind to prevent the dirt from battering his face when he rode.

Galavon kept talking. It felt good to talk to no one. "I should have cracked her harder with the staff. I bet then I wouldn't be in this situation. Torvil too." The wind blew his hair back out of his face, allowing him to see clear. The cold wind felt good on his arms. They were burnt from riding beneath the sun for so many days.

They came to the small troll hovel, but Galavon would have considered it more of a burrow with barely enough room for the horses. The highway was nowhere in sight now, gone from vision for many days, and only stunted trees and plenty of grass stretched in all directions. Galavon felt alone.

He didn't listen to Ceridwen snap out orders. He dismounted from Kid and sat in the grass away from the hole. He kept a loose hold on the reins but allowed enough slack for the horse to wander a small circle around him. He unstrapped the bent harp and started to play.

His fingertips were sore and felt thick. They rubbed against the wrong strings, causing sounds that could have come from a banshee. He didn't care. Despite the poor performance, it felt good to have his hands on something he knew he could control even for just a moment.

The clouds moved in overhead, darkening the plains. Galavon felt the cold wind that brought the clouds pick up and tussle his hair. His fingers moved to play a different tune, one he had thought forgotten. It was a song he had learned from one of his maids who claimed his mother used to accompany it with a slow verse. Galavon did the same.

> *"The wind blows through the branches of trees,*
> *Alongside mountains, fast and free.*
> *It fills the sails of traveling ships*
> *Riding the waves with each rise and dip.*
> *It blows by fast, so listen close,*
> *Wind always sees and hears the most."*

No one paid him any attention. Ceridwen was yelling at the biggest of the men. Judging by the red tint to her face, she was furious. Spittle flew from her lips like venom.

I wonder what he did.

Galavon didn't know of anyone besides Ceridwen who could make their eyes resemble flames when they were angry, and she did it well despite their crystal blue color. He continued playing the simple tune on the harp.

What were the words she said earlier? I wonder if it works both ways.

"*Veho Affatus.*" The words came from his mouth, but they were accompanied by something else flowing up from his lungs. Energy Galavon had never felt before flew from his lips with the strange words. Tiny green sparkles disappeared in the air in front of him.

The wind blew down from the sky, catching Ceridwen and the man's dirty clothes and whipping their bodies with it. It continued on to Galavon's ear, gently caressing his cheek on the way.

"And how in Shiva's fiery prison am I supposed to know where we are? You live around here, take us to real shelter so I don't have to huddle with you no good..." It came in a whispered version of Ceridwen's voice. Galavon smiled.

"Veho Affatus."

Again the odd sensation flowed out with the words. "I'll burn your hide until it blackens and leave you for the manticores or the Crows, whichever finds you first. Don't think..."

It was nice to know he wasn't the only one she directed her anger toward.

"Veho Affatus." Nothing happened.

"Veho Affatus," Galavon said again. Nothing happened.

"VEHO AFFATUS!" he yelled, yearning to feel that strange energy flow through him again, needing something to work.

Ceridwen heard his outburst and turned her head. Galavon couldn't help but look at the dirty, blood-matted hair where he had hit her with his staff days ago. Her beak-like nose made the look she gave even more threatening. "You're all worthless!" Ceridwen let loose a howl of anger. The big man stepped back, disappearing in the hovel. The mage stared at Galavon and stomped toward him.

"How in Shiva's fiery prison are any of us supposed to know where we are?" Galavon started to walk toward her as well, dropping Kid's reins without a second thought. "Wandering out here in a sea of grass where manticores or Crows will find our blackened corpses isn't exactly what I signed up for!" The man she had been yelling at only moments before looked at Galavon questioningly.

"Ahhh, so what did you sign up for? I thought it was to learn Wind Magic, and you seem to have utterly failed at that!" They continued toward one another.

"As a matter of fact, it did work! That's how I know we're lost!"

Ceridwen stopped and Galavon followed suit. Her rags combined with her angry menace made her look every inch of what Galavon pictured a mage from the Albus Venificus would look like. Normally one to avoid confrontation, Galavon was unsure of what to do now. The frightening image of the woman in front of him stole his frustration and anger and replaced them with nervousness. He wasn't sure what he was supposed to do now that he stood facing her.

The other Albus Veneficus left their horses in the hollow and got in a position to watch the showdown. They kept a safe distance from the two.

"A seer, huh?" She called out. "It's about time; I tire of babysitting a child." She glared at him from under her dirty hair. "So let's see if you ARE a seer. You should be able summon a little wind, then? Stop fire if I throw it at you? If not, you're no longer a burden. We could use the extra horse. I hope you remember the first word I taught you."

Panic began to set in. *She can't be serious!*

Galavon looked to the men and found no support. He knew they were as afraid of the mage as he was, and he also knew they were glad it was Galavon who found her fiery temper.

Galavon did remember the word though. *Brevis.* She had made him repeat the word over and over again as though he was too stupid to remember it after the first twenty times. It meant "brief wind."

Ceridwen lifted both arms above her head and extended all her fingers. The sleeves of her dirty shirt fell to her elbows, revealing gangly arms beneath. Scars decorated her skin like brands, and Galavon imagined that they were from the constant use of fire.

"Incendia Inflatus."

The air itself grew warmer. The space between her open palms gave birth to flame; orange, yellow, and red swirling in a circle, hissing and crackling. The colors formed a ball of fire the size of a large fist, and it floated between her hands.

Ceridwen didn't wait long. She threw the ball of flame, and it raced across the space between them, leaving a smoke trail to follow behind.

She was serious!

"Brevis!"

The wind, a comforting feeling, blew past Galavon even as the green sparkles began to disappear in front of his mouth. It pulled his pants legs tight and pressed his tunic against his back. His hair flipped and danced in a wild manner, a mirror image of the grass below. The zephyr shot past him and intercepted the fire ball. The wind dissipated and the hungry flames ricocheted not far from Ceridwen's left shoulder, straight at the men. They jumped aside in all directions to avoid the fiery missile. The fireball exploded when it hit the grass, creating a resounding boom after its impact. Horses reared in the troll hovel and fled across the plains.

Galavon avoided Ceridwen's stare from across the field by watching the men try and stomp out the flames. The fire seemed hungrier than common flames and rapidly created burning patches in the grass. Sounds of frightened horses mixed with the shouts of the men.

"Congratulations," Galavon heard in his mind. He knew she was using White Magic to talk only to him. "You're a seer now. I knew the wind would choose you. It's in your blood." The flames spread fast in the grass, the men running around in a craze trying to stomp them out.

Galavon ran to help. He heard the men cursing their luck, cursing him, and cursing Ceridwen for trying to kill them. The hungry flames ate the grass in a mad fervor, spreading and growing. If they stepped on one flame, another two grew in its place.

"The flames will lose their hunger as my anger fades," Ceridwen called out in a calm voice. "The rain will beat down the natural flames they cause." He remembered the last rain he experienced in this region, and he was not looking forward to a repeat.

A giant drop fell from the sky and splattered on his hand. "Here it comes," he said to the wind. No one else was close enough to hear him.

"Grab the horses before we lose them in the storm!" Ceridwen barked. The men jogged out toward the wandering horses, trying to calm the timid beasts. Luckily for Galavon, Kid hadn't wandered from the first spot he left him. The horse filled his mouth with grass and continued to rip more off the ground.

Galavon retrieved his harp and replaced it on his belt. The staff lay on the ground near the horse, and he picked it up as well. Kid nibbled away, unperturbed about what just happened. Galavon felt the soreness in his legs but walked him where the others were gathering with their spooked horses.

"Take the horses as far back as you can into the hole. We'll try and make enough room up front."

The abandoned troll hovel was bigger than Galavon originally thought. The ceiling was low, but the hole was surprisingly deep after a sudden turn. The troll-made-cave had dirt floors, but it offered protection from the rain for the full party.

The men pushed the horses to the back as they were told and began taking off saddles, bridals, and reins. Thunder sounded from outside, and they kept the horses calm. Ceridwen went to a pile of sticks one of the men brought in and uttered a single word.

"*Incendia.*"

A small flame lit the pile, and one of the men edged closer with a pot. Ceridwen pushed Galavon to the front of the cave, making sure he left the harp and staff with the horses. They were so close to the entrance that the falling droplets splashed mud onto his already dirty boots.

After an awkward moment of silence with the two staring into the storm, Ceridwen spoke. "Do you have any questions?"

Why should I ask you? He thought bitterly. *You hardly know more than I do.*

He shook his head.

"You can speak to people at great distances now, once you learn how to find them," she explained. "The wind will carry it for you, which is quite different than White Magic – I can only speak in your mind as far as I can shout."

"Do you even know how to find someone with wind?"

"No, seer, I don't," Ceridwen responded acidly. The beating sound of the rain hitting the ground outside created a constant rhythm in the background. "You will have to figure that out on your own." Lightning struck outside, and in that quick flash Ceridwen planted a leg behind Galavon, shoved him to the floor, and filched the pouch containing the emerald from his belt. The mage put her foot on his chest and held the pouch above him. The gray clouds outside kept the hovel dark, but not so dark Galavon couldn't see the pouch dangling above him. Ceridwen tossed it into the rain, no more than ten or so span from the entrance.

"*Brevis!*"

Nothing happened.

Ceridwen held him to the ground, and no matter how Galavon squirmed he couldn't get up. Eventually he stayed motionless.

"Magic jewels have a price," Ceridwen said. "You've only won half the battle to join us as a seer.

"It only takes one spell to become addicted to its power. The more time you spend away from your first gem, or the farther apart you go from it, the more it will call for your touch. You're nothing without your stone."

Ceridwen removed her foot and Galavon got to his feet. "I'm not addicted to anything." Galavon was quickly becoming frustrated again. No talent, they kill you. Find a talent, and they take it. He took a step toward the pouch, but Ceridwen stopped him with a hand to his chest.

"Of course you feel nothing now. The emerald has been out of your possession a short time. The feelings will grow stronger. The Albus Venificus can't have this sort of weakness. We will make you immune to the flaw. You will endure the call of the emerald and live, keeping the power and killing the gem, or you will die and the emerald will remain intact with its power." Galavon walked away from the entrance of the hovel back to his harp, where he idly plucked at a string.

Ceridwen shouted at him from the front. "Let me say it again for you, seer. If you survive the emerald will die and you will require its assistance no longer to cast Wind Magic. If you die, the emerald will survive and we'll find another who can survive this."

Ceridwen walked into the storm and retrieved the pouch. She came back and sat with her back against the dirt wall.

"*Aridus*," she said. Even with the space between them Galavon could feel heat emanate from the mage. It didn't take long before the droplets running down her face from her tangled hair dried off her skin. Steam climbed up from her body before dissipating in the air above.

"I suffered the same with my pearl, except my own mother did it to me. It can only be done with your first, and if you learn other magics, you can't die when those stones are taken away. If you survive you will thank me for this."

If I survive.

"Enjoy your sleep tonight. It will be the last good sleep you get for a while."

Chapter 8
(Galavon, Anne)

"Ceridwen, I need to rest," Galavon gasped. Sleep was hard to come by, just as Ceridwen had promised. He often found himself short of breath since the day she took his emerald, and every now and then a sharp twitch would convulse his body. He couldn't separate the days, instead they all mingled together into one long, dizzying dream. Galavon remembered seeing a huge band of trolls many hills over and finding two men in the plains. He didn't know the order of these events or how long ago they occurred.

He couldn't even eat his meager portion of the rations. Since the day she took his emerald, he had only managed to get a small amount of bread and water down.

"No time, seer. Now that we know where we're going, we make haste. You should be thankful. If I had waited until the stone's hold was stronger you would feel worse."

The two men they had found were part of the Albus Veneficus, sent to direct members to a meeting. It seemed their luck had turned with Galavon's discovery.

Had it been three days since she took his emerald? Four?

Why must everything in my head revolve around the day she took my emerald? Galavon angrily thought to himself.

Galavon attempted to pull Kid beside Ceridwen's horse. It was difficult to muster the energy necessary. "Ceridwen, how did you not suffer when we took your ruby on the road?"

"It was my second stone. The pearl was my first. I told you, you only become one with your first."

Galavon held out a shaking hand. *When did I become so weak?* His body trembled with the effort. "Give me back the emerald. We can start this over once we get to where we're going. I need it."

"Not a chance, seer."

"I don't think you understand," Galavon said through gritted teeth. He held his hand farther out. "I must have it back." His body convulsed, and he barely managed to keep his saddle. A chill gripped him, and he shivered. The air was cooler than the beginning of their trip, but he knew he was the only one who got cold.

"As I said, Galavon, the answer is no." She spurred her horse to a faster speed.

Galavon's hand fell to his side.

I must have the stone.

He dug his heels into Kid's side to keep pace.

"Give it to me!" Galavon snarled, leaping at the mage. His body betrayed him, however, and dizziness washed over him. The feeble attempt resulted in a thud as he fell to the ground. The smell of dirt and grass filled his nostrils before another chill raced through his body and a spasm shook him uncontrollably. He started to see black spots wash across his vision

"To Shiva's own prison with you!" Galavon heard faintly in the background. The voice was hazy, but he was sure it was Ceridwen. He thought he heard her spit. *Why does she always spit?* The spasm faded, but even with control of his muscles he felt too tired to move. It was an effort to breathe. "Tie him to the horse; we're too close to stop."

The spots filled his vision until there was only darkness.

Galavon opened his eyes to a slit. The faces of the men were blurred, but Galavon could still smell the sour stench of sweat and grime. He felt rough hands loosen the rope that tied him to Kid. He had no energy, and his muscles felt like mud.

"I think he's done for. How long has he been like this?"

"Days. I don't have time to waste on him. Throw him with the horse fodder. Theres nothing we can do at this point. He either lives or he doesn't."

Live or die... does it matter which I do? Yes, it does. If I die I'll never see Anne again.

The voices sounded far away, and even the ropes sliding off felt distant. His stomach churned, and he dry heaved, the effort of it stealing energy that Galavon wasn't even aware was still in his body.

One of the men jumped back and a rope loosened too fast around Galavon's waist. He felt the wind fly by as he plummeted to the ground, still dry heaving uncontrollably into the dirt. Bits of dirt stuck to his lips.

"By the fire of Shiva! He's in enough pain as it is!"

Darkness filled his vision.

Galavon sat up and gasped for air, his eyes popping open. Sweat drenched his hair and his brow. His head felt like fire. Tremors suddenly shook his body with violent force, and his eyes rolled back into his head.

"Shhh. Easy, seer, easy. Lay down." The voice was gentle and sweet, that of a young woman. Galavon felt a soft hand push him down and hold him. A cold sponge dabbed against his brow. He continued to shake.

"Might as well leave him, girl. Ceridwen says it's up to him if he makes it or not," said an older voice.

"It's terrible that they do this," the gentle voice said. The cold sponge continue to dab at his head. "I can't just leave him here to die. Why can't they just give him back the stone?"

"That's not for you or I to decide. Come, there's nothing you can do here. There's work to be done."

The shaking continued, and the cold sponge left. Darkness filled his vision.

Galavon woke to the cold sponge. It felt good on his hot head. He could feel loose straw underneath a thin blanket poking his naked back. He dared to open his eyes and was greeted with a blurry vision between the darkness that still hovered along the edges and the light in the center. It was clear enough to make out the hazy form of a young woman hovering above him. It smelled musty, like a barn.

"Anne?" he asked.

"No, not Anne." The dabs continued. Even with his blurry vision, he thought he could make out a smile forming on those hazy features. "The stone's hold over you broke," she whispered, much quieter than before. "They were wrong. Shouldn't be long now, and you'll be back to normal."

Galavon tried to bring a hand up to brush the dark blur he knew was the woman's hair. "Anne..."

The darkness at the edge filled his vision.

The sharp pain of hunger woke Galavon. He rested on a thin blanket that sat over a pile of straw that smelled of sweat and sickness. The room was small and empty of furniture besides a splintery table and chair. A dented pitcher sat on the table. Horse bridles hung from the walls on nails. Galavon put both hands on the floorboards and pushed his way up to a sitting position, blinking his eyes to get used to the sunlight pouring through a single window. An easy, cool breeze blew in fresh air. He could hear the bustling sound of a busy street.

Where am I now?

Galavon wore nothing but a ragged blanket that covered the lower half of his body. His hair now fell just far enough to cover his eyes. He tried to brush it away with his fingers, but it fell back.

Has it really been so long since my father and I left Mecca?

Galavon's stomach rumbled again in an effort to tell him none too kindly that he hadn't eaten a real meal in days. His tongue felt like sandpaper and begged for moisture. He wondered if the pitcher still held water. He slowly rose to his feet and shuffled to the pitcher. He lifted it to his mouth and drank. The breeze blew in again and ruffled his hair, sending goose bumps across his bare body with its chill.

Footsteps creaked from outside. Someone tried to open the crooked door that led into the room with no success. Galavon lowered the pitcher from his mouth and put it back on the table. Then came a loud thud and the door burst open, sending a woman stumbling into the room with a basket in her hands.

She must have seen around twenty or so Twil, maybe more. Her body seemed soft, not fat, complete with full curves that would make some men look twice. She had dark straight hair that fell down around big gray eyes. She looked up at him.

And he remembered he wore no clothes.

His face turned bright red. He backed toward the ragged blanket on the floor while making an effort to hide below his waist with his hands. Galavon fell into the hay and pulled the blanket over his mid-section.

The young woman couldn't suppress a laugh. It made Galavon's face turn even more red in embarrassment. "Don't worry; I've already seen the rest of you. And if you were curious, you look just like every other man I've seen."

She walked to the table and set the basket down. "It's good you're feeling well enough to move around." She looked in the pitcher. "Even found the water I see. I imagine you're hungry, too. You've been living off water and honey."

The woman looked back to him, nodding approvingly as though convinced he was well enough to move around. "There's bread and cheese in the basket. If you think you can hold down a real meal, come down to the common room." The young woman turned and moved toward the door.

"Wait," Galavon said. His voice sound hoarse and little shaky. "Where am I? Who are you?"

"You're in the stables of the Riverbend Inn in Marcil. Mistress Dana rarely caters to your... friends... but everyone believed you were going to die. As for myself, I am Sama."

I'm in the shadow of Castle Conwy? We must have traveled further north than I thought.

"And my belongings?" he asked, though he feared the answer.

"Everything they left is in the corner. They took the horses." She turned toward the door. "Your strength should return quickly. I've seen some recover from your... affliction..." She grabbed the door knob and yanked the stubborn portal open.

"Wait, where did they go? What am I supposed to do?"

"I really must go." She curtsied in her bar maid's dress and exited the room.

Galavon wasted no time in getting to the basket. The breeze coming in was chilly without any clothes on, but he didn't care. He drank more of the water and tore a chunk out of the bread with his teeth. He was ravenous. Every bite seemed to strengthen his body.

After finishing the meager amount of food in the basket, he walked to the corner where his belongings were piled in a heap. Only one pair of clothes remained: a patched gray tunic, brown leggings and belt. They showed wear from the rough travel, but they were clean. His boots lay underneath the pile of clothing, and his pouch of coins, harp, and staff were beside those. He still wore the iron sun and moon pendant from his father.

Feeling vulnerable, Galavon first put on his leggings. He then inspected the pouch of coins his father had given him. Galavon remembered removing the silver and single gold mark, but he knew the pouch had been three times heavier than it was now. He looked inside to discover only copper pennies and a few copper lots.

So much for them being my friends. They stole most of my coin and left me to die in the stables of an inn. They probably left this for the innkeeper.

He sighed, thinking of the silver marks he had put in his baggage, all of which were gone with the rest of his clothes. He did a quick search of his boots and was pleased to find the gold mark still hidden there.

After finishing the pitcher of water, Galavon put his tunic, boots, and belt on. He strapped the harp on its frog and moved to the window. The free blowing breeze continued to swirl around him.

Looking out, Galavon had a good view of Marcil. He knew the town well, stopping at it on every trip of the Great Trade Circle. They usually stayed at an inn just under the walls of Conwy Castle. The King's Respite it was called, a richly decorated inn built for wealthy merchants passing through on the trade route.

The alley that ran under the window Galavon looked out of was small and had little traffic. It led to a much busier street at the end where Galavon could see a number of townspeople walking past to complete their daily chores. Hovering above the roofs across the busy street loomed Castle Conwy.

The castle was huge. It had eight enormous towers that rose from its stone walls to protect trade down the Southern Holy River. Though Galavon couldn't see it from his window, he knew the castle was built on an island complete with a bridge to connect it to the town.

Many castles that Galavon had seen, such as Bled Castle, Albrechtsburg, and Alcazar were built for war and beauty. Galavon had even heard that the castles Himeji and Matsuyama, built before Reproba Caelum with outlandish architecture, were as beautiful as they were martial. There was no denying the one strict purpose of Castle Conwy.

The castle was built when tension in the Fire Pass Province was high. The merchants and soldiers needed a safe way to Farrow, so Castle Conwy and another castle, Castle Almourol, were built to protect that passage. Attraction was not in the mind of the architect who designed the castle, only war, though the looming defensive structure did have its own sense of beauty.

Galavon's stomach rumbled again – the water and bread weren't enough. He turned from the window and went out the door. It led to an open second floor that looked out over an empty barn. A single ladder connected the ledge with the barn floor, and Galavon climbed down slowly, still not at full strength. Exiting the barn through its main doors into the bustling street, it wasn't hard to find the door to the inn. A sign with a curving blue line and a house marked the entrance to the Riverbend Inn.

The common room was as Galavon expected. There were a few patrons looking for a mid-day meal, but there were many open seats. A small stage was in the corner, and Galavon suspected they got a much larger crowd at night when their was someone entertaining.

He sat down apart from the rest and laid a copper lot on the table. In no time at all Sama walked up with a steaming bowl and laid it down in front of him.

"It's a cheesy trout soup, made with fish from the river, and cheese from the cows outside of town. Should be a potato or two in there as well. Hope you enjoy."

"Sama," Galavon started. He could hardly resist not diving into the soup – the smell of trout seemed to take away his ability to think. He lowered his voice. "Where is Ceridwen?"

Sama's smile disappeared in an instant. "Don't ever say that name here again!" she whispered in a harsh tone. "Do you want us all to end up as dinner for the Crows?" She looked around to see if anyone had noticed. They were all too far away to hear. Sama put a pleasant smile back on her face before curtsying and going on her way.

What have I gotten myself involved in?
Uneasy now, the soup didn't taste as good he thought it would. Still, he finished the bowl and sat in silence watching the others in the room. He felt awkward sitting alone. He wasn't sure what he should do or what was expected of him.

Mecca isn't too terribly far away, he thought. *I could always go to the mansion... and return as a failure. And eventually be arrested as a heretic.*

At a loss, Galavon rose from his chair to walk back to his room. At least there he wouldn't feel awkward sitting alone. As soon as he stepped into the street, a rough looking man grabbed him by the arm and whispered in his ear. "Keep quiet, seer, and follow me." The man dropped Galavon's arm and walked away through the crowd.

Normally Galavon's courage would have failed him, but when the man said "seer," there was a hint of respect there Galavon wasn't used to.

Galavon followed him down the bustling street and into an alley. They made turned into a smaller alley, hardly big enough for a person. The man he followed was forced to turn sideways. Little light found its way to the narrow passage, and worse, it smelled like a wet dog. The man disappeared in a door, and Galavon followed him inside.

The dimly lit room had only candles in the corners to light it. No windows decorated its sides, and there was only one other door besides the one Galavon came through. Crates were piled against the walls, and Galavon noticed rolls of fabric leaning in the corner.

Three others occupied the opposite side of the room, and all three wore a scarf across the lower half of their face. A man dressed in new, well-made cotton clothing sat in a chair between the others. Wrinkles were etched around his eyes. To his left hunched a woman with disheveled gray hair in a worn dress. The lines around her eyes were more numerous and deeply etched. To the right stood a boy that couldn't have seen half as many Twil as Galavon.

The older man nodded, and Galavon's guide exited back into the alley, taking the light from the open door with him. Only the flickering of the candles were left to brighten the room, casting shadows on the walls.

"You must be Galavon," the man said. "It's a pleasure to have you here." He repositioned the scarf around his face. The old woman glared, and the boy twiddled his thumbs.

"Ceridwen told us the stone accepted you, though from the state you were in when she brought you here, we all believed you would die." He reached into a pocket. "Here, you can have this now." He tossed something the size of a fist to Galavon. In the dim light it was difficult to see, and the object bounced off Galavon's fingers. It struck the floor with a thud. Galavon hoped they couldn't see him turn red. He bent down and picked up a large emerald. It didn't glow. "Many like to keep the stone as a keepsake."

The stone sickened Galavon. It wasn't a sign of accomplishment to him, but rather a reminder of his near death experience. "You keep it." He tossed it back. "I don't care to ever see it again."

The older man handed it to the boy. "I'm sorry that we must keep our identities hidden from you, but we must be careful. The Holy Order of the Black Wing are moving in mass further south, burning those who are not devout enough Followers as they go. Just yesterday they beat a man for threatening them with a look."

"How many of you are there?" Galavon asked. "Is there another seer I can learn from?"

"There was a meeting in the plains outside of Marcil," The man said. "Ceridwen was the last to make it. It was the largest meeting we've had in many Twil. There was one mage besides

Ceridwen, a druid, three sahagin, eight shaman and a dozen clerics."

Galavon didn't miss the fact that he didn't mention a seer.

"You've joined at an interesting time," the man continued. "Besides those of us here to keep an eye in Marcil, everyone rides south."

"What's happening south? My father is there." *And Anne.*

"That we can't say. For the time being you're to stay here. Rest, recover. From what I understand you traveled a great distance in a short amount of time. Rest will benefit you."

"Stay here? How long? Can any of you teach me Wind Magic?"

"We aren't sure how long, and well, Juliana, I mean, my friend here is a sahagin and can…"

"She can teach me no more than Ceridwen could." Galavon said, interrupting. "And where would she teach me? Here, in the storage room of a tailor's shop?"

The light of the candles reflected off of a bead of sweat on the man's face. "It's all we can do. We're all that's left in Marcil."

"And I could at least teach you some manners, boy," the old woman, Julianna Galavon guessed, snapped. She lifted a frail arm to point at him and her scarf fell from her face.

"And this isn't the only storage room we have, it's a big shop!" the boy said through his scarf. The man ran his fingers through his hair.

"You can't go traveling on your own. The Crows look for us everywhere. You're safe here in Marcil, and you will stay. That is final. If you wish to practice Wind Magic you may do so in here."

"Father, doest he even to be with the wind to use it?"

"Um, well, I'm not sure," the man said. "But…"

"I believe I'd be safer on my own," Galavon said. *No wonder they left them here. One has seen Twil more times than she can remember, one is too young, and the leader is a dunce.*

"You will be safer here, I assure you. We'll contact you when we find a safe place for your practice." He rose from his chair. "It has been a while since we've had a seer in our ranks. The stones are rare and finding someone outside of the Mountains of Hope to use one is even more rare. The seers there are protective of their stones and their magic." He stretched out a hand for a handshake.

The man's grip was weak, his skin soft. Galavon nodded to the others and left the room.

Galavon walked back to the inn's barn. His room was the same as he left it. The staff leaned up against the corner with the rest of his things. He touched the moon and sun pendant around his neck. It's touch reminded Galavon of everything he'd been through. He knew he couldn't stay in Marcil or go to Mecca. If he truly wanted to learn what it meant to be a seer, he needed to go to the Mountains of Hope. It was his best chance to make it back to Anne. Or even survive.

The road didn't always stay near the cliffs that looked out over the gulf, though Anne wished it did. Sometimes it would loop away and the great expanse of water that made up the Cliffside Gulf would disappear behind trees, but they never went so far that they lost the roaring of waves or the cries of gulls in the warm, salty air. More than once she saw small beaches below the cliffs, and more than once she asked if they could stop and spend a day at one of those sandy respites. But Captain Philial-boring-Marlowe only said that they must continue.

Anne pulled off a piece of a kerplum leaf she had snagged from a low hanging branch and tossed it out the back of the wagon. It fluttered for a second before falling to the dirt road. She ripped off another piece and did it again. The trip had begun with such excitement, but day after day, traveling soon grew boring. She threw the rest of the leaf off the back of the wagon at Porter, but it fell to the road before it hit him. He eyed her with confusion.

By now she knew the names of everyone in the party. They were pleasant enough, but there was only so much to say. Porter still refused to talk with her. For that matter, they all treated her a little different now that they knew she was a monk… well, a cleric.

That will take time to get used to. I guess all the monks will be considered clerics in our province if the Duke's plan works.

It was their uneasiness around the idea of someone other than a monk or priest using magic that kept Anne from practicing it on their trip to Castle Himeji. Isabella was an exception, but she was always kind and encouraging. The wagon hit a bump, and Anne bounced up before coming down hard on the wooden boards. It wasn't the first jolt of the journey, nor would it be the last.

The wagon came to a bend, and as they rounded the corner the gulf came back into view. It was a sheer drop off to churning water below filled with jagged rocks protruding from a foamy surface. Out on the water, however, was a sight she had not seen yet during the journey.

Three ships bobbed on the waves. One of them was a large bulky thing with a single square sail rising in the middle. It towered above the smaller vessels and looked to sink in the water hiding even more levels below.

The other two ships were long and sleek. They boasted a number of triangular sails, and could only be considered small when compared to the large blocky ship. All three were too far out to see much more detail, except that they all had black sails.

"Isabella, look at the ships!" Anne exclaimed, getting to her feet on the back of the wagon. She could feel the breeze from the gulf blowing her curly hair back. One strand landed in her mouth and she brushed it away. "I've never seen them with black sails. They're so far away, they look like toys." The wagon hit another rut in the road, and Anne had to steady herself in order to sit back down with any dignity.

The maid laughed, catching Anne's waist to help ease her down. "Aye, they be a sight, my lady."

"Hmmph," said one of the guards. "A terrible sight. Black sails mean pirates."

"Aye, and slavers," another put in. "They don't often be sailing ships that size – at least not along this coast, thanks to the Duke. Usually they sail off to the curators-know-where for 'em. They must smell trouble."

"Could you imagine being a pirate?" Anne asked. She fingered the black ribbon she wore in her hair. She continued to wear it every day. "Adventures to unknown lands, treasures, and sword fights."

"Ye mean death, dirt, and thievery," the first guard said. "Pirating be no job fer a pearl like you."

"Well," Anne replied, giving him a sideways look. "I wouldn't be that sort of pirate. Besides, if I had to fight against men like you for any loot, I'd stay away from these shores too."

That elicited a chuckle from the guard, and he hefted his heavy axe further up his shoulder. His grin seemed to take up his whole face.

Isabella smiled in approval at the compliment Anne gave to the guard. The woman leaned her head back against one of the satchels and closed her eyes.

Great. Bored again. Anne tapped her fingers against her knees in quick succession. She truly wished she could at least attempt some White Magic without spooking them. She eyed her things beneath the bench in the cart. There was a trunk and a bag, and though the bag was mostly soft and full of clothing, something stiff created a sharp edge. It was the book Larith had given her. This wasn't the first time she wanted to pull it out on the journey, but she worried about the others.

Maybe I'll just read it and not practice any spells.

Anne reached over and pulled the bag toward her. In no time she had the old book in her hands. She ran her fingers down the cover, smooth except for a few lines and bumps the old leather must have suffered from years of use and travel. The wagon lurched again, but Anne almost didn't notice as she unwound the cord that held the book closed and opened to the first page.

A diamond was drawn on the page. The top point had an "H" to mark it. The right a "B," the left a "C," and the bottom an "E." A circle was connected to the bottom of the diamond, and Anne saw the seven pointed Elemental Star drawn inside of it with all the elements Larith had taught her: fire, wind, black, water, earth, white, and dragon.

So the E stands for Elemental. That's easy enough, but there's three more. Does that mean there are three more types of magic?

Anne flipped the page and hoped to find out. This is where the text began. She recognized the script of the old nuncio.

Blood Magic

During my stay in Afrikaar, I moved across many kingdoms, starting in the powerful Sheba to the east before moving west across the war torn central kingdoms. Songhai, Kanem, and Fulani were a few of their names, though I'm not sure how long these struggling kingdoms will last.

There is a great difference between the wealthy and lower classes. Despite the ongoing wars, the wealthy are pampered by huge numbers of slaves with heritage from the Kingdom of East Ager, the Gold Desert, the Sauromation Jungle, and even bronze skinned folk from islands I've never seen on any map. Though they originate from all over Mundus, most are bred for beauty at slave farms. Young girls with pale skin and perfect teeth are the most expensive. They're the back bone of the economy, and I'm often reminded that though I may be free, the white color of my skin means I'll never be equal to these dark skinned people in their eyes. The poor often spend long days working fields in terribly harsh conditions.

I was given the rare opportunity to join a group of mercenaries in Ghana who were hired not to fight one of their never-ending wars, but to march into the Sauromation Jungle and put an end to a "blood band" that was raiding small towns along the outskirts of the jungle.

A "blood band" I was told, was a group of young women led by a witch doctor seeking to kill their first men. The tribes that roam the thick jungle live in matriarchal societies where only females fill the roles of warriors, chiefs, and spiritual leaders. They call their warriors

Amazons, and it is custom that they must kill a man before being allowed to give birth to a child of their own. These murders were the intention of the blood band, and by all reports, they were doing it well.

As interesting as this alien culture is, it was not my purpose to go with the band to further explore the roles of the Amazon warriors, or even the roles of their men who are rarely seen. Instead, I freely gave my skills as a cleric so that I may gain an understanding of the magic used by the witch-doctor. A witch-doctor is a sort of priestess to the tribes.

The group I was with was known as experienced Amazon hunters. They were successful in driving away the blood band, though I would say that killing two of the Amazon warriors and losing five men is less than success.

While I didn't have the opportunity to question the witch-doctor, the attack on their camp yielded certain items that granted a great store of information. They included a bronze sheet with words pounded into the metal, three dolls, a great number of candles, dried herbs and roots, several vials filled with oddities, and even a stiletto styled dagger. I quickly cast a clarity spell on the dagger and discovered its true name. "Alius."

"*Alius!*" she said out loud. One of the guards gave her a funny look.

That's my dagger! It did come from the Sauromation Jungle!

Anne thought about Larith's last words to her before she left Caernarfon Castle. "Its secret lies in its name," she whispered. She looked at the dagger thrust into her belt.

No magic here Anne, you need to keep some friends.

Sighing heavily and barely able to refrain from trying to use the stiletto, she continued reading the text.

The candles were all different colors, but my attention was drawn to the vials. They were filled with hair, blood, fingernails, and personal trinkets such as a brooch or a ring. The mercenaries I came with took these from me and had them destroyed. They claimed the witch-doctor used these to track and hex the blood band's targets.

The dolls were rudimentary things. They were made of straw and bits of old rag. These too were taken from me, but they were not destroyed as the vials were. Instead, the mercenaries handled them delicately. They searched the dolls carefully until they discovered a small pebble hidden amongst the straw. They then deftly removed it, trying to damage the doll as little as possible. Once the stone was removed, they set the doll on fire.

The sheet of bronze was a puzzle. I was unable to decipher all of the words that were beaten on its surface, but enough were revealed to understand its purpose. It was a ritual guide for a hex. The middle of the plate was domed, and it's safe to say this was the resting place for the contents of the vials. They were placed there for the witch doctor to practice their magic on their intended victim. I was sure not to leave any bits of hair or personal items in the jungle.

Though I didn't gather as much information from this journey as I had hoped, I did learn more about their magic than most who don't live in close proximity to the Sauromation Jungle. After piecing together my findings, I have to come to the following conclusions:

The magic used does not fall under the Elemental Magic star. It's something older, unique to this region. I shall call it by the name given to it by the people of Afrikaar – Blood Magic.

The magic is performed by a priestess known as a witch-doctor. They require a piece of their target, such as blood or hair, though personal trinkets like jewelry might work if their target has spent enough time with the item.

A ritual is required to cast a spell. They do not require specific stones to cast, nor do the effects happen instantly as spells do with Elemental Magic.

Judging by the small number of witch-doctors said to be with the Amazon tribes, the secrets of Blood Magic are heavily guarded. They seem to be an essential part of their culture. With the finding of the stiletto Alius, it is obvious they recognize the ability of other peoples to produce magic of their own. They're capable of putting aside their desire to remain hidden to trade for these magical items at a city known as Kampaia. I have been told by a few brave merchants who ventured there there that it is filled with great pyramids they use to worship their gods.

There was so much more of Mundus than just East Ager. The thought of witch-doctors and blood magic made Anne's imagination run wild. She forgot about the boring trip as she pictured the women warriors. Her mind wandered to adventures in the Sauromation Jungle, exploring all the way to the fabled city of Kampaia and the pyramids. She wondered how the matriarchal tribes would treat her since she wasn't a man. She flipped the page, ready for a new adventure.

Cosmos Magic

This is the third type of magic I came to discover, following Elemental Magic and Blood Magic. As I neared my sixtieth sighting of the shooting star Twil, I had gathered a great deal of information and become a mage, practicing a number of the Elemental Powers. The Elemental section will expand on these. I mention this to highlight the great amount of time and land covered before coming to this information. I had already seen each of the failing independent city-states, endured the heat and blowing sands of the Gold Desert, experienced the might of each of the cathedrals in the Kingdom of East Ager, collected exotic flowers from the Sauromation Jungle, watched the never ending wars in Afrikaar, walked through the cold emptiness of the White Desert, and even gazed upon the magnificent halls of the Dwarven Strongholds. Though each of these regions had a beauty and culture of their own, none of them prepared me for Twilight Laender, the home of the elves.

I was taken at the border by a group of elves who called themselves The Scouts. From there I was blindfolded and taken to their capital, the Crescent City.

The city is a forest. It's a common misconception that the elves build their homes in the trees, but this is not true. They build alongside the trees, mimicking their grace to fit in as though they a part of the forest.

Each "building," for lack of a better term, is in the shape of the great trees they live beside. The trees rise high into the sky, taller even than the white oaks of the Mountain Province in East Ager. They're complete with leaves, vines, and flowers, which the elves somehow grow out of the "buildings." Walkways span from one "building" to another to create streets above the forest floor, whether grown or built I'm not sure. Thin archways of interlacing branches decorate these walkways. There are no sharp turns or rigid edges. Everything melds together as though shaped in nature.

No sort of waste can be found littering the city, hardly any d irt at all is noticeable on the walkways. Canals act as their streets on the forest floor, with cobblestone walkways along their sides around the bases of the trees. Bridges of thin branches and natural beauty span the canals constantly. Long boats with high prows crafted in the shapes of exotic creatures are poled through these canals, each of the elvish boat masters able to control them with a grace that matches the city's splendor.

The city sits beside Moon Lake, which feeds the great river that flows through the Sauromation Jungle. By simply being allowed to view the city, I was given a great honor.

I was escorted at all times and kept from visiting many of the larger, grander buildings closer to the lake. The elves were kind and gracious hosts in their own secretive fashion.

They're a race that is of a similar height to humans. They're more agile and infinitely more patient. Their eyes are all a deep purple, and their ears are pointy things that rise nearly above the tops of their heads. No freckles or moles mar their pale skin. They hold their chins high and look down on other races. I put this aside and learned what I could.

A council of elves I never saw answered my questions. My guide of the city, Dahareuch, was a member of The Scouts who took me at the border. He referred to this council as the Elders. Each question had to be submitted in writing, and I was given a written response. After questions of a personal nature that dealt with my past, I asked of the elves' history.

They had traveled to Mundus from a land across the Barren Ocean. In their old home they had been more numerous and built cities that put this one to shame. The origin of their home and how it was lost to them was not surrendered to me. They arrived over a thousand years ago to find this "New Land" already populated by diverse races. As elves, they live long life spans but rarely have children, creating a slow expansion in this new world.

They were familiar with Elemental Magic before arriving, however, they see it as a lesser magic. The Elves claim to be able to heal better, produce more potent magical items, and control more power. They call it Cosmos Magic, though they sometimes refer to it as High Magic. No other race that I am aware of can use it.

They revealed little, offering only enough to gain an idea of how Cosmos Magic works. During the day they use the power of the sun, and at night they use the stars and the moon. They spells they cast depend on the source of the power. This restriction makes me think less of Cosmos Magic, but the secrecy behind it and the limited answers I received hint that it is capable of much more.

The following conclusions can be drawn about Cosmos Magic:

It is a type of magic used only by the elves. They draw upon the heavens above to fuel their power: sunlight during the day and moonlight and starlight during the night. They claim to be able to accomplish all the things of Elemental Magic, though what I learned of the art revealed no such abilities. Its secrets are well protected, even more so than those of Blood Magic.

Anne looked out the wagon to the west where the sun came closer and closer to the water with every passing moment. The brightness of it would not let her stare directly at it, but she closed her eyes and let its warmth wash over her face.

The power of the sun harnessed into a spell. Anne wasn't sure what the stars and moon could offer, but everyone knew the power of the sun in the Peninsula Province. Though the sun felt warm now, it was the start of the cold season, and its intense heat had the power to kill during the hot summers.

Cosmos Magic. Elves. So much more than just the Kingdom of East Ager.

Anne flipped to the next chapter, a single page.

Holy Magic

> *The last of the four I learned from the Elves as well. They claimed there was another, more rare magic. Holy Magic cannot be learned or taught. No rituals are required, no words, nor a source of power. The Elves say that once every thousand years somewhere a being is born with the blessing of the Creator. As they grow older, their power grows stronger. They're able to watch events from a great distance, see the future, read minds, and eventually at the height of their power control the emotions of others. They call this person an Oracle.*

The entry ended suddenly, far shorter than the other two. It was the only thing written about Holy Magic. Anne glanced at the next page and saw Elemental Magic written at its top. That section seemed to cover most of the book. It would cover magic Larith was familiar with, magic he knew and used regularly.

"We stop here. We're not far from Himeji."

Isabella opened her eyes and smiled at Anne lazily. The cart came to a halt and the woman sat up and stretched. "Come, let's get yer things settled fer camp. It will be nice fer both of us to 'ave a good stretch."

Chapter 9
(Anne, Galavon)

The coast around Castle Himeji was much different than the coast around Caernarfon Castle. Instead of cliffs, the land gently sloped downward to meet the Southern Ocean. Where land and water came together, thin strips of sandy white beaches were formed. They were littered with shells that hid beautiful pink interiors, scuttling hermit crabs, round sand marks complete with the Reproba Caelum star, small black pods her father had claimed were mermaid's purses, and many more treasures from the sea. Seagulls flew overhead calling out, and the ocean bellowed out a rough song with every wave that crashed on the shore.

Anne wasn't allowed outside the castle without an armed guard. There were more tales of pirate ships along the coast than just the three that Anne's party had seen. The guards said it was because the pirates knew trouble was stirring in the province. Porter Mann was entrusted to keep guard over Anne while she sat on the beach within sight of Castle Himeji's white walls. He kept his distance from her and tried to emulate Captain Philial's vigilance.

What would Porter Mann do if pirates attacked us? Anne giggled. The young soldier would likely flee. *It's not like there are any pirate ships in sight anyways.*

Castle Himeji and Castle Matsuyama resembled no other castle in all of the Kingdom of East Ager. They were built before the influence of Reproba Caelum came so far south. Anne was used to their architecture, having traveled all over the Peninsula Province so her family could be feasted by this Duke or that Count, but Castle Himeji still took her breath away whenever she saw it.

The people called it the "White Heron." The castle rose from the top of a hill, and was comprised of a main keep of 6 floors and a basement, as well as having three smaller towers. The walls and bottom part of the buildings inside were stone, but as the structures rose into the air they were painted white. The roofs sloped downward in a steep descent, but at the tip they rose again, giving the buildings a proud look.

Anne felt safe in the castle. It was filled with the Duchess' men. The castle was far too strong for pirates to attack, and even the goblins avoided fighting beneath its walls during the War of Fire.

Duchess Hamilton, or the Lady Ayn as many called the powerful woman, was a much different woman than Lady Ignava or Duke Briel's wife, Duchess Dara. Lady Ayn was strong willed, one who did not have to command respect or obedience. It was freely given. She was the only child of her father who had been Duke of Castle Himeji. She had been married three times in her life, one of her husbands succumbing to a disease the monks were unable to heal, one dying to pirates, and the last perishing in the War of Fire. When Lady Ayn was not parading her sons in front of Anne, the Duchess talked with her about White Magic.

Anne must have shown her the globe of light a dozen times in the privacy of Lady Ayn's own chambers. The Duchess said the time was not yet right to discuss Anne's abilities openly, especially with the number of monks in the castle. Lady Ayn was hungry for the knowledge though, Anne could see it, and Anne wondered how long it would be until the Duchess procured her own pearl.

Anne was able to learn about her brother, Cecil. An exhausted rider had ridden all the way to Castle Himeji. He had gone the normal, faster route, passing through Asaph and by the Cathedral of New Beginnings.

There had been a trial. Well, what passed as a trial. The priests of the Fire Pass Cathedral had accused Tarik Ziyad of being a traitor and a heretic, plotting the assassination of their high priest. They had also accused Cecil and the two Lieutenant commanders, Varro and Paulus, as having plotted with him.

Somehow, Cecil evaded being found guilty, though they found their father Tarik guilty of all charges and stripped her family of their noble title. Cecil would not become the next Constable, and they lost all of their property except for the small manse outside of Pearl.

But I don't care, Anne thought. *I just want my brother back. Safe.*

There were also reports of numerous attempts on Cecil's life, and a strange attack on the Army of Truth by a horde of trolls as they passed through the Fire Pass Province on their way home. Cecil survived it all still, and marched south with the army to the Cathedral of New Beginnings to see who would be named the next Constable by High Priest Denis.

Though Anne was scared of losing her brother, she knew if he could just make it to Pearl and meet with Duke Briel, everything would be all right. He would join with the rebels and be safe from Reproba Caelum. She would be safe from Reproba

Caelum. There would be no more need for this secrecy that kept Anne from using magic openly.

But even with the need for secrecy, Lady Ayn supported Anne's desire to grow stronger with White Magic. It was unfortunate she couldn't talk to the monks, but that was why Anne was sent to this particular beach, far from prying eyes. Well, away from all eyes but Porter's. She had to practice so she could help her brother and Duke Briel take the Peninsula Province from the curators and their priests.

It was the perfect sunny day to practice. Anne stripped her shoes off her feet and dug her toes into the sand. She pulled out the leather book and rubbed its brown cover before opening it to the first chapter on Elemental Magic.

Elemental Magic

Elemental Magic, the New Magic as the elves call it, is the primary magic used in Mundus. While they call it the New Magic, it's just as old as the others. It's comprised of fire, wind, black, water, earth, white, and dragon, each listed in order as they appear on the Elemental Star. The first three, the right side of the star, are Wayward elements. The second three, the left side of the star, are Tame elements, each directly across from its opposite on the star. Dragon has no opposite. Wayward and Tame Elements should not be mixed unless it is with their opposite, as opposites are attracted.

Ugh, ok Larith, I know this stuff. Get to the spells!

The individual Elemental Magics are most commonly used by themselves, though they can be combined if the user is trained in two or more of the Elemental Magics. When Wayward and Tame Elements are combined, the resulting spell is difficult to control. This is why it should only be done if the caster believes their abilities are strong. Those wield more than one type of Elemental Magic are called mages. Each of the elements will be discussed individually, as well as hybrid combinations. First, however, I shall explain the source of Elemental Magic.

Dragons embody the power of an individual element. Every dragon is a female. Every wyvern is a male. Once every hundred years the wyverns go through courting rituals and mate with the dragons, each in their own unique fashion. If another female is hatched, the elder dragon will battle it as soon as it reaches maturity. It takes many Twil for a dragon to reach maturity. The eldest nearly always wins, unless the dragon is very, very old. In my travels, I have discovered that none of the current dragons have seen less than 2,000 Twil. Shiva is the oldest, and though her exact age is unknown, I estimate she has seen over 6,000 Twil. There has never been more than one mature dragon of any elements for longer than a few Twil in recorded history, written or oral.

Wyverns are powerful elemental creatures in their own right. Though they may not "use" magic as we do, they also embody the qualities of the element they are related to. In rare instances, a caster may use a spell unique to each element to forge their soul with that of a wyvern. This is atypical due to the many requirements that must be met: a spell must be cast, the wyvern must deem the caster worthy, and both the wyvern and the caster must be near death.

The men and women who achieve this feat are called summoners. They are shunned by most societies as abominations. Reproba Caelum has labeled them as heretics.

A summoner? Anne had heard the name before. In fact, she was sure one was executed by the priests at the Cathedral of New Beginnings a few Twil ago, before the War of Fire. It was the first time Anne had encountered the Holy Order of the Black Wing and the Holy Order of the White Wing, both of which sent representatives to see the summoner destroyed. Summoners were rare, and his destruction brought a huge swathe of those loyal to Reproba Caelum. Anne flipped the page and was greeted with only more script. She flipped again, and again, until the words "White Magic" graced the top of a page.

White Magic can be...

Anne turned the page. *I'll come back and read these...*

The casters are called...

She flipped another page.

Subluceo – A simple spell that summons a globe of light under the caster's control. Must be wary of putting...

Finally, the good stuff. Another page flip.

Aperio – A simple spell that summons the true name of a magical item. Often referred to as a clarity spell. The caster must recite the spell while hovering their hand over the item, never touching. The caster must also imagine the item slightly vibrating to give it a voice. Must be wary, as always, of letting too much White Magic flow into the *item, or it will shatter. A relatively simple spell that most beginning cleric's do not attempt due to the chance of losing the magical item.*

Anne placed the book down. She withdrew *Alius* from her waist cinch and placed it on top of the book.

It'll be fine, she thought. *The book says it's a simple spell.* The last sentence of the page echoed in her mind. Still, she hovered a hand over the stiletto and took a deep breath.

"*Aperio,*" she said, picturing the dagger vibrate. Nothing happened. She didn't feel the power swell up inside her, she didn't see the dagger vibrate, and she didn't hear a name.

"*Aperio,*" Anne said again. Nothing.

"Aperia, Aporio, Apopo…" Nothing. A seagull cried out, mocking her failed attempts. Anne glared at the bird, but she knew it wasn't the bird's fault. It flew low, this time right by Porter Mann, who was still looking out along the shoreline as though a gang of pirates might attack at any second.

Anne reached down and grabbed the dagger. *Maybe this will work at least. I already know its name.*

"*Alius,*" she said staring at the stiletto. Nothing. "*Alius,*" she said again, closing her eyes and focusing on the dagger in her hand. She could feel its weight, uneven due to the long, thin blade, and the edges of the twisted metal handle rubbing against her palm. And then she felt… a tingling sensation.

A flash of green brightened the area, followed soon after by a white one. Another form materialized in front of her, and she felt an odd link, like a cord, connecting the two. It was as though she was staring in two mirrors at the same time. Both girls wore a light blue, loose-fitting silk chemise with a dark brown waist cinch and a white underskirt. All four feet were bare and covered with sand. Anne stared at her own crystal-blue eyes. The only thing that wasn't the same was her hair. The curls on one blew behind her, billowing in the wind with the black ribbon, the curls on the other blew in her face, the black ribbon dancing loosely.

Though they looked the same, Anne could feel the difference between the two. One felt weightless. It reminded her of a cloud. Her real body felt solid. It was confusing looking through two sets of eyes, hearing the waves with two sets of ears. It was disconcerting, but Anne shook away the dizziness and reached out with her real body and touched the cheek of the illusion.

It was an odd sensation touching her own cheek. It felt like skin to her real hand, but on the cheek of her illusion, it felt... clammy. Cold. Unreal.

Anne tried to raise the hand of her second body, but instead raised the hand of her real body again.

This is going to take a lot of practice.

She had to concentrate hard to move the second body and not her own, but she managed first to raise a hand. Then take a step. And another. The dizziness faded soon after she was no longer looking at herself, but it was still difficult to comprehend what body was sensing what. Anne tried to run. Her second form ran stiffly, but it did run, though somewhat slow. She could see through its eyes and feel the wind whipping her back.

"Come on Porter!" she made herself cry from the second body. Her voice sounded different than she thought it did. "Hurry!" Illusion Anne ran past the young soldier.

"What?" Porter said confused. "What's wrong? Where are we going?" He took off after the illusion, and though he ran somewhat more fluidly, his brigandine armor, spear, and shield slowed him down. "Wait, Anne! What's going on?"

"Over here, Porter!" Anne called from her real body. She jumped up and down waving a hand in the air. "Over here!"

Porter turned and Anne doubled over in the sand laughing. The young soldier's face was a mixture of confusion and fright. He looked from one to the other, both giggling hysterically in the sand, Anne unable to stop the l aughter from reaching the illusion. Porter's eyes were the size of a silver mark as he looked first at one and then the other.

"Anne? Wh-what's going?" he stuttered. "What have you done?"

Anne stood up wiping tears from her eyes. She focused on the odd connection, and somehow, she severed it with a thought. The illusion disappeared, and once again Anne could only see through two eyes, smell through one nose, and listen through two ears. *Alius* felt cold in her hand.

"You should have seen your face, Porter!" Anne laughed.

The soldier turned red with embarrassment. "So there's nothing wrong? That was just... magic?"

"Yes, Porter," Anne said. "It was just me. I'm still the same girl you grew up with." He gripped the spear haft tight and nodded.

"Come on, what do you say we go back in for the mid-day meal. I know Lady Ayn will want to see us." She replaced *Alius* in her waist cinch and retrieved her book before skipping to Porter and grabbing his free hand. His eyes grew huge. "Now tell me all about this girl in Caernarfon Castle."

"Well, uh, you mean..."

"Of course! The serving girl with the beautiful hair! I saw you two when we were leaving, trading kisses in the dark. Porter Mann, I never thought…"

They walked back to the castle through the maze of walls that defended the entrance. Though Anne asked Porter questions about his girl, she still managed to do most of the talking as they wound their way around one corner and the next.

The black ribbon she wore fell in her face, and Anne brushed it aside, her pearl necklace bouncing on her chest.

Galavon wasted no time returning to his room in the Riverbend Inn's stable. It was small, smelled of dust and horse, the furniture was splintered, and the air was stagnant. He went to the corner and packed his meager belongings into the satchel. With the bag on his back and his staff in hand, he left the stable and turned onto the busy street with Castle Conwy looming above.

Having been in Marcil before, it wasn't difficult for Galavon to find his way to the market. There farmers and fishermen sold their wares to the townspeople, though there wasn't much of a crowd or many stalls. Once there, he swung into a tailor's shop for a cheap, woolen cloak. It was drab brown and itchy, but just walking in the town reminded Galavon it was the start of the cold season, and he was farther north than he used to be.

It wasn't difficult to find what he needed in the market. A red-faced farmer sold him apples, dried meat, and cheese. A shrewd little woman forced the rest of his coppers out of him to buy four wineskins, one full. He would have bought more, but he knew none of these folk would be able to provide change for a gold mark, and if they knew he had it, he'd be robbed. He filled up his three empty skins with water from the public fountain.

These small towns need a bank, Galavon thought. Gold was no good when you couldn't use it for the things you needed. He considered buying a horse, since Ceridwen had stolen Kid, but he didn't know the difference between a horse worth its own weight in silver or a horse barely worth a copper lot. Not to mention, as demonstrated, he wasn't the best rider.

Of course Ceridwen would take my horse. Poor Kid.

Not bothering to go back to the Riverbend Inn, Galavon left the town and walked west along a dirt road for the remainder of the day. The Mountains of Hope rose in that direction, hazy due to the distance. Galavon wasn't used to walking so far, and it didn't take long for his feet to get sore. Still , he kept walking, and his strength returned as though he'd never been sick at all.

Farms were situated along both sides of the road. They were large structures, often times with young boys on the rooftops with horns watching cattle in close pastures. Galavon knew that when a son got married in these farms they simply built on to the structure for him and his bride. This created sprawling farmhouses of different shapes and sizes.

Night came as the plains opened up before him, and the farmhouses grew further apart. Now the boys on the roofs were replaced with men hold short bows. The sight didn't make Galavon feel any better traveling alone. His thoughts drifted toward manticores and trolls. He thought about turning for the last farmhouse he saw, but a light breeze pushed at his back giving him encouragement, though it had a slight chill to it. Galavon was grateful for his cloak. Luckily the stars shone bright and the sky was clear of clouds. Every sound he heard made him step faster, and he knew he wouldn't be able to sleep even if he stopped.

When the sun rose from behind him, painting the grasslands gold, Galavon was unable to take another step. His eyelids drooped, and his feet felt as though he had walked with rocks in his boots. Looking around off the road, Galavon could see no spot that looked better than any other. So, finally, he wandered into the tall grass and slept curled up in a ball using his satchel as a pillow and his itchy cloak as a blanket. Laying his head down, he saw the tops of the grass bend around him from the wind. *Maybe something is watching out for me.*

The nap was short due to the sun, the hard ground, and Galavon's uneasiness. He lifted his head above the grass and looked back where he had walked from, still only seeing the loneliness of the plains. A small flock of sheep roamed back along the road, but no shepherd stood watch over them. Galavon brushed his hair away from his eyes, the breeze ruffling it as usual.

Stay in Marcil and rest until they return. Why had that sounded so bad?

He turned his head west, the direction he was traveling, and he saw the mountains. He must have traveled far in the night. They still loomed in the distance, but now they looked huge, as though Galavon might actually reach them.

The nap was poor, but it revived him enough to continue pushing through the rest of the day. He passed small houses with fenced in pastures, but these seemed mostly empty and were far apart. Likely the herders had taken their cattle or sheep into the grasslands to graze.

The road climbed to the top of a low hill, and Galavon scanned the plains. To the south he saw his first manticore standing over the corpse of a dead cow. The giant stinger that dangled over its red mane frightened Galavon into a run, the wind at his back as though pushing. The creature looked like an overgrown cat with a scorpion's tail and fluffy mane. He hoped the monster didn't see him. They were known for being aggressive.

Out of breath from his run, Galavon looked up at the sun and hoped night wouldn't come any time soon. He knew he wouldn't be able sleep, especially not after seeing the manticore. He sat down on a large rock to recover and eat some of his poor rations.

Unable to sleep, Galavon walked through the night. He considered himself lucky not to have to suffer through bad weather, but the long walk with little rest began to take its toll. He fell asleep before morning and woke after the sun rose high into the sky. The road came to an end, fading into the grassland, but still Galavon continued, all the while staring up at the peaks ahead. At the end of that afternoon, he finally reached the mountains.

The Mountains of Hope ran north and south, but a small chain of low peaks reached out close to Marcil. The grassland became more rocky the further he traveled, until he came to the foot of the mountains. They were rigid and steep, with huge boulders strewn around the base. Galavon could see no clear way to travel deeper.

Exhausted, Galavon sat with his back against one of the boulders. He reached for a skin but found it empty. That meant he only had the wine left. His food was beginning to run low too. His adventure was looking like a disaster.

Ever since I was given a little responsibility, I've only fallen further and further.

A cool wind blew. It was never cold enough to make him shiver, just enough to let him know it was there. It blew his hair around and caressed his cheeks. It was his constant companion, and though it wasn't the sort of companion Galavon wanted, he accepted the friend gladly. A particularly strong gust pushed his harp away and then back against his leg in rapid succession.

"I've nothing else to do." Galavon reached for the old harp he carried with him. He plucked a string or two, testing the sound. Unhappy with it, he turned the broken tuning pegs the best he was able. He started a simple tune.

"The wind blows through the branches of trees,
Alongside mountains, fast and free.
It fills the sails of traveling ships
Riding the waves with each rise and dip.
It blows by fast, so listen close,
Wind always sees and hears the most."

The wind slowed down once Galavon finished. The short song reminded him of his mother and helped him feel at ease. His heavy eyelids closed and he drifted into sleep deep in the shadows of the Mountains of Hope.

He was woken by the sharp, piercing cry of a beast.

Startled, Galavon got to his feet and grabbed his staff. His cloak fell to the ground beside his empty wineskins and satchel. He scanned the fields before him and looked up at the mountains, but he couldn't find what made the sound.

"You grab the staff first. Interesting." A man looked down at him from one of the lower ledges of the mountain. The face was hidden by a hood and a leather mask painted to look like it had scales, but two reptilian green eyes stared back, long thin pupils in a sea of green. He jumped off the ledge, and just as he neared the ground, he called out.

"*Lente.*"

Wind flew past Galavon and created a cushion below the man, slowing his descent. Despite the help of the wind, the man rolled out of the fall as though he didn't know if his jump would be cushioned or not.

Silver scales with a hint of green created a cuirass that covered the top of the man's chest and back, leaving the lower part of his abdomen unarmored. It looked old and well used. The hood didn't come from a cloak, but rather from a sleeveless tunic worn underneath the cuirass. Grey straps wrapped around his well-muscled forearms, which were also covered in scars. On his hands were fingerless gloves with brass knuckles. Loose leather pants with more scales on the thighs and calves, as well as worn leather boots, finished off his attire.

He looked hard and dangerous.

"Who are you?" Galavon asked tightening his grip on the staff. He didn't think it would be of any use if the stranger decided to attack him. He stepped back until he was against the rock wall.

The man nodded to Galavon's harp. "The wind brought me to you. I assume you're a seer?"

Galavon hesitated before speaking. "Well, yes. I suppose."

Another shriek pierced the air, this time echoed by more cries.

"We don't have much time." The strange man brushed Galavon's staff aside and grabbed his tunic. He pulled Galavon away from the face of the cliff.

"What are you doing?" Galavon asked. He tried to pull free, but it only caused him to stumble.

He swung Galavon around to face him and spoke quickly in a gruff voice. "My name is Myson, and I'm also a seer. I found you because the wind brought your song to me. It so happens that it also brought the song to the ears of a green wyvern I was about to save from a pack of red wyverns. You pulled him away from his course toward me, so now you must help me save him. Follow me and on three, we jump. Come!"

Myson turned toward the cliff and kept his grip tight on Galavon's tunic. He sprinted toward the steep cliff with Galavon in tow. Galavon tried to keep his feet under him, but Myson's grip on his tunic was the only thing that kept him from falling.

"One, two, three! *Tripudio!*"

Myson jumped in the air and Galavon stumbled forward. Nothing happened though, and the pair ran straight into the rock wall.

Galavon rubbed the top of his head and shoulder. Myson showed no frustration or pain.

"It's the same with all you seers chosen away from the mountain. You're like hatchlings. We're trying again," he said. "This time jump. And say *tripudio*." He yanked Galavon from the ground and walked him away from the cliff.

"What was the word? Tripoduo?" Galavon asked.

"*Tripudio*. Now run!" The pair ran at the wall again, this time at full speed. "One, two, three!" The pair leapt as high as they could, Myson still keeping a firm grip on Galavon's tunic.

"Tripudio!" they both cried out. The familiar tingle in Galavon's chest flowed out with the word.

The wind rushed in from all sides and swelled beneath the pair. It pushed upwards with great force and their jump extended. The low ledge they jumped toward came closer and closer, but Galavon could feel his ascent slowing.

He reached out with a foot to the edge, but it only skimmed the top. His attempt sent a shower of pebbles dancing down to the bottom, and Galavon could feel his body starting to fall.

"No, no, no, no, no," he said in rapid succession. He struck out with his other foot, but only the toes of his boot made it to the edge. His tunic went taut and Myson hauled him the rest of the way.

"Focus on moving forward, not up next time." Galavon was breathing heavily, his eyes big. "That's about the highest you can jump with the spell. You wouldn't have died from a fall at this distance, but you can still break a leg if you don't land right. Now quickly, they'll be flying in from the north and we need a better position."

Myson took off again, leaving Galavon to follow behind. The man never lost his footing leaping over the boulders and small chasms. There was only one more instance where the pair had to use the spell *tripudio,* and it was much lower than Galavon's first attempt. At last they came to a crater, forming a small valley of pebbles and rocks.

"They'll come through here. Use *corruo* to bring down the first big red you see, I'll take care of any others."

"Bring down what? A big red? *Corruo?*" Galavon whispered. His tone was frantic. "What do I do then?"

Myson punched his fists together twice and then held them up at chest level. "We train to use our fists as focal points for our spells. I see you have a staff. You're a seer. Use them together to..." Myson was cut short by a loud cry from above. The wyverns were getting closer.

"What if my spell doesn't cast?" Galavon could feel sweat gathering under his arms. The fight against the Albus Venificus was nothing. He was about to fight wyverns.

"You're protecting the wind's own get – it'll do as you ask. More often than not, at least." Another cry pierced the air, and the green wyvern became visible above.

The green wyvern was nearly the same jade color as Galavon's old emerald, only a little lighter. His torso was the size of three Chargers, his entire body as long as two of the river boats used to haul goods along the Holy River.

Right behind flew the first of the red wyverns Myson called 'big reds.' It was larger than the green, though not quite as long, and its wings were shorter. Galavon couldn't imagine it ever catching up with the green in front.

"Pull it down! Now!"

"*Corruo!*" Galavon said.

Nothing happened. Two more big reds appeared behind the first.

"*Corruo!*" Myson yelled, his deep voice filling the crater in front of them. Galavon watched in wonder as the first red plummeted downwards, its wings flapping limp above its body as though a hammer were pushing it down.

I messed up again. With his failed attempt at the new spell, Galavon turned to Myson for guidance.

The man stood tall beside him with his arms spread wide. The hood was pulled back, hanging limp behind his back plate.

Small scales covered the back half of his bald head, and instead of ears he had small holes like a lizard. He held the leather mask in one hand, revealing more scales that lined the bottom of his eyes and the top of his nose. He looked half dragon.

"*Voco Zoe!*" Myson called out. "Protect your kind!"

A jade mist in the shape of a green wyvern sprung from Myson's chest. First the head came out, followed quickly by the long neck, body, and tail. The man's eyes went wide and his arms stretched out even further. The veins on the visible part of his arms bulged as though they were going to pop. The wyvern shade quickly took a corporeal form upon exiting and flew toward the second of the big reds.

Myson jerked forward and fell to one knee. He sucked in air before returning Galavon's stare. The scales were gone beneath his eyes, replaced with the smooth skin of a human. His ears had returned, and he looked normal. A crash sounded on the other side of the crater as the first red wyvern smashed into the ground with a resounding thud. "Time to kill a big red," Myson said. He jumped back to his feet and went into a sprint toward the fallen wyvern.

Now that the beast was closer, Galavon could see it clearly. It truly was huge. Its skin was a multitude of overlapping crimson scales. Tall spikes ran down its neck all the way to the tip of its tail. Two spiraling horns grew from the top of its head, just above rows of teeth the size of daggers. None of this deterred Myson from charging the dazed creature.

Galavon looked back toward the sky and saw the beast that came from Myson pummel into the second big red. They crashed together in a tangle of talons and teeth. Flames shot out of the red wyvern's mouth as they plummeted to the ground in a rolling ball.

The green wyvern being chased turned to confront the last of the red wyverns. The big red unleashed a mouthful of flames in its direction, but the lithe green used its spade-shaped tail to dart underneath the blast. Rather than having the spiraling spikes of the red wyverns, two straight spikes grew back toward the green's neck. Its face was more pointed than that of the red's as well. Where one looked deadly, the other looked graceful.

Galavon could see, however, that the left wing was blackened. It was a scorch mark, and that must have been how the reds managed to keep up.

Another boom sounded, and Galavon turned to see Myson's green and the red wyvern he attacked crash into the cliffs amongst a shower of rocks and pebbles. They fell from view behind a large outcropping, and Galavon turned his eyes back to the fight above.

The big red mostly lashed out with its tail, equipped with more spikes, every now then attempting to bite at the darting green. He hung motionless while the other wyvern zipped around him, snapping at all sides. The red was nearly twice his size.

A roar sounded across the crater, and Galavon saw Myson closing in on the wounded red. The wyvern blew a blast of fire toward him, but Myson jumped away into a roll, dodging the blast. Coming out of the roll on his feet, he yelled *"Brevis"* loud enough for Galavon to hear and punched out toward the creature, once, twice, three times. Green flashes hit the red square in the face, knocking him back. The big red got on its two feet and roared in protest. He jumped back in the sky and flew away, rocking as though he sat too long at a tavern.

Looking back at the pair in the sky, Galavon saw the big red lash out with his tail at the green again, but this time, a spike sunk deep into the side of his torso. The green wyvern bit down hard his opponents tail, and together they fell from the sky. The red tried to stay airborne, but the green wyvern weighed too much. They hit the ground with a crash in the middle of the crater, the green wyvern on bottom. The red pulled its long neck around and bit down on the green's back.

Galavon rushed toward the pair. He looked at the red's head and swung his staff in that direction. *"Brevis!"* he yelled out.

He felt power in his voice coming from his lungs. Wind circled around his arms and moved to his staff, where it projected out in a slash of wind. The strike covered the distance quickly, knocking back the red wyvern's head. The creature snarled and leapt to its feet, ripping its tail free of the downed green's jaws. Galavon tried the attack again, but no wind accompanied his strike.

"Back! Get back!" Galavon heard from behind him. He came to a stop.

The red wyvern drew in a deep breath before stretching its long neck forward and blowing a blast of fire in Galavon's direction. His vision turned red in the swirling mass. It raced toward him, threatening to devour him.

I'm going to die.

"Minimus Parietis!" The flames directly in front of him slowed down, and those along the side raced past. It gave Galavon enough time to duck and hide his face behind his arms and meager cloak before the slowed flames washed over him.

The pain only lasted a second, but the fire continued to burn for many more. Flames ripped away at his skin like a hungry animal. He couldn't stretch the muscles on his arm because his skin hardened to a black crisp. His tunic burned away in an instant. When the flames stopped, Galavon fell to the ground facing the red wyvern.

It let out a final roar before it jumped back into the sky and flew away. Blood dripped as it made its wobbly flight.

From his angle on the ground Galavon could see the downed green wyvern clearly. Its scales were a beautiful jade, though blood flowed from the wound on its side and made some of them a shiny crimson color. Many of the scales were missing from its neck where the big red must have dug his talons in to try and dislodge the creature. The green wyvern's teeth were bloody too, a testament of its own success in wounding the red. Its big eyes stared back at Galavon's charred form.

Myson raced to Galavon's side. "Can you hear me? Are you still alive?"

Galavon nodded meekly. The world was beginning to fade from view.

"Listen to me. Repeat my words, but direct them to the wyvern. *Veho Affatus Unus.*"

Galavon tried to repeat the words, but no air would come out of his throat.

"To Shiva's own prison with you! Say the words!"

A soft thud sounded behind. This green wyvern was the size of one of the big reds, a giant compared to the dying green in front of Galavon. His hide was marred with claw marks as well, and scars decorated his pointed face.

"Say them!"

"Veho Affatus Unus," Galavon whispered. He felt the familiar sensation of the wind carry his words. The green sparkles flew through the air, where, Galavon could not tell before they blinked away.

"Do you hear anything? Are you there? Do you hear anything?"

Myson's words faded. The brown and gray cliffs became blurred, as did the blue sky above. Galavon only had his thoughts.

Good-bye Mundus. Perhaps the curators will forgive me. I wish I could've seen Anne once more. Just another failure.

A gruff, primal voice disrupted his thoughts. *"Veho Affatus Unus, Rorrik."*

Chapter 10
(Sheik, Sao)

Sheik Nasseri stretched out the miniature hands of a child up toward a shelf in the kitchen. There, just out of reach, sat a ceramic jar in the shape of a squirrel. Sheik knew inside were dozens of gingerbreads baked earlier in the day. Just the thought of them made his mouth water, and he could still taste the two or three he had been allowed.

"Darla," he said. His voice had the sweet sound of a child's. "I can't reach the gingerbreads."

Across the kitchen a skinny maid scrubbed hard at pots and pans. She was covered in grease up to her pale elbows and somehow managed to get some on her forehead as well. She had brown, stringy hair and a warm smile. She turned from the soapy water and directed one of those smiles toward Sheik.

"Little Master, you've already had some today. Lady Nasseri asked me not to give you anymore."

"But I want them."

"After dinner, little one." She turned back to the pots and focused on an especially stingy bit of grease.

Sheik continued to reach upwards, all the way on his tip-toes. His little fingers just managed to brush the bottom of the jar, and it rocked left, then right, before crashing down on his head. It shattered into a dozen pieces, and Sheik fell back on his bottom.

"Oh, little master!" Darla rushed to the boy. She produced a rag and wiped blood from his forehead. Sheik was dazed, and his head rang, but he didn't cry out.

The door to the kitchen banged open, and Sheik's father walked in. In a glance he took in the broken jar and gingerbreads laying all over the floor. Sheik scuttled backwards away from Darla.

"What is the meaning..." Sheik's father demanded. For a man he was short, but to Sheik he was a giant.

"She threw it at me, papa," Sheik said. "She said the cookies were all for her, that she wouldn't share, and she threw it at me. See, I'm bleeding." He reached for his head and felt warmth. His hand came away with a little red on his fingertips.

His father looked long and hard at him. Sheik couldn't read his stare. "And what do you propose we do about this, Sheik?" he finally asked.

"Punish her father! Throw a jar at her like she did to me!"

"My lord," Darla said getting to her feet, "you know I would never dream of harming the little master, I..."

"Do you call my son a liar?" he asked her, interrupting the woman. His stare turned to her.

Darla licked her lips and rubbed her hands against her apron as though they were wet. She looked at Sheik then, petrified. "N-n-no, my lord, never, but..."

"If he isn't a liar then there are no buts." He looked back at Sheik. "If you wish to punish her, you will administer the punishment. Jars are expensive. We will take her to the courtyard and throw a brick instead." He tilted his head slightly to consider the servant. His stare was vile and dangerous. Even Sheik recognized the look despite being a child. "Servants are expensive as well. Leave her face and her arms. Hit a leg. She can still do dishes with a limp."

Darla looked at Sheik, her eyes wide. Her mouth parted. "Please, little master, you don't want to…"

"He does," his father snapped. "I can see it in his eyes. No more words from you until the punishment is complete, unless you want me to throw the bricks. Now get this over with Sheik. The servant has dishes to tend to."

The three of them walked out a small door in the kitchen that led to a side courtyard. The branches of the bushes along the wall of the kitchen were bare of any leaves. The grass was brown where it was not trodden to dust. Cobblestones separated the bushes from the rest of the courtyard.

Sheik bent down and scooped up one of the cobblestone bricks. It felt heavy. Dirt was caked on one side where it was half buried in the earth. He wiped it off, sending the dark grains flying back to the ground. He looked up at his father.

And then he felt the iron grip from the small man on his soft arm. He was frightened. He was no longer himself, no longer the little boy, but now he was Darla. She stumbled over her skirts, tears silently streaming over her cheeks. Her hair felt greasy and itched the back of her neck. Through blurry eyes she saw the child-version of himself holding the cobblestone brick, looking unsure.

Darla was shoved hard against the low brick wall of the courtyard. She stretched out her hands to stop from slamming into it, calloused hands from years of washing dishes. She felt the lord reach to her ankles and pull her skirt up over her bottom. Her legs were bare, as were her underclothes. Shame and embarrassment filled her.

"Throw it, Sheik."

Her vision was blurry from tears, and she stared down at the base of the wall. Something hard pounded into her left thigh. Her buckled leg snapped forward from the blow and her knee hit the wall. She could feel blood trickle down her leg, just like the tears that trickled down her face.

"Another."

This brick came in lower, only scraping her right calf. She continued to cry.

"Another."

This one was harder, and rammed into her right calf again. The force again caused her leg to jolt forward, hitting the brick wall. It took all her strength to continue standing, but she knew worse would come if she fell before the end. Uncontrollable sobs shook her shoulders. She wept.

"Go inside, Sheik. I'll administer the rest of the punishment."

And then there was fire. Searing flame. The pain was abominable. Sheik screamed, a howl that didn't sound like himself. First it was the deep voice of a man, then the cry of a woman. Then a child's. He burned and burned, again and again feeling the pain of those he had burned.

Sheik was reliving the cruelty he imposed on others during his life. It began when that boy, Cecil, drove a sword through his heart. Sheik had set an ambush, but he failed to realize the extent of Cecil's heresy. One of the boy's followers was well-versed in elemental magic and had saved him.

The fire stopped. He was a young man, dressed in black. He was short, and an evil grin was stuck on his face. They were in a forest, the Mountain Province by the look of it. Huge trees grew skyward, leaving open spaces in the darkness. It was cold. He was not himself, but a commoner named Gendry. He wore dirty, torn wool.

Behind the real Sheik was another man, finely dressed in black with gold buttons, standing in front of a fire that gave the little light they had in the dark forest. The man held a matching black rod with gold butt caps. "You will be taught to fear the curators. Fear of the gods is the beginning of wisdom."

Gendry felt sweat run down his face. Sheik reached forward, grabbed his hair, and yanked him around. There on the ground on top of dry leaves that blanketed the forest floor was a black box with iron wrapped around it. Gendry was forced into it head first. With the pushing he couldn't get all of his limbs inside, and he was punched on the back. It was a hard punch, the punch of a man who was used to using his fists. The lid slammed shut.

The fire disappeared, and there was nothing but darkness. One of Gendry's knees was at his chest, the other at an odd angle from being shoved in the box. The tight squeeze made it impossible to turn. A splinter from the box pierced one of his shoulders, and he was forced to try and hold himself up just an inch to prevent it from digging in further.

Gendry tried to breathe evenly, but the tight space made it hard. He tried to stay calm, but he felt trapped. The air was stale, and the edges of the box were so close. So close. He was squeezed so tight he could hardly move, and his joints were cramping. And the edges were so close, so close. He tried harder, tried to stay still and calm, but he couldn't.

He screamed and shook the box. The splinter dug into his shoulder, but he didn't care. He had to get out, he had to move! He rocked back and forth, screaming. He was sweating despite the chill, breathing even harder, screaming, screaming, and screaming. The box fell to one side, driving the splinter in even further. Gendry breathed heavily. His legs cramped. The one at the odd angle had a dull pain. Finally, he stopped and regained control in that awful position.

How long he stayed like that he didn't know. He was unable to sleep due to the discomfort. At one point light filtered through a slim crack in front of his eyes, but it too faded as time continued. He urinated on himself twice, the scent of the warm liquid filling his nostrils with a putrid stink. His stomach growled in hunger, and his tongue swelled for water. Something bit his ankle, an ant most likely, but he couldn't reach to swat it away. The itching, nagging pain was almost a relief from the rest. Eventually he became numb, and the world inside that box a haze.

Another light came through the crack. This one flickered, small at first, and then it grew. The chest was pushed back to its original position, and Gendry felt the splinter dislodge from the wood and break off into his skin. The top was hurled open, and hands gripped him.

The throbbing pain in his knees became sharp as his legs extended. The hands threw him on the ground, and he was unable to keep his feet due to the soreness of his limbs. He gingerly tried to extend them, rustling the leaves as he did.

And then the fire returned. Searing the flesh off his body, leaving nothing but charred bone. His screams were not his own, but instead the shrill cries of women, deeper screams of men, and the wailing of small children. Scene after scene Sheik relived the horrors he dealt to others during his lifetime, always experiencing it from their point of view. The physical pain was often dwarfed by the fear and shame he forced upon others.

Mostly he burned. The hungry red, yellow, and orange flames licked at hair and skin, its fiery touch igniting pain.

Suddenly he was a giant of a man, probably a blacksmith, huddled over a small child. A glance over his shoulder revealed the real Sheik with the black rod of a marshal of the Holy Order of the Black Wing. The black rod rose and fell, rose and fell on his strong back. The child cried in terror beneath his body.

Then he was an old woman, huddled in a great hall. There were cries and screams all around him, but a Lady sat tall in one of the two chairs set on a raised dais. Smoke swirled in beneath the two great wooden doors at the end.

"Lady Ignava, what be we to do?" she asked. The lady looked so calm on the chair, dressed in a neat black dress with her hair in a bun.

"We do nothing, Margaery. My fool of a husband did this to us. We await Anuke as regally as we can." The fear in the hall was palpable as children screamed and servants cried. Sheik, as Margaery, could feel her own tears fall down her wrinkled face. The heat was becoming unbearable as they sat in the stone oven. The smoke burned her old lungs as though a fire grew in her chest. Margaery turned to see three of the guards by the door gripping their weapons tight as though preparing to storm out.

"Do not..." Lady Ignava began, but the three guards ignored her. They threw open the doors and raced out into the smoke. Margaery could see their dark forms through the haze open another pair of doors, the main doors, and charge out of the building, weapons held high. Though she couldn't see them, she knew dozens of bolts flew at them, and the men crumbled to the ground.

A ball of flame became visible through the smoke screen on the other side of the open doors, lighting up a man Margaery knew was himself, Sheik. She pulled close a young servant girl, her granddaughter, and wept as the ball of flames flew into the hall.

It was Sheik's final act before death. He had waited in the ruins to complete his mission and kill Cecil. But that nuncio, a nuncio of all things, had saved him! The memory was faded, blurred by his endless tortures, but it was there. And now Sheik was dead. Suffering. Burning. Reliving the pain he caused.

"*Domito mortis,*" a voice demanded. The visions swirled to black, a tornado of voices and tears. Around and around they went, faster and faster until they converged into an indistinguishable blackness. And then there was nothing.

"Awaken," a voice commanded. Sheik could see. Above him he saw the stars and moon shining down. Their light revealed the blackened walls of the Ziyad manor.

He put his hands to the ground and pushed up to his feet. His limbs were stiff, and he couldn't feel with his hands or his feet. Standing in the courtyard was a curator.

He was tall and broad. His jaw line was strong, his cheekbones high. His brown hair was cut short, and his face shaven clean. His nose was strong, but not large. It was the youthful face of a young man, the most handsome face Sheik had ever seen, despite dark circles around his eyes and the pallid coloration of his flesh. His chest was covered with a silver cuirass, armor plate etched to look like muscle. Matching pauldrons protected his shoulders, shining in the moon's light. Layers of long blue robes flowed out from beneath the cuirass to his knees, and underneath were leather sandals with long straps that wove up his calves.

As impressive as he was to take in, the most impressive of his features were the giant white wings neatly folded behind him. Though the memories were cloudy, hidden by a haze of torment, Sheik knew what he looked at.

I've been blessed by my gods. It is Ares himself.

Monks were scattered behind him, as well as two priests. A few soldiers in the leather brigandine of the Army of Truth were scattered around as well.

"Conjure a small flame in your hand," the curator demanded.

Sheik reach out with his hand, palm facing up. It didn't feel odd to obey, there was no choice. He opened his mouth to speak, but no words came out.

"God of my gods, protector from the fire, something has eaten half of his tongue. We've come too late." This was said by one of the priests, a priestess, the only female in the gathering.

Too late? Even that simple thought was hard for Sheik to conjure. He hadn't been commanded to think, and therefore it was next to impossible for him to do so. He felt like a puppet, the words of Ares his strings. If the string did not move, neither did he. He let his hand fall to his side.

"Heal it," Ares said.

"God of my gods, protector from the fire, he's dead. The tongue won't grow."

Ares turned his head to those behind him. "*Brevis*," he called. A short gust of wind soared in from the sky. A soldier fell forward in front of Ares on his knees, looking straight ahead at Sheik. The soldier looked confused, but he didn't move. Ares drew his short sword and buried it behind the man's helmet into his neck.

When Ares retracted the blade, the man slumped down to the ground, his crimson life force flowing freely on to the grass.

It reflected the light of the stars and the moon. "Take his tongue then, and make it work."

Though fear shone in the priestess' eyes, she pulled a small knife from her belt and cut out the man's tongue. She came to Sheik then and grabbed his chin with her free hand. The priestess held the other man's tongue in Sheik's mouth.

"*Resarcio*," she commanded. Sheik couldn't see what took place in his mouth, nor could he feel, but the pleased look from the priestess told him he had a new tongue.

Ares spoke again to Sheik. "Conjure a flame," the curator demanded again.

Sheik raised his arm, an odd thing to do without feeling. He tried his new tongue.

"*Incendia*."

A small flame appeared in the palm of his hand.

"Good. Move from the corpse, I shall raise him. They are far more obedient soldiers in death than they are in life."

The bustle of Asaph astonished Saoirse. He had made the trip to the small cathedral town with his father to trade horses nearly every Twil, but even during the small fair the town was not as busy as it was now. Crowds uncommon to the town walked up and down the dirt streets. It was impossible to find rooms at an inn and difficult to find even a seat at a tavern once the sun set on the horizon and darkness settled in. Tents had sprung up outside of the town, creating a maze of streets of their own. Sao was thankful the crowd came during the cold season, because even with the colder weather the press of bodies made him sweat. Then again, it was never really cold in the Peninsula Province.

The town had no walls and no definite shape. It was built around the Cathedral of New Beginnings, which took up a great deal of space in the center. Unplanned streets ran around it on all sides, creating a small but complex network of alleys and side streets. The lack of organization or a central street made the crowds seem thicker than it really was.

More often than not those walking the streets were armed men. Most were soldiers of the Army of Truth, distinguishable by their leather brigandine armor with the patch. Sometimes even cavalry were seen, falchions at their side and shiny steel breastplates of woven metal strips. Few attempted to ride horses through the streets though. They were not as wide as those in Pearl, and the crowds of people and small streets made it difficult for riders to push through. They had all come from the packed garrisons to the east, soldiers left as a buffer in case the goblins came again. Why they had been brought to Asaph, Sao was unsure.

Sao discovered through conversations with men deep in the bottom of their ale cups that the other armed men were household guards of the nobility. So far he knew of three Counts and a Duke staying in Asaph, along with numerous of the less powerful Viscounts and Barons. Somehow the news that Cecil Ziyad wouldn't be named Constable had traveled faster than even Sao had. Day after day the crowds huddled around the Cathedral of New Beginnings, few but the most powerful getting inside to try and influence the decision of High Priest Denis.

The Cathedral of New Beginnings itself didn't resemble a cathedral at all. The walls were circular, and a rainbow of veins snaked their way through the stone. Though the walls were thin and left just enough room on the catwalk for a single man to walk, they were high and efficient at keeping out the crowds. From the outside it resembled a fortress more than a cathedral.

Though Sao was unable to get inside, he knew what it looked like from past visits. Inside the circular stone wall stood a single building. The front room consisted of seven altars to the seven curators, each altar having a statue of the curator to whom it was designated for. A staircase in the back led to the living quarters of High Priest Denis and the priests and acolytes who resided in the cathedral on its upper floors.

The most beautiful part of the Cathedral of New Beginnings was what lay between the central building and the wall. In that ample space, except where a stable and outdoor kitchen was set up, grew the most magnificent garden in East Ager.

The climate of the region made growing plants easy, and with enough care, species not native to the province were able to flourish as well. A natural spring ran beneath the cathedral which fed various fountains and streams where colorful fish with sweeping tails swam. There were statues with pouring buckets, great creatures of the sea that Sao didn't have a name for leaping over gushing water that looked like waves, great dragons spewing waterfalls, magnificent curators poised with aquatic creatures, and more.

Lilies grew close to the streams, showing off vibrant yellows and reds. Two-colored lilies graced the ponds as well with pink and white. There were bright blue asters, their thin petals spreading wide to reveal their color. White, pink, and even golden yellow daisies sprung up in carefully tended areas.

Goldenrods filled spots that would have been vacant of color with yellow petals. Helenium, tiny flowers with copper colored petals, rose in areas where the fountains and waterfalls left damp soil. Pansies of all colors were placed against the walls to add even more color to the rich garden.

Despite the range of colors and the beauty of those fountains and flowers on the ground, none of them matched the splendor that was the hanging gardens that were visible even over the wall. The central building went up in sections, leaving flat areas meant for gardening on the roof, creating a pyramid. There were seven tiers, and the plants grown on these high areas grew long so that they hung over the sides. Waterfalls starting from the top of the cathedral cascaded down as well, making the inside look like a paradise.

The tiered garden was just barely visible from the window Sao looked out. He was staying in his aunt's home, his father's sister, sent to gather information for Cecil like he had done in Zephyr Hills. The situation here was different, though. The soldiers were unsure why they had been called from the garrisons, and the women and children in Asaph knew little as well, only that some of their men were home and they were glad for it. Only the guards of the nobility seemed to have a purpose, and they were tight-lipped. Still, with most of the local men absent, the newcomers were causing quite a bit of trouble with the women.

The rumors he did manage to hear wouldn't help Cecil at all. Monsters in the graveyards outside town, men and women disappearing in the night.

With so little information being gained, Sao wished he could have accompanied Cecil in Pearl instead of rushing to Asaph. Somehow Cecil had known about the attack on his family's manse, but it became more real when they heard the story from a group of outriders from Pearl. Everyone inside had been burned or shot with quarrels when they tried to flee.

He's had a lot to deal with, Sao thought. First his father, then the trial, the assassination attempts on his life, the battle at the bridge with the trolls, and now the rest of his family burned in their own home.

Sao rubbed the beginnings of a beard on his chin. *And now he leads a revolution.*

He had heard that just last night in one of the crowded taverns. The news had spread like wildfire among the patrons. The bulk of the Army of Truth, those not in Cecil's honor guard, were supposed to arrive in Asaph later this very day, and with their absence from Pearl, Cecil along with Duke Briel had claimed the city.

Times were changing, and Cecil needed Sao to keep him well informed if he was going to survive. *I suppose I should get back to it.*

It only took one step over the small pile of blankets on the floor that served as his bed to reach a narrow staircase. His room was more like a large closet than a bedroom, one that was normally filled with spare fabric, needles, and thread. His Aunt Fi was a widow and survived off mending clothes in the small town.

Upon coming down the stairs he caught sight of his aunt sitting on a low stool in front of splintery desk patching a pair of coarse cotton pants. She was much older than his father, the oldest of their siblings. Her hair was gray, and her wrinkled eyes were kind. She didn't have freckles like Sao did – they came from his mother. She did have his charm, however, and was much liked in Asaph.

"Are ye headed out fer the day looking fer horses?" she asked.

That was the lie he had told her. Though Asaph was no Farrow, it was the best place in this province to find a good horse. The best in all of the Kingdom of East Ager if you wanted a Southern Jiggler.

"Yes, auntie. Don't wait up for me." He opened the door and scuttled out under her frown. She was no fool; she knew he was off to a tavern, she just didn't know where his fat coin pouch came from.

Spying pays far more than shoveling horse manure. Who would have thought I'd be getting paid to listen to rumors?

Sao walked among the crowd heading toward the tents outside town. He took his time, leisurely squeezing between armed men, boys running errands, and women scuttling through trying to be invisible. It was an odd gathering, not quite as crowded as it had been days before. Most of the soldiers seemed to be in their camp outside of town.

"Aye, it's true," Sao overheard from a young boy speaking to a friend against a wall in the street. "Derve saw his sister with a soldier, and I'll bet ye a copper penny she be..."

Sao walked on. Not everything he heard along the street was important. In fact, most of it was worthless. But most rumors had some truth to them, so he continued walking and listening.

There wasn't much to hear. Some girl kissed a soldier, monsters in the field outside town, a boy skinned his knee tripping from the crowd, there were more disappearances, the cathedral was in need of more wine, etc. Things either not true or not important. Sao walked through the town to the tent-city outside.

Most of the tents were arranged in neat rows. These were the tents of the garrison, a small cohort under the command of some lieutenant Sao had never heard of. The rest, close beside the others, were less organized but just as numerous. They were the tents of the nobility and their household guards. There were no guards stationed to keep people from wandering from the town to the tents. Some of the townsfolk and surrounding farmers took advantage of this and set up stalls for their wares.

The sound of hammers took Sao to the edge of the tents. There he saw dozens of soldiers constructing a palisade wall. Some of them dug holes while others put in wooden stakes at an angle that were then sharpened to a point. The wall snaked around the southern part of the camp to the west where construction continued. The palisade wall was built a good distance from the town where they were building it on this side, leaving an open field.

He leaned up against a nearby stall where an old woman attempted to sell quilts. Her jaw jutted farther forward than the top part of her mouth, which gave her a stubborn look. Her skin, due to years in the sun, was as dark as leather. Sao assumed it felt like leather too. The woman was hunchbacked and didn't look the least bit friendly. Still, he figured he could try and talk to her.

"What are those soldiers doing over there?" Sao asked. He tried to sound curious, and nodded his head toward the construction.

"Use yer eyes boy," the woman snapped. "They be building a wall. Now, if ye aren't gonna buy ye 'ave to be moving! Ye be blocking view of my quilts."

Sao looked down at the quilts on her stand. They were thin, too thin for any province but the Peninsula Province during the cold season. He flipped through them as though interested.

"Mmm, this is a nice one," he said picking up one. He pretended to examine it. "Of course, a wall. I wonder why they'd be doing that around Asaph?"

"They be soldiers, boy, they be doing as they be told be my guess. Now move on! I bet ye 'aven't a copper to yer name." She reached forward and ripped the quilt from his hands before placing it back on the table.

Sao dug his hand deep into his pouch and pulled out handful of coins. He filtered through them until he found a copper lot. He put it on top of the quilt and returned the remainder to his pouch.

"I'm rather fond of quilts, but I believe I'll keep looking for another." He moved to a different stack and feigned interest. "Orders, huh? Who would give orders like that?"

The old woman scooped up the copper lot and bit it. Satisfied, she put it in a pocket on her apron. "From the lieutenant, though my daughter says he got the order from Duke Marlow." The woman finally understood why he was there. "Aye, and the word be he 'as all but been named the new High Commander. Suppose they be waiting fer the ceremony to make it official." She looked Sao up and down. "Are ye married boy? My daughter might 'ave seen a few more Twil than ye, but I bet..."

"Yes, this one will do," Sao said taking the original quilt. "May the Mother watch over you." He walked back through the tents leaving the woman behind.

All but named, huh? At least this gives me something to look into besides disappearances and monsters...

Chapter 11
(Anne, Galavon)

The town outside Himeji Castle was named after the Castle – Himeji. Though not as large as Pearl, or even large enough to be considered a city, it was the largest town in the region. The southeastern parts of the province were the most populated, but most of the people were spread out in small farms. Still, towns such as Himeji existed to serve as places for the farmers to sell their goods and buy what they couldn't make on their own.

It was the Day of Victory, the eighth day since the last, and many of the Followers of Reproba Caelum who lived out in the farms came in to the towns to hear the monks give the Brahma. For those not overly concerned with hearing the monks, the day also served as the perfect opportunity to catch up on the latest rumors and spend a coin or two at the market.

Anne's father had never been overly concerned with making it to every Brahma, but Lady Ignava made it a point to at least have a monk give it at the manse. The Brahma was actually only phase two of a four phase ceremony, but the whole thing was often called the Brahma as well. Anne didn't mind listening to the Brahma, but she enjoyed the third phase: The Lessons. In the Lessons, the monk or priest told stories from long ago when Reproba Caelum first began. The stories contained morals, and they were truly enjoyable from monks skilled in orating.

Although if Duke Briel and Lady Ayn's plan works, I suppose I won't be hearing the Brahma anymore.

Anne wandered the streets of Himeji with her maid Isabella, perusing the wares set out by the peddlers, the shops that lined the street, and even the fruits and vegetables the farmers set out. Most of the women who came in from the farms sold fabric made from the stalks of kerplum trees. The kerplum fabric was light and airy, but a little itchy for Anne. She preferred her light wool and silk. Still, the prices for the garments were cheap, and most of the commoners on this end of the peninsula wore it.

It was warm outside despite the beginning of the cold season, but for someone born and raised in the Peninsula Province, it was the perfect day. A light breeze that was almost cool kept Anne refreshed.

"Ooh, Isabella," Anne exclaimed moving to a small stall with shell jewelry. "These are magnificent," she said to the man. There were bracelets and necklaces stacked full of small, white shells of different shapes. She lifted one up and clasped it on her wrist.

"It looks fine on yer wrist too!" The man exclaimed. He was a squat fellow, short and plump. "It be my boys who go to find these beauties on the shore, but it be me who creates the jewelry."

"The white of the shells seem so pure," Anne said. She twisted the bracelet on her wrist. There was a single, glossy black shell there among the white, a chip of something larger it seemed, but still bigger than the white shells.

"What is this?" She asked the merchant. "One black chip amongst all the white? It's so smooth."

"Another shell I suppose. My boys found it on the shore with the rest of 'em. Never seen a thing like it on the shore. I can remove it if my lady prefers."

Anne thought about her pearl hidden beneath the neckline of her dress. "I'm partial to things found washed up on the shore," she said. "It adds character to the piece."

"Aye, that it does, my lady! Will ye be purchasing, my lady? It be said that Anne Ziyad herself wears my jewelry!"

Anne giggled and looked at Isabella. The maid smiled back, a little distant. Something was on her mind. "So you know Lady Ziyad herself? I heard she's monstrous and quick to get in trouble."

"Oh no, my lady!" he said back. "She be a beauty, and as mild mannered as a doll!"

Anne gave the merchant a sideways look and began to unclasp the bracelet. His eyes followed every movement of her fingers. It was fun not being recognized on sight like she was in Pearl.

"Oh, but, well, of course she can be a bit of trouble, if ye believe the rumors! And she be not quite a beauty, I only say such things because of her family."

Gotcha.

"Isabella," Anne said over her shoulder clasping the bracelet back in place on her wrist.

"Yes, Lady Ziyad?" her maid asked.

The man's mouth dropped. In fact, a number of onlookers from around the peddler gaped. It was fun making these merchants eat their words. Anne produced a copper lot from a pocket sewn into her dress.

"You do believe I'm beautiful don't you?" she asked Isabella, feigning sadness and looking away from the peddler.

"Ye be as beautiful as a rose," her maid said.

"That's what I was going to say!" exclaimed the merchant. He wiped sweat from his brow. "My lady, what I meant..."

His sentence trailed off, and he looked to be at a loss for words. By now a crowd had gathered to watch. There were children squeezing through their parents' legs, a monk, men and women from all walks of life.

"It's quite all right, sir," Anne said smiling. "No harm done." Those words might not be completely true. Anne wasn't sure if the man was going to have a heart attack or not. It wasn't often that nobility bought jewelry from street peddlers. "I'll take this bracelet." She pulled one of his hands open and placed the copper lot in it. "And how many boys do you have?"

"Uh, I 'ave three my lady," he said in a shaky voice. He ran his hands over his head, as though he was unsure what to do with them.

"These are for them." She handed him three copper pennies. "Good fortune to you and your boys."

And the legend of Anne Ziyad grows, she thought.

The stares from the crowd followed Anne and Isabella through the town. Anne was used to them, she sometimes received them in Pearl when she pulled similar stunts. Among these stares, however, she felt something different. Something dangerous. It seemed her shopping day in Himeji was at an end.

"Isabella, lets gather our own shells," Anne suggested as they passed through the small gate of the town. Having Himeji Castle within walking distance should be protection enough.

"My lady, ye know we be expected back at the castle," Isabella said. "We don't 'ave any guards fer ye. Here and back the Duchess said."

"Isabella, I've seen sixteen Twil. I think I can decide where and when I want to go somewhere," Anne responded. "We're leaving early, and have you seen any danger on the beach? I haven't. Not a single pirate. We'll be within eyesight of the castle walls. And besides, the Duchess left yesterday with half of her guard. Even Captain no-fun Philial left. She won't find out."

Isabella looked worried. There was definitely something on her mind. "Aye," she finally said. "Who be me to tell ye no. Lead away my lady, but be careful." Her worried look turned into a smile. "I know he be a little young fer me, but yer captain no-fun sure be fun to look at."

Anne ignored the comment and darted toward the white beach. She wanted to lose the watching eyes that made her feel uncomfortable. She heard Isabella scrambling behind trying to keep up. They both giggled as though neither had seen more than ten Twil.

The pair made it to the beach without incident and out of breath. Anne fell back in the sand and let her chest heave up and down as she sucked in air. She looked up at Isabella, and her maid smiled back. Anne didn't like to think of her as a maid. She was more of a friend.

The two walked down the beach laughing. They scooped up shells when they saw them, quickly filling their pockets. The strip of beach grew smaller as they continued walking, the thick tangle of trees and brush edging closer.

"Did ye ever learn a new one? A spell?" Isabella asked. Her hands held the hems of her skirt to her knees so they wouldn't get soaked.

"I've gotten better at healing," Anne said. She had scoured the castle looking for minor cuts and scrapes once Lady Ayn sent away the monks. Bruises were much more difficult, but with

Larith's book she was able to figure them out after only a few minor mishaps.

Maybe more than a few, but all minor.

"I would love to use White Magic," she said. "Healing people. Aye, it must be a joy." The maid twirled in the shallow water as a wave swept back out to sea. She pulled up her skirt as it crashed back in. "What about the other trick ye were working on? Speaking to someone's mind ye said."

Anne bent down for a small, white shell. They were her favorites, and the ones that decorated her new bracelet. Many already had perfect holes in them for a string, though she didn't know how they got there.

I bet Larith would know. He knows everything.

"I couldn't get it. It's not like healing. I have to 'picture my voice in their head,'" Anne said in her best imitation of Larith's wise, deep voice. "At least that's what Larith says in the book. I'm not really sure what that means. The first time you cast a spell is supposed to be the hardest." She stopped examining the small shell and put it in her stuffed pocket.

There wasn't much of a beach now before the trees. "Ye will figure it out, I be sure of it." Isabella walked through the shallows and placed a hand on Anne's waist. "Anne, there be news from Pearl this morning." She spoke slowly.

"What was it?" Anne asked. She reached down for another shell.

"I be sorry Anne. The Crows... they burned down yer manse. I be truly sorry." Anne straightened. Isabella embraced her and rocked her back and forth.

They burned down the manse?

"The servants? The guards?"

"Aye. I be so sorry."

"My mother?"

"Her too," she said in a soothing voice, continuing the rocking as though Anne were a baby. Anne turned around and returned the embrace. The two stood there in silence, wrapped in each other's arms. Isabella stroked Anne's hair. Anne didn't cry. She couldn't believe it. It didn't feel real.

"They've killed my father and my mother," Anne said blankly into Isabella's shoulder.

"This may not be the best time to tell ye... but Anne," Lady Isabella hesitated. She took a deep breath. "Lady Ignava wasn't yer real mother. Many Twil ago, Tarik and I, well, his marriage to Lady Ignava was for political..."

Isabella was jerked toward the beach, nearly taking Anne with her. Anne stepped back to regain her footing and looked up. She saw a man with his hand over Isabella's mouth and a knife to her throat. "That be touching, very touching," he said. Two more came out of the trees with nasty curved swords. Behind them came another, nervous and disheveled, as though he had slept little the night before and was still trying to recover. He wore the kerplum fabric she saw in Himeji.

"That's her," the last one said. He was an average man in size and bulk, but his eyes held greed. He pointed at Anne. "She said she be Anne Ziyad." He grabbed his forearm and looked down at the feet of the other men. "Can I 'ave my money now?"

The closest of the other two snarled and slashed at him with a sword. That man was big, at least a span taller and two span wider at the shoulders than the others. He wore a dirty vest and loose fitting trousers. The blade sliced close enough to cause the man to yelp and jump back.

"Bugger off," the big man snapped. "Ye get nothin, ye drunk. To Shiva's own prison with ye!"

"Easy on the language, Bruce," the second man with the sword said. "There's a lady in our presence." This man was of similar size to the drunk and had big, brown eyes. His clothes, while dirty, looked to have been fine at one time, though in their current state they looked far from it. His hair was neatly combed. "Why don't you just come here, my dear? We won't hurt you. Come now, come on."

The third man with the knife to Isabella's neck had a wicked smile that he flashed to the other men in spastic motions back and forth as though he was about to burst with energy. His hand jerked around as much as his head, and a thin drop of blood formed on Isabella's neck.

"Come now, my dear." The man took a step toward her and held out his free hand. "Come on."

Anne drew *Alius* from her belt. She held the long, thin bladed knife pointed toward the strange men.

"Hah!" the big one barked. "By the fire of Shiva, she be thinking to fight us off!" The man with the knife giggled and smiled even brighter with a slight twitch. She saw Isabella strain her neck as his knife carelessly moved up and down.

"Now, now, girl, let's put that away."

"*Alius*," Anne commanded. The flash of green came, then the white, but as soon as Anne felt that strange link and saw out of four eyes, she spoke again.

"*Subluceo.*"

Two white globes of light the size of her head appeared in front of the real Anne. She hadn't only focused on learning new spells, but also on perfecting the ones she knew. She sent the two globes racing toward the group of strange men, straight at their faces before willing them out of existence.

Even with her practice, controlling two bodies and two globes of light was beyond her. As soon as the lights blinked away, Anne darted down the beach toward Himeji Castle and sent her stiff limbed copy leaping at the blinded rogues who held Isabella.

Running with her real body, even in her dress, was easy compared to controlling the fake Anne, so she focused on her illusion. The men were all stunned by the sudden bright light, except the drunk, who dashed off into the trees. The illusion's movements were stiff, but it bounded through the shallow water and leapt at the big man. It stabbed forward with *Alius* and drove the thin bladed stiletto into his right shoulder. The dagger sunk halfway through before the man grabbed the illusion's wrist. Its head whipped to the left as he backhanded it with his other hand. She assumed it was backhanded, because she couldn't feel a thing. She saw Isabella sprinting the other direction fumbling with her skirts.

Good. Maybe she'll escape as well...

Her thoughts were interrupted as her real body was tackled to the sand. *Alius* went flying. She was dimly aware of the odd connection between her and her false image dissipating. There was only the real her now. She could just barely make out the top of the castle above the trees. Anne turned her head and saw the drunk on top her.

"Oh, now they have to pay me!" he said. His breath smelled like stale ale and his body was grimy from dirt and sweat. He held her down and tried to look into her eyes, but Anne turned her head away, kicking all the while. "But you be a pretty thing. I be seeing why they want you."

He let go of one of her arms, and Anne struck him across the face with her free hand. He struck her back. "Aye, but ye don't act like a lady do ye?" He stood up with a tight grip on Anne's wrists.

"Help! Please, no, help!" she screamed, a loud scream she hoped they could hear at the castle. The drunk tried to drag her into the trees, but Anne jerked and kicked, anything to prevent him from getting her out of the open.

"Quiet! Quiet!" He said jerking her arms painfully. Suddenly, a knife appeared in his wrist. A look of horror came over the man's face. A curved sword slid out of his chest. The drunk looked down at the red blade, but it slid back out. He looked at Anne, his face trembling, and whispered, "I don't want to die." Then he was pushed over to the side to land on the beach. The man with the combed hair took the drunk's place and grabbed her with his free hand.

"I don't envy you, stabbing Brutus like that," the man said. Behind him was the fidgety one, grinning again, leaning down to retrieve his knife. "I suppose the thought of how much you're worth will keep you safe, but you better hope he doesn't find your mother."

Galavon's entire body hurt. He felt mangled and ached from the inside. His chest felt tight. He managed to open his eyes to a slit. He could see a figure bending over his middle clad in white. He blinked to clear his vision, and looked again.

There, bending over him, he could see the right half of a girl. No, a young woman. Most of her body, including her face, was covered by a white cloak made of some sort of fur. All he could see of her were thin white hands hovering over his body, blonde locks that escaped from the hood of her cloak, and the right half of her face.

Her skin was pale and smooth, her face fragile. Her nose was thin and ended in a point. The eye he could see was green. She was focusing hard where her hand hovered above him.

She's beautiful, in a delicate way, he thought to himself.

Galavon took a deep breath and found the strength to use his voice. "Is... is this the Sacred Isle? Are you a curator?"

The young woman jumped to her feet and backed away, startled. Galavon could see the left half of her face now, and he gasped. It was scarred, twisting her lip into a grimace at the corner and spreading up her delicate cheek like an angry red fire. Her eye was white, dead, useless, obviously seeing nothing. No hair fell from beneath her cowl from that side of her scalp.

"Do you hear that Lisbeth?" A hard voice said. "He believes you as beautiful as a curator." Galavon turned his head to look at his surroundings.

He was in a tent with a fire burning from an iron brazier in the center. The walls of the tent looked to be hide, and they danced back and forth often, as though a strong wind pushed from outside. There was another pallet laid out on the hard ground.

On the other side of the brazier were two men. One was Myson, dressed in his odd scale armor and wearing his mask with the hood pulled over his head. He wore a short, thin jacket over his bare arms now.

The other man was similarly dressed, except for the mask and scale armor. He had his hood down. His face looked as though you could break a stone over it. He had a strong chin and green eyes like the girl's, though they seemed to bore holes through whatever they looked at. His head was bald, and he stood a head taller than Myson.

"And no, this is not the Sacred Isle." He walked from around the brazier with powerful strides. He held his head high and spoke as though he was used to giving commands. "Thank you, Lisbeth. You may leave now."

The girl spun and darted out of the tent. Galavon could see nothing but darkness outside the tent, and in the brief moment the flap was open a cold wind poured in and sent goose bumps down Galavon's skin. His bare skin.

Again!?

His cheeks turned red and he reached down to pull up the woolen blanket he could feel low, too low, around his waist, but his hand stopped short, and Galavon froze. The top of his right arm had a patch of green scales.

Panic set in. "What? What is this?" He sat up quickly and stretched his arm out in front of him. The quick movement blurred his vision, but he was in a panic. Just the one patch there, but now that was sitting up he could see that the left side of his abdomen was covered in green scales as well. "What have you done to me!" he wailed, scratching at the scales on his side.

"Easy!" The man commanded in a deep voice.

"Galavon, breathe!" Myson yelled.

Galavon tried to pull off one of the scales and was successful. Blood immediately filled the spot where the scale had been. He dug his nails under more and began to pull up, trying to yank them from his skin. Two strong hands gripped his right arm at the same time two more gripped his left. Galavon screamed, twisted, yanked, and pulled to no avail. Their grips were too strong. "What have you done to me!"

"Calm down!" The man yelled over him. "Calm down! *Filius!*"

Galavon didn't hear the soft breeze brush back the flap of the tent, but he could feel its gentle caress over his skin. He stopped fighting, dizzy and out of breath, and fell back. The breeze continued to blow, but the grips on his arms loosened. Someone threw the blanket up to his chest.

"What have you done to me?" he asked quietly between breaths.

"Galavon," Myson said. "You're a summoner now. You're a seer summoner."

A summoner... Galavon thought. He stared up at the roof of the hide tent and watched the smoke from the brazier escape out of the hole in the top. *Myson is a summoner.* He reached up with his left hand and touched the right side of his face. It was smooth skin. He touched the left side, and he felt hard, cold scales running from his forehead down to his chin. *I'm a monster...*

"You've achieved something that few are able to," the strange man said in his hard voice. "A gift that many of us wish for but only few are granted."

"But I'm not one of you!" Galavon yelled back. Then in a whisper, "I made no deal with Shiva."

"That's right; you're not one of us." Somehow, despite the hard stare, there was not a hint of anger in his voice. "You don't know who you are. You're a Follower, yet you're a seer. You're weak, yet you show strength. You can't be all of these things. If the path isn't in front of you, you can't choose to walk it. You must choose from the paths life has given you." The man let his hard gaze linger on Galavon.

I don't want any of this. I only wanted to find my place in Mundus.

"But it is your gift, and you may choose to squander it however you like." He gave Myson an unreadable look and left the tent.

Galavon tried to remain calm.

"Myson," he said. "Why is there a tightness in my chest?"

"Because you share it with a wyvern," he said. "It was the only way to save you." He reached down by the other pallet and put herbs in a pot. He hung it over the brazier. "But you both are right – you're not one of us. I'll teach you what I can, but we seer summoners don't often stay in one place for long. The open air beckons."

"Who are you, Myson? All of you, I mean?"

Myson stirred the pot. "We are the Viridian. Viridia was the name of our kingdom. That was our king, Viriathus. Similar to the Albus Veneficus some say, but we're much more. We're the remnants of the people who lived in the Mountain Province before Reproba Caelum. We continue to wage war against them in our own way."

Myson turned and picked up a wooden bowl. He scooped a brown liquid out of the pot and put it in the bowl. "Drink this. Lisbeth did what she could, but you need your rest. This will help."

Galavon grabbed the warm bowl and took a sip. It tasted like mint, and warmth filled his insides. It didn't help the tightness in his chest. He pulled the blanket farther up to keep his shoulders warm. Well, that and to hide his demonic traits.

I'm a monster.

Galavon forced the thought away. "I've never heard of the Viridian. How do you fight back?"

Myson sat on the other pallet. "We stay hidden in the peaks of the Mountains of Hope. This is where Reproba Caelum harvests rubies and sometimes finds emeralds for their priests and acolytes. They go deep in the crevices where the Northern River of Flame flows and searches for them. We raid them and take the stones for ourselves."

Galavon suppressed a yawn. Whatever sort of herb Myson put in his drink was acting fast. The blanket slid down, and he saw the green scales on his arm. There were more on his shoulder. "So many of you are shaman as well as seers? Mages?" His head was cloudy, and it was getting increasingly difficult to think.

"Our ways make learning Fire Magic difficult." He held up his arms showing the thin coat. "We focus on controlling all aspects of our body. We don't allow cold to touch us or fear to seize us. With so much control over our emotions, there's no way we could learn Fire Magic."

Galavon's head tilted forward, his eyes half closed, and he jerked his head back upright.

"Myson, are my eyes... are they like yours? Are they wyvern eyes?"

"Sleep, Galavon. You're a seer summoner now. But yes. We call them dragon eyes."

Galavon woke to Lisbeth leaning over him again. He scuttled backward, jerked upright, and pulled the blanket up to his chest. The sudden movement startled her, and she moved back against the tent wall, head down.

"Sorry, I'm not used to being, uh, exposed." Galavon said with a blush creeping up to his face. "I mean, I know you aren't... down there... but..."

Lisbeth looked embarrassed as well. "Yes, I was careful not to," she said in a quiet voice. She kept her face turned so Galavon couldn't see the left side. "I was only checking your progress." She scurried to the flap of the tent and moved into the sunlight before Galavon could say a word.

He felt a little better today. He managed to get to his feet at least. The tent had a chill to it, and the brazier was no longer lit. At the foot of his pallet he found his charred boots, his father's amulet, and a folded pile of clothes similar to those that Viriathus had worn, and Myson for that matter, except the scale armor. The sleeveless tunic and thin jacket did little to protect him from the chill, but Galavon at least felt covered. He also slid on the amulet.

He ventured out from his tent into the cold. There was no snow, but everything was covered in a thin layer of ice, even his tent flaps. Set up all around him were more tents, perhaps fifty or so of them. Shuffling between them were men, women, and children. The men were all bald and clad in the same clothing, some without the thin coat and only in the sleeveless tunic with the hood. The women had thick hair and similarly thin clothes. The children didn't seem to notice the cold either.

Galavon kept the hood of his sleeveless tunic up, but he could feel their stares. At least, he thought he could. He pulled his cowl lower over his face.

I'm forever marked.

The tents were put up in a circle on the flat surface leaving an opening in the middle. In the opening were older children, boys with their hair completely shaven like the men. They balanced on one leg, shirtless, with the cold wind whipping around them. An old man watched in silence.

Galavon pulled his own thin coat tighter. The chill didn't seem to bother these people at all. That was good, because it was only the beginning of the cold season, and Galavon couldn't imagine how cold it would get this high in the mountains. He spotted Lisbeth in her white cloak watching from beside a tent, protected from the wind.

"Hi," Galavon said. Lisbeth glanced in his direction but didn't respond.

He searched in the silence for something to say. "Do you know someone out there?"

She looked down at the ground. "They call it the field. But no. My brother died with my parents."

"I'm... I'm sorry for asking."

She nodded, still not looking at him. She stared across at the boys, now on their other leg. Galavon tried to wrap the thin coat even tighter.

"Having trouble with the cold?" Lisbeth asked in her soft voice.

Is her voice soft or sad?

"Uh, I'm all right," Galavon said. He shivered as an especially cold wind blew around him. He wasn't up against the tent like Lisbeth was. "I suppose I'm used to a thicker tunic with sleeves."

She nodded from within the shadow of her hood. Another gust of cold wind blew, harder this time, and it pulled the hood from Galavon's face. As quickly as he could manage, he pulled it back up.

Lisbeth giggled. It wasn't a giddy, joyous giggle full of mirth like Galavon had heard from Anne, but a gentle little laugh that just managed to escape before she could hold it back.

"I could use a higher collar too, the wind can't blow that off." He smiled. He hadn't expected to hear the shy girl laugh.

"It truly is an honor here, to be what you are," she said. "You've cheated death and come back even stronger."

Galavon pulled down the sleeves of his thin coat in an effort to cover the scales on his hand. He didn't want to be reminded of what he was.

"It may be an honor here, but in the Kingdom of East Ager I'll be an outcast. I'll be hunted down by the Holy Order of the Black Wing. No one will accept me."

Will Anne be able to accept me? Will she accept me as a beast, as this monster that I've become?

"I used to live in the Kingdom of East Ager, when I was a little girl. My father was a monk, but he abandoned Reproba Caelum so he could be with my mother. We were outcasts."

Galavon edged closer so he could hear better. The sad, gentle voice grew quieter with each word.

"Healing was my father's purpose, and he couldn't help but heal those around him. He was a cleric after all. When I was only eight he gave me a pearl he had stolen from Reproba Caelum. He taught me White Magic."

She stopped. Galavon was afraid to press, afraid she would leave. So he waited. After a few moments she continued.

"The Crows found us eventually. We ran into the mountains, but they caught us and killed my family. Viriathus was able to save me, but only me. They had saved me for last, and were taking their time with me." She pulled her own hood down. She stared straight ahead though, and Galavon could only see the golden blond hair and delicate side of her face. Lisbeth brushed back her hair and revealed a large pearl dangling from an earring.

"This one is mine. It reminds me that I still breathe, that I still live. The Viridian say it reminds me that I still have a path to tread." Lisbeth hesitated, took a deep breath, and turned her head.

The other half of her face was ruined. Her lip twisted in a sick grimace at the corner. Red scars marred that half of her face, and the flesh around her pale eye was swollen. No blonde hair fell from her bare scalp. But there, hanging from her ear, was a large but faded pearl.

"This pearl was my father's. It reminds me of the steps I've already taken." She quickly turned her face and buried it back in her hood. She left him.

Galavon reached up and stroked the scales on his face. They were hard and rigid. As difficult as it was for him to accept them, he wasn't sure how Lisbeth could continue. He felt foolish.

"*Filius,*" he called out. It was the same word used by Viriathus the night before. The cold wind flew around him, and Galavon raised his arms. It rustled his tunic, flew down his sleeves, and sent shivers through his body. It was comforting. The gust blew back his hood, and Galavon closed his eyes so he could focus on feeling it. The wind ruffled his hair and blew it all directions before dying down.

Galavon returned to his tent. It wasn't long before Lisbeth came with a small meal. They ate in silence. She left, darkness fell, and she returned to the light the brazier. She told him Myson had gone the previous night with many of the other men, but it was for the best since Galavon needed rest. Again she left, and Galavon slept.

Galavon returned to the Field when he woke the next day after nibbling on a cold heel of bread and cheese he found at the foot of his pallet. Judging by the sun, he had slept through the morning and into early afternoon. The students were in a line now, punching the air in front of them with the same teacher.

Two students were separated from the others. These two attempted to project gusts of wind at buckets placed on the ground. After several failed attempts, they were changed out with two more.

They must be experimenting to see who the wind will accept.

"Why don't you join them?" Lisbeth's soft voice asked from beside him. Galavon turned. He hadn't heard her walk up. She handed him a staff. It was slightly thinner than his wrist, and there were bumps where smaller branches had been cut from it. The top was a gnarled knot that almost looked like the open maw of a wyvern. It looked like the entire thing had been hardened by fire, blackening the outside but making it stronger with ash and heat. "Myson mentioned you had a staff, but it was destroyed. This was going to be an extra tent pole, but I took it before they could carve away the knot."

It felt right in Galavon's hands. "Thanks," he said. He pulled down his hood and walked across the Field. It was a slow walk, which Galavon hoped made him look determined, but it was really due to the aching he still felt all over his body.

The old man turned to face him. He looked wise and patient. He wore the same as the other men – leather pants and sleeveless hooded tunic with the thin linen coat. A plain thick belt decorated his waist and held a shining emerald on the front. They stood in front of each other for only a moment before the man reached out with his palms up.

Galavon wasn't sure what to do. Lisbeth was too far away to ask, and the students were busy punching in sync. The old man didn't utter a word or move his hands. He nodded towards the staff.

Galavon put it in the old man's hands. He bowed, took a step back, and pointed the staff at Galavon. With his free hand, the man pushed the back of the staff and sent it into a whirl. The old man spun as well, keeping the staff in one spot, whirling around so fast it looked like a shield. Somehow it seemed to pick up more speed before the old man lashed out, stopping it just short of Galavon's head. He stopped then, handed it back to Galavon, and sent him to the line of students.

Time passed by slowly, and Galavon thought he would see the next Twil before he was told to stop. There was no break for water or food. Only whirling the staff around and around. Blisters formed on both hands, and the achiness in his body got heavier. More students replaced the pair. Darkness began to fall, and Galavon grew hungry, thirsty, and exhausted.

What am I doing? Even Viriathus said it, I'm not one of them.

Through the day one of the boys was successful in creating a blast that knocked over a bucket. There was no exclamation of joy, no hoot of congratulations. There was only a smile, a bow, and a pat on the back before he was sent away. The testing continued, but only for one boy at a time.

Darkness began to fall, and the repetitive movements with the staff were no longer enough to keep Galavon warm. Finally, the last boy left with no success of knocking over the bucket. A giant emerald, just as Galavon expected, was carefully placed in a chest before the boy carried it off. The old man picked up both buckets and placed them a few paces in front of Galavon. The old man then stood beside him facing the buckets.

The old man punched out with one hand, then the other the other hand. He punched again with the first, this time with more force.

"Brevis!" he commanded, the first word Galavon had heard him utter, and a surge of wind shot down his arm and sped toward the bucket, sending it flying through the air.

"Onis!" he cried again. He opened his palm and bent his arm back toward his face at the elbow as though motioning for the bucket to return. Nothing happened though, and the bucket continued to sail away.

The old man didn't look pleased, but he nodded toward Galavon and stepped back to observe. Galavon gripped the staff in both hands, preparing to lash out. He took a deep breath but was stopped by the old man. He moved Galavon to the position he had been practicing all day.

"Momentum," he said. He separated his hands as though he was holding a staff as well. He made the motions Galavon had practiced before stepping back.

Galavon made the motions. The staff created a slight burn when it passed over the blisters on his hands, but he sent the staff into a whirling blur. Finally, it neared the end of its cycle, and Galavon lashed out.

"Brevis!" he called. Galavon felt the power in his voice and saw the tiny green sparkles leave his mouth. Cold wind swirled down the staff and shot toward the bucket in an arc. It missed, but not by much, leaving a streak in the thin layer of ice that covered the dirt.

The old man nodded for Galavon to do it again.

Galavon repeated the motion and called out, *"Brevis!"* No green sparkles. Nothing happened.

Again Galavon repeated after receiving a nod to continue. This time the arc of wind struck the bucket hard, sending it flying through the air. Galavon slammed the butt end of his staff into the ground and mimicked what the old man had called earlier.

"*Onis!*" A small whirlwind spiraled forth, picking up bits of ice along its path. It scooped up the bucket and sent it swirling into its vortex before spitting it back out toward the pair. The whirlwind continued though, slowly fading until it hit the nearest tent. Luckily it had lost much of its power by this point and only shook the cloth structure. A startled woman ran out of the tent. When she saw it was nothing, she gave an angry look at the old man.

The old man smiled at Galavon and patted him on the back before walking away. Galavon felt pleased with himself, but he was also tired and cold. He returned to his tent where he and Lisbeth ate a small meal. She left, and he slept.

The next morning he woke to Lisbeth rushing into his tent. "Galavon, they've returned." She left just as quickly. He rose from bed, surprisingly feeling better despite his sore shoulders and blisters. He dressed and made his way to the Field.

There were a number of bows being given all around, and a few hugs. Galavon saw a warm smile and a congratulatory pat to the boy who had become a seer. Viriathus was bowing to a woman and sharing hugs between three young children. After a moment of this, Viriathus raised his arms and everyone quieted down.

"The attack was successful, and not a man was lost. This is the path we've been given, the path that we've chosen to walk. We must leave this place in the morning, it's no longer safe." There was no applause, only a murmur and many smiles as the crowd departed.

These people don't show emotion even in victory.

Galavon found Myson then, behind Viriathus and his family. Only Lisbeth was there beside him, neither speaking a word.

"Galavon. It's good to see you've accepted who you are," Viriathus said before Galavon could get to Myson. In his rush he had forgotten to pull the hood down. Viriathus smiled at the woman, his wife Galavon assumed, and tilted his head. In response, she gathered the children and herded them away.

"I've brought you something." He reached for his belt and there, beside a large pouch was a thick, wool, wide brimmed hat with a pointy top. He grabbed the dark gray hat and handed it to Galavon.

"In the Sparkle they have divers to search for pearls. In the mountains we have miners. They search for rubies in caves with walls of lava. These hats help to shield their eyes in the caves and keep them warm in the mountains. We found a lost miner wandering back to Trikkle, and this was his hat."

"I don't understand," Galavon said. The thick wool felt warm, and he was tempted to put it on his head right then.

"The words we exchanged when we first met. You said you weren't one of us. This is to remind you of the path you tread before you found us. You were lost, much like the miner. Now, you're a summoner. The past is our strength, the future our goal, the present our prison."

Galavon nodded, though he was still confused. He put the hat on. It fit well, though he did feel awkward with the wide brim. It cast a shadow across his face.

I don't really care how it looks, it's a thousand times warmer than those thin hoods.

"Galavon," Myson said walking up. "I must leave tomorrow for the Gold Desert. No one can traverse these mountains faster than we can with our wyverns. I would appreciate the company, and I can show you a thing or two about being a seer summoner."

The Gold Desert?!

"I, I don't know how to summon," Galavon stammered. "I'd just slow you down."

"I can teach you the basics today, enough to get us started. It's an important journey."

This is my path now, I guess. I can choose to walk it, or I can be forced. At least, that's what Viriathus would say.

"I'll do it," he said. "Why the Gold Desert? More green wyverns?"

"Not quite," Viriathus said. He pulled the large pouch from his belt and emptied a large, shining ruby into his hand. "The barbarians pay a hefty sum for these. They dream of the day they can take back their land just as we do, and this makes them our allies. It's how we survive, Galavon."

"How many do you have?" he asked.

"Three," Myson said. "They'll provide more than enough to get us through the cold season."

The ruby glowed, much like Galavon's old emerald before Ceridwen stole it. "I'd like to buy one."

The two men smiled. Galavon figured it was the equivalent to laughter for those who were not Viridian.

"Galavon, these stones fetch a gold mark each, and they're worthless to us. Our strength lies in controlling our emotions, not embracing them. That is how you use Fire Magic, embracing your anger."

Galavon pulled off his right boot. It was in near ruin from the flames of the red wyvern, but the thick leather remained intact enough to wear. He turned up the boot and a gold mark fell into the palm of his hand. He pulled the boot back on. It was too cold to leave it off for long.

"As you have so kindly reminded me, I'm not one of you." Galavon grabbed the tip of his new hat. "My past is different, and it's my strength."

There was no laughter this time, only wide-eyed shock. "It's hard to argue with my own words." Viriathus took the gold mark from Galavon's hand and replaced it with the ruby. "Be careful with it, Galavon. We teach control for a reason. He's yours now Myson. May your path be clear." Viriathus left then with the departing crowd.

"It's a day for surprises," Myson said. "Come, Galavon."

Galavon followed Myson and Lisbeth through the crowd among the tents. The people were already hard at work preparing to move. It seemed as though they would be ready long before the morning.

They came to a small tent, perhaps half the size of the one he had been staying in. It sat apart from the others. It was complete with its own brazier and simple cot. A trunk sat against one of the leather walls.

"If you're going to travel with me, you'll need more than just the clothes you were given. As we keep reminding each other, you're not one of us. You weren't taught control of your body, nor are you used to the mountain weather. Just as Lisbeth needs her thick cloak, you too need something more."

"I had this made for you," Lisbeth said. She pulled out a dark green tunic. "It has sleeves for your arms, and it's thicker than the coats the Viridian wear." She held it up for Galavon to see. The back of it would come down to his calves while the front would only come to his waist. Along the edges of the sleeves and along the collar was silver stitching in the shape of three bands weaving in and out of each other. "The needlework is my own."

"It has a high collar," Galavon said. He smiled, and Lisbeth looked away.

"It's thick enough for this as well," Myson said. He reached behind the chest and pulled out a short cuirass long enough to cover his chest and upper back, leaving his lower abdomen unarmored. It was covered in silver scales with a hint of green. It matched the one Myson wore except it included pauldrons attached at the shoulders.

"You're a seer summoner. I had our master craftsmen work on it as soon as you arrived. It's made out of the scales of your wyvern." He produced leather pants like his with more scales on the inside thighs and calves, as well as a new pair of boots. "And you'll need these to ride your wyvern."

My wyvern, Galavon thought. *I truly will be a seer summoner.*

"I'm not sure what to say," Galavon said. "You two have been so kind. I'm not sure I'll ever be able to pay you back. I just gave away my last coin..."

"It's not your coin we want, Galavon. We want your friendship. You're a seer summoner, and you've embraced it."

Galavon nodded. He wasn't sure what else to do. These people showed so little emotion.

"Put them on. You have much to learn before the afternoon is over."

Galavon met Myson at the edge of the tents. He felt awkward in his new garb. The scale breastplate was heavier than he was used to and felt odd being so short. Though the tunic kept him much warmer than before, the high collar and low back sometimes got in his way. Even his new hat felt as though it would blow off at any minute. He strapped his ruby to an arm band as Ceridwen had and wore it on his left arm beneath the tunic.

"You look good," Myson said. They were alone behind an outcropping of rock. "How does it feel?"

"Off-balanced," Galavon said. "Why does the cuirass stop so high?"

"For flexibility while we ride."
Galavon nodded and shifted the armor on his shoulders. It was going to take a while to get used to.

"First you call your wyvern. *Voco Zoe!*" Myson's body tensed, and his back arched. His eyes went wide. His muscles strained. A green mist in the shape of a snapping wyvern emerged from Myson's chest. Once the full form was free, it landed on the ground and became corporeal. Myson pulled his mask off and walked up to the huge beast and stroked its neck.

The green wyvern was as huge as Galavon remembered. It sat back lazily on its two feet. Dragons were said to have four legs instead of just two like wyverns.

"Galavon Zoe, Zoe Galavon." Myson patted the wyvern's neck and turned back to Galavon. "It's *voco* then the name."

Galavon's eyes were wide with fear. *One bite, one snap with those jaws...* The green wyvern Zoe simply stared back. It craned forth with its long neck and sniffed at Galavon's hat.

"I-I-I don't know his name," Galavon stuttered. "I can't remember."

Zoe opened his mouth revealing a row of sharp teeth, and green specks like dust in a ray of a light flowed out to wash over Galavon. "*Vestra Rorrick,*" a heavy, deep voice said to him.

"N-nevermind," Galavon said. Myson chuckled.

Galavon took a deep breath. "*Voco Rorrick.*"

Galavon's arms were thrown wide. It felt as though his chest was ripping apart, his rib cage being pulled in opposite directions. He screamed out loud and fell to his knees in pain. A green mist flew from his chest and took the form of a green wyvern in front of him. Galavon fell forward on his hands and knees and gulped in breaths of air.

"You'll get used to the pain," Myson said.

Galavon's chest was no longer tight. He reached up with a hand and felt his cheek. It was smooth. *The scales are gone.*

He looked up then and saw Rorrick. He wasn't as big as Zoe, but he was magnificent. His scales glistened in the icy sunlight, perfectly overlapping one another down his long body. The greens only had two horns that came back toward their neck making them look sleek. Rorrick leaned forward on his two legs and let his long tail that ended in a spade wave up and down. He seemed to be scrutinizing Galavon as much as Galavon was scrutinizing him.

"They don't speak often," Myson said. "And when they do, it's often hard to understand because they speak an ancient language, the same we use to cast our spells." Myson turned back to Zoe. "All right Zoe, let me up."

The green wyvern squatted down and Myson jumped on his back. "Don't sit on the neck, it'll strain them. Don't sit too far back either, or you'll slide. If you do fall, *lente* will help cushion it. That is, if the wind feels like cushioning it. To the sky!"

Zoe's wings extended out, reaching at least three times the length of his body. He pushed off the ground with powerful legs and took to the sky.

Galavon was left with Rorrick. The wyvern still eyed Galavon as if deciding what to do with him.

"All right, Rorrick," Galavon mimicked. "Let me up." Rorrick turned his head sideways, the long sleek face looking puzzled.

"Uh, let me up," he said again, motioning with his arms. Rorrick turned his head the other way like some hounds did when they were confused.

This is getting us nowhere.

Galavon edged forward slowly with his arm outstretched. Rorrick pulled his face back with a questioning look. He didn't step back though. Galavon continued to inch forward until he stroked the green's neck. The scales were hard as rock, perhaps harder. They felt smooth under his touch. Galavon reached up and patted as high up Rorrick's back as he could reach. "Come down Rorrick, I'm getting up."

Rorrick was still unsure, but the pats must have been a good enough clue. He squatted down. Galavon hoisted himself up clumsily.

And I thought riding Kid was difficult?! I'm on a wyvern!

Rorrick squirmed and let out a roar. The sound was sharp and deafening. He bumped Galavon up once, twice, three times.

"Ok, ok, sorry," Galavon said. He edged back. His legs were set comfortably where Rorrick's neck met his body just before the wings. Rorrick was no longer squirming, but he swung his long neck around to stare at Galavon.

"I'm new to this, too," Galavon told him. He took another deep breath. *What am I doing?* "To the sky, Rorrick!"

Again, Galavon got a confused look from the wyvern. "Uh, up?" he asked. He pointed a finger to the sky.

The green wyvern's wings rose. They came up arched and created a wall between Galavon and the mountainside. Galavon felt his legs stretch wider as Rorrick took a deep breath and squatted. In a rush the wings shot down, Rorrick's legs sprung up, and the air in the wyvern's belly was released in a deep exhale.

Galavon squeezed his legs together as tight as he could to prevent from falling back. He dropped his staff and leaned forward to grasp Rorrick's neck with his hands. He closed his eyes while the air rushed past. His new hat was ripped off by the sudden propulsion. His hair whipped around his face. Finally, Rorrick straightened out, and Galavon dared to open his eyes.

Stretched out before him was the mountain range. He remembered looking out over the plains of the Fire Pass Province from the top of a low hill, but it didn't come close to what he saw now. The peaks of mountains rose below him, clouds floated below and above, and even the Viridian village looked tiny from this height. The wind seemed to flow through him rather than around. Zoe flew in beside the pair, and Myson called from his back.

"Amazing isn't it?" he yelled. Galavon nodded. "I wouldn't recommend flying too far, remember you share the same energy. You could die from exhaustion if you push too hard." The two wyverns swooped to the right in sync. Galavon hugged Rorrick's neck with his arms.

"Just use your legs to hold on! They fit perfectly in front of the shoulder, so don't fear falling back! The real danger is falling forward!" Galavon pushed his way upright. It did feel more secure.

"It takes such a toll, I don't recommend flying far and then fighting," Myson yelled. "Especially if the odds aren't in your favor like when we fought those big reds. Better to save your energy for the fight." Galavon nodded.

"That's it! Easier than it looks, eh?" he asked. Again Galavon only nodded. He was focusing too hard on not falling.

I hope my face isn't as pale from fear as I believe it is.

"Why don't we use saddles?" Galavon asked. It was his first words from Rorrick's back. "I think I'd be more comfortable, and less likely to fall."

Myson grinned from across the empty sky between their wyverns. "And what would we do with the saddles in the wild when the wyverns return to us? They aren't horses Galavon! And you can't ride them like one! You tell them where to go and let them take you there. Down, Zoe, we're done."

The two wyverns swooped back down to the ground. The landing was lighter than Galavon thought it would be, but it still sent chunks of frozen earth jumping from the ground.

Myson jumped from Zoe's back. He stroked under the wyvern's neck, which caused him to stiffen his back and close his eyes in pleasure. "The wyverns are a part of us. We share the same body most of the time. Only we can ride them, and maybe a passenger if we don't go too far and the wyvern will accept them. Endurance, though, that is what you must learn now."

Galavon could understand the truth in that. He was already breathing hard, and all he had done was a short ride.

Myson patted Zoe. "It's always hard to watch them go, but they must."

With one last pat, Myson said, "*Voco Zoe.*" The green wyvern looked sad before fading into a green mist and going back into Myson's body. Myson managed to keep his feet this time, but it still took his breath away. He put his mask back on to cover the scales that returned to his face. The wind picked up in a sudden gust of warm air.

"Help! Please, no, help!"

Anne?

"Galavon! It's time to come down."

"Did you hear?" Galavon asked, alarmed. "It's Anne! She's in danger!"

"Galavon! Relax," Myson said. "Who's Anne? What are you talking about?"

I nearly forgot her!

"The wind! It carried her voice to my ears. Myson, I must go to her! It came from the south, the wind was warm. I must go!"

Myson's eyes came down at the corners, but he nodded. "When the wind brings us a message, we must take heed. That's how I found you, after all." He scooped up Galavon's hat and staff. He walked to Rorrick's side and handed them to Galavon.

"It's your path to tread," Myson said. "If you must go, you must go. Rorrick should be able to find you water to stop at." He handed up a dented, tin cup from his own belt. "If not, melt some snow. Fly fast and high over the Fire Pass to avoid any big red's. Once over the pass you should be fine, but don't fly over the Sparkle, it's nearly the mating season for the whites, and you don't want to get caught up in that."

Galavon felt terrible for leaving after all Myson had done. "I'll return."

Wrinkles formed beside Myson's dragon eyes and Galavon knew he was smiling beneath the mask. "I know the ways of seer summoners. Be prepared for a lonely journey Galavon, but you're right. We'll see each other again." He stepped back. "If you need me, send a message on the wind."

Rorrick squirmed beneath Galavon. "You never told me how."

"Just say my name after *veho affatus*. It's as simple as that. The wind will deliver the message if it wishes. Now go."

Galavon pulled his hat down tight and gripped hard with his calves. He held his staff out wide.

"To the sky, Rorrick!"

Chapter 12
(Galavon, Anne/Galavon)

The cold moon shone down on Galavon. It was bright this night, and thankfully so, because Galavon wouldn't have been able to see a thing. He pulled his hat lower and sunk down into the high collar of his shirt to try and find some warmth. The wind seemed to mock his effort though, and blew in around him.

Galavon didn't know if the moon was actually cold or not, but it felt that way on his mountain perch. He was so high that if he went to the edge and looked over the Cliffside Gulf below, he couldn't hear the waves crash against the rocks. He hadn't been warm in two days.

Looking back on his sudden departure, he felt like a fool. How could he have forgotten Anne? Even with the acceptance of the Viridian, how could he forget her? He felt even more the fool for leaving with no food or water. The only water he had so far was snow melted in his mouth, and that only made him colder. Rorrik had been able to kill a goat before Galavon dispelled the wyvern, but it lay useless beside a similarly useless frozen pond and the dented tin cup Myson gave him. He had never learned to start a fire, and apparently it was a tricky endeavor.

I've never been able to do anything right. The wind swirled in around him even harder, and its breath might as well have been ice. *I thought you were on my side?*

He unstrapped the ruby he bought from Viriathus and gripped it tight. This wasn't the first time he had tried to use it. Every night so far he had gripped the ruby and called out the word he remembered Ceridwen say in the troll hovel. That day felt as though it had happened a Twil ago.

Galavon knew Fire Magic fed off anger, so he had tried to make himself angry. He had thought of his mother dying, he had thought of his father never treating him like a son, he had thought of Torvil treating him like a child, he had tried thinking of Kavar's treachery on the road outside of Farrow, and he had even tried thinking of Ceridwen abandoning him in Marcil. But he still sat frozen in the mountains surrounded by food and water he couldn't cook or melt.

This always seems to be the way of it for me. I wonder if I'll actually be successful in dying this time. I can't even seem to do that right. He knew if he summoned Rorrik to fly lower he was likely to pass out. The wind blew again, this time warm.

"No, no, please no!"

Galavon jerked upright. It was Anne again, on the wind. The sound came from the southeast.

"*Incendia!*" he called out with his hand facing a small pile of sticks he had gathered. Nothing happened.

"*Incendia!*" he said again, louder. Still, no flames appeared. The wind became cold again, freezing, and managed to work its way past his collar and hat.

"Yes, I'm cold all right!" Galavon yelled. The wind blew even stronger. It's bite was ice, sending a chill that ran along Galavon's spine. "If I can't get warm and get any rest she could be hurt, or worse!" The swirling air became colder than ice, whipping at his clothes. He stood and thrust his hand out into the air.

"Incendia inflatus!"

A burning in Galavon's chest, a fiery glow between his ribs, sent an energy racing up his arm and flowed out through his palms. The energy he felt well up inside of him began to form a ball shape. Galavon hooted in sheer joy, until he realized the ball continued to grow.

"Uh, stop! Stop!" He swung his arm to the side in a panic, and the ball of flame flew forward and struck the frozen pond. The swirl of fire exploded into hundreds of smaller flames on impact in a great blast that sent Galavon flying on his back against the ground and his hat soaring through the air. Bits of ice and fire fell down around him.

Galavon propped himself up on his elbows. The small flames were dissipating with nothing to latch on to. He wasn't concerned about keeping the flames alive though. He could still feel that glow burning in his chest.

The wind blew again, not nearly as cold as it was a moment before. It swirled above his head and dumped his hat on top of it.

This wind is worse than Rorrik, he thought bitterly. Still, it had helped him learn to use Fire Magic. Learn Fire Magic. *I'm a mage! I'm a mage! I can use fire and wind!* He jumped to his feet and laughed out loud to congratulate himself. He had taught himself! Maybe he wasn't so bad at everything. Maybe Elemental Magic was his thing.

Galavon rebuilt his little pile for the fire, the original being blown away from the blast of his spell. He hovered his hand over it and said *"Incendia."* He drew from the small amount of anger that burned in his chest, a very small amount, and a lick of flame lit the sticks and leaves. Galavon nursed it carefully and soon had a fire.

It took no time for him to heat up a glass of water, and the warm liquid soothed the cold in his insides. The mountain goat was a much more difficult task, but the pain in his stomach demanded food. With a sharp rock, Galavon managed to separate most of the hide from a section of meat. The merchant guards had skinned wild game on the road every now and then when they were lucky enough to fell a deer or rabbit. Without a knife starting at the tail was difficult, but the sizzling flesh that came off of his makeshift spit tasted like hot success, even if there was still a hair or two on it.

He sat back against a rock he was grateful he didn't land on during the blast and warmed his body. Tonight he would actually get some good rest.

"*Veho Affatus*, Anne Ziyad," he said getting as comfortable as he could on a hard rock above the world. "Hold on, I'm on my way." The words flew from his mouth as green specks before being scooped by the cold wind and carried away.

Galavon was up with the sun the next day. His fire had burned out, a dead pile of ash now, but he felt invigorated. Staring south as the sun came up on his left, Galavon knew he would find Anne.

I wonder if she even remembers me.

But there was no time to think. She needed him, and whether she remembered him or not, he would be there to rescue her.

"*Voco Rorrick!*"

The pain racked his chest, pulling a scream out of him as the green mist formed into Rorrick. The green wyvern looked refreshed as well. He swung his narrow face around on his long neck and nudged Galavon.

"I'm coming, Rorrick, just a second," Galavon said, raising one hand and breathing hard. "It takes a lot out of me to summon you."

Rorrick coo'ed at Galavon. In the little time they had spent together, Galavon already knew what the low vibrations coming forth from his throat meant. It was the green wyvern making fun of him.

He acts like I whine all the time!

It had started when Galavon was having trouble the first night using Fire Magic and continued since then. Galavon tilted his eyes and glared at the wyvern in a friendly way and scratched his throat as he had seen Myson do to Zoe. Rorrick's neck stiffened from the scratching.

"Ok, time to go Rorrick. We have a lady to save."

I wonder if he remembers me.

It didn't really matter now if the merchant boy did remember her though. She didn't believe she would ever see him again. She didn't know if it really was Galavon's voice that accompanied the cold wind two nights before, but it was a nice thought at a time when nice thoughts were hard to come by.

After she was caught, the band of men bound her hands together at the wrist, tied a rope to her waist like she was a puppy, and put a rag in her mouth so she couldn't scream. The rag came out the next day, but she was awarded with a none-too-gentle slap every time she made a noise. From there they moved north along the coast back in the direction of Caernarfon Castle. They stayed off the road though, which made the journey slow.

The few days felt as though they were never-ending. She spent them quietly crying herself to sleep, silently hoping that the men wouldn't touch her while she slept and that the few guards left at Himeji would find her. Her captors took most of her things except her necklace, the shell bracelet, and her black ribbon. She often kept a firm grip on the latter. It reminded her of her father and those who died in the manse. Each morning she woke with streaks down her dirty cheeks from the tears and prepared for another long day of walking through the thick tangle of underbrush.

The one with the combed hair, Tsai, seemed to be in charge of the group, with Brutus as a big, close second. The fidgety man they called Twitch was in charge of holding her leash. More rough, ragged men joined them through the days, bringing their number to ten before they stopped on a sandy beach beneath the cliffs along the coast.

Anne wasn't abused, but she was kept under close watch. At first she was let off the rope and allowed some privacy to do her business, but after a failed escape attempt and a purple bruise on her arm she was only given the privacy of a large maltree with the rope still tied around her waist whenever she had to relieve herself. She received two more bruises on her thighs after she picked up a heavy limb and smashed it down on top of Twitch in another failed escape attempt. Twitch grew more careful of her then, making her walk in front of him to be sure she wasn't up to anything.

Sometimes Anne wished she knew more than just White Magic, or at least more of it. Casting a globe of light or healing a scratch wouldn't help her escape.

At least Isabella escaped. Maybe she can help them find me.

Tsai didn't allow any of the other men close to her, and Anne was glad of it. At one point Twitch had walked off and handed her leash to another man, who wasted no time in pulling her close. With the rag gone from her mouth it only took one scream for Tsai to come running. They were brutes, all of them, and Anne feared Tsai wouldn't be able to restrain them for long.

"How long be we waiting here fer?" one man asked Tsai. It was the early evening, and the band had a fire roaring and fish burning. It would be their second night on the beach. The group had pulled out a rusted, metal cage from a shallow cave, making Anne believe kidnapping wasn't a new thing for these pirates. She sat in it now, apart from the circle around the fire, but still close enough to hear their words.

"Not much longer," he said. Tsai pulled off the cork of a bottle with his teeth and took a gulp. "We're a few days early, but the ships will be here yet, long before any sort of patrol finds their way to this beach."

Pirates. These men are pirates. Does that mean... they plan to sell me?

More corks were popped and bottles were passed around. One pirate with a tattoo of a fish across his face started to play a tune on a flute. Some of the men raised their bottles and took even deeper swigs of the amber liquid. Anne could smell the drinks from where she sat, cheap maltree wine, stolen she was sure.

Twitch sat in front of her cage. He nursed a bottle of his own in one hand and fiddled with his knife in the other. The unusual man always seemed to have a long-bladed knife in one of his hands. Anne was surprised he still had all of his fingers considering the spasms. His strange smile lit his face when the music started, and he trembled slightly as he looked at the others. None seemed interesting in talking to the peculiar man. Anne could see *Alius* in the back of his belt. She thought if she could somehow get the stiletto off him she might be able to escape.

"Beorn, why don't ye try that harp ye stole? Ye used to play a bit didn't ya?" One man yelled out between bites of fish. His bottle was nearly empty.

Another man, this one bald with a scar running across his cheek, dug through a satchel and pulled out a harp. It looked to be new, fresh wood with carved clouds running along its stem. The man plucked at a string, obviously out of tune, nodded, and tried to play the instrument.

"Bah!" was the response. Most put hands to their ears.

"Put the Shiva blasted thing away!" Brutus roared. He stood in front of the others and took a great tear out of a fish. "Give me the tune to 'The Ballad of the Sea Man,' just on the flute," he roared, bits of fish coming out with every word. The harpist looked disappointed, and the flutist stopped his song, nodded, and started again. Some of the other men joined in by hitting their knees or seats like drums in a slow rhythm. Brutus tossed the fish, emptied a bottle of maltree wine, and started to bellow out a verse.

"I knew a man who sailed the seas,
From the Cape of Good Hope to Tripoli!
He forsake the shore, the trees and bees,
For on the ocean he was free!"

"Har har! Ain't that the truth!" one of the men yelled out. Brutus shot him a look that promised death for interrupting and stole his bottle of wine.

> "He left the land of East Ager,
> Sailing south in the heat on a wild hair!
> The weather was good, and fair out there,
> Then he felt a chill in the air!"

Brutus upended that bottle as well, and he sent it sailing straight at the man he stole it from. The other pirate fell backwards in the sand to avoid being hit, and the bottle shattered into a thousand pieces.

> "'Pull the sail down!' the captain cried,
> By then the ship was along for the ride!
> The poor boat it rocked, from side to side,
> And then the ropes were ripped untied!
>
> A huge wave crashed over the rail,
> It seemed they were in the heart of a gale!
> Sailors did their best, with pails to bail,
> But all their work was to no avail!"

Anne had never heard of "The Ballad of the Sea Man," but from what she heard so far it wasn't something she imagined pirates wanting to sing.

> "The man grabbed on to floating wood,
> And held on for his life the best he could!
> The man prayed out loud, 'he would do good,'

And against the storm he withstood!

He washed right up on to dry land,
A sunny beach with trees and sand!
The man soon was saved along that strand,
Nursed to health by feminine hands."

Suddenly the rest of the pirates joined their voice to Brutus'.

"And now this man who knew the seas,
From the Cape of Good Hope to Tripoli,
Forsake the ocean, for trees and bees,
And for the refuge he found between a girl's knees!

"Bahaha!" the pirates roared. Wine spilled on to the sand with their laughter. Now Anne understood why the pirates liked it.

"Ey, Brutus," the smallest of them said. He was skinny and had long dirty hair that stuck together in clumps. He handed Brutus his bottle. "I've never heard of 'Tripoli."

"Bah," the man said. He put the bottle to his lips and then had to wipe his face clean with a dirty sleeve after spilling half on himself. "Far away, made up. I don't care." Brutus sat back down on his stump heavily, the wine beginning to take the desired effect.

The drinking continued into the night. More songs and verses were repeated, though most came out slurred or incomplete. The verses they did sing only made Anne more nervous. She wished they would sing song with a happier theme.

The fire began to die down as the night went on, until one of the pirates said, "What, what do-say," one pirate slurred, "we get the girl to do a dance. That wouldn't hurt 'nothin, now would it Tsai?" Others joined in, calling for a dance. Anne moved to the back of the cage, as far out of the fire's light as she could manage. It wasn't the men who called out who bothered her, but those who stared at her through the bars.

"The answer is no," Tsai said. "Unless you want to explain to Tew how his priceless treasure became nothing more than any other girl."

"But we don't 'ave to tell him," another said. "It be just a dance."

Twitch pulled out a second knife, one in each hand. He spasmed nervously.

"Do ye hear that?" one man asked. The others fell quiet. Anne couldn't hear anything over the beating of her heart.

"It be not a ship," another said.

Then Anne heard it. It was a rhythmic whoosh, whoosh, whoosh coming closer. Suddenly a huge beast, a wyvern, landed in the middle of the fire and sent sparks flying in all directions. The pirates brought up their arms to shield their eyes, and most rose to their feet. The wyvern's long neck shot out at one of the pirates and bit down on his shoulder. The man screamed and beat at the wyvern's face, but the sleek head pulled back like a snake and let out a deafening roar into the faces of all the pirates on that side of the fire. Anne saw Tsai and others fall backwards.

A man jumped off the wyvern's back. He landed on his feet, but stumbled forward in the sand. His face was covered by the shadow of a wide-brimmed hat and a high collar. Twitch pulled back his arm and let loose one of his knives at the intruder. The man's staff was already whirling in a practiced motion, and he swung it in Twitch's direction.

"*Brevis!*"

A slash of wind followed the tip of the staff and blew the knife back into Twitch's chest, as well as knocking two of the other pirates down. Twitch fell back against the cage. Anne lunged forward and grabbed *Alius* through the bars. She found the keys to her cage as well.

"*Incendia inflatus!*" One of the man's hands came up and a fireball formed. He threw it at two of the pirates regaining their feet. The camp brightened as though the sun was shining when the fireball struck between them, raining bits of fire and flesh from the sky.

Anne managed to get the key into her cage and unlock the door. She looked up in time to see the wyvern knock Brutus to the ground with a whip of his spade tail, but another pirate swung down hard with a curved cutlass on the wyvern's back. The blade didn't pierce the scales, and the creature brought its head around and grabbed the pirate by the legs with long pointy teeth and threw him toward the water.

Beorn, the one who failed playing the harp, grabbed Anne's hair and her hand holding the stiletto. He began to drag her down the beach. "Come on, you're coming with me!"

Another strange word called above the cries of the wounded pirates. "*Onis!*" Anne didn't see the effect of the spell, but she had a battle of her own to fight now.

She yelled out "*Alius,*" and suddenly she felt two of her. The real her was still tightly grasped by the pirate, but Anne's illusion stuck her dagger deep into Beorn's stomach. His hands loosened instantly, and she pushed him away, keeping a firm hold on her dagger.

She looked back where the campfire had been. Two men lay screaming in the sand, their bodies full of teeth marks. Brutus lay unmoving next to a rock by the cliff, his neck at an odd angle. Twitch was no longer twitching, and his knife was still embedded up to the hilt in his chest. There were scorch marks on the ground where two more pirates had stood. The others were fleeing into the night.

"Anne?" The voice sounded anxious.

It can't be.

"Galavon?"

The man swept his hat down from the top of his head and held it to his chest. "It's me."

Anne lost her concentration, and the illusion faded. She forgot about the wyvern and ran forward, wrapped her arms around him, and buried her head into his chest against his cold scale armor. She began to sob.

She could feel Galavon's confusion, but he eventually brought his arms around her. "Shhh, it's ok, it's all right. They're gone, Anne."

Anne pushed him back to arms length and looked up into his eyes. His face was smooth and his eyes were green, just as she remembered. "Can we leave?" she asked. She felt a tear run down her cheek. "I want to leave."

Galavon nodded. He looked tired. The wyvern turned its long neck and coo'ed at the pair. A smile crept up on Galavon's face, and he patted the wyvern's nose. The creature then looked at Anne and then back to Galavon. "Rorrick's right. We can only go a little ways, but perhaps we can find something." Galavon looked around the camp then, picking up a satchel and stuffing it with bread and empty bottles. He even picked up the harp.

"Rorrick?" she asked. She moved forward and felt the wyvern's neck. His scales were hard as rock, but placed perfectly to overlap one another. The wyvern inhaled deeply, but soon exhaled as Anne found a tender spot on his neck to rub.

"He's safe, I promise. Well, it's not like you're afraid I suppose. Come on, you can sit in front of me." Galavon jumped on the wyvern's back just behind the neck. He put his hat back on, pulling it tight, and held out a hand. Anne took it.

"We'll have to stay low," Galavon said. "It'll take too much energy to fly up on the cliffs. Maybe we'll find another beach." With that, Rorrick jumped into the air and with a few beats of his massive wings, they were gliding over the water.

Anne let her arms reach out to either side like wings of her own. The wind swirled past her, the waves roared below, and the moon shone above. It was exhilarating and freeing, especially after the cage. She felt safe riding Rorrick with Galavon's arms wrapped around her waist. She laughed out loud and grinned, leaving her troubles further and further behind with each beat of Rorrick's wings.

But Anne could tell Galavon was getting tired. Even Rorrick seemed to be struggling. The beating of his wings slowed, and the water began to loom closer. Everything just looked dark along the shore.

"*Subluceo,*" she said. The familiar energy ran through her body and produced a glowing orb above her shoulder. She sent it out along the cliffs, speeding ahead of them.

"There," she said. The globe of light stopped in front of the opening of a sea cave. It looked as though the water flowed right in. "It looks deep. Perhaps it's dry inside."

As they got closer, Anne commanded her globe farther in. There was a small beach filled with crabs, but further up a bit of rock jutted forward to make a shelf above the crashing waves. Rorrick landed just before the small beach in the shallows, no longer able to beat his wings in the tight space. He walked to the beach and Anne and Galavon jumped off his back.

Galavon truly looked exhausted now. He was fighting to stand. "Anne," he said pulling off his hat. "Please, remember me like this."

"What do you mean?" she said. Her globe of light still lit the cave, and she could see Galavon's tired green eyes, his shaggy straight brown hair. There was no hair on his face, and Anne doubted he would ever really be able to grow a beard. He didn't have big muscles like Captain Philial, but he didn't look as soft as he had in Pearl. He was still the merchant boy, everything Anne could have hoped for.

"*Voco Rorrick*," Galavon said. The wyvern gave one last regretful look at Anne before turning to mist and disappearing into Galavon's chest. Galavon gasped in pain before dropping his staff and hat and falling to his hands and knees. Anne rushed over to grab his shoulders. He gasped for breath before turning back to look at Anne.

Half of his face was covered in scales. His eyes looked like cat eyes, a single slit among green. Though he was still breathing hard, Galavon looked sad and worried. He looked at her with those cat eyes as though waiting for something.

No, not cat eyes. Dragon eyes.

"I'm a monster," he whispered. He turned his head away.

"No, you're not," Anne said. She stroked his hair. "Those men were monsters. You, you're my hero." He looked back again and smiled. His green dragon eyes seemed to say thank you.

"Have you ever... killed a person? I think I killed three men tonight, not including those that Rorrick killed." He looked down at his hands.

Anne hadn't thought about their actions. She was just glad to be safe. "If you wouldn't have killed them, I'd be worse than dead." She continued to stroke his hair. She too had killed a man, but she had no regrets. She knew the look in his eyes.

Anne helped him up the shelf away from the sand. There was plenty of room for the two of them. Galavon put his hat on the stone and laid down on his back. Anne curled up against him with her head on his chest. His scale armor was hard, but she liked listening to the rhythm of his heart underneath. He managed to put one arm around her before passing out from exhaustion. She could feel more scales from beneath the sleeve of his tunic.

Anne felt safer in his arms than in any castle. She allowed her light to dissipate, and she stared out at the opening of the cave where the waves slowly crashed in. There was a streak of moonlight sparkling with the choppy water. She wished they could stay forever in that little cave.

The moonlight continued to glitter with the movement of the water, and Anne's eyes began to close. It was the last thing she saw before falling asleep.

Anne woke first. The sun was up, but they were far enough in the shadows that it wasn't overwhelmingly bright. She looked up at Galavon's face for nothing more than to be sure she hadn't dreamed the whole thing. It was the first night of sleep she hadn't had any nightmares. She had dreamed of riding on Rorrick in Galavon's arms. Galavon slept soundly still. She reached up with a hand and caressed the scales on his cheek. They were hard and cold.

My Galavon. You came to rescue me. And I thought you had forgotten me.

Anne managed to get out from under his arm without waking him. She stood and stretched, arching her sore back and stiff neck until they cracked. She didn't much care for sleeping on rock.

Now that the sun was up, she was able to see the cave in its entirety. The sandy beach was wider than she remembered, and crabs ran up and down the sand. The shelf they slept on didn't go much further back, but it did end in a small puddle of clear water that trickled down from above.

Anne went to the puddle and tasted it. It was fresh water, clean and so clear she could see small grains of sand at the bottom of the bowl shape where the water dripped. She scooped some up with her hands and drank. She then attempted to clean her face. She used the puddle as a mirror in an attempt to straighten her disheveled and unruly hair.

"Anne?" She heard from behind her just as she finished. "I, I thought I might have been dreaming. It really is you, isn't it?"

"It's me," she said smiling. "And are you truly Galavon? You're not exactly the merchant I remember from the Harvest Festival."

Galavon scooped up his hat and tried to disappear beneath the high collar of his shirt.

"No, no, in a good way. I just meant it seems like a lot has happened since that night." She lifted a hand.

"*Subluceo.*" A small white globe appeared above her palm. "I'm not the same girl you knew either." She let the globe dissipate.

Galavon nodded and looked out at the mouth of the cave. He was avoiding eye contact with her. "I'm sure it's a little awkward having me rescue you, having only met once before."

I'd rather no one else.

"Not at all," she said. "There's some fresh water here if you're thirsty. There might be some mussels in the sand, too. You wouldn't believe everything that's happened…"

Anne spent the rest of the morning telling her tale. When she told him about Ares' corpse, Galavon looked surprised, but not shocked to learn that Reproba Caelum was a false religion. She told him of Larith and his teachings. He listened intently, and Anne could tell that he still felt unsure of himself around her.

He's changed so much, but he's still nervous around me. I hope that never changes.

Galavon remained quiet through the tale and offered sympathy when she spoke of her father and her old home. She couldn't stop all her tears, but she managed to keep them under control until she finished. At the end, she sat down next to him against the wall of the cave and rested her head on his shoulder against the pauldron. "And what of you, Galavon? How did you become a seer, a shaman, a summoner, a mage!" She took her head off of his shoulder. "You're a mage, Galavon!"

Her excitement finally brought a smile to his face. He told his tale in few words, though in truth, Anne knew it should have taken longer than hers. He too had been through a lot since they last saw each other, yet it took him half the time to recount his adventures.

"So, Rorrick is his name?" she asked. "He's a beautiful creature." Anne looked toward the mouth of the cave. With the tide pushed out, the waves were much smaller. An idea came to her.

"Don't take this the wrong way Galavon, but you stink." His eyes grew big and a look of shock came over his face. "Don't worry, it's nothing a swim can't fix. Come on!" Anne stood and grabbed the hem of her filthy dress before pulling it up and over her head.

"Anne, wait!" he said averting his eyes. "You're, eh, were the daughter of the Constable, I can't..."

"Oh, shut your mouth," Anne said playfully. "I'm not just wearing a dress. I have on a smock and short breeches."

Galavon finally lowered his hands and turned around. Anne climbed down to the beach and waded into the water.

She heard Galavon take off his scale armor, but she focused on the little crabs that went scurrying whenever she walked near. Eventually he waded up beside her clad only in his braies, the underclothes most men wore.

Galavon was skinny, but not too thin. He didn't have huge muscles, but Anne found herself drawn to him. Scales crawled up on different areas of his body, and he was embarrassed by them. Anne ignored them and splashed water in his direction.

The two swam together, Anne finally getting a laugh out of Galavon when she threw one of the tiny crabs in his direction. He jumped back with a smile on his face and returned fire with a ball of seaweed.

Afterwards Galavon picked up the harp, tuned it, and began to play. He played a tune she'd never heard before about the wind. It seemed fitting for him. He played another about the dragons, but Anne had heard this one before. Both were simple, but pleasant.

"Can you play 'A Harpist's Broken String'? The one from the Harvest Festival?"

Galavon grimaced. "That's a fast one. I'm not sure I can keep up."

Anne playfully pushed him. "Come on! You have to at least try! I'll sing while you play!"

> *"In the city not far from here,*
> *Gathered a crowd,*
> *A harpist to hear!"*

"All right then," he said laughing. "Keep going, I'll try to keep up.

Anne laughed back and started the first verse again.

> *"In the city not far from here,*
> *Gathered a crowd,*
> *A harpist to hear!*
> *It was said he could win a tear*
> *From all the beautiful maidens dear."*

The pair did find some scallops along the beach in the cave, and they feasted upon them with some of the bread they had pilfered from the pirates. When the sun began to go down, sending rays of brilliant colors stretching into their cave to fill it with oranges and yellows, they sat together on the ledge of their shelf watching the light. Anne had her head on his shoulder again, but this time he wasn't wearing the pauldrons, and her head fit perfectly.

A perfect day.

She lifted her head from his shoulder. She grabbed his face, turned it toward hers, and kissed him. It wasn't the faint brush of lips as it had been on the steps of her manse. It was a full kiss, her lips pressed hard against his. She pulled her head back when the moment passed.

Now a perfect day.

They slept in a similar position as the night before, but this time they used their clothes as a meager cushion between them and the stone. While they positioned everything, Anne noticed she had lost her black ribbon during Galavon's rescue. She thought of her father and all those lost, including Lady Ignava, and smiled knowing they would be glad she was safe.

When Anne woke, Galavon was standing on the beach with wind swirling around him and rustling his shaggy hair. In an instant it was gone, and Galavon turned back to the shelf.

"You're up early," Anne said sleepily. "What are you doing down there?"

"You said there was a mage who should be with your brother, so I sent him a message on the wind. Larith." He kicked at the sand. "I figured he would know it was real message, not just a voice in his mind."

"What did you say?" Anne asked. She propped up on an elbow. "And how does the wind find him? He could be anywhere by now, probably staying at Pearl. He's the oldest man I've ever met, and he doesn't move much. He could have gone back to Caernarfon Castle I suppose, but he could be anywhere really."

"I, uh, the wind…"

Anne laughed. She was going to have to slow things down. "What did you say to him?"

"I figured we couldn't stay here forever," he said. "Although I'm enjoying it! I am! We just need food, a proper bed. So I gave him my name and asked him where I should take you."

What does he think I am, a helpless farm girl?

"Take me?" Anne responded dryly. "You mean where we should go?"

"Yeah, where we should go," he said quickly. "That's what I meant."

"You should've just asked me," Anne said. She stood and picked up her dress. She had managed to clean it to an acceptable level yesterday, but sleeping on it did the fabric no favors. "We need to go to the Cathedral of New Beginnings. That's where my brother will be. That's where all the nobles will be for that matter." She kept talking while her head disappeared inside the dress. "That's where the future will be decided, and that's where we'll be." Her head popped out, and she put her arms through the sleeves. "My brother needs me, and the people will need me. I must be there to help them. How fast can Rorrick get us there?"

"We can't ride him far," Galavon said. "Two of us is too heavy, and we share energy."

"Can you get us above the trees so I can see where we are? We need to get there as soon as possible."

Galavon sighed, but he nodded his head.

"Then get dressed, merchant boy. I'll fill up these bottles with water. We need to find a farm if we expect to eat today, and we should have left yesterday."

Galavon and Anne crashed down among the maltrees on Rorrick in front of two soldiers. Though shocked, the two leveled their spears and shouted an alarm rather than turning tail and running.

These must be real soldiers, not recruits like I saw in Pearl, Galavon thought.

Anne jumped off of Rorrick before Galavon was even done thinking. She walked to the pair with her hands held high.

"Lady Anne?" one asked. He dropped his spear and ran forward grabbing her, pulling her away from Rorrick.

Galavon jumped down from Rorrick's back as the green wyvern let out low roar at the sentries. At least, that's what Anne said they were. Sentries to the force that camped just to the Northwest of Asaph and the Cathedral of New Beginnings.

"Yes, it's me, I'm fine," Anne said, struggling to get out of the soldier's grip.

"We were told just yesterday ye were captured by pirates," he said, stunned, looking back and forth from her to Rorrick.

"Well, I was. And I was saved."

Galavon tore his gaze away from Anne. He loved looking at the feisty girl and the way her curly hair swayed in the breeze above her crystal blue eyes, but he knew she had the soldiers handled. Instead, he scratched Rorrick's chin before muttering *"Voco, Rorrick."*

The green wyvern turned to a mist and surged into Galavon's chest. Galavon did his best to stifle a cry of pain, but it came out as moan as he fell forward in the grass. He wasn't sure how Myson managed to do it without falling, the pain was unbelievable.

The sentries stared in horror at Galavon. Still breathing hard, he pulled his tall collar higher and his wide brimmed hat lower to cover his scales and eyes. It was the first time he was around people as a summoner who would not accept him. He was nervous.

Well, more nervous than usual.

Anne demanded to be taken to her brother despite the early morning, and the guards were unable to deny her request as shocked as they were. They walked through the trees, the soldiers obviously wary of Galavon, until they came to the camp.

The tents were all organized, and the pathways were kept clean of any clutter. They strode through multitudes of soldiers sitting outside of their tents. Those who recognized Anne pointed and said things like "The pearl of the province!" or "The Constable's sister!" They all seemed more interested in Anne than Galavon, and it made him feel a little more at ease until they came to the large tent in the center of the camp.

There was a boy with a crutch dozing on a stool outside the tent along with two guards. He snapped awake as soon as they came close, and he hobbled to his feet. "Eh, Lady Anne? Do ye wish to see..."

"Of course I do, Tim!" She pushed him back down on the stool.

Is there anyone in this Province she doesn't know or boss around?

Galavon shrugged at the boy as an apology before following Anne inside.

The tent was sparse except for a writing desk, a chest, four stools, an armor stand, a cot Galavon guessed was the boy Tim's, and Cecil's bed. Cecil Ziyad was standing in front of the desk embracing his sister, quill still in hand.

Anne was saying something Galavon couldn't make out, but Cecil stared hard at Galavon from over his sister's shoulder. It was the same stare he remembered from the feast, a look that said Galavon was out of place here. Galavon stepped to the side of the tent entrance and tried to blend in with the furniture.

Anne and Cecil ended their embrace, and Anne went into her story, vividly explaining her adventures. Cecil listened, occasionally smiling, sometimes grim if the story demanded it, but in-between these he studied Galavon as though he was a wild animal. Galavon did his best to ignore the looks while studying him back.

Cecil had changed a great deal since Galavon saw him on the raised dais of the Harvest Festival. His eyes were harder, much harder, his already well muscular form now tighter. He had the start of a beard as well, making him look a full grown man. There was also a thick air of authority about him now, and a slight worry along the edges of his eyes.

As Anne's story came to an end, she grabbed Cecil's hand. "And here we are. What about you? You look older with that beard!"

Cecil rubbed the hair on his face. "Yes. Anne, did anyone, have they told you about mother...?"

"Yes, I know." A look crossed her face, like she wanted to say more but thought better. "How did you come to be here?"

Cecil stared down at her and a slight smile came to his lips. "Duty, vengeance, but mostly truth. It's been a hard journey Anne, I'm sure you already know most of it."

"Well, sure," she responded. "I heard some, but I want the details. Like what exactly happened in Zephyr Hills? Or the battle with the trolls? And the manse..."

"He'll have to fill you in on the details later, Anne." An old man walked in then wearing the robes of a nuncio. Galavon assumed this was Larith, the mage Anne had spoken about. He had sent a message back on the wind telling Galavon which camp was Cecil's. He gave Galavon a nod and said, "Summoner," as though it was nothing out of the ordinary. He then looked at Cecil.

"Ah, yes... another meeting," Cecil sighed. He walked to the chest in the room and put on a dark blue coat with brass buttons. Anne gave Larith a hug before standing by Galavon.

"Did you dream again, last night?" Larith asked Cecil as he buttoned the coat.

"I did. The vision was similar to the one I had the night before."

Larith nodded, and Anne looked up at Galavon with confusion on her face. He shrugged.

"I believe you should put a great deal of faith in these visions. I know your dream of the trolls proved to be true, and with that precedence, it would wise to use the information they provide."

"I will," Cecil said. "But it's easier said than done. It's difficult to convince others when I say I had a dream." Cecil's voice was stern, resolute. Commanding. Galavon couldn't believe anyone could argue against that tone.

"Yes, I imagine so. Let us go then, they wait. Come along Anne, Galavon."

The three of them left Cecil's tent and strode through the camp. Galavon noticed others mixed in with the soldiers, household guards of the nobility.

They walked into a large tent with a long rectangular table. A map was strewn out across the top of it. Where there wasn't ink, it was yellowed. The old map depicted Asaph.

Everyone around the table stood as the four of them entered. Cecil went in first, followed by Larith. Anne came through next, and there was a gasp. No one noticed Galavon, and he used it to slip into a crowded corner.

"Lady Anne!" this came from a woman at the table. "We had news you were captured right outside Himeji Castle! Are you well? Are you hurt?"

Anne opened her mouth to respond, but Cecil spoke over her, no small feat Galavon knew. "She's fine now, Lady Ayne. You may all be seated. Another chair for my sister, please." Cecil didn't slow as he walked to a chair at the head of the table, and Larith took another along the edge. Soon a stool was produced beside Cecil's chair. Anne sat down in it and made it look as though it were a throne.

They truly are Ziyad's, Galavon thought looking at the brother and sister. It was sometimes hard to remember that the spirited Anne was the daughter of a Constable and a high ranking noble in her own right. Cecil, on the other hand, never looked less than the very image of a powerful noble.

Galavon could feel someone staring at him through his high collar and the shadows created by the brim of his hat. Along the edge of the table he caught the glare of Ceridwen. The gaze wasn't angry but questioning. He looked away from her eyes quickly and did his best to ignore the mage.

Cecil acknowledged everyone around the table and greeted them by name. He started with those to his right. Directly beside him was Duke Briel, the man Anne had told Galavon about who resided in Castle Caernarfon. Then came the

Lady Ayn, or as Cecil said in his formal tones, the Duchess Hamilton. Beside her was Count Marcus Berthier, who received a special thanks for his brother's sacrifice in defense of Cecil's life. Anne's eyes got large at the thanks, and Galavon could see worry in her face.

Next was Count Rolf Kyburg, a balding Lord, then Count Warin and Count Guiscard who seemed to be good friends with one another. After the pair came Lord Gregory White, and then a man named Lord Will Tyrol. Cecil wished his father count Tyrol many more days in his old age.

From the little Galavon knew of the Peninsula Province, they accounted for two of three duchies and six of eight counties. It was a significant portion of the Peninsula Province.

Cecil then went to his left down the table, announcing these men as representatives from the Army of Truth. First came Lieutenant Commander Varro, a man who looked every inch a soldier. Next came Lieutenant Herzen, a grey haired man with a long dangling mustache, who did not have the look of a noble. Then there was Lieutenant Gherro, who looked young beside the old veterans.

Cecil announced the next three as representatives of the Veneficus. Larith was first, all dignity with his snow white hair and wrinkled smile. Then came Ceridwen, demand already plastered on her face, and another woman who looked like an old farmer's wife. Hulda was her name, and though she didn't look as though she belonged at the table, it didn't seem as though she believed she didn't belong.

The Albus Veneficus already managed to join with them. It must have been why they were in such a hurry.

"For those of you who are new to our cause," Cecil began, "the Veneficus is an order of magic wielders sanctioned by myself and all of the nobility who sit at this table." There was a stir among the men and women around Galavon who he assumed were the lesser lords and ladies of the province. It didn't surprise him many were angry and shocked at their inclusion. Again Galavon wondered how Ceridwen had managed to weasel her way in with Cecil in such little time.

"I know many of you are concerned about their loyalty, but their assistance is necessary if we are to continue gaining ground. We have no priests of our own, and only a small number of monks have defected. Larith, a trusted friend and advisor of my mine, acts as their leader. He is known as the Archmage of the Veneficus, and these two women sit on the Council of Mages. The three of them, and any other mages who join their ranks and thus sit on the council will make the rules governing those who wield magic."

"That's too much power!" one man said from the crowd of lesser nobles.

"Whoever is selected as our leader once we have reclaimed the peninsula will have the right to veto their laws if they see fit to do so, but they cannot make laws of their own concerning magic."

Talk erupted among the crowd. Galavon saw Ceridwen smile in delight as she leaned over to discuss something with the woman Hulda who sat beside her.

Anne said something to Cecil Galavon couldn't make out due to the chatter. The voices around the pair died down though as they looked at Anne.

"What did she say?" asked Ceridwen, disbelief evident on her face.

"I said Galavon is a mage," Anne stated. *Oh no, Anne. Don't say it.* "A mage summoner. That means he deserves a seat on your Council of Mages. And a seat at this table then, for that matter."

Anne turned her crystalline gaze on Galavon, and the crowd parted around him. He could feel sweat beading on his temple.

"Him?" Ceridwen asked in the silence. "A mage? A mage summoner?"

"Bring him a chair," Cecil demanded in a despondent voice. Another stool was brought and placed at the end of the table by Hulda. Galavon took the seat, feeling every bit out o f place.

Wine was brought in on trays while Cecil continued. "As most of you know, we have secured Pearl after minimal fighting. The lands controlled by the lords and ladies present are also considered ours. Duke Marlow and Count Macedon, now known as the Devout, stand against us as supporters of Reproba Caelum. Count Desmond and Count Raitin have not chosen a side." Galavon watched as Cecil accepted a separate goblet. It wasn't the dark red of wine, but rather water. "Over two-thirds of the Army of Truth stand beside us as well. Lieutenant Commander Varro, if you will continue."

Varro stood. "What you're all looking at is a map of Asaph and the Cathedral of New Beginnings. Our forces currently triple, if not quadruple, those of the Devout, who are camped around the town. We have four full infantry cohorts and three cavalry cohorts, though some are filled in with household guards. The objective tomorrow is to seize control of the cathedral. With the cathedral in our hands and the forces of the Devout sent scattering, the entirety of the province will be ours."

"What about," Count Kyburg said jumping in, "Count Raitin and Count Desmond? We can't leave them unaccounted for."

Duke Briel began to open his mouth, but Cecil silenced him with an upraised arm. "They have assembled their household troops around their homes. They number too few to cause us any real trouble if they choose to attack. Messages have been sent, but it is likely they wait to see who will win out in the end. Either way, we can't afford to wait for them to choose a side while we have Duke Marlow and Count Macedon in one spot. A victory here at Asaph means the province is ours, and it buys us time before an army from the Kingdom of East Ager arrives. You may continue, Varro."

"Easy for you to dismiss, but your home doesn't border Count Desmond's," the Count retorted.

"That's right, Count Kyburg, it doesn't because I don't have a home. Reproba Caelum took it, just like they took my mother and my father. I hope you don't have to suffer as I have."

"Hmmph. Do we at least know why Duke Marlow has decided against joining us?"

"My personal sources say Duke Marlow believes he will be named the new Constable, so he has much to gain if we fail in our endeavor. Varro."

"Before we left, the Army of Truth began construction of a palisade wall here." The Lieutenant commander motioned to a miniature palisade wall sitting on the map. "As you can see, the wall covers the south and north side of Asaph, but it leaves open the fields to the west and east. Due to our superior numbers and the lack of any real fortifications on this side, we'll drive the bulk of our army through there to capture the town. A cavalry cohort will be sent to the east side to prevent any from escaping in that direction and to put pressure on that side of the town."

"The strength of our enemy lies with its magic. Their number of magic wielders outnumber those of ours at least two to one. Most on both sides are monks or clerics as I'm told they're called, but they may still cause a problem. Those in the Veneficus who practice White Magic will be spread throughout our lines to shield our troops from magic barrages, while those who wield more destructive magics will be divided into two groups."

"High Priest Denis put that palisade wall up like that for a reason," Lieutenant Gherro said. "Look how far from the town he had it built. He crafted the field. Are we sure we should allow him to pick the spot of this battle?"

Duke Briel barked out a laugh. "It's not like we have a choice in the matter. The fight will be in Asaph."

"But does it have to be there?" Count Kyburg asked.

I don't know this Count Kyburg, but for someone who looks as though he's never seen a battle, he seems to have an opinion on everything.

"It's possible he didn't have the time to finish the palisade, but it's also possible he is funneling our attack here, " Varro answered. "However, with our numbers…"

"If magic is his strength we could be marching right where he wants us," the Count insisted.

Ceridwen spoke. "The grouping makes it easier to block the spells, now shut your trap and let the men who do this sort of thing for a living talk."

Count Kyburg's jaw dropped, as did most in the tent. Lady Ayn stifled a laugh, Larith chuckled, and the soldiers nodded approvingly. Galavon felt as though he should be shocked, but he knew Ceridwen better than most at the table.

"As I was saying," Varro said, "with our numbers we should be able to easily overwhelm them and take the city."

"Also," Cecil said, "I believe I know why he is bringing us to that spot." All eyes turned to him.

"I believe there's an army of undead laying beneath the ground there. As Larith informed me, this is a common tactic used by necromancers and mages who practice Black Magic. The undead spring up amongst the ranks to create chaos and confusion."

"How do you know this?" Duke Briel asked. He looked as surprised as the others around the table.

"There have been a number of rumors of disappearances around Asaph, as well grave robberies. We will need to send a scout to confirm the ground is dug up in that area, but I'm confident they'll find loose dirt."

"That's hardly enough evidence to come to that sort of conclusion," Count Kyburg said. "What else do you know?"

"I had a dream."

Silence ensued. Galavon was part of that silence. *A dream?* A few of the lords and ladies along the tent wall snickered. None of the soldiers did.

"If the Army of Truth would have listened to his last dream, we'd be a great many men stronger," Varro said. The other officers at the table nodded.

"He speaks true," Lieutenant Herzen said. "I was there, I laughed, and I was wrong. I watched men die at the hands of the trolls because we didn't listen."

Galavon looked at Anne, and she looked back down the table. Apparently there was more to the story about the battle with the trolls.

Lady Ayn looked across to Ceridwen. "Then what do we do? How do you combat Black Magic?"

That's odd that she would ask Ceridwen over Larith. Have they been talking?

"There are White Magic spells to banish the undead," Ceridwen said. She looked to Larith for confirmation.

"They exist. For minor undead such as zombies, they must be raised from a fresh corpse. Even a novice cleric can dismiss them, for they are raised with a minimum amount of Black Magic," Larith said. "Skeletons are a combination of magics in order to hold the creature together. Ghouls require even more skill, as a necromancer must invest a great deal of Black Magic and more into the creature."

"So we're actually putting faith in this 'dream' Cecil had?" Count Kyburg asked.

"Constable Ziyad," Lord White said as several of the officers in the room bellowed out the same.

"It would be foolish not to at least prepare," Duke Briel stated. "Will the... Veneficus be able to handle this?" The question seemed hard for the Duke. The question was directed to Larith, but the other woman, Hulda, spoke.

"Zombies, yes, unless there are thousands. Even our newest clerics will be able to dismiss them with a simple thought, though we'll have to teach them. These spells are not common knowledge. The combination of magics used to raise a skeleton make them difficult for any magic wielder, but the soldiers can bring them down with a little effort."

"It is possible they have raised an arch-zombie. Simply put, the necromancer deposits just enough Black Magic and White Magic for the undead to think. Useful for raising shaman or the such. Still, they're fairly easily brought down."

"All of the spears have butt caps on the end," said Lieutenant Herzen. His dangling moustache moved with every word. "They're not as sharp as the tip, but they do come to a point. If the soldiers sharpen them, it will be easier to stab the creatures if they come from the ground."

"And we'll put more clerics with the infantry," Cecil said, "to help protect the troops against magic and to dispel the undead."

"Ghouls though, those creatures are difficult." Hulda said, starting again. "Like a zombie they feel no pain and are mostly whole, but like a skeleton they are fused with other magic that makes them resistant to spells. These abominations are cruel and take a serious toll on the necromancer who raises them. I would say you have one person able to destroy a ghoul, and he is sitting at this table." Hulda nodded to Larith.

Galavon didn't know how this woman had such knowledge of Black Magic, but the thought of fighting undead unnerved him. First bandits, then mages, wyverns, pirates, and now undead. Why was he sitting at this table? How was he supposed to help with any of this?

"The chance of a ghoul being present is slim," Larith said. "Even High Priest Denis lacks the knowledge to create such a creature, and he isn't fool enough to surrender that much of his life force to its creation. If there's a ghoul, then it's not the ghoul we should fear so much as the mage who created it. It would mean a curator is present."

"I've seen the body, Ares is dead," Lady Ayn said. "Are you saying it's a fake?"

"No, no, Lady Ayn," Duke Briel answered. "It's his corpse to be sure, but he has been dead for some time now. The curators could have sent a replacement."

"A single curator," Larith said, "will change the course of this battle. They were rumored to be gods for a reason. They are the masters of elemental magic."

"There is no evidence that we've come across that indicates the presence of a curator," Cecil responded. "Please Lieutenant commander, continue."

Varro spoke again. "Once the three cohorts who make up the battle line have engaged, a cavalry cohort will sweep around from the south, and another will do the same from the north. We should completely surround them in the field outside of town. Once we reach the houses of Asaph, our soldiers will split into maniple's to clear the streets. We want as little damage to the buildings as possible. Once the town is clear, we'll gather as many Veneficus as we are able to and clear out the Cathedral."

With the plan laid out, the discussion became mostly minor details. These were laid out by Varro and the other officers. Lunch was brought to the table, miniature pies with a moist crust filled with vegetables and chunks of chicken. Galavon devoured his small pie, his first real meal in days.

The meeting came to a close as the meal ended. Ceridwen and Hulda left immediately to teach their clerics how to battle undead. Ceridwen didn't leave without thumping Galavon on the head however, and demanding him to find her later that day. The nobility left to organize their own men, and the officer's of the Army of Truth gathered at the far end of the table going over the lists for the divisions of the army. Larith stayed seated at the table.

Galavon let the others clear the tent before he stood. Anne was a holding a conversation with Cecil, about the trolls he was sure. "Cecil!"

Sao, the stable boy Galavon had met in Pearl, burst in the tent out of breath. He no longer looked like a stable boy, however. His clothes were much finer, and like Cecil, he had the beginning of a beard on his face that made him look a great deal older.

"The high priest proclaimed Ares the King."

The king?

"What?" Someone bellowed.

"A curator king?" Anne asked.

"Are you sure? He declared a god king?" Cecil asked. The officers as the end of the table stopped their discussion.

"Ares was there! A curator Cecil, accepting a crown! The high priest said that the province would no longer be a province, but a kingdom. The Kingdom of Niveus."

Suddenly a sound like thunder shook the ground beneath them. Once, twice, and then a third time the boom sounded.

Varro wasted no time. "Berthier, get your cohort ready at the edge of camp. I want riders discovering what that was. Now!" Several of the Lieutenants darted out of the tent.

"That's not everything, Cecil," Sao said. "He proclaimed a Constable. He gave the title to Tarik Ziyad."

"Father?" Anne said. "He's alive?"

Galavon kept quiet but watched the news wash over Anne and Cecil. Anne's face was a mix of excitement and confusion, but Cecil held a straight face masking his emotions.

"That's impossible," Varro said. "I saw his body. Tarik Ziyad died in the Fire Pass Cathedral from arrow wounds and magic. His body was mangled and broken."

"I saw him," Sao said back. "He was bigger, his skin darker and black around the eyes. He wasn't the same as I remembered, but by the fire of Shiva, it was him!"

"He's a ghoul," Larith stated. The others in the tent quieted.

"Then our worst fears are confirmed; we face a curator tomorrow," Cecil said. "A rogue curator. It would seem we may not have the advantage despite our numbers."

From Galavon's seat he could see confidence fading from those who were left at the table. What looked like certain victory was no longer so certain.

"The revelation that Reproba Caelum is a false religion has brought you all to this point," Larith said. "You knew it would not be easy to separate from the Kingdom of East Ager and its curator overlords. However, it is not just the curators we face. It's time you knew who we're really fighting against." Larith said.

Galavon turned to look at the old Archmage. *Who we're were really fighting against? As if a rogue curator and the rest of the Kingdom of East Ager isn't enough!*

"I'll tell it."

A man at the edge of tent stepped forward. He wore the garb of the nobility, plenty of silk and even a fashionable beret that hid the top of his ears. "The elf who failed to kill you, Cecil; his name was Beretheor Sunsphere. He was three hundred years my senior, yet still born in Ager." When he looked up his purple eyes caught the light, and he pulled off his cap to reveal pointed ears.

Varro was the first to pull his blade, followed soon after by the others, and the sound of steel sliding out of leather erupted throughout the tent. Men jumped between Cecil and the elf as if expecting an attack at any moment.

"Darak!" Galavon said. "He's a friend! Put your weapons away!" Galavon put his arms out to stop them, but none of the guards moved to replace their drawn weapons.

"This elf is more than a friend," Larith said with a smile on his face. Tension relaxed in the tent and sword tips lowered, but none of them were returned to their sheaths.

"Lower your weapons. We all want answers, and this Darak can provide them." Cecil said forcefully. "Speak elf."

The elf nodded in thanks to Cecil. "As I was saying," he began, "the elf you killed was Beretheor Sunsphere, a middle-aged elf and a fellow agent working in the Kingdom of East Ager. My name is Dahareuch Starshine, also an agent of the Crescent City, as demonstrated by this." He pulled out a talisman on a chain with the sun and moon sharing the face. Galavon pulled his own out from beneath his tunic, the one his father had given him.

"Many years ago the elves ruled over a mighty empire across the Barren Ocean, The Dawn Empire. The empire was prosperous and soon became overpopulated by humans, a race the elves considered lesser due to their inability to use Cosmos Magic. They forced many of the humans to leave and settle new lands, the furthest of which were here.

"As you can imagine, the humans weren't pleased with being sent away from their home. There was an uprising. Despite not having magic of their own, the humans were winning due to sheer numbers. Finally, the Emperor combined his power with those of the elvish nobility, called High Elves, and used more Cosmos Magic than had ever been unleashed on the world. They called down a mighty meteor and crushed the entire army of humans.

"So great was the meteor that its destruction went beyond killing the humans. Dust rose into the air and blocked out the sun and stars. There was no light for crops to grow. Low Elves died of starvation, and even more died to powerful tornados that wrecked the lowlands. Soon the remainder of the High Elves were forced to search for a new land in Mundus. They sailed east hoping that their colonies had managed to escape the destruction they had called upon their own home.

"Once they arrived here in Ager, they vowed to never allow magic to destroy their home again. As the population slowly grew, the ruling class known as the Elders sent out agents throughout Mundus to determine threats and keep magic in check. What they discovered frightened them. They didn't trust humans due to the war they fought in their homeland, even those native to Ager. They made a pact with the curators to control Elemental Magic.

"The curators may have subdued Shiva, but you can't trap the living essence of an element with Elemental Magic. Elves forged Shiva's prison beneath the rock at Fire Pass. Their influence spreads far and wide all over Ager. As agents, it was our job to travel the different cities of these lands to be sure there was no growth of power that could threaten the land.

"You're father was an agent, Galavon, though a human one. That is why he possessed that charm. But they do more than identify agents. That piece of jewelry has the ability to negate magic spells when they touch your skin. You're father gave you the pendant when he decided he no longer wished to work for the Elders. He joined the revolution Galavon, and now resides in Pearl."

Galavon fingered the pendant. All this time and he never knew what it did.

"This new Ares is ambitious," Darak continued. "He has separated himself from the other curators, similar to what you all have done. With this discovery, Beretheor and I were ordered to assassinate you Cecil Ziyad, and then him, so that Reproba Caelum could once again claim this land and control Elemental Magic."

"What made you change your mind?" Cecil asked.

"I was born in Ager. This land is my home. I have those I call friends in this very peninsula, and even those I claim as family. In my travels I have seen the oppression the curators use to keep their end of the bargain struck with my people, and I don't believe it's right."

"This battle will not be the last or the most difficult we will face if we wish true independence from the elves," Larith stated. "There will be many difficult times ahead, but despite the odds we face, there are others who wish an end to the tyranny as well, other allies we must use."

"Then you stand with us, elf? Can you help us take down this new Ares?" Cecil asked.

"I will do all that I am able to further your cause," Darak responded.

"Well, I don't intend to be ruled over by priests, elves or a curator," Lieutenant Commander Varro said. "I intend to put someone I can trust on the throne! I say we bring the fight tomorrow against this King Ares, curator or not!"

There was a murmur of agreement around the table. Galavon wasn't sure they understood exactly what they faced. If Darak spoke the truth, than even if they won the battle tomorrow against a curator, the revolution would not only be fighting the Kingdom of East Ager, but all those that the elves influenced as well.

Berthier strode into the tent and bowed. "Defenses are set, Constable."

"And the thunder? What was it?" Cecil asked.

"From what we can tell it was Duke Marlow and his sons riding for our camp with more soldiers. Their flags and gear still lay about on the ground, but there are no bodies."

"More undead," Larith said. "He's using them to create more undead."

"They were rounding up some of the townspeople even as I came here," Sao said. "You don't think their turning them undead, do you?"

By the fire of Shiva, would they kill innocents to boost their lines?

"It doesn't matter. We'll face nothing new," Cecil said. "Preparations continue as we discussed before. Tomorrow, we ride to battle!"

Chapter 13
(Galavon, Ceridwen, Anne, Larith, Galavon, Ceridwen, Anne, Larith, Galavon)

What am I doing here?

That was the question Galavon asked himself over and over again. Yet, no matter how many times he asked himself the question, no matter how many times he replayed recent events in his head, he still had a hard time believing where he was and what he was doing.

He stood in one of the two groups of spell casters. Due to Anne's insistence, he was inducted into the ruling council of the Veneficus, the Council of Mages. When it was revealed he was a summoner, most of the Veneficus were awed rather than distrusting. Galavon wished that could have been said for the others in the camp. Though they were fighting against Reproba Caelum, some still made signs of the five-pointed star in his direction.

Regardless of their thoughts, as a member of the Council he was given command over one of the two groups of Veneficus that were to throw magic missiles at the enemy. He only knew two fire spells though, and one was only useful for starting a campfire. Luckily it seemed to be the preferred spell for most of the shaman in his group. His wind spells would help little from such a distance.

"Brrrrrrrr." It was a long note, blown from a conch shell, and after it sounded more began to emit the blast from amongst the ranks. It was the command to march. Galavon gulped. It was the command to engage in battle and face death.

What am I doing here?

Galavon still had the amulet his father had given him safely tucked away beneath his tunic. He had tried to convince Anne to take it, but she refused, stating it was his only protection against magic since he couldn't use White Magic.

Galavon nodded to those around him with a false air of confidence. He was glad they couldn't see his pale face or the fear in his eyes due to his hat and high collar. He had a druid, a sahagin, and four shaman. Two clerics also walked with them, and it was there job to shield them from any spells sent their direction. His orders were easy enough. He was to wait until Ceridwen gave them a target, but Galavon knew how battles went. He had read plenty of histories. They never went according to plan.

Galavon wished Anne was in his group. She had managed to bully her brother into allowing her to be in the battle. Even Larith had joined her cause, saying it would be a waste not to use a cleric when they had one. Cecil had relented, allowing her in the other group as one of two clerics who were supposed to shield them from magical attacks. He gave her a bodyguard, the stable boy Sao, but Galavon would rather have her safe in a castle somewhere.

Or with me. I could protect her.

Ceridwen walked amongst the ranks of the infantry cohort in the center of the advancing line. She felt empowered, as though she was finally where she belonged. It would have made sense for her to be with one of the two groups of Veneficus throwing spells at the enemy, but she was a woman of action. She wanted to lead, to curse those who had held her down for so long with the very air from own lungs. Where better than in the thick of battle?

Well, that and these clerics that are meant to protect the soldiers are nothing more than foolish children without an ounce of strength.

She knew some of the clerics were strong, but they were mostly farmers' wives who had hid their use of White Magic and old men who used to be pearl divers and decided to keep rather than sell one of the pearls they found. They were cowards in Ceridwen's mind, hiding and hoping to never be discovered by the Crows. Sure there were a few who had fought in the War of Fire against the goblins, but there were few of them trusted enough to walk amongst the ranks because they used to be monks.

Little more than dirt in my opinion. Except for the Duchess, of course. She's brave. For a noble.

Ceridwen spit, barely missing the boot of the soldier in front of her. Thoughts of the nobility disgusted her. Men and women pampered in comfort , given everything, claiming to be special because they were born with ten times more than everyone else. They were handed power rather than earning it. They didn't know what it was to truly live. The Lady Ayn, however, was a strong woman and a fast learner. It had only taken her days to learn the basics of White Magic.

Ceridwen honestly hoped the basics were enough to keep her alive.

There were three other mages on their side in the battle. Larith rode with the Ziyad boy, Hulda commanded one of the two groups of Veneficus, and Galavon commanded the other.

Ceridwen chuckled at the thought of him. She remembered when he was a worthless yelp of a boy. Now he was a mage summoner! She hated to admit it, and she never would to his face, but she was proud of him. Shocked, but proud.

"Shields!" One soldier said beside her. Judging by the stripes on his shoulder, he was a marshal. The call came from others along the line as well, and the well-trained soldiers lifted their shields above their heads.

But Ceridwen saw the fireball hurtling through the air. *Incendia inflatus* were the words. A simple, devastating spell that caused more damage with its explosion than with its fire. Nothing she couldn't handle, but also something those shields could not.

"*Contego.*"

She pictured a globe surrounding her and the soldiers around her in the maniple she marched with. She felt the familiar swell of power, a comfort really, a soothing force she expelled to form a shield from the attacks. She couldn't make the shield big enough for the entire cohort without jeopardizing its strength, so the key was to put the shield where it needed to be to minimize the destruction.

The ball of fire hit the magical barrier and exploded, creating a boom that made some of the younger soldiers flinch. Ceridwen buckled underneath the blast, and she felt her skin burn briefly as though the fire had hit her instead of the shield. It was the cost of blocking magic – you still felt some of the blow.

But Ceridwen welcomed the pain. She laughed out loud, and she knew she sounded crazy. She had never held anything back, including her honest, true, screeching laugh. "If that's all those grave-robbing dragon-turds have to throw at us, this will be a slaughter!"

Some of the soldiers grinned, but the marshal beside her kept his eyes on the sky. More flames shot along the line, even a bolt of lightning struck. A distant call of "Brace!" came from somewhere, and Ceridwen saw a wave in the ground approaching from above the heads of the soldiers in front of her. The ripple in the earth struck a shield similar to the one Ceridwen had created. A cry went up, and Ceridwen saw an old man she had taught the spell shield to only the day before launched through the air as he took the full brunt of the spell.

Amateur, wyvern welp.

The marshal beside her made the call again. "Shields!" If he would have paid attention the first time, he'd know there was no need for the call.

"Contego."

White Magic surged through her and Ceridwen put up her barrier. Another fire ball soared through the air. This one seemed bigger than the others, perhaps larger then all of them combined.

The raging ball of flame hit the shield hard and drove Ceridwen down to her knees. She sunk into the loose dirt, her skin burning. She gritted her teeth and screamed through them, eyes clutched shut. She forced her eyes open and screamed at the sky. "By the fire of Shiva that burns!"

The marshal gripped her elbow and hoisted her to her feet. He helped her stumble along with the marching men.

That one had some built up anger. Maybe even a bit of pain.

"Did you see where it came from?" Ceridwen asked. The marshal pointed straight ahead. There, on the edge of town, was a building with people on its roof. She nodded and pushed off his helping hands.

"Subluceo."

A small globe of light formed in front of her face. She commanded it to the building. As much as she would have liked to utterly destroy them herself, she knew what her job was in the ranks of these soldiers.

The globe dissipated as soon as it neared, not by her own command. Immediately fireballs flew to the spot, even a boulder hurtled through the air. A druid's she was sure, probably Fargo. The man was proud of what he was. The fire attacks crashed against a globe of protection similar to Ceridwen's, harmlessly dissipating above their target. Even the boulder struck the shield and turned into a million pebbles that showered a group of soldiers beneath.

And that's why I'm with the soldiers. We'll see how they like these spears being shoved up their arses.

Anne watched the shaman in her group throw fire at the building. The sahagin claimed they weren't close enough for their magic, but the shaman unleashed a torrent of flames that were repelled by the enemy's magical barrier. Similar spells were thrown at the marching line of soldiers.

"Now they know where our casters are," Sao said to Anne. "They should be targeting us soon."

Sao was the only non-spellcaster in their little group. It was one of the conditions Cecil had set to allow her in the battle. She didn't mind Saoirse Ire being there, she had known him her whole life, but she didn't like feeling as though she had to be babysat.

Anne kept her eyes on the sky as they walked behind the lines of marching soldiers in their small group. The front ranks were nearing the opening in the palisade, and if Cecil w as right, they were about to be attacked by undead. Sill, her job was to protect this group, and she kept her eyes focused on the clouds.

And then it was her turn. Balls of fire soared over the heads of the soldiers in front of her, coming directly at her. This was part of the plan, to try and distract the magical attacks from the soldiers so that the clerics marching with them could focus on fending off the undead.

Anne was told the further away the spell was thrown, the easier it would be for her to block. She had learned the spell yesterday, and she hoped she was ready to receive a real hit.

"*Contego,*" she said. The other cleric in their group muttered the same word.

Their shield went up, and together they weathered the attack. Anne felt a burning along her skin with each hit, and light blows from each strike. It reminded her of one morning when she had helped her maid Isabella make breakfast. It was similar to the popping bacon grease that hit her skin.

Not my maid. My mother.

"Anne, are you all right?" Sao asked. He clutched that odd weapon of his, a claw, as though it would be helpful against the ranged attacks. The weapon was like her dagger, *Alius*. It too had a name and a power, one that Larith had told Sao yesterday.

"Of course!" she said with a forced smile. "It's like swatting flies!" She hoped they didn't launch anymore any time soon.

"There they are," Varro said. They could see undead rising from the ground. Some came behind the ranks, dead flesh reaching up to pull out the rest of their rotting corpse. Some, the fresher ones it seemed, jumped up from their holes, grabbing and slashing with bare hands at anything within reach. These were mostly among the soldiers.

"Congratulations on being correct," Count Kyburg said. He sat on horseback with some of the other nobility who weren't going to take part in the fight.

"I'd rather have been wrong," Cecil said.

Yes, the boy has become a man, Larith thought, keeping his gaze on the fighting. *He has become a man of steel, toughened and sharpened by circumstance.*

"Go on," Duke Briel said. "The battle has started."

The Count turned his horse and fled with the others. Larith didn't bother watching them go. Only he, Cecil, Duke Briel, the elf Darak, and a few of the nobility stayed to fight with the regular soldiers. Larith watched more of the undead crawl up from the earth. Flashes of light went off like fireworks, each one marking the end of one of the zombies at the hands of a cleric.

Larith glanced a look at Cecil. Without his dream the soldiers there would have been caught unaware. Larith questioned it before, but now he was sure: Cecil was an Oracle, gifted with the rarest of magics, Holy Magic.

"By the fire of Shiva, I'm glad Anne isn't down there," Cecil muttered, barely audible.

The group of enemy soldiers, living enemy soldiers, beneath the outermost building with the spell casters began to move forward, marching where the Army of Truth's infantry battled the undead.

"There's the move we've been waiting for," Varro said.

"Signal the wings to charge and surround them," Cecil said. Larith was no general, but the infantry ranks held their formation, a good sign.

Varro turned and raised a conch shell to his lips.

"*Adiuvo*," Larith quietly said.

Two short blows from the shell rang loud and clear, green speckles coming from the end. The signal would be heard.

"There," Gherro said to Cecil. Larith looked to where he was pointing. The space between the Palisade was large, too large for the infantry line to completely fill it in. Cecil and the officers had planned for the cohorts to ride through the openings on either side of the infantry in order to surround the enemy when they engaged. It seemed Ares had anticipated the maneuver. Undead rose from the left side to block their path, and another force of soldiers marched to intercept those on the right.

"It's too many," Duke Briel said. "We need to send in the Veneficus hanging back. Our maneuver will fail if the cohort isn't strong enough to break though."

Larith's horse shook it's mane. He could feel its nervousness through the saddle. He continued to observe with the others, but it seemed too early to commit the reserves.

Suddenly the sky above the south side of the Army of Truth's infantry line seemed to catch fire. The clouds turned red, and all the air, even where Larith sat on his horse's, seemed warmer. Over a dozen balls of flame, one bigger than any that had yet been launched, covered that portion of the sky before descending down upon the line.

"Shiva's own breath..." Duke Briel murmured.

A magical shield came up, followed by explosion after explosion on its surface. Before the last fireball fell though, the shield shattered like glass, and the fireball fell in among those fighting the rising undead.

"Give the signal for the Hulda's Veneficus to move in with the cavalry on their side. Send Galavon's to the infantry," Cecil ordered. "We also ride for the breach, but we charge through and then support the cavalry cohort. Yah!" Cecil dug his heels into Babieca's side and flew into a gallop. Larith gathered his reigns to follow. He felt as though his old bones would shake free. Duke Briel, Lieutenant-Commander Varro, Marshal Gherro, and the elf Darak followed with him.

That's the signal. We have to go in there.

Galavon gripped his staff tight, his knuckles going white. He thought the skirmish on the road to Farrow was a real fight. He was wrong then, and he was scared now.

He saw zombies spring up from the ground in front of him alongside skeletons wielding rusty blades. The infantry didn't even break stride, crushing the undead beneath their heels and the butt caps of their spears. If one did manage to cause a disruption, the clerics banished them with a thought and a yell.

That was before the rain of fire. Now there was a hole in the line, infantry being flung alongside the undead. Most of the soldiers who were not in the direct blast were merely dazed and regained their feet as soon as they were able, discarding their shields to use their spears with both hands. The fight there was wild, more single combat now, and that was where Galavon and his band were to go.

One of Torvil's sayings came to mind. *The things we do for women.*

"To the breach!" Galavon yelled, holding his staff in the air. His small group of casters ran with him to the open ground in the wake of the passing cavalry cohort coming in between the side of the line and the palisade. Before Galavon's group could make it, another cavalry cohort, the reserves commanded by Cecil Ziyad himself, stormed past them. Despite the dust their horses threw in the air, Galavon was glad to see them galloping past to the breach as well. None of his group seemed to look forward to what they faced.

Well, maybe except the druid, Fargo. He seems eager enough.

But even as the cavalry rode by on their Southern Jigglers who seemed to dance across the field of battle, hands came up from beneath the dirt. Galavon felt the rumble of another blast, though he didn't see where. His attention was focused on the skeleton sitting up from the ground, the bottom half of its body still covered in dirt.

What did they say about skeletons? They were hard for the clerics, but the soldiers could bring them down.

"*Brevis!*" Galavon shouted, swinging his staff in front of him even as he ran toward the skeleton. An arc of wind flew forth from his swing, knocking the skeleton back just as it got its legs free. It sat back up as Galavon got closer, and with a double handed blow from his staff he sent the head bouncing off its shoulders.

Following in from behind, the druid Fargo, a large man, placed a boot on the skeleton's ribcage and pushed the torso back against the ground, shattering bone and sending splinters in all directions.

"We 'ave to use force fer the skellies!" he said between laughs. He laughed! The druid reminded Galavon of Torvil without the beard.

More undead were springing up around them. Galavon saw one of the clerics dismiss a zombie in a brilliant flash of light, and one of the sahagin go into a trance and send hundreds if not thousands of tiny needle-like droplets into a running zombie. They moved forward and soon came to where the fireball had crashed.

Some from the reserve cavalry were leaping from their horses and picking up shields to try and reestablish the line. The others were busy battling undead covered in armor with long spears, a difficult match up for the men on horseback.

Wait, those are our soldiers they're fighting! Our own dead are rising against us!

It was Galavon's only thought before he was forced to the side by the thrust of a spear. He looked into the soldier's helmet and saw a charred face. His eyes were black. Galavon batted away another thrust with the end of his staff before swinging out in an attack of his own.

"Brevis!" Nothing happened.

The zombie soldier pulled back his spear and swung it like a staff at Galavon's head. He just managed to duck beneath the swing and take a few steps back. He reached out his hand again.

"Incendia inflatus!"

This time he pulled from the fire burning in his chest. He only allowed a small orb of flame to form before sending it crashing into the zombie's chest. The small ball exploded, separating the zombie into two.

From the corner of his eye he saw a cavalry officer pulled from his horse by an undead woman wielding a frying pan, and a shaman brought down by a skeleton. Galavon had no way to help them as he was forced back by another thrusting spear. A man on horseback rode by and sliced down with his falchion, knocking the zombie forward off balance. Galavon took the opening and sent his own thrust toward the zombie's face.

"*Brevis!*"

Wind swirled down Galavon's staff directly into the bloodied face of the zombie. Galavon heard a crack as bone broke and the head snapped back. The back lip of the helmet the zombie soldier wore dug through his leather brigandine and held his head looking skyward. The corpse dropped its spear and walked in circles, arms outstretched.

More of their own soldiers rose. With each death the enemy army grew. Galavon even saw a three legged horse plow into one of their mounted soldiers, bringing him crashing down in a pile of kicking hooves.

"There, above! Bring him down!"

Galavon turned where he heard the voice and saw Darak leap from the saddle of his horse. He fired two arrows before landing in a roll on the ground, then standing to fire more. Galavon followed the flight of the arrows to Ares hovering above the battle.

His wide, white wings kept him bouncing in the air. It looked as though he was scanning the field. Every now and then he would point to an area and the dead would rise to fight for him. The arrows were brushed away by wind as though they were nothing, and the fake god continued to make the Army of Truth's casualties his minions.

"It be Ares himself!" Fargo yelled looking up. "Use yer spells on him!" He then roared in a primal grunt, knelt on his knees, and drew runes in the dirt. The shaman commanded balls of fire to their hands and threw them into the sky. Bullets of water followed just behind the fire, with a huge boulder flying in last. Galavon added a fireball of his own to the barrage.

Ares didn't bother to even try and dodge the attacks. The fireballs, boulder and water bullets struck a shield around him. Galavon lost sight of him due to the spray of earth and fiery explosions. When it cleared, Ares still bounced in the air, his white wings keeping him afloat.

"Darak, can you use Cosmos Magic to break that shield?" Galavon asked. He smashed his staff across the face of a zombie with a broken leg lumbering toward him.

"I use the moon and stars," he said, firing another arrow at the curator and dodging a lunge from what appeared to be a dead baker. "I can do nothing under the sun."

Looking around, with the spear wall gone, it was hard to tell who was winning in the breach. A huge explosion sounded to the north, and Galavon guessed the formation there was broken as well. The reserves had continued their charge through to strike at the new oncoming force with the other cavalry cohort, and still more of the dead dug themselves up from the ground. Galavon was at the back of the fight with Darak, the others having moved forward with the advance. Ares made another motion with his hands, and Galavon knew he called more soldiers from death to fight for him.

He has to die, or all is lost.

"Voco Rorrik."

Galavon's muscles tightened all over his body. He dropped his staff unknowingly and hunched over in an attempt to stay on his two feet. He screamed up at the sky, and a mist in the shape of Rorrik's head burst free from his chest followed soon after by a neck, body, and tail. The wyvern shot straight into the sky toward the curator.

Galavon stood upright and inhaled deeply, desperate for air. He kept his eyes open and watched Rorrik.

If horses could fly, that graceful wyvern would have been considered a Southern Jiggler, but he looked more like a Charger now the way he hurtled himself through the air at Ares. The flying green let out a piercing roar. Galavon wished he could see the shock on the curator's face when he finally saw the wyvern coming straight at him.

A beam of white so bright it left spots in Cecil's vision cut through the air, but Rorrik broke into a roll, barely dodging the attack, and the beam struck the open ground behind the battle. A wall of flames came up then, but Rorrik charged straight through, and in an instant it looked as though a fireball was carrying the curator straight into the air. The pair did a loop back around, both of them upside down, before falling to land behind the battle.

Galavon grabbed his staff from the ground and raced to where they landed, only steps behind Darak.

Ceridwen spit a mouthful of dust to the side. All around her the soldiers of the Army of Truth pushed forward, their shields interlocked like dragon scales and their spears stabbing ahead. They were moving forward, pushing against a smaller shield wall in front of them. She could feel hands gripping at her ankles. There was no room for her to stop them, but no room for them to crawl out of their holes either.

The dust came from a blast to the south. She knew that meant someone's shield had broken. She hoped the caster had died in the following blast. A broken spell shield meant the loss of sanity for the caster.

Even squished together like they were, she managed to protect the line from more magic attacks. The men and women who threw the magic, judging by the clothes they wore, were priests. There was one however, the one who's blasts were stronger than all the others, who wore faded black. They were now away from the building and behind the soldiers on the field.

"Push!" the marshal yelled beside her. "They'll break soon! Push!"

She heard the soldiers around her heaving. The line surged forward with the effort, and Ceridwen knew they would soon to be trampling over the living and the undead.

There, just over the heads of the soldiers in front of her, she saw a huge, low fireball land among the enemy soldiers just behind their front line. *By the fire of Shiva, they're killing their own troops to break our formation!*

The explosion scattered bodies all over. Ceridwen went sailing through the air herself, landing dazed on her back. She looked up through the dust and saw how lucky she was. Corpses were littered all over the ground, mostly their enemies, but some of both due to the closeness of the impact.

It didn't take long for the burnt bodies to rise again. Some still gripped weapons, some used their blackened hands like claws. Soon the living were fighting their comrades' corpses in a wild battle.

One such undead soldier came running at Ceridwen. Zombies were the least of her worries. They were thoughtless creatures, intent on accomplishing the task they were assigned by their necromancer. They required the smallest amount of Black Magic to create, and they required a similar amount of

White Magic to destroy. Ceridwen raised an open hand in front of her face and stared at the approaching zombie, imagining it as it really was. Dead. No spark in its black eyes.

"*Expello,*" she cried, squeezing her hand into a fist.

A silver light flashed in the zombie's chest, and it fell to the ground. There were other ways to kill zombies, but this was the easiest. She saw more flashes, and Ceridwen knew that the other clerics who walked in the ranks with the soldiers had survived the blast. It wouldn't be long before they had control of the field again.

With the formation broken, she could see through to Asaph. She saw what looked like the priests running back, but there, striding forward, was the one dressed in black with a monk behind him. He was a short man, deathly pale, with sharp, angry features. He held a black rod with gold butt caps in his left hand.

Arch-zombie.

The arch-zombie raised a hand and a thin line of fire struck out toward one of the clerics. The cleric quickly brought up a shield, and for a moment the two were locked there, the thin streak burning into the shield. Ceridwen knew that spell, the words were *incendia telum*, and that streak would not end until the shaman stopped pumping energy into it or the shield broke.

"*Expello!*" Ceridwen called in an attempt to save the cleric.

The silver light flashed just before the zombie shaman, striking a shield. The monk behind him must have brought up the shield. She didn't contemplate it for long though, as a skeleton shambled forward on stiff legs with a rusty plough in its hands.

Ceridwen jumped back from a sideways swing, then leapt forward and grabbed the handle of the plough. The skeleton smelled of dirt and worms. In an instant the skeleton ripped her hands free of the plow and shoved her back with a shoulder rush.

Falling, Ceridwen saw a living soldier swing his spear and displace the skeletons head. The skeleton crumbled to the ground as the soldier exploded from a fireball. Flesh flew all around her. Ceridwen could see the zombie shaman striding toward her and readying another spell.

"*Contego!*" she called out swiftly from the ground.

A shield appeared in front of her and blocked the fireball. Ceridwen felt the burn of the attack, but the quick spell was nothing compared to the one she had blocked earlier. She struck with her own spell then, just as the arch-zombie did the same.

"*Incendia Telum!*"

Fire streaked from her outstretched hand and struck the shield she knew would be around him. His fire streaked out as well, meeting the shield she still held in front of her.

Ceridwen gritted her teeth. Her shield blocked the spell, but she still felt its searing burn on her skin. Her only chance was to break the other shield first, but controlling both white and fire was difficult. She could feel the glow in her that was the source of her White Magic depleting, draining her of energy, and only half of her attention could focus on her rage that was Fire Magic. She knew her shield couldn't hold for much longer, but she managed to get her feet beneath her. A piercing cry split the air above her, a frightening, bestial sound.

"To Shiva's burning prison with you!" she cried. She cut off the energy to her shield the same time she leapt away. The arch-zombie's streak of fire blasted into the dirt where she had been laying. Ceridwen focused her full energy on her rage, and poured forth all she had into her thin streak of fire.

The shield shattered and her streak slammed into the arch-zombie, knocking him back and ending his spell. He caught fire immediately, the dried up corpse no match for the hungry flames. Ceridwen got to her feet and ran toward the downed zombie.

Even on fire, the undead shaman got to his feet. He stretched out a hand to throw another spell at Ceridwen.

Eat worms, corpse!

"Expello!"

With no shield to block her spell, the silver light lit his chest, and the shaman fell back to the dirt.

The undead who pushed at the northernmost section of the spear wall fell away like leaves in the cold season. Well, at least the cold season farther north, kerplum trees were always green.

The spell to dismiss zombies was easier than casting a globe of light. Anne could manage three at once if the undead were grouped. Sao trailed behind watching her back.

Blasts could be heard elsewhere, but Anne focused on her line's steady advance. A skeleton ran at the spear wall swinging an old axe, allowing one of the spears to slide through its rib cage. The axe was blocked by the shield of the spear wielder, and then the shield of a second soldier crashed down on top of its yellowed skull. The rim of the shield created a crack, and the soldier sent it crashing down again, shattering the skull.

Anne advanced on the far left side of the infantry line. Hulda's group of Veneficus had been ordered to support the cavalry swinging around on their side. The casters had been unable to keep up though, and did what they could from behind the safety of the shields on that end. The end of the advancing cavalry cohort was far enough to begin its turn when a wall of fire sprung up from the ground. The flames caused a sudden stop, and then arrows the size of a grown man flew through them, lighting on fire as they soared through the blazing inferno.

Anne saw one of the giant missiles take down a horse. Another flung a man from the saddle before impaling the next soldier. Cries rose from men and horses. The wall of fire in front dissipated into a mist, one of the sahagin's doings Anne was sure.

With the wall gone, a gale of elemental attacks fell upon them. Anne called up her shield and stopped first a fireball then a wave of falling icicles. The burning and stabbing pain from deflecting the attack made Anne close her eyes and tense her muscles in an effort to keep the shield up. The pain far exceeded that which she felt earlier.

If my shield falls more than just me will die.

The pain stopped and Anne looked around her. She could see a small tornado filled with rocks battering into a shield similar to her own, and even a dark cloud of shadowed figures descending upon soldiers who were unable to find protection in a dome. The advancing wall of shields and horses turned into small pockets huddles under shields while the stragglers were torn apart by combinations of different Elemental Magics.

"The priests must be on this side!" a captain called out over the booming of explosions, howling of wind, and roaring of fire. "We must advance and take out the scorpions before they can reload them and focus our clerics down!"

A thick bolt of lightning arced in from the sky and crashed down upon one of the pockets. The shield shattered into shards like a broken glass. A second lightning strike followed with boulders and fire. In moments that maniple was wiped out.

Anne stared in awe. *I can't stop that lightning. There's no way.*

"Anne come on! We're moving!" Sao yelled. He grabbed the sleeve of her robe and pulled her behind him. They were in a single century now, moving at a sprint across the field.

They weren't the only ones. Other groups began to charge, some with horses, though it seemed most of the cavalry had lost their saddles in the rain of magic. What was left of the undead in front of the priests came running forward to meet them.

"Save your strength to protect us from their magic!" the captain yelled. He was handsome despite a scar running down his cheek. His eyes were alight with courage. He had lost his shield at some point in the advance, and now wielded his spear in two hands. "We'll handle the undead!"

One of the giant arrows from the scorpions flew through their group. The brave captain was impaled, only steps away from Anne.

Still, the group ran on. Anne could hear another strike of lightning with booms of magical attacks following. Another cleric down. Their lead runners crashed into the undead coming at them. A piercing cry echoed from above, and Anne knew Galavon had released Rorrick.

"Keep moving forward!" Sao yelled in the absence of the captain. "We must get to the priests!" Anne could just manage to see through the fighting in front of her. There, just beyond the undead, were two groups of casters.

There were acolytes dressed in white robes, and priests in white tunics and pants. In the middle of the two groups was

High Priest Denis, in a feather tunic with a circlet on his head decorated with a single black chip. A fireball was launched from one of the shaman in the ranks of the Army of Truth, and the acolytes immediately put up a shield.

"There's no way any magic is going to get through that shield," Anne said. She ducked down to avoid the swing of a zombie corpse, the first to make it through the soldiers.

"*Auliya!*" Sao cried as he sliced down with his odd claw.

Sao's body erupted into fire. His freckled face was hidden by the licking tendrils of flames, but they didn't stop there. They ran down his arms and legs and danced wildly on the top of his head. They burned all the way to the tip of his claw, burning even as it sliced through the undead's corpse as though it was butter.

The zombie instantly lit up in flames. Sao caught the undead in a backswing across the face, and he kicked the burning remains back before it had time to attack again. The zombie tried to rise, but the fire burned quickly, and the corpse soon stayed still.

"That's what your claw does?" Anne asked, startled.

Anne pulled out her weapon from its sheath on her belt while she ran. It was her stiletto. She gripped the handle. She couldn't afford to split her mind just yet. She had to focus in case of the lightning strikes.

A century of cavalry barrelled into one of the groups of priests and acolytes. Most fled, running through the field for the safety of Asaph. The cavalry charged past to hack at those fleeing. Another century of infantry charged toward the other. The priests who stood their ground unleashed elemental fury on the foot soldiers. Heat radiated from the encounter, and rocks blasted through the air. Somehow the cleric's shield didn't break, and the foot soldiers crashed into the enemy casters, slaughtering the magic wielders with their spears.

All sound stopped. Anne watched her group join in the slaughter of the enemy casters, no need for a shield. She watched the white robes become red, the tunics become crimson. She couldn't hear screams, and she couldn't hear breathing.

Sound returned in an instant, a huge boom with such great force that it blew back Anne and the soldiers. The remaining cavalry were thrown from their saddles, the horses fleeing. Her ears rang and her vision was blurry, but she tried to get back to her feet. She saw Sao get up beside her. Many didn't move. Where the slaughter had been stood only one man. High Priest Denis.

His mouth moved to speak words Anne had never heard. His gray eyes were wide staring up at the sky. A swift breeze blew around him, rustling the white feathers that made up his tunic and pants. His arms stretched down at his sides, tight with strain, and his palms were open, fingers separated. He lifted off the ground and levitated, toes pointing to the ground.

"By the fire of Shiva..." Sao muttered beside Anne.

Fire began to circle his floating body mixed in with the wind. The swirling flames took the form of five eagles that flew around him in a whirlwind of flame. One of the soldiers leapt forward, spear jabbing. The soldier was thrown aside like a rag doll, his arm catching fire. The high priest floated forward.

A cleric cast an anti-magic bubble in front of the high priest. It lasted for less than a heart beat before shattering once contact was made. The cleric collapsed on the ground.

"How do we stop that?" Anne asked to no one in particular. A few soldiers threw spears to no avail. They were caught in the whirlwind and shot back at the thrower as a fiery missile. The eagles of fire swooped out of the whirlwind to attack any who came close. He seemed unkillable, but at least the dead had stopped rising.

"*Profundo.*"

It was one of the sahagin. The word was echoed by the other in her group. Somehow both had managed to stay alive. The air around them seemed to dry up, and suddenly a great gush of water streamed forth from their hands. One stream was directed toward the high priest and got caught in the whirlwind, flying harmlessly around the floating mage. The other struck a flying eagle, but it hardly diminished in size. It did catch the eagle's attention though, and it flew toward them leaving flames in its wake, dive bombing the sahagin. Its strong talons ripped apart one of their throats, and while the other sahagin managed to dodge the attack, his robes caught fire.

The soldiers continued their attempts to get through. If the high priest made it to the pitched battle, there would be massive losses. They danced around the whirlwind trying to find a way through, those with shields trying to deflect the attacks of the fiery eagles. The cavalry were using their arrows, but they burned before coming close to the high priest. The lucky soldiers received burns, the unlucky ones with talon marks across their eyes, arms, and throats. Many were dying or screaming in pain.

Anne could still hear the rest of the cohort fighting undead behind them, but even the thought of that battle faded as one of the birds streaked toward her. *They're so fast!* She dove to the side as it struck at a soldier.

Even with no more undead joining the fight, they had to bring down the high priest. She watched his advance as she returned to her feet. Sao helped her up.

That's a lot of focus to control that whirlwind and five birds, Anne thought. *I have a hard time with three globes of light.* Then she had an idea. It was just like stealing that apple pie before the Harvest Festival, except instead of Cecil and a dove she had Sao and five fire eagles.

"Sao, can you feel fire when you use your claw?" she asked "I mean, you're covered in flames, so you must be immune to it, right?"

"I don't know. I suppose."

Well I suppose "suppose" is going to have to be good enough.

Anne scooped up a torched shield from the ground. It was painted dark blue with a white circle in the middle. A fallen soldier's shield. It had talon marks scratched along its surface. "Take this, use your claw, and distract those birds. All of them if you can. It must take all of his concentration to control them."

Sao looked unsure, a look that Anne was unfamiliar with seeing on his freckled face. He was always confident, which is why most of the girl's back home liked him. But those girls were women now, and this freckled boy a man. His face hardened and he nodded.

"Anne, a cleric has already tried to stop him. You can't do it."

She locked gazes with him. "I have to try. I can't let my people die."

"*Auliya!*"

The flames covered his body, the shield, and his claw. They moved in a wild dance on the top of his head, like the flame of a candle caught in the wind. He ran toward High Priest Denis.

I hope I'm stronger than whoever that cleric was.

Anne pulled her stiletto and began her own run in High Priest Denis' direction. She swung around the outside though, trying to get behind his swirling mass of destruction. There weren't many soldiers left around the high priest, and those that were there were in flight away from him. It wasn't long before Anne was running alone.

She managed a look over her shoulder and saw Sao. He had two of the birds diving at him as he stood alone in front of the advancing high priest. Two of the other fire eagles were harassing the running soldiers, but they soon made a turn for Sao.

Where is that fifth eagle?

A screech was the only warning Anne received. She dove to the side barely dodging razor talons. The fire still burned her arm though, and she was forced to pat out flames on her robes. She wasn't directly behind the high priest, but it would have to do. Sao had four of the fire eagles, he wouldn't be able to last long.

"Alius."

There were two of her now. But while there were two of her, there was only one fire eagle. She sent her illusion running, doing her best to make the movements look fluid rather than stiff. She hoped the high priest was too caught up in the fight against Sao to pay attention to which was real.

The fire eagle flew toward the illusion. Anne took her chance and sprang to her feet. She ran toward the high priest. In the back of her mind she tried to keep the false Anne running, but it didn't take long for the eagle to swoop down and rip out the illusion's throat. Anne lost her connection, but she was at the edge of the whirlwind now, and no eagles were around to attack her.

Maybe a smaller bubble, with all my strength, just enough to get inside.

"*Contego!*" she called.

Anne felt the power rising from deep inside her. It was more familiar now than it had been at first, but it was still exhilarating. She let the energy fill her before allowing it down her arm to her hand where she would create the shield. Her shield would either hold or she would die.

Anne focused hard on her spell. She followed the course of the energy carefully, knowing it meant life or death, putting in as much strength as she could afford. As it streamed forth though, she stopped before it escaped through her hands. There was another point of exit at her wrist, a path she had never noticed until now. How long had it been there? In her mind's eye it seemed vibrant, powerful. She directed the white magic out of this opening instead of her hand.

Time seemed to slow. Anne knew she imagined it. The air before her had a purple hue. A frustrated caw from a fire eagle sounded in the distance. Anne focused her bubble on the edge of the whirlwind. The wind instantly swirled around the obstacle, like a river flowing around a large rock. Anne wasted no time.

She ran through the tunnel, and out of the corner of her eyes she saw all the fire eagles flying toward her. The high priest's eyes look glazed over, as though he was in a trance, like the sahagin. She grabbed one of his legs and stabbed him in the thigh with her dagger.

The birds dissolved in thin air. The wind stopped. High Priest Denis fell from the ground in a crash. He looked at her with rage in his eyes. He kicked her legs out from beneath her. It was Anne's turn to fall, and the high priest stood towering above her. He was a tall man, a man who would have been comfortable in armor as well as robes. He held both hands forward and uttered words Anne didn't understand. A sword of lightning appeared, and he raised the weapon.

Three blades with fire dancing on their tips cut through the air and the high priest's neck like a knife going through an overripe kerplum. The lightning sword disappeared, and the high priest's head slid forward. Somehow the high priest caught his own head, blood oozing from his neck, and he ran across the field, his head clutched in his hands, before falling dead to the dirt.

The flames around Sao went out, and he threw away his ruined shield. He was missing chunks of armor from his arms, and a long scratch from what Anne could only imagine was a narrow dodge from one of the eagles still dripped with fresh blood from his neck. Sao reached down with his free hand and pulled Anne up from the ground.

Larith watched Cecil swing from the right side of Babieca as he charged through a knot of the undead. His hand-and-a-half sword smashed into the head of a zombie. An interesting choice, for it strayed from the usual falchion used by most of the cavalry. The blow wasn't strong enough to cut the skull in half, but with his horse's extra strength the blade ripped free from the skull and sent the zombie to the ground in a spiral.

Cecil's command to charge couldn't have come at a better time. The concentrated blast in this area had destroyed the line of infantry. Now small fires burned on the ground, and dead soldiers from the Army of Truth were rising against the living. For every undead they brought down, one of their own rose.

Despite having numbers, if it continued, Larith knew they would lose that advantage if they had not already.

Larith rode behind Cecil, followed closely by Lieutenant Gherro. The man seemed intent on keeping him safe. Larith didn't bother to tell him he needed no protection. He was saving his strength in case the rumor of the ghoul was true, or worse, they found Ares.

The cavalry cohort continued to charge through, leaving downed zombies and skeletons in their wake. Cecil stopped to survey the field, Duke Briel beside him. Larith rode to the group.

"Cecil," Duke Briel said pointing ahead. "There!"

Their young constable turned to look. It was difficult to see past the cavalry soldiers riding in front, but then Larith saw four horses and their riders flying back through the air, their woven steel armor crushed in by a heavy blow.

A huge man stood alone swinging a giant flail. The handle was a blood red rod as thick as a soldier's arm, and it was connected to a spiked ball crafted in the shape of a skull. The skull was so heavy that when it hit the ground it sank deep into the dirt. Larith knew only one creature strong enough to wield such a weapon.

It looks as though we've found the ghoul.

Despite having no hair on his head, bulging muscles held together by black iron straps, and pointed teeth the creature showed when he snarled, Larith recognized the late Tarik Ziyad's face. His crystal clear blue eyes were filled with rage. His lips were twisted and his teeth bared as though hungry for blood.

"My father... that's my father!" Cecil said. "We have to do something, we have to free him!"

"That's your father's body," Larith said, "but that is not your father. He has been twisted through pain, agony, and magic into a ghoul."

The four dead cavalry rose from the ground. Cecil's eyes stayed on the ghoul. "Cecil, look at me!" Larith demanded. The constable looked back. "He is not your father." Tarik lifted the great spiked skull from the ground and swung it in the air again, knocking more riders from their horses.

"Can we kill him?" Cecil asked. He watched as one of the cavalry soldiers made it inside the great swinging flail only to be grabbed by the front of his armor and beat with the rod.

"I can disable him," Larith responded. "It will take time, and he'll only be vulnerable while I hold him in a stasis."

One of the undead charged at the group, his bloodied falchion held high. Gherro spurred his mount to meet the attack.

"We can give you time," Duke Briel said. "Come on boy, we'll fight the ghoul ourselves!" He too spurred his horse forward. Cecil squeezed Babieca and urged the warhorse to follow.

A small group of cavalry were already charging the ghoul from the opposite side. It looked like a captain with ten or so men from his century. Tarik began to swing his massive flail as they charged.

The cracking noise of metal crushing bone sounded across the field all the way to Larith's ears as the skull struck the side of a horse. The man flew forward from the saddle, and the horse crashed into the one that rode beside him, sending that man sprawling as well. The iron skull continued through crushing two more soldiers and flinging them from the saddle. The chain caught the next soldier and knocked him from his horse as well.

The giant skull fell to the ground sending up bits of grass, its weight burying half of it in the ground. With a primal roar, he leapt at another soldier and tackled him from the saddle. The others in the charge rode by, swords swinging, and while their blades buried deep into the dead flesh, they did nothing to stop the undead beast from ripping out the soldier's throat with his teeth.

A screeching roar echoed across the battlefield, sounding like it came from the sky.

Our summoner has released his wyvern. He has found Ares.

But Larith had no time to think about what could be happening across the battlefield. He dismounted from his horse and allowed the different magics inside his chest to come alive, filling his aged body with power. He dropped runes to the ground before entering into a trance as he mumbled old, nearly forgotten words. He funneled the anger from his youth to add more strength. He felt wind swirl around him as he said the words, and a part of him die as he placed his own life force into the mix. All the while Cecil battled Tarik in front of him.

Cecil stabbed forward with his sword like it was a short spear as he rode past. Duke Briel slashed with his own weapon, both scoring solid hits. Cecil's sword was left behind, embedded too deep in his father's flesh. Tarik straightened, and with a quick jerk of the black rod, the ghoul sent a wave through the chain of his weapon. The heavy iron links caught the legs of Duke Briel's horse, sending both mount and rider to the ground. He then reached behind his back and slid out Cecil's sword before running toward the Duke with the weapon clutched in his free hand.

Larith continued his chanting, the power growing around him. Black, green, red, blue, yellow and white streak swirled around him. Pulling so many elements together was difficult, interlacing the spinning colors into a unique pattern even more so.

The monstrosity that was Tarik leapt into the air, the thick chain following behind him like a tail. He soared through the air for the last fifteen steps to plunge Cecil's blade through the Duke's chest.

Cecil turned to charge back but was stopped by an undead soldier. The once living stabbed up at him from the ground. Larith watched through the rainbow of colors as Cecil grabbed the shaft of the weapon with his armored fist. The soldier abandoned the weapon and pulled Cecil from the saddle.

Babieca reared back, front hooves flailing, catching the zombie on the chin and knocking him back. Without his rider, the warhorse gave in to fear and galloped away.

Cecil stood and smashed the butt-cap of his stolen weapon into the head of the zombie soldier until it no longer attempted to rise. All the while the ghoul continued to ravage the soldiers around him.

Then Larith felt the cruel stare of the ghoul wash over him. Tarik strode toward him, aware of what he was doing. The ghoul then said something in a guttural, deep voice Larith couldn't understand, but he soon did. The undead around them on the battlefield abandoned their fights and similarly charged at him.

Larith continued to cast his spell. It was intricate, so intricate. He needed more time to thread the green here, place the black there. He could only hope that Gherro was able to protect him. Cecil broke into a sprint toward the ghoul.

Good, he understands. His father's armor fits him well.

Cecil jumped over a section of the long chain that held the spiked skull of the flail. He cracked the sharp end of the spear across the ghoul's face. It ripped through dry skin, but no blood came out of the wound. The attack made Tarik turn.

There! Larith thought. He sent the weave of light at Tarik, connecting the two of them together with a writhing cord of magic. He could feel the anger inside, the strength of the mage who had created him. But there, underneath it all, was the old Tarik. Larith struck there first, driving his swirling tendrils of colors between the old Tarik and the darkness beyond. He poured more power into the cord, causing it to pulse and grow thicker.

Larith was part of the ghoul now. It's movements and thoughts his own.

"My son," Tarik grunted. The angry eyes looked feverish with excitement. "I'll not feed on your bones. I'll make you one of me. Together for eternity." Larith pumped more of the energy through the cord, pushing the anger away. The old Tarik broke through for an instant.

"Run," Tarik whispered to Cecil.

The red rod swung across suddenly, but Larith poured more energy, the connection between the two writhing like a live snake. The ghoul's attack slowed, and Cecil ducked beneath the attack. He stabbed forward with the spear catching the ghoul in the shoulder before retracting the weapon. Cecil sidestepped a slowed uppercut from the ghoul's free hand. He swung the shaft of the spear to crack against Tarik's side. He jumped back to avoid another attack from the rod, but Cecil's feet hit the chain, and he fell backwards to the ground. He rolled to the side to dodge a heavy stomp, Larith doing all he could to press back the darkness that enveloped Tarik and slow him down for Cecil until enough of the energy flowed into the abomination. Cecil rose on his knees with the spear to block a heavy downward strike from the rod, but the blow broke the spear in half and the force sent Cecil facedown to the dirt. If it had been any longer it would have crushed his skull. He clutched the broken ends of the spear.

"You see," the ghoul said. "You will not..." Larith forced his magic to fill every crevice of the inside of the ghoul. Tarik dropped the handle of the flail and floated above the ground as the ribbons of light pulsed. A clear diamond of magical energy surrounded him, slowly rotating. His arms were thrown wide within the stasis prison, unable to move.

"Kill him now!" Larith heard behind him. It was Gherro's voice, nearly pure panic. The marshal battled half a dozen zombies with more flooding in. It was all Gherro could do to keep them away. Cecil gripped what was left of the spear in his right hand.

Do it... I can't hold back the darkness for long...

Cecil turned to the ghoul in front of him. Larith could see him through Tarik's eyes.

"I will set my father free," Cecil said. He stabbed forward with the ruined spear, plunging it deep within the chest of the ghoul.

Black liquid poured from the wound as the ghoul screamed in his deep, raspy voice. The liquid steamed and disappeared before it hit the ground. The bulging muscles shrank, and even the earlier wounds inflicted on the ghoul began to leak the vile blackness. Cecil released his grip on the ruined spear and got to his feet, backing away from the dying ghoul. The screams grew distant, and then the corpse hung limp in the stasis prison.

The crystal shape blinked out of existence, and the ghoul's remains fell to the ground. Larith fell to his feet coming out of his trance. He saw Cecil turn with a smile of triumph on his face through a horde of ghouls desperately being fended off by Gherro. Then he felt a blade pierce his side. Then another. And another.

All my life for this moment. I created a new world and freed the oppressed. Rule with justice and compassion Cecil, especially compassion.

Rorrick and Ares hit the ground with a soft thud behind where the armies crashed.

He must have used a spell to soften their landing, Galavon thought running to the pair.

Rorrick reacted instantly, using the claws on his wings to push himself back to his feet. His long neck reached forward to bite at the curator. Though Ares was still on the ground, a ball of flame smashed into Rorrick's face, driving back his snapping jaws. The wyvern struck out with his spade-shaped tail next, but Ares was on his feet, and with a flap of his white wings he sailed unharmed over the attack. Ares punched forward with both hands as though he was strangling Rorrick. The wyvern's head went stretched up to the sky, his muscles tense as black globs raced from the curator's hands into his chest.

The spell only lasted a few moments before Rorrick broke through the paralysis and leapt forward. Ares seemed to explode at that moment with dark energy, blowing the wyvern back across the field to land on his side.

Darak used his speed to come at Ares from a different angle than Galavon, and he only now slowed down his pace. He fit arrow after arrow to his bow and loosened the bolts at the hovering curator. Ares turned and muttered a spell, but the small whirlwind that surrounded him came too late for the first arrow. It buried deep into his left shoulder, only inches from his heart. Ares' left wing stopped beating, and he fell to the ground in a heap. His whirlwind caught the other incoming arrows, and they swirled around him with the wind.

"To Shiva's prison with you elf!" he screamed. Darak stopped firing into the whirlwind and instead ran forward. The arrows that were caught shot out then, flying back. Darak dove to the side rolling, leaving a line of arrows in the ground behind him. A few even sailed above as the agile elf cut back the other way, but one caught his leg and sent him sprawling to the ground. A fireball that burned as black as the night sky flew in at the downed elf.

"*Brevis!*" Galavon called out.

The wind reacted by sweeping past Galavon and pushing the black, burning ball to the ground. The spell erupted with an expulsion of air that threw the elf back in a heap as though he were weightless, the black flames somehow dying on his skin.

"*Incendia inflatus!*"

The source of anger burned in Galavon's chest, and he felt it surge through his arms and out into his hands. It quickly gathered into a fiery ball, and he threw it at the curator. It left a streak of smoke in the air behind it before crashing into a spell shield around Ares. Though Galavon saw the curator flinch from the flames, he knew he wasn't even close to breaking the shield.

The whirlwind swept up the flames from the blast and threw them back at Galavon. The fire came at him in swirling streak.

"*Brevis,*" Galavon said swinging his staff. The arc of air pushed the flames aside, though they flew past close enough for Galavon to feel the heat.

"*Brevis,*" he called out again swinging his staff. This arc of air pushed forward to slash against the magical barrier.

He repeated the spell over and over again as he swung the staff in the practiced rhythm he had learned from the Viridian, each swing bringing him closer to the fallen curator. Not every swing produced the arc of air, but the wind accompanied enough of the attacks to produce a rapid barrage against Ares' shield.

Galavon stopped his attacks and watched the curator. He was pale and bony, his thin hair tangled from the tiny tornado that had surrounded him. Still, he was magnificent. Despite his bedraggled appearance, his strong cheekbones, glaring eyes, perfect white teeth, and lean figure made him handsome. He stood slumped from Darak's arrow, but he still managed to have an air of confidence. Or maybe it was arrogance. Still, his confidence made Galavon feel uneasy.

"So, wind and fire is it?" Ares said. Galavon was breathing hard after the sprint and his last attack, but he stood with his staff at the ready. "Here's some advice to you mage summoner – though I don't intend to leave you alive long enough to use it. Learn White Magic to shield yourself from magical attacks. The wind will fail you eventually. Second, combined elements produce a far greater power." He muttered something Galavon didn't understand. Black and red droplets floated up from Ares' shoulders and head, along with green and yellow, black and white, even purple. They swirled together, the red and black beginning to dominate. They took the form of Rorrick, only three times as large and with four legs instead of two.

It's a dragon.

The dragon seemed to be made of black and red flames. It continued to grow as it took shape.

"*Incendia inflatus!*" Galavon cried, hurling a ball of flame into the growing beast. The dragon absorbed the fireball.

"*Brevis!*" Galavon said slashing. No arc of wind accompanied the swing.

"*Brevis!*" he tried again. Nothing.

"You see, the wind will fail you. That is why it is the weakest of the elements," he said. The dragon was at least five times the size of Rorrick now, Ares not even coming halfway up his front legs. The giant magical beast stretched its neck forward and roared at Galavon, the strength of the blast pushing him back.

An arrow flew at Ares, but it was caught by the whirlwind. Galavon looked to the side and saw Darak struggling to put up another arrow. "My final lesson is to never go against your betters. I am Ares, curator and ruler of this burned peninsula." The second arrow flew in and was again caught.

Ares' magical creation pumped its wings and flew up in the air, and then higher still. Galavon was sure the entire battlefield could see the massive beast. It roared one more time before inhaling, preparing to breathe pure destruction.

This is how it ends, at the maws of a magical dragon created by a curator I used to worship.

Galavon stood firm. If he was going to die, he would face it as a man, as a mage summoner, not as the boy who cowered and somehow managed to escape death. He gripped his staff in his right hand and watched as a torrent of black and red flames mingled with lightning was hurled at him.

The attack descended over him, but Galavon felt nothing. He saw the fire, heard the pops of lightning, knew the blackness reached, but none touched him. The very force nearly knocked him back. It sent the long back of his tunic fluttering, and it blew his shaggy hair into tiny whips that lashed across his face. Galavon felt something warm of his chest. He pulled out the medallion from his father. It glowed a bright silver.

The attack faded. As Galavon's eyes adjusted to the light of day, he saw Ares on the ground. His eyes were lifeless.

Darak, with ash on his face and an arrow in his leg, looked at Galavon from across the field. His pendant glowed on his chest like Galavon's, and he held his bow. "It was the wind," he said. "It didn't stop that arrow. It failed him."

Chapter 14
(Anne, Galavon, Cecil)

Anne sat in the Goblin Fire Inn's common room. Porter, now her full time body guard, stood watch outside the inn. The place was lavishly decorated, obviously an inn intended for nobility visiting Ehime, the town outside of castle Matsuyama. Cecil had paid for the entire building. She had accompanied him here for the ceremony of naming Captain Philial as Duke Marlow since his father and two brothers were killed in the lightning strikes before the Battle for Asaph.

It's a dumb name. No one wanted Asaph. It was just a convenient place to kill each other.

Anne still mourned Larith, and she had even replaced the black ribbon in her hair in memory of him. He had died a hero, but what had the revolution really lost with his death? They lost an understanding of Elemental Magic surpassed by none, a counselor for the newly formed Veneficus to keep them in line, and a wise man with endless advice.

And I lost a friend.

She sat on a cushioned chair waiting for someone to retrieve her so she could speak with her brother. Her own brother. After his dream won them the battle and with the death of Duke Briel, he had become more than just a supporter of the revolution. He had become the revolution. Anne had seen the change in the tent before the battle, but even the hard, concise, determined Cecil she had seen there had changed. The steel had been iced. Even the strong Lady Ayne and the fiery Ceridwen succumbed to his words.

"He's all yours, Anne," Sao said walking in from a hallway. His eyes seemed darkened around the edges as though he had received little sleep. Cecil was even working his friends hard. Still, it was nice to see Sao and his familiar freckles. He was always a good friend to Cecil.

"Is he alone, Sao? Or does he have a council in there with him?"

Sao walked to Anne's table and leaned against a chair on the opposite end. "He's alone," Sao said. "But Anne, there's a lot of changes taking place. Necessary changes. Sacrifices. For this to be successful, we all have to sacrifice."

"I know more than most about sacrifice," Anne replied. "I've sacrificed my father, my home, and more than one friend. I believe I know as well as any that sacrifices have to be made."

Sao nodded and let go of the chair. "Well, I'm off. Another mission for the kingdom. It's always nice to see you, Anne." He strode across the polished wood floor underneath a gilded chandelier to exit out the door, his odd claw hanging easily on his waist.

What was that about?

Anne rose from the chair, grabbing the folds of her gown and tugging them to get them out from beneath the table. The voluminous folds were the new style in Mecca, and a merchant from Farrow had brought the dress with him as a gift for the new ruling faction in their province. Well, not province anymore, but the Kingdom of Niveus.

Anne gathered up her skirts the best she could and walked down the hallway with a determined step. If he was a king, that made her a princess. And, unlike the others, she would not bow to his word. She grabbed the brass doorknob, twisted, and pushed the heavy door inwards.

The room was dimly lit, but Anne could see clearly enough. Cecil had made the library of the inn his reception room. It had a lush carpet and multiple chairs, each with a side table. Cecil had two books sitting on the table beside him, and he absently thumbed through the pages of another. He looked up and smiled.

"Do you remember this book? It's *The Complete Tales of the Harpist*. It's where the song comes from. It's one of your favorites, isn't it?"

Anne sat down. That song always reminded her of Galavon. "Of course. I didn't hear it tonight."

Cecil laughed. "You know they can't play that at a Title Ceremony. It's more formal, not like a Harvest Festival."

"Well, I prefer the festivals," Anne said. "At least at those I don't have to wear a dress like this."

"Oh, come on Anne, the dress is…"

"Horrific!" She said. "Do you remember what father used to say about fashion in the Kingdom of East Ager? 'Fashion means uncomfortable and expensive. Give me my boots any day.' Well, I say this dress is uncomfortable, and I want my riding pants back!"

"Or as mother used to say, 'no one will take you seriously unless you take fashion seriously," Cecil retorted, laughing again before falling silent with Anne.

That's what your mother used to say. Do you even know that we're only half brother and sister?

Anne broke the silence by motioning to the heavy crown that sat in his lap. It was a bulky thing, crafted of white gold, with the single, black chip High Priest Denis had worn. "I noticed you put the shell on the crown."

"I did, yes," Cecil said. He picked up the crown to study it. "I had no clue what it was at first. That mad woman Ceridwen tried to demand it from me, which led me to believe it was of some value." He shook his head in disbelief. "Dragon shell. More rare than any jewel. Who would have thought we both would end up with one?"

Anne held up her wrist and rattled her bracelet. The vendor hadn't lied when he said it was a shell necklace. Sea shells and dragon shell. It made the trinket priceless, and Anne intended to return to Himeji and reward the street vendor handsomely.

"Anne," Cecil started, "you know after the ceremony I met with people not from here. There was the merchant from Farrow, one of Sao's spies from Zephyr Hills, and an envoy from Tew."

"Tew? Cecil he's a pirate. He sells women to slavers in Afrikaar, he robs vessels, and kills men. He's the reason we can't trade with those kingdoms! He's a thief, and a murderer! What business could you have with a man like that?"

"The Army of Courage is marching south from the Fire Pass Province led by curator Anuke! They're sending ships from Farrow with Esus as the admiral to block trade in and out of the kingdom. That's two curators, Anne! Two! And how long will we have until the Army of Triumph marches from the Point Province? Or the Army of Honor from the Mountain Province? After the Battle for Asaph, I don't think we can win a war with the Kingdom of East Ager alone. We've only won one battle, and the revolution is just beginning."

Ugh there's that name again!

"That doesn't explain why you met with a pirate. Have you forgotten they captured me?"

Cecil shut the book, folded his hands in his lap, and leaned forward. "I have named Tew a Duke and Admiral. With his ships under my command, we might be able to win at sea against East Ager. With his islands as part of the kingdom, I can open safe trade with Afrikaar to help feed our people while we fight. More importantly, I can send an emissary into the Gold Desert to make a treaty with the barbarian tribes. They've always claimed the Fire Pass Province was theirs. I say let them have it."

Anne fumed at the idea of making Tew a Duke, but as much as she hated to admit it, she could see reason behind the decision. The added ships alone might be worth naming him Admiral, not to mention the trade that would open.

But besides all that, the journey to the Gold Desert sounded dangerous and filled with adventure. A chance to see more of Mundus, parts few people from the Kingdom of East Ager have ever seen. Surely this is what Sao was hinting at. Who would make a better diplomat than the sister of the king?

"Cecil, I'd love to..."

"I've decided to send the summoner."

Cecil was sending away her Galavon. She had found someone, Cecil disapproved, and so Cecil sent him away.

"The choice is obvious," Cecil said. "The man is a powerful mage and familiar with travel. He sits on the Council of Mages. It would be honorable to receive him. He won't travel alone. The elf, Dahareuch Starshine, he will will go as well. Anne, he explained to me why the goblins attacked from their isles.

"Before Shiva was imprisoned, there was another fire dragon born. That dragon is almost mature and lives on the

Goblin Isles. The goblins want to release Shiva before the new fire dragon is fully grown so that the cycle can continue. The elves and the curators refuse to release her and have to battle her again. There's already reports of more fire wyverns than normal in the Fire Pass Province."

"What does that have to do with the revolution? With sending Galavon?"

"I want to release Shiva. It will balance the elements and possibly fight our war for us. Surely she will want revenge."

Anne stared at him with wide eyes. "You want to release Shiva? Cecil, she's the epitome of chaos and destruction! She is the essence of one the Wayward elements! What makes you think she will stop with the curators?"

"It is a risk we must take. We can't win a war against the curators alone."

"Can she even be released? She sits under a magical fortress in enemy territory! It's a suicide mission! I'll not let you send him away to his death!" Anne said standing up. "I love him Cecil! He saved me when no one else could, and I love him! You will not take him away from me!"

Cecil rose from his chair, now yelling. "If it means victory than we will try anything, no matter who must die!" Cecil sighed. His next words were controlled. He looked her in the eyes. "Anne, you have to marry Admiral Tew. They were part of his conditions for becoming a part of our kingdom."

Marry a pirate?

"I won't do it, Cecil. I'd rather slit my wrists."

"If you don't marry him Anne, we don't get his ships, which means we have no navy. The curators will sail their armies right around ours and kill hundreds if not thousands of our people. They'll sack castles and burn towns. Even if we somehow hold them off, without outside trade we won't have enough food to feed everyone and the army. People will starve."

Anne sat back down and stared off into the distance. Her back was straight, and her hands rested on her knees. She felt her hair bounce on her shoulders.

I find happiness, and it's ripped away.

"I know you like the summoner, but Anne, it could never be. We must not live for ourselves, but for others. Tew is now Duke of the Tew Islands. He brings us a navy. I need you to do this. The Kingdom of Niveus needs you to do this."

Anne nodded and stood on wobbly legs. She held back tears. She wouldn't cry in front of this man that used to be her brother. It was the second time in her life she had been at a loss for words. The first had been when she met Galavon. The second was now, when he was taken away.

Galavon sat in a small clearing in the middle of a kerplum tree copse. He was far enough away from Ehime to keep the noise from the celebration low, and the trees hid most of the light from the town. He was still unsure around people with his scales and dragon eyes. At least it was peaceful beneath the stars, and the cool breeze of the cold season this far south felt like the perfect weather.

He was getting used to traveling with only the bare necessities. He kept the sun and moon amulet, his staff, a water pouch, a small roll of blankets, the tin cup from Myson, and the harp he stole from the pirates that night he saved Anne. Rorrick was a proficient hunter when they weren't near a town, and that's where Galavon preferred to be, away from towns. Even after his role in the Battle for Asaph, it would take many Twil for the people to accept him.

No fire burned in his camp. The stars and moon provided enough light, and Galavon nibbled on a small dinner of dry venison and bread. He sat with the harp in his lap and plucked out a song.

"The wind blows through the branches of trees,
Alongside mountains, fast and free.
It fills the sails of traveling ships
Riding the waves with each rise and dip.
It blows by fast, so listen close,
Wind always sees and hears the most."

Wind blew in from between the trees and wrapped its elf around Galavon. It tussled his hair and even vibrated the strings of his harp to add a final, mournful hum. That was his mother's song, and though Galavon never knew her, he felt as though he was closer to her every time he played it.

I can feel fire burning inside me, and even the other glow, but neither comforts as the wind does.

After the battle, Cecil honored those who played significant roles in the victory. To Ceridwen he gave one of the sapphires discovered in the cache of rare gems in the Cathedral. It took her little time to discover its secrets. The Cathedral itself and the lands surrounding he gave to the Veneficus. Galavon was also given a gift for bringing Ares to the ground – a pearl from the same cache. It was the other glow he felt inside.

Learning to use the pearl had been frustrating. It didn't come as easily as the ruby he carried, and took even longer than the emerald. However, with Anne's help, he finally unlocked it's secrets along their travels. That was Galavon's new responsibility – to follow Cecil and act as the Veneficus' representative. Ceridwen was elected the new Archmage, and she appointed Galavon so he could be closer to Anne.

The cold season so far had been the happiest days of his life, but he knew they wouldn't last. Already there was word of the other provinces preparing to march. Though their coordination would take time, no one suspected that the warm season would begin before the next battle. And at the next battle, the Venificus would be needed.

It was odd to think that because he knew three different Elemental Magics that he was considered the second most powerful mage in the Veneficus. Galavon smiled, proud of his accomplishments for once, and felt the tightness of the scales on his face.

But some still refuse to accept me like this… as a summoner, half wyvern.

His father was one of those. On their way back from Caernarfon Castle to name the new heir, they had stopped in Pearl. Galavon had been informed by Torvil at the door to his father's home that Patrick's son had died in the Battle for Asaph. Torvil was back to his normal, jovial self, even congratulating Galavon, but he still didn't allow him inside to see his father. It hurt, but Galavon didn't expect any less.

The wind then carried a sound to his ears. It was the crunching of fallen leaves beneath running feet. Perhaps slippers. Galavon set the harp on the ground and stood, searching for whatever was making the sound.

Anne burst through the trees at a sprint and wrapped her arms around him. She cried into his chest. Not long ago he would have felt awkward in a situation like this, but time had only strengthened their bond.

"Shhh," he said stroking her curly hair as it bobbed up and down with her sobs. The wind was gone now, leaving Galavon holding Anne in the middle of the trees. "What is it Anne? What happened?"

She sniffed and looked up at him with crystal clear, blue eyes. She was the only person he didn't mind looking at his scales. Her curly hair was in a tangle, and there was a smudge of dirt on her tanned face. But even with all that and the tear stains streaked down her cheeks, Galavon wasn't sure there was a more beautiful girl in all of Mundus.

"He's sending you away. To free Shiva."

To do what?

Galavon felt his eyes widen. Surely he misheard her.

"To where?" he asked, hoping she would say something else.

"To Shiva, Galavon! To Shiva's own prison! He is literally sending you to Shiva's own prison!" Anne trembled.

There was no place he desired to go less than there. In Reproba Caelum it was a place of fire and torment for those who did not follow their rules. It was supposedly buried underneath the Fire Pass, which caused the twin rivers of lava to flow, but where would he even begin to find his way inside? And what would he do if he made it inside? Shiva was there!

By the fire of Shiva, he's sending me to death itself.

"And I'm to marry the new Admiral Tew, the former pirate, so the Kingdom of Niveus will have a navy." Her words came out strong, but once they were out, her lips quivered, and a new tear ran down her cheek.

"We'll leave then, Anne! We'll leave right now. We'll go north and stay with the Viridian in the mountains, they'll accept us, I know they will. We can…"

She balled up a fist and hit it against his chest, not in anger but frustration. "Galavon, I can't," she said. "If I don't do this, Cecil will lose the war, the revolution. More people will die. I can't let them die."

They stared at one another for a moment. Hair stuck to Anne's wet cheeks where it came in contact with the remnants of her tears. Her eyes were red around the blue from crying. Galavon could see anguish and determination plastered on her perfect face.

"So, we lose each other then?" he asked. He held back tears of his own. He knew his voice sounded shaky, he could hear it himself. "After everything?"

"No. We'll always have our time in the cave. And tonight. I won't let him take that from me." She put a hand behind his head and pulled him forward. Their lips met, and she pulled him harder, forcing their lips so tight Galavon could taste a small drop of blood where his teeth cut the back of his lips.

There in the moonlight, with the wind swirling around them, Anne and Galavon embraced and wished that the night would never end.

What have I become?

Cecil sat in the library of the inn still, surprisingly alone. It was rare for him to be alone, except in his dreams. Gherro had a huge number of soldiers outside and around the inn, but in this room he was alone. He allowed his hard exterior to fade, to soften. He twisted his goblet filled with water idly in hands before throwing it in a rage. The metal goblet crashed against the wall, spilling water across the floor.

What have I become?

How could he so easily use his sister? He used her as easily as a tool, as he would a sword. Anne Ziyad was a loving, kind girl, and he had used her.

Not a girl, but a woman now.

That thought was hard to accept, but he knew it was true. Twil would light the night sky any time now. Already people waited up to watch the sky for a viewing of the star. This would be Anne's seventeenth. She had fought in a battle, and she had found love. Yes, she was definitely no longer a girl.

"But why him, Anne?" he said out loud. If it had to be anyone, why not the new Duke Philial Marlow? Or even a commoner he trusted, like Sao or Lieutenant Gherro? They would have been acceptable. But not him. Not a monster.

The new kingdom was still struggling to accept the Veneficus. Cecil knew they would in time, and he also knew the Veneficus was a necessity if he planned on winning this revolution. Still, Cecil had to be careful about what the people thought of him. He needed their support. The public marriage of his sister to a commoner would be damaging. Still, if this was all, Cecil would be able to stomach it. It was no worse than a former pirate.

But this Galavon was a summoner. Scales marred his face, and death stared back from those unnatural eyes. The new Archmage Ceridwen claimed it was remarkable how fast he picked up Elemental Magic, even claimed he was lucky to have been chosen by a wyvern to share the same body. But the commoners saw only a monster. Cecil could not be seen as the king who gave his sister to a monster. So instead, Cecil sent the monster to either secure victory, or to his death.

Perhaps if my luck runs true, both.

Two former monks came in then. They were considered clerics now, and members of the Veneficus. They had changed sides soon after the Battle for Asaph. Whether their faith had truly been shaken or if they were just desperate to have their pearls returned, Cecil was unsure. Either way, he and Gherro felt as though they could be trusted.

Most clerics, even those who were not former monks, continued to wear white cotton robes and leather sandals. These two were no exception. Their robes seemed freshly washed, probably because they knew they were serving their king tonight.

One of the clerics bent to pick up the goblet and replace it on the table. Neither asked why it was there. It wasn't their job to ask questions.

"Lieutenant Gherro is escorting him in now," one of the clerics said.

"And you two can handle him?"

"Yes, my king."

Cecil nodded in acceptance of the answer. Still, just to be sure, he said the name of his armor.

"*Alveus Silicus.*"

The weight of the armor faded, but Cecil knew it only became stronger. The silver runes that were etched up and down the length of the dark blue armor enforced its strength and made it lighter. Even if his guest made a move to kill him, it was unlikely he would get past the strength of the armor that had once been his father's.

The door pushed open, and Lieutenant Gherro walked through. He was clad in armor as well, the woven strips of armor that the cavalry wore. His falchion hung at his waist. Behind him walked in a shorter figure with a limp huddled beneath an oversized cloak.

"Welcome, Muha," Cecil said. "I'm pleased to see you have accepted my invitation."

The hidden figure threw off his cloak and put it on the back of the chair that sat across from Cecil. Muha could not have been more than six span, barely reaching Cecil's chest. His skin was a yellowish green, similar to the trolls Cecil had fought. He had wiry black hair cut into a low strip that ran down the center of his otherwise bald head. He had no ears, small eyes the color of blood, and his nose and lips were wide and full. He wore gold arm bands wrapped around well muscled biceps, one with a ruby embedded in it, and another with runes. His chest was bare save crisscrossing leather straps with an empty frog, and he wore leather pants with a layer of chainmail sewn over the top. Scars decorated all parts of his body.

"You father," he said pointing to Cecil, "give Muha bad leg with spear. Now Muha live, and he dead." Muha climbed into the chair across from Cecil. His legs didn't touch the ground. "Him great general. Muha come in respect."

Cecil nodded. He didn't expect this from the goblin chieftain. All the stories he heard from the War of Fire were tales depicting the goblins as butchers and fanatics, but the little creatures did not seem dumb. This one was obviously bilingual. Sort of. "What you want for trade? Goblins and man not friends for long time."

"Muha, what are the curators to your people?"

"The winged-men?" Muha asked. He slammed a fist into his chest, making a dull thud that was similar to a drum. The goblin chief's eyes narrowed. "They bring us few stones. Promise to help goblins. They say now is time to wage war so goblins release old dragon. Restore balance. That when Muha meet your father." He drew a thumb across his neck and bared his teeth, making a hissing sound. "Now many goblins dead."

The goblin chief didn't stop. "Winged-men say goblins must stay on islands. Then winged-men say goblins must fight. Winged-men are treacherous, but strong. They bring goblins stones." He pointed to the armband with the runes. "Goblins need stones. Can't get them trapped on islands."

"Muha, we're fighting the winged-men. We drove out their Followers. We can trade stones." Cecil stood and walked to the corner of the room where a sack sat on the floor. He brought it to Muha and placed it on the table beside his chair.

Muha looked suspicious, but opened the sack. His red eyes grew large. He emptied the sack into his lap, three glowing rubies falling out. "What you want for trade?"

"The winged-men are sending ships to try and steal our land. We have ships of our own, but they aren't enough. I ask for your help in fighting the winged-men on the water."

"Ha!" Muha laughed. "Ha! Ha!" The goblins laughter reminded Cecil of a barking dog. "Winged-men have much magic. You will lose."

"We have more magic," Cecil responded. "We beat them here, didn't we? No more priests. No more winged-man. We killed him. But we need more ships if we're to keep winning. Goblins are users of Fire Magic, are they not?"

"Goblins best with fire!" Muha proclaimed. "But goblins need more than trade. There can be only one dragon. There two dragons now. Free Shiva to fight our Ishum. You bring fire to sky, goblins bring fire to ocean."

"I can make that promise, Muha," Cecil said, "but the goblins will have to fight before Shiva will be released. The winged-men's ships will sail soon. I can't promise that Shiva will be released by then. Or if my men will even succeed."

Muha looked displeased. "Who you send? How they free?"

"I'm not going to discuss the logistics with you Muha," Cecil said. "Just know I'm trying, but if we defeat the winged-men, you will be free to march across the Fire Pass Province and free Shiva yourself if I fail."

"You give Muha much to think on." He put the rubies back in the sack and jumped down from the chair. He threw the cloak around his small body to conceal it. "Muha will send word. Much to think on."

"Keep the stones Muha, as a token of good faith."

Muha nodded and grabbed the sack with his small green hands before walking out the door. Gherro and the two clerics escorted him out.

That Dahareuch Starshine, or whatever his name is, was right. The curators' reach expands much further than the Kingdom of East Ager. They control the pirates, the goblins, and more than likely the kobolds, trolls, and giants. And the curators are controlled by the elves.

Cecil stood from his chair and ran a hand through his hair. Once he stole apple pies, now he traded his sister for a navy and made deals with the enemies of his father.

It will all be worth it soon enough. Anuke comes south with her army.

Anuke. According to Larith before he died, she was the oldest surviving curator besides Neith and responsible for many of the horrible acts committed by Reproba Caelum. He had said she was cruel, malicious, and vengeful. She was the curator who killed his father. He would show her vengeful.

Cecil walked to the windowsill and looked out over the town. He could see lights burning in the windows of other common rooms where the people of Ehime still celebrated the new Duke. Cecil didn't feel like celebrating. Things had changed, and he was no longer a boy, but he wondered if he was making the right moves.

Then, in the sky, as bright as a full moon, was Twil. The large star was impossible to miss as it slowly flew across the sky. All down the street people wandered outside to watch the star. Sleepy-eyed children were pulled from bed, and older folk looked upon it with a familiarity that only the aged knew. Fingers pointed up, and drunks hooted and hollered. It faded slowly away around the other side of Mundus.

It was a new Twil, and Cecil was king

For more information on author R.P. Miller
check out his author page at:
https://www.facebook.com/rpmillerauthor/